The
Silk Weaver's
Wife

ALSO BY DEBBIE RIX

The Girl with Emerald Eyes
Daughters of the Silk Road

The Silk Weaver's Wife

DEBBIE RIX

Bookouture

Published by Bookouture
An imprint of StoryFire Ltd.
23 Sussex Road, Ickenham, UB10 8PN
United Kingdom
www.bookouture.com

ISBN: 978-1-78681-228-5
eBook ISBN: 978-1-78681-227-8

For Charlotte and Joe

One day, as Empress Hsi Ling Shi, wife of Emperor Huang Ti, was sipping tea under a mulberry tree, a cocoon fell into her cup and began to unravel. The empress was so enamoured with the shimmering threads that she discovered their source, the Bombyx mori silkworm found in the white mulberry. The empress soon developed sericulture, the cultivation of silkworms, and invented the reel and loom.

Thus began the history of silk.

Prologue

As he left her for the night, locking the door behind him, Anastasia felt her heart quicken. She lay on the bed, a solitary candle flickering beside her, casting shadows around the room that formed the boundaries of her world. The light reflected in the myriad of tiny panes of glass in the casement window overlooking the Grand Canal, scattering beams of light, like fireflies, around the room. The iron bars that had been fitted over the windows were a constant reminder of her incarceration. She had been imprisoned in this room in Venice for so long and had endured his nightly assaults – until tonight, when she had set in motion a train of events that once begun could not be undone. If she failed, or weakened at any time over the next few days, she feared she would be trapped here, forced to submit to Anzolo, for ever. It was vital that she delayed any visit from a doctor for as long as possible. Locked in her airless bedchamber, she was as helpless as ever. What she needed to do now was persuade her husband that she should be allowed to leave this room.

Then, and only then, would she have a chance to escape.

Part One

Silken Thread

'Do not be afraid; our fate cannot be taken from us; it is a gift'

Dante Alighieri, *Inferno*

Chapter One

Villa di Bozzolo, near Verona, Italy
May 2017

She wakes. Sun is stealing round the edges of the darkened shutters, channelling the light into a sharp laser-like beam that highlights the knots and nail heads of the stained-oak floor. She pulls herself up in the large bed, leaning against the unyielding carved headboard, momentarily confused. There is an unfamiliar smell: slightly musty, overlaid with beeswax polish. She runs her fingers over the white linen sheets – they are old, not yet threadbare, but soft.

The last time she had lain in a large bed in soft, white sheets in Italy he had been there with her. They had gone to Florence to celebrate her birthday. She had reached out to him but he had turned his back. She had watched as the muscles that ran along either side of his spine flexed at her touch.

'Millie… Don't.'

'Don't what?' she'd asked, not yet understanding.

'You know. This. It's over. You must see that.'

She had lain silently then, hardly daring to breathe; the marks left by her fingernails just a few moments before, as she climaxed, were developing into red weals near his shoulder blades. Perhaps, she thought, if I don't say anything we can both forget what he just said. We can get up in a moment and go out into the sunshine. We can sit at our favourite cafe and I can order us coffee just how he likes it – strong and short, with a little *pasticceria* that I will dip into my milky latte. We will wander round the market, or along the banks of the Arno. Later, we will come back to our white bed and make love again before falling gently asleep. I will listen to his breathing as it becomes even and I will lay my hand on his thigh. It will comfort me as I too slip into sleep. We will wake as the sun sinks low in the sky, take a shower, and I will put on the dress he likes – the coral linen that I bought in the market yesterday; the dress he says makes me look like a ray of sunshine. I will brush my dark auburn hair and twist it into a chignon and he will kiss my neck.

He turns finally to look at her. His eyes are cool pools of water.

'Well?' He sounds irritated. As if this is an editorial meeting he is chairing back at their offices in London and he is waiting for a verdict from one of his best journalists on an idea he has just floated. She almost expects him to say: 'Will it fly? What do you think, Millie?'

'What do you want me to say, Max? Why is it over?' She is trying to stay in control. She won't cry, won't beg. He wouldn't like that; won't respect her for it – better to challenge a little, as she would with a story.

'Isn't it obvious? I can't keep lying to Katje. She sent me a text this morning, wishing me a great day. It's just wrong, Mills. You know that.'

'Wrong for who?' Millie says, bridling slightly at the use of this most private of diminutives – only Max and her brother Freddie ever call her 'Mills'. To use it now seems like a further betrayal.

'You, me, Katje, the kids.'

This was a low blow. At thirty-eight, Millie, with no children of her own, tried hard to excise Max's kids from her mind. He had already acquired two families: three boys – all grown men now, from his first marriage to 'Lady' Jane, and two 'adorable' blonde girls with Katje. Any mention of them was out of bounds for Millie. He knew that. She had laid it out for him fair and square when they began their affair six years earlier, as he nuzzled her neck in the taxi after the awards ceremony where he had taken his team and finally made his move.

'I like you, Max, I really do, but anytime you bring your wife and family into our relationship it's over – OK?' He – a little drunk, randy, intoxicated by his star reporter and the award she had just won for 'best feature', would have promised her anything to get into her bed that night.

And so it had begun…

Millie had gone from one-night stand, to lover, to mistress. The early days were a whirlwind of whispered conversations on office phones, fleeting meetings in corridors, kissing in the lift. The excitement and adrenalin of it all was somehow life-affirming. Over time that early lust had turned to love, or at least what she thought was love. There was passion certainly, on both sides, a mutual sense of longing, and tumultuous lovemaking. But six years on, the harsh reality of what they were doing had set in; the passion had subsided a little and had been replaced with something else. On her part a sense of disillusionment: she was sad and lonely much of the time, with a creeping guilt about those little girls living in the tall house in Notting Hill with their Pilates-toned mother. But most of all, she had an overwhelming feeling that life was passing her by. She had a chic flat in Spitalfields, a good job and three awards displayed on the mantelpiece above the designer fake fire. But there was emptiness at the core. Her kitchen – which should have been filled with the comforting chaos of loving meals for two, three, or even four – was more often just a place for coffee for one. No family casserole dishes graced her cupboards. No rolling pins or cookie cutters cluttered up her drawers. No children's drawings were stuck magnetically to her fridge door. There was none of the muddle created by two, three or more people jostling for position in a household. Just a clinical set of matching white china – chic, expensive and somehow soulless.

'You deserve more,' he had said at last, sitting up in bed. 'I know how much you want kids… I just can't give them to you.'

Her eyes stung with tears now. He always could get right to the heart of any story. That was his genius as an editor. He would sit in editorial meetings patiently waiting for all the hacks and researchers and editors to bring their ideas to the party and then would say, with a slight air of resignation, 'OK, so this is what we're going to do…' And he would proceed to outline ten, or fifteen, stories that scarcely anyone had mentioned, all brilliant, relevant and right on the money.

And now it seemed, their relationship was at an end. He packed his in-flight bag that morning in Florence. He kissed her 'one last time'. He told her the room was paid up till the end of the week. She must 'order anything she liked'. She had an open ticket back to London. 'Take your time, do some shopping,' he'd said, passing her a credit card he had opened specifically for their time together. He slid the plastic card guiltily over the bed towards her – as if a new dress or designer handbag could wipe out six years, anaesthetise the pain. She thought back to a month or so before, when they had stayed in a little boutique pub on the South Downs; a rare weekend as a couple. They had talked over dinner of their fantasy home: a cottage in Sussex where they could 'really be together'. Looking back, she realised that it was she who had talked about the cottage; he had just not disagreed. He had never lied, but he had allowed her to fantasise; she saw that now. Had allowed her to dream that they too could have a loving family of their own, if he could just tell Katje that it was over. But he never could. Now, instead, they were over.

She stayed in the hotel for one more night before flying home. She was back in the office the next day, at her desk working on a story, when Max came in. He looked surprised to see her.

'Welcome back,' he said. 'Good trip?'

She nodded silently, fighting back the tears, and turned away. Later that day she left an envelope on his desk marked 'private'. When he opened it, clipped pieces of a credit card would fall onto his desk.

She had considered including a letter of resignation, but common sense got the better of her: she had a mortgage to pay. But she needed a way out, a way not to have to see him every day.

The solution came a few days later. The women's page editor – a glamorous and experienced journalist named Sonia – called her into her office one morning.

'Millie, darling, pop over and see me a bit later? I've got a little story I think you'd do so marvellously.'

The Italian government had recently given financial support to an initiative to reinvigorate the silk industry in the Veneto region of northern Italy. The initiative was being spearheaded by a local entrepreneur, who was determined to revive the indigenous silk industry, to wrest it from the grip of the Chinese, who had been flooding the market with cheap silk for decades. Silk had been produced in Italy for hundreds of years, but the increased use of pesticides in the 1950s had damaged the delicate balance between the mulberry trees and the silkworms. The entrepreneur was keen to get a tiny foothold back in the market of which they had once been leaders. In future, 'Made in Italy' would regain its significance. A revitalised silk industry had the potential to make a difference to thousands of people's lives, providing work and an extra source of income for local landowners.

'Get over to Verona, darling,' said Sonia. 'Verona, Lake Como, Venice – that's just the start of it. I think you'd do such a lovely job... a real "feature" piece. Romance, fashion, the EU, China, biodiversity, economics – it's all there. Tickets on your desk.

We've booked you into a fabulous-sounding villa near Verona, fifteenth-century originally, been in the same family on and off ever since. Run now as a B&B. Vineyards, silk farm, even a swimming pool. Enjoy!'

On the flight over, she wondered if Max had had a hand in it. Had he 'had a word' with Sonia? They went back over twenty years. Sonia had seen him through two marriages and many more 'liaisons'. Rumour had it that they had been lovers too, back in the day. Had he said, 'Sonia, darling, find something lovely for Millie. She's had a rough time of it lately.' Is that how it went? Was she simply a disposable commodity – like a flat that never got used, or a piece of designer clothing that had once been loved but was now destined for the charity shop?

Either way, it was a good story and the locations were undoubtedly beautiful. And now here she was in the villa near Verona. Her room overlooked the rear of the house; the swimming pool was to one side, the garden to the other. It was overgrown, in need of some tender loving care. By contrast, the vines that stretched away from the end of the garden were meticulously kept and reached down to a river that carved its alluvial way through the valley. To the other side of the garden were the mulberry orchards: neat rows of trees, their branches stripped bare to feed the hungry caterpillars that, even now, were ingesting their own body weight in mulberry leaves each day, before spinning their silky white cocoons.

The villa and the surrounding estate were owned by brother and sister, Lorenzo and Elena Manzoni, both in their mid-forties. Elena was divorced and lived in the villa with her two young adult sons. Lorenzo was a widower. He had one child, a nine-year-old daughter named Bella. He had greeted Millie warmly when she arrived in the hire car. Had solicitously shown her where to park in the shade of an old barn. She glimpsed barrels stacked up in corners. Huge wooden racks lined the remaining three walls. Lorenzo gestured towards them.

'That's where we used to keep the silkworms in the old days. We've got a bit more scientific now,' he said. 'I'll show you tomorrow.' The sun was beating down on the pale apricot walls of the villa. He carried her case up the grand but crumbling stone steps and opened the heavy oak doors that led to the high-ceilinged entrance hall. He smiled slightly as she gasped in admiration at the decoration; the walls were painted with frescoes – faded and peeling, but beautiful. He asked for her passport.

'Ah… Camilla Caparelli – you are Italian?'

'On my father's side,' said Millie. 'My great-grandfather was Italian but I was brought up in England – Berkshire, in fact, about as English as it gets. I don't even speak Italian that well, I'm rather ashamed to say. Just a bit of restaurant Italian, you know?'

'Where were they from, the family, do you know?'

'Lucca. They were in the leather trade, I think.'

He showed her to her room.

'I hope you like it… It's one of our best rooms.'

'Oh that's so kind. I hope you don't need it for a proper guest.' Millie's newspaper was being given the room free of charge in return for a good plug for the Manzonis' business.

'No, no, it's our pleasure. It's not really the season yet. May, you know, is quite early for most of our regular guests. I don't know if they told you, but we don't normally serve dinner – just breakfast. There are several nice restaurants nearby. And my sister Elena, she's a wonderful cook and breakfast is quite special. I don't think you'll need much lunch. But we would like to invite you to dinner with us, this evening.'

'That's really kind,' said Millie. 'Please don't feel you have to, but it would be good to chat and find out a little about your business.'

'Yes, of course. We live just over there.' He pointed out of the window towards an old gold-coloured stucco barn. The end wall was decorated with small regular openings, forming a triangular pattern up into the eaves.

'You have a dovecot,' said Millie delightedly. Five pairs of creamy white doves sat contentedly in the early-evening sunlight on the ridge of the steep terracotta-tiled roof. 'I love the sound that doves make. It reminds me of my parents' house, which was surrounded by woods. That cooing always takes me back there somehow. It's comforting… you know?'

Lorenzo smiled.

'I understand. A sound from your childhood that makes you feel safe.'

'Yes, exactly.' She smiled at him. 'So you don't live here in the villa?' she asked, back in reporter mode.

'No, we keep the rooms for guests. But in the winter, when we are closed, we move back in for a few weeks – for Christmas and New Year. It's fun with lots of family around but a little cold, if I'm honest. We are more comfortable over there. It's cosy, you know? See you at eight.'

The Manzonis' kitchen was at one end of the barn. It was simply and inexpensively furnished with an elderly electric stove on which stood two ancient pans, bubbling gently, alongside an extra double-electric ring on the chestnut worktop. It was not elegant, but serviceable. There was a freestanding fridge and a shallow, stained stone sink, beside which was plumbed an elderly dishwasher. Opposite this run of units was a table topped with a huge slab of grey marble, obviously well used, dulled with age. A tomato salad, sprinkled with basil, had been laid out on a colourful maiolica plate. Bread lay invitingly in a basket. A long chestnut table ran down the centre of the barn, surrounded by wooden kitchen chairs with rush seats. French windows looked out over a small terrace, upon which stood four elderly, rusted wire chairs with pale blue cushions. A bottle of red wine stood open on the table with several mismatched glasses and a turquoise pottery bowl filled with pistachios.

'Elena,' Lorenzo called out to his sister, 'here is our guest. Camilla Caparelli – her family are from Lucca originally.'

Elena emerged from a door at one end of the barn. Behind her, Millie could make out a large double bed with a lace bedcover. Elena, dressed in jeans and a black shirt, extended one elegant hand. Her fingers were long, the nails cut short but beautifully shaped. She wore no wedding ring, just a large silver ring on the small finger of her right hand. She was tall, like her brother, and had a few silver hairs among the lustrous dark hair that was twisted into a chignon. The siblings looked very alike. Both had an aristocratic bearing, with high foreheads, but Elena's dark brown eyes contrasted with her brother's, which were the colour of faded denim.

'It's a pleasure to meet you.' Elena's English accent was impeccable. 'From Lucca, you say? A beautiful city. Do you visit often?'

'No, not often. We went as children a few times and stayed near Viareggio with some distant cousins. Although I did go back just recently; I was visiting Florence with a friend…'

An image of Max cycling along the medieval walls of Lucca, shouting to her over his shoulder: 'Come on, Mills, race me,' flooded her mind. They had been so happy that day.

She looked away momentarily, aware that tears were close.

Lorenzo, sensitive to her sudden distress, handed her a glass of wine.

'I hope you like Valpolicella. It's from our own vineyard.'

'Thank you,' said Millie, blushing slightly. 'I love it.'

'Dinner won't be long,' Elena said, as she turned to her brother, and dropped her voice a little. 'Lorenzo, *quando torno a casa* Lino?'

He responded in Italian. Millie understood a few words. Lino was clearly one of Elena's sons, who was at university in Padua.

'My nephews,' Lorenzo said, by way of explanation, as Elena wandered through to the kitchen. 'They are on their way back from Verona now. Lino is a student in Padua – he's back with us for a week or so. His brother Angelo works with us here full-time; he graduated a couple of years ago. He's been out delivering wine to the cooperative this afternoon.'

The boys arrived twenty minutes later; tall, handsome, slender, like their mother. They chatted easily with their guest, clearly relaxed in any social situation.

'I'm sorry that my daughter Bella cannot meet you this evening,' explained Lorenzo, as he refilled Millie's glass. 'She is spending the night with a school friend.'

Dinner began with pasta and rabbit sauce, followed by sea bass, simply cooked and served with tomato and basil salad. As the boys helped to clear away the plates, Millie placed her phone on the table.

'That was delicious, Elena, thank you. Your brother was right – you are a fantastic cook.' Elena smiled graciously. There was something inscrutable about her, Millie felt. She was not easily flattered, that was clear. Perhaps it was her aristocratic bearing, but there was an invisible wall around her, as if she was anxious to protect herself from this stranger in their midst.

'Should we talk about the silk farm now? I hope you don't mind if I record our chat?' Millie gestured towards her phone. 'It saves me making endless notes.'

Lorenzo and Elena nodded.

'Tell me a little of the history of the house and the farm. Have you always kept silkworms here?'

'Traditionally, yes, as the name of the villa suggests.' Lorenzo gestured towards a business card lying on the table, decorated with a pen and ink sketch of the villa, its name emblazoned above.

'What do you mean?' asked Millie.

'Villa di Bozzolo, House of the Cocoon.'

'Oh, I see – I didn't realise. How interesting. So silk is what you have always produced here?'

'Yes, silk and wine. But the house and the estate have been through enormous upheaval over the years – even in the last century

during the two World Wars, it was very difficult. It's a long story…
I should start at the beginning.'

Later that night, as Millie lay in bed, her fingers touching
the soft white sheets, listening to the doves gently calling to
one another, she thought once again of Max. He hadn't said
goodbye to her when she left the office the previous evening. In
fact, he had not spoken to her at all privately since they parted
in Florence a week earlier. She had sat with him in editorial
meetings, but he had pointedly avoided her gaze. He had been
polite enough when she had suggested ideas for features but
there was a distance. It was unfair of him, of course. And yet
what had she really expected?

She thought, sometimes, of her own parents; so upright, honest
and faithful. Her father was a civil engineer, now retired and living
in Berkshire; he was a pillar of village life. How would she have felt,
as a child, if he had abandoned her mother? She knew the answer
to that: she would never have forgiven him.

No, it was not a victimless crime, this love affair with Max – far
from it. There were multiple victims: Katje, the girls, as well as
herself. And however much he promised her that she meant something to him; that he loved her; that, yes, he was capable of loving
two people and that he could cope with it – for her, increasingly,
it was just not enough. When they were together there was an
intensity, a passion neither had felt before; at least that is what he
had told her. And yet, when she really needed him – if she had a
nightmare in the middle of the night, or when she'd had a bad day
at work – he could not be there. His real life happened elsewhere.
It was Katje who lay in his arms at night; it was her neck that he
kissed when he got home from the office. It was his daughters he
sat with and watched TV; it was his family he took on holiday to
Greece, or skiing in Austria. She was allocated just one evening a
week, and the occasional weekend or business trip. It wasn't a life;
it wasn't really love.

Max had told her that he loved her; that he loved to be with her – that she brought him so much happiness. And yet, she had to confess that she wasn't happy… ever. When she was with him she was waiting for him to leave; and when she was not with him, she was waiting for him to arrive. She had been waiting too long. And yet… as she felt the sheets that night in the villa near Verona, and thought back to their three glorious days in Lucca and Florence to celebrate her thirty-eighth birthday, before the moment he told her it was over, she began to cry.

Chapter Two

Villa di Bozzolo
May 1704

Anastasia and Marietta silently shut their bedroom door. Pale shafts of early-morning light spilled round the edges of the shutters. They could hear their father snoring loudly from his room further along the corridor. Sometime during the deep darkness of the previous night they had listened as he shouted at his wife. They heard the slaps; later, they had heard their mother weeping softly. They wanted to go to her, to lie with her and comfort her, but they had learned long ago to resist the temptation: it would only exacerbate the situation. They could only comfort her when she was alone – when their father had gone out to the vineyard, or to harangue the workers on the silk farm.

'Marietta,' whispered Anastasia to her sister, 'you must stay here. There's no reason for us both to get into trouble.'

'No, I'm not letting you go on your own. Besides, I'd rather be with you than alone here when he finds that you've gone.'

'But... what about Mamma?'

Marietta stopped on the staircase, a look of resignation spreading across her face.

'You think I should stay here to protect her?'

'Well, when he finds that I've gone, he's going to be so angry. And maybe if you are here, and say that you know nothing, he will believe you and leave Mamma alone. Otherwise, he'll blame her, you know he will.'

Marietta nodded her head sadly. Her sister was right; their father would certainly blame their mother for Anastasia's disappearance. Her fear was that she too would take a beating as he sought to discover the whereabouts of his eldest daughter. But she smiled bravely, kissed her sister on both cheeks and held her to her, inhaling the sweet, familiar scent of her dark hair.

'Are you sure Marco said you were to come today?'

'Yes, I have his letter here,' said Anastasia, taking the folded paper from the pocket of her skirt. She read aloud:

Come to me at the villa on the lake. I will be waiting for you.

She clutched the letter to her breast and kissed it before putting it back in her pocket.

'But I still don't understand,' said Marietta, 'how he thinks he can marry you without our father's permission. And with no dowry?'

'Marco will see to everything…'

Marietta saw on her sister's face a combination of desperation and hope.

The sisters heard their father moan in his sleep – a loud animal-like groan that normally preceded his waking. 'Marietta,' said Anastasia hurriedly, 'I have to go.'

Anastasia kissed her sister, pulled her cloak around her shoulders and ran down the last few steps into the large hall. It was just before dawn and she hoped none of the servants were awake. Her little Bolognese dog, Bianca, slept peacefully in her basket beneath the large hall table. Anastasia bent down to stroke her head. 'Goodbye, my little darling,' she said to the bundle of soft white fur. The dog looked up lovingly and licked her hand. Anastasia heard the distant clanking of the grate down in the basement kitchens. Realising the cook or kitchen maid must already be at work, she kissed the little dog briefly on the top of her head and ran to the heavy oak door. As she turned the key, causing the mechanism to slip back, it emitted a loud clunk. She held her breath to see if the noise had disturbed anyone, but the silence was interrupted only by the sound of the doves cooing in the dovecot nearby. She pulled back the long bolts at the top and bottom of the door. She had oiled them a little the night before, and the top bolt slid back almost silently; but the bolt at the base of the door remained stubbornly stiff, and its sharp edges cut into her small fingers painfully as she yanked. It sprang back suddenly with a loud crack. Bianca jumped out of her basket, wagging her tail.

'No, Bianca, go back to bed. Go... shoo,' whispered Anastasia.

The dog turned and lay down on her bed, her ears pricked, her head cocked to one side, questioning, her little black eyes alert and watchful. Anastasia paused briefly, listening for the sound of footsteps on the cellar stairs, or from upstairs. But there was silence. She pulled the door open and stepped outside. Her father's hunting dog Arturo lay across the doorway; she stepped over him, brushing his long back with the hem of her dress. He raised his huge shaggy head morosely from sleep and watched as she ran deftly across the yard, holding her skirts high, and opened the stable door. Her horse, Minou, shook his head from side to side in greeting. She stroked his ears and kissed the side of his head, shushing him. She closed the stable door silently behind her and pushed the horse gently to one side of the stall. Taking the saddle that lay across the door, she threw it over his warm pale grey back. His ears pricked. As she buckled the girth beneath his soft underbelly, she heard the unmistakable sound of her father coughing loudly. She peered over the top of the stable door. He was standing on the steps of the villa in his nightshirt, looking around him. He rubbed his large belly and scratched his balding head. He looked left and right, then straight ahead, towards the stables.

Anastasia shrank into a dark corner of the stable; the horse peered round, watching her intently as she crouched in the shadows. She held her finger to her mouth and looked into the eyes of her beloved Minou, willing him to stay silent. Some unspoken understanding flowed between them; he stood stock-still. Normally when she was saddling him, he would shake his head happily, or paw the ground a little, impatient to be off. But that morning, as the sun rose slowly over the villa, Minou was like a Carrara marble statue. He closed his eyes and exhaled almost silently through his soft pink nostrils.

Her father coughed loudly, clearing his throat, spat on to the marble steps of the villa, scratched his backside, patted his dog's head and turned to go back into the villa.

Anastasia breathed finally, and stood up, stroking Minou's pale grey flank.

'Good boy,' she whispered.

She pulled the bridle over his head, fixing the buckles, all the while whispering, 'Shush, boy… good boy.'

When he was saddled, she looked up towards the house. Her sister Marietta stood at their bedroom window; she raised her hand nervously as Anastasia led her horse out of his stable. Hitching up her skirts, she climbed into the stirrups and onto his back. In minutes she was gone, galloping through the archway and onto the open road.

Chapter Three

Breakfast at Villa di Bozzolo was just as Lorenzo had promised. Half a dozen tables were arranged around the dining room, laid with colourful maiolica china. Four other people were staying at the villa – middle-aged couples who ate their breakfast in virtual silence, interspersed with *sotto voce* comments about needing more coffee, or another slice of cake.

A long table stood in the middle of the dining room, covered with white linen and groaning under the weight of home-cooked cakes, breads and pastries. Little glass dishes of jam, all home-made and neatly labelled, were arranged next to silver dishes of butter. Elena drifted into the room, wearing a long black apron, offering 'any kind of coffee. We can do latte, cappuccino, espresso… Or there is filter coffee and all kinds of tea.'

Millie sat down at a table in the corner, next to a window that overlooked the garden. It was curious, she reflected, how solitary diners preferred corner tables, as if the walls around them could provide some sort of protection. She ordered a latte and looked around her. The walls were painted a pale shade of apricot. The panelling was highlighted with faded gold leaf. Family portraits adorned the walls in heavy gilt frames – strong-featured men and women dressed in dark Victorian garb. From the window she could see the edge of the swimming pool, behind a long hedge. Angelo, Elena's son, walked up and down methodically, dragging what looked like a long-handled fishing net through the water to collect fallen leaves and debris. A little girl – tanned and slender in her pink swimsuit, her brown hair streaked gold by the sun – climbed out of the pool, giggling. She tried to take the pole from the young man, but he lifted it high above his head, laughing. The child picked up her towel and ran through a small gap in the hedge towards the barn where Millie had eaten supper the previous evening. This, she realised, must be Bella.

Millie felt a small frisson of guilt. The child looked about the same age as Max's two girls – Charlotte and Tabatha. She had never met them formally, of course, but had seen them once. In the early days of her relationship with Max, she had gone with a friend, ostensibly to look around Portobello Market, but in her heart of hearts, she had really wanted to find out where Max lived; to find his house on the edge of a square in Notting Hill; to observe him in his 'other life'. It was wrong, she knew, reckless even, but she felt powerless to stop herself. She was driven by a combination of curiosity and envy. After she and her friend Kitty had walked from one end of the market to the other, Millie had suggested they have coffee in a trendy cafe in Elgin Crescent. As they ordered lattes and beetroot cake, she noticed a tall man attempting to pull a double buggy backwards over the threshold of the cafe, cursing under his breath as he did so. She realised at once, and with some horror, that it was Max. Overwhelmed with shame at just being there, Millie ducked down beneath the table, hissing at her friend: 'Oh God, that's my boss! I don't want him to see me.'

The friend, who knew nothing of Millie's relationship with Max, whispered: 'Why?'

'I… I'm late with a story. Oh, don't let him see me.'

The waitress chose that moment to bring their lattes and cake.

'Does your friend still want this coffee?' she asked, peering around the cafe. Millie sat scarcely concealed beneath the table, her body folded up as tightly as it could be; her face in her hands.

'Yes... yes,' said Kitty nervously, shifting her chair slightly so as to further conceal her friend from the tall, harassed silver-haired man at the counter. 'She's just had to... um... to pop off and find something.'

The waitress raised her eyes heavenward, and put the coffees and cakes down on the table.

From her vantage point underneath the table, Millie observed her lover.

He wore a pair of chinos and an old denim shirt; she had never seen him in anything so casual. At work, he was always impeccably dressed. But they suited him – the blue denim brought out his grey eyes and highlighted the silver hair pushed away from his tanned face. Max was always tanned, perhaps because he played tennis most mornings before coming to work.

A tall, slender woman came into the cafe behind him. She had cropped blond hair and wore a black leather jacket and very tight jeans. Her eyes were shaded by a pair of oversized black sunglasses; they were the only 'oversized' thing about her. This, then, was Katje. The two children in the buggy, both with fine blonde hair, wore navy and white striped T-shirts tucked into denim skirts.

Katje discussed the various cakes on offer at the counter.

'Max, what do you want? It's your sons who are coming to tea, after all.'

She sounded impatient.

'I don't mind... anything.' The twins chose that moment to start fighting, pulling each other's hair and pinching one another. One poked the other in the eye and the indignant victim screamed loudly. Max crouched down by the buggy and remonstrated with them, his voice remarkably calm and conciliatory.

'Now, Tabby, that wasn't nice, was it? How did you think Lottie would react? She was bound to be furious with you.'

The sight of the man she loved negotiating with his little daughters was almost unbearable for Millie. The harsh reality of observing him in the midst of his own family – being confronted by his domesticity, his gentleness – was agonising. All the fantasies she had nurtured over the years of the life they might one day share, the children they might have, were exposed for the insubstantial flights of fancy they truly were. Millie blinked back the tears. Meanwhile, Max's wife looked on dispassionately as her husband continued his attempts at mediation.

'We'll have the carrot cake,' she said, abruptly, to the man behind the counter, who took it off the plate and put it into a large white box.

Millie had a fleeting realisation, looking between the crack in her fingers, that she and Max were virtually on the same level. If he turned round now, he would see her hiding beneath the table.

Fortunately, Tabby chose that moment to poke her sister in the other eye.

'Oh for heaven's sake, Max, take them outside,' barked Katje impatiently.

Max leapt up and began to back the buggy clumsily out of the door. Katje paid for the cake and left the cafe hurriedly. Millie could see her remonstrating with him as they walked up Elgin Crescent in the sunshine towards Portobello Market.

Millie crept from beneath the table, wiping her eyes, red-faced with embarrassment.

'Bloody hell, that was awful.'

'Millie, what on earth— are you all right?'

Kitty noticed the unspilled tears.

'Yes, of course; I think I got some dust in my eyes under there.' Millie wiped her eyes roughly with the back of her hand and ate a forkful of beetroot cake.

'I mean…' Kitty continued, 'OK, you're late with a piece, but did you really need to hide from him? It is Saturday after all, you're allowed to have some time off.'

Millie brushed her comments aside.

'You don't understand my business; he'd expect me to be working on it. Anyway, I don't think he saw me... did he?'

Later that evening, as she poured herself a lonely glass of wine, she was overwhelmed by a sense of shame and self-loathing.

'This has got to stop,' she said to herself, out loud, not for the first time. But it was not that simple.

Now, as she watched Lorenzo's daughter Bella, she thought of Max's two little girls. Would they still be blonde? Or would their hair have begun to darken like Bella's? Would they be laughing now, in the large open-plan basement kitchen of the house in Notting Hill? What would Max be doing? Reading the papers probably, maybe with the girls on his lap. Or was he, perhaps, thinking of her? The longing she had felt for him the previous evening, as she lay in the large white bed alone, seemed sullied suddenly. He had been right to end it. She should have done it herself years ago. She should never have allowed it to start. She had been brought up as a Catholic; what would the nuns at her boarding school in Sussex have made of her behaviour? She knew the answer to that.

Before guilt completely overwhelmed her, she stood up and examined the groaning breakfast table. She chose a small pastry, a piece of cardamom cake ('freshly baked this morning'), and allowed Elena to talk her into a boiled egg.

'I know how the British love their boiled eggs,' Elena said as she headed back through the swing baize door towards the villa kitchen.

Lorenzo had arranged to take Millie on a tour of the estate at nine o'clock, after breakfast.

'Let's start with the silk farms,' he had suggested the previous evening, 'then we can look at the vineyards, and visit the cooperative where our wine is made.'

She came out of the villa forty-five minutes before the appointed time, to scout around a little on her own. As she closed the heavy door behind her, Lorenzo and his daughter emerged from the barn. The child she had seen at the swimming pool earlier that morning was now dressed in bright pink jeans and a T-shirt, her hair carefully plaited. She carried an unfeasibly large backpack, which seemed in danger of dragging her to the ground. Her father removed the backpack and threw it onto the back seat of his elderly Fiat car. Then, gathering his daughter up in his arms, he swung her onto his shoulders and ran around the derelict fountain in front of the villa making wild-animal noises, as Bella laughed and screamed.

Lorenzo came to a sudden halt in front of the villa and looked up at Millie, who stood mesmerised by the scene.

'Wow! That was quite something,' Millie said, laughing. 'Your daughter, I presume?'

Lorenzo swung the child off his shoulders.

'She is. This is Isabella. Bella, this is our guest, Camilla Caparelli. She is staying for a few days and will be writing an article about the villa.'

The child smiled shyly.

'*Buongiorno*, Bella,' said Millie. '*Come vai?*'

She held out her hand to the child, who shook it politely.

'OK, *andiamo*,' said Lorenzo. 'Bella came back early from her friend's house, to have a swim and change, but we need to get her to school now. I'll be fifteen minutes – the school is just in the village.'

'No problem, I'll see you shortly. *Ciao*, Bella.'

Chapter Four

Villa Limonaia, Lake Garda
May 1704

Anastasia rode Minou hard during the three-hour ride to Villa Limonaia. Every few minutes she looked anxiously over her shoulder, expecting to see her father's chestnut stallion bearing down on her. But after an hour, and then two, she began to hope that perhaps, miraculously, he had gone back to bed without realising she was missing. Then uncertainty crept into her thoughts. Surely, she reasoned, he had noticed the front door was unlocked. He would start to wonder why. Would he walk over to the stables to check on the horses? And if he did, and found Minou gone, it would be a matter of moments before he was rushing up the grand marble stairs of the house, and shaking her poor mother and sister awake, demanding to know where Anastasia had gone at this hour of the day. He would press his face close to Marietta's; she would feel his hot breath on her cheek. She might manage to persuade him that Anastasia had just gone for an early-morning ride. He might believe her… but when she did not return in an hour, or maybe two, he would start again. He might even hit her, or their mother. It had happened before.

She remembered a time, not so long ago, when he had lined them all up against the wall of the drawing room and had threatened to kill them, holding his pistol to each of their heads in turn, if they did not confess to some misdemeanour or other. She could not even remember what they had been accused of, but she remembered the stinging pain as his large hand connected with her cheek; his hot, rank breath as he pulled her face close to his; the cold steel of the gun's barrel as he pressed it against her temple; the clinical sound of the gun being cocked. She remembered the terror and sense of helplessness she had felt as he held their mother by her hair, yanking it so hard that a clump came away in his hand. Later that evening, as they welcomed guests to their house, he had been the convivial host, telling the assembled company what a wonderful wife and daughters he had. She had watched her mother's face contort itself into a smile to please him, her hair dressed with an elaborate stiffened lace headdress to conceal the missing hair, and had realised that he would never change, and that none of them would ever be free of him until the day he died. That night she had prayed for that day to come sooner rather than later.

The sun was directly overhead, and the heat intense as Anastasia turned into the private lane that led down to the villa by the lake. The road meandered through mixed woodland – tall cypresses and pines interspersed with more exotic trees and shrubs – which provided welcome dappled shade. As Minou trotted contentedly through the woods, Anastasia saw occasional inviting glimpses of the dark blue lake glistening beyond the dense vegetation.

Marco's father, Vicenzo Morozoni, was a keen plantsman and an enthusiastic follower of the new and exciting Baroque style of gardening. He had travelled all over Europe and beyond – as far afield as the Levant – to gather rare and unusual plants for his gardens. He had a passion for tulips from the Netherlands, but had also filled the gardens with lilies, and lemon and orange trees which grew successfully in the warm moist microclimate of the lake. He was a keen amateur painter, recording each plant's structure carefully in pen and ink, or watercolour, in a set of leather-bound notebooks that were arranged neatly on the shelves of his study. He had shown the pictures to Anastasia on her last visit and had encouraged her to take his pencils and paints into the large garden and make some sketches of her own. She had a talent for painting and sketching and had spent a delightful hour or two drawing a rare lily that he had recently brought back from a visit to the Netherlands. Later, he had remarked on her ability.

'That is very good, Anastasia; you have talent. You should draw and paint more often.'

'I love to paint plants, like you. I draw my horse Minou too. But there is something special about the intricacies of a flower, or a leaf, that make it a wonderful study.'

By contrast, Anastasia's father, Ludovico Balzarelli, disapproved of her painting. In fact, he disapproved of any occupation that took women away from their domestic duties. He allowed for the normal social intercourse that a family in their position was required to display, but he discouraged any kind of academic improvement for his daughters. They played the spinet, which he tolerated, and Marietta had a good singing voice. When people came to the villa he would proudly demonstrate his daughters' talents and encourage them to entertain their guests. But the pursuit of painting, or the study of languages, or learning for its own sake was effectively forbidden. The girls knew better than to challenge him; it would only result in punishment. But secretly, they continued to draw in the privacy of their bedroom – a leaf, or a flower gathered on a walk in the garden and secreted into a pocket, to be drawn later. Their mother occasionally managed to smuggle books into the house too, but that was a rare treat. Small leather-bound volumes of poetry, or perhaps a play or novel. A particular favourite was *Persinette* – the latest work of the French novelist and poet Charlotte-Rose de Caumont de La Force, known as Mademoiselle de La Force. The girls fell on the new romantic novel, and took pleasure in reading to one another when they knew that their father had gone for the day. But they could not risk leaving any books in plain view. Instead, they were hidden away in a chest at the back of their wardrobe, covered with layers of undergarments to discourage any unwanted discoveries.

One morning, as Anastasia walked in the vineyard, she was overwhelmed by the desire to draw a bunch of grapes hanging down from the vine. There was something intoxicating about the dew on them, the sharp morning light casting shadows on the leaves, the strong dark stem of the vine. Their father had not long gone out for the day, and so, thinking she could work undisturbed for an hour or two, Ana went to her room and brought down her easel and sat contentedly sketching between the rows of vines. She was startled suddenly by a rustling sound, followed by an angry roar. Ludovico was bearing down on her, his face puce with rage. He ripped the paper from the easel and tore it up in front of her.

'You should be inside, helping your mother sort linen,' he barked, as he pushed the hapless girl towards the house, dragging the easel behind him with the other hand. The following morning, when Anastasia looked once again for her easel, the kitchen maid, Magdalena, told her that her father had ordered it be destroyed. Anastasia's rage at this act of vandalism burned brightly that day. Far from discouraging her in her artistic ambitions, it only served to crystallise her determination that she should be allowed to pursue an artistic life of some kind – if she could just escape the controlling influence of her father.

To meet a man like Marco, whose family encouraged her artistic ability, had been a joy. She had grown up socialising with his family. She and Marco shared a love of nature and a passion for horses. But there the similarities ended, for Marco's upbringing had been very different to her own. Marco's mother had died when he was a child and Vicenzo, his father, had taken on the role of mother as well as father, managing to combine the ideal qualities of each. Vicenzo was intelligent, gentle and nurturing, and gave his full attention to his son. Marco was educated by tutors at home; he was introduced to the family business as he entered his teenage years, and taught about the extraordinary legacy of the Morozoni family. Anastasia observed all this and could not help but compare it with her own upbringing. She was particularly touched by Vicenzo's demonstrative affection for his son. He would often put his arm around Marco's shoulder as they talked; and he encouraged him to entertain guests at dinner with a funny story, or an amusing anecdote, laughing loudly at the boy's jokes.

The Morozoni and Balzarelli families had known each other for several generations. Vicenzo and Ludovico's fathers, both significant landowners of the Veneto region, had been good friends. The Morozoni family's wealth had been built on the manufacture and trade of plain silk fabrics known as *ormesini da fodera,* which was cheaper to produce than silk brocades or velvets. Manufactured in mills dotted across the countryside between Verona and Trento, this plain silk proved popular and profitable, undercutting the established silk mills of Venice. The Morozonis' silk empire had created enormous wealth, and they had acquired vast tracts of land and property across the north of Italy. Vicenzo's grandfather had bought an old monastery on the shores of Lake Garda, which he converted into a summer residence for the family. It was an ideal retreat for them to get away from the heat of city life in the summer months. Vicenzo and his son were the first generation of the Morozoni family to base themselves permanently on Lake Garda, where the artistic, aesthetic Vicenzo concentrated on the estate and family farms, while his two younger brothers, Giancarlo and Alessandro, developed the family silk business.

The Balzarellis, by contrast, were essentially farmers. They had owned their land since the fourteenth century and were proud of their farming heritage. As well as extensive vineyards, they also farmed arable crops and, through a network of smaller tenanted farms on their land, manufactured silken thread for the mills and looms of Veneto. Most of the land had been acquired by Ludovico Balzarelli's father, a determined, ambitious man. A disciplinarian, he was perhaps a little too firm with his only son. Ludovico's elder brother had died as a child, and the younger brother grew up sensing his father's disappointment that his favourite son had been taken from him. When his father died, Ludovico was determined to achieve financial success and prove himself to his dead father. Under Ludovico's stewardship, silk production had become increasingly important to the family, as the region became one of the major silk-manufacturing centres in Italy. The city of Florence and the northerly region of Piedmont also prided themselves on the quality of their silk, but Veneto considered itself pre-eminent. In fact, it was said that the extraordinary career of the sixteenth-century architect Palladio, who designed over four thousand villas in the area for wealthy clients, was based almost entirely on the production of silk in the Veneto region.

Ludovico was driven essentially by two things: money and envy. He resented the Morozoni family's massive wealth and was determined to build up his own empire to equal theirs. He had ambitions to own his own silk mill, to see his silk turned into a product that would one day grace the great and good of Veneto society. But Ludovico had a fatal weakness: he gambled. Lacking the capital to acquire a silk mill, he had borrowed, using the farm as security. When he lost at cards, parcels of land were sold to pay the debt. The large estate he had inherited from his father was sadly depleted and the dream he had of owning his own mill retreated day by day. Of course, he took no responsibility for this state of affairs. He was incapable of appreciating the risks he took, seeing his gambling as a necessary part of business life. The next game, the next hand would bring him the wealth and success he craved. But the more he lost, the more he turned his anger on his wife. If she could produce a son with whom he could work, who could inherit his business, his luck would surely change.

*

Villa Limonaia stood on the edge of the lake among lemon and olive groves. As Anastasia rounded the side of the villa, she saw Marco seated on the large veranda overlooking the lake. The villa had a small landing station and she could hear the waves of the lake slapping the underside of the wooden jetty. Marco looked up when he heard the rhythmic thud of the horse's hooves. Seeing Anastasia, he rushed down from the stone veranda and took the reins, helping her dismount.

'*Cara* – you are here… you must be tired. Come inside, we will get you a little wine and something to eat.'

Anastasia laid her head against Marco's shoulder as he swept her off her horse. He put his arms around her.

'You are safe now, *cara*… come.'

He called for the groom, who led Minou off to the stables.

Sitting on the veranda, watching the sunlight play on the surface of the lake, Anastasia's fear began to fade a little. It was so peaceful – just the sound of lapping water and the rustle of the trees in the wind.

'I have made all the arrangements,' said Marco as he handed her a glass of wine. 'We shall travel today, by coach, to Lake Como. My cousin Tobias and his wife Caterina have agreed we can have the ceremony at their villa. They have asked a local priest to marry us.'

'That's kind of them, but isn't that rather a long way to go? Why don't we just get married here?' asked Anastasia.

'I am anxious that we get as far away as possible, just in case your father comes after you.'

'Yes… I understand.'

'You left early, as we agreed, before your father got up?'

'Yes – at least I tried. But he did get up. I was saddling Minou when I heard him come out. He stood on the steps in front of the villa. I thought he had seen me but I crouched down in the corner of the stable. Minou was so clever and brave. He didn't move, he gave no sign I was there. My father went back inside. But I made a mistake – the door was unlocked. He always locks it at night. I am worried he might have realised that something wasn't right.'

'You didn't ask Marietta to lock it behind you?'

'No!' wailed Anastasia, leaping to her feet and pacing the terrace. 'I have been reproaching myself all the way here. But I was fearful she would be discovered. I wanted her to go back to bed, I didn't want to get her into trouble.'

'I understand, Anastasia,' said Marco soothingly. He stood and wrapped his arms around her and led her back to her chair, encouraging her to sit down. 'Here, drink your wine. Calm yourself, *cara*. I'm sure that was the right thing to do. But it won't be long before he realises you are gone, and forces Marietta to tell him your secret. I know she is loyal to you, but from what you have told me he will not allow her to remain quiet for long. He will find a way of getting the truth out of her, or your mother.'

'My mother doesn't know… I didn't tell her. But you are right. Oh, poor Marietta! I should never have taken her into my confidence. She wanted to come with me, but I persuaded her to stay to protect Mamma.'

'Of course. Your poor mother. Let us hope he is not too angry with either of them. And by the time he finds us it will be too late.'

'And what of your father? Does he know our plans?' asked Anastasia.

'No, I decided not to tell him. But when he returns from his travels, you will be here with me as my wife. I'm sure then that he will be happy for me.'

Anastasia was not so sure. Even a family with land and income preferred their sons to marry a woman with a good dowry.

'Are you sure? He might be angry, too. He might force us apart.'

'No, no! You know my father – he is a gentle man. He has a tender heart. And he is fond of you, Anastasia. Now, we should go.'

He stood up and called the servant for the carriage to be brought round to the front of the villa.

'I did not risk bringing any luggage with me… I have only the clothes I stand in.'

'Don't worry,' said Marco, 'we will buy what you need in Como.'

Chapter Five

The journey to Lake Como took two days. Anastasia was tense, peering constantly out of the rear carriage window, terrified that her father would follow them.

'Anastasia, he's not there. He has no idea where you have gone. You're safe, I promise.'

'Yes, yes, I know you're right. It's just… you have no idea what it's like to live with a man like that.'

'I know he has been harsh sometimes but you've told me so little.' Marco took her hand and kissed it. 'Tell me now.'

'I am ashamed.' Anastasia's dark eyes filled with tears.

'What have you to be ashamed about?'

'He's not just harsh; he did such a terrible thing – to Mamma, the night she told him of our plans to marry.'

'He was angry, I know. He forbade the match – that's why we've been forced to run away.'

'It was worse than that, much worse.'

'What do you mean?'

Anastasia had never confessed the full extent of her father's terrible cruelty to anyone outside the family. It was their awful secret, buried deep within them. Somehow Ludovico had managed to persuade his family that the cruelty he meted out to them was their responsibility. Throughout her young life, Anastasia had often wondered why he felt the need to be so cruel. Was he simply, as she often thought, just a wicked man? Was it her mother's inability to produce a male heir? Four sons had been born over the years, but all had died in infancy and her father often referred to his 'terrible luck' in only having daughters. With each death, her father's behaviour became more erratic, more violent.

Sometimes, Anastasia feared her father's cruelty to them was caused by her mother's acquiescence at his ill treatment – her complete inability to fight back. Anastasia had observed her mother's passivity over the years, and she understood. If you fought against Ludovico his rage could be uncontrollable. But, nevertheless, Ana railed against it. Her hatred of her father was intense and visceral.

What she could never reconcile was that the brutality he displayed towards his wife and children was in such contrast to the love – the almost pathological passion – her father had for dogs and horses. Their unwavering loyalty, she presumed, gave them a special place deep in his heart. She knew nothing, of course, of his childhood. Of the love he had felt for his first dog as a little boy, or of the terrible pain he felt when the dog died and how he swore never to love another living thing. Unable to keep that promise, he wept, still, when a favoured dog died; he would sit all night with a sick horse, washing it down, stroking its flanks. And yet he was incapable of showing any affection for the people he should have loved most, his own family.

'When we left your house that night, the night you asked me to marry you, we were so happy – Marietta, Mamma and I. Mamma seemed so delighted for me. I know she was hoping that it would give us all the chance for happiness; she and Marietta would be allowed to come and visit me at Lake Garda… they would have the chance to get away from my father. But I know too that she was fearful of telling him about us.'

'Go on,' encouraged Marco.

'"I'm sure all will be well, Ana," she said that night on the way home. "The families are old friends. The Morozonis are highly respected and it would be a good match – but we must tread carefully with your father."'

Marco took Anastasia's hand in his own.

'She was right. My father is… unpredictable. He likes to be in control. I was naive. I assumed because the families have known each other for so long that he would ultimately be happy with the match. I was wrong.'

'What happened?' asked Marco.

'When we got home, we were standing in the hall, taking off our cloaks and gloves. We were laughing and happy. "You are in good spirits, wife," Father said. He'd come out of the small salon with a glass in his hand. His tone was accusatory, as if he resented our happiness.

'"Yes," my mother said, so innocently, "we have had a fine time."

'We thought nothing more of it, Marietta and I. We said goodnight, but my mother looked anxious when I kissed her. I should have realised, then, what a terrible thing I had asked of her – to intercede for me with him.'

Anastasia's eyes filled with tears.

'Go on,' urged Marco.

'The following morning, after my father had left the villa to visit the vineyards, we crept into their bedroom. The shutters were still closed. The room was hot and airless. Marietta went over to the window and opened the shutters. And then we saw her… Mamma… lying there in the bed. Her body was crumpled, there was blood on the pillow – her lip had been split. Her face was covered in bruises. She held up her hands to shield her eyes from the light, so I closed the shutters again.

'"Mamma," said Marietta, "what has he done to you?"

'Mamma tried to pull herself up in her bed, but she sank back on the pillows, clutching at her ribs. She was obviously in pain. I told her, "Don't move, Mamma… don't move." Marietta lay down on the bed next to her, trying to comfort her.'

'Had *he* done this terrible thing to her?' Marco was appalled.

'Yes. She had asked him, you see, if I could marry you. But he refused.'

'He had promised you elsewhere, you told me in your letter.'

'Yes – to a mill owner.' Anastasia almost spat the words in disgust. 'What I didn't tell you was that he finally confessed that he had lost me in a game of cards.'

Marco stared at her in disbelief. 'That cannot be true.'

'Oh, it is true. They met in the casino in Venice. This man beat my father at cards and would not let him off the debt. He threatened to ruin us, if Father backed out. If, on the other hand, the marriage took place, my father's business would prosper. The contracts have already been signed.'

Anastasia stared miserably out of the carriage window.

'Ana, Ana… I can't believe he could do such a terrible thing.' Marco pulled her towards him, embracing her, kissing her hair, her cheek. 'But I am with you now. I will protect you, I promise.'

Anastasia pulled away from him for a moment, wiping her eyes with the back of her hand.

'I was so angry with him at that moment. I said to my mother, "He cannot do this to me. I am not something to be sold, or handed over. How dare he? He cannot make me. He cannot."'

'And what did your mother say?'

'"You know he can. He has the power, you cannot defy him."'

'Thank God you wrote to me…'

He squeezed her hand comfortingly.

'Are you sure *your* father will forgive you for marrying me in secret?' Anastasia asked anxiously.

'Of course he will. He loves you, Anastasia; he admires you – you know that. I think he will be delighted to have such a beautiful daughter-in-law.'

'Not if my father decides to sue him.'

'Don't think about that – even he wouldn't do such a thing.'

Anastasia smiled, ruefully.

'You are so lucky to have such a kind father. Ever since I've known you, I've never seen him angry with you. He is always so full of love, so encouraging.'

'He is. He has always told me that I must follow my heart and that's what I'm doing now. You'll see – he won't be angry once we're married.'

They stopped overnight in a small tavern in the village of Rovato. The horses were stabled nearby and the carriage driver was billeted off the main road at a farm where the carriage could be concealed in the barn. Marco had arranged for a suite of rooms in the tavern for himself and Anastasia, and asked the serving girl if she could bring their supper upstairs. He was anxious they should not be observed. She returned with a jug of wine and a large tureen of soup that she laid on a small table in the window of the little sitting room. He knocked gently on Anastasia's door.

'Anastasia… *Cara* – there is a little supper laid next door. Come, darling, you must eat.' He pushed open the door. Anastasia lay fully clothed on the bed, fast asleep. He kissed her forehead and finally she opened her eyes. She was instantly awake and alert.

'Oh Marco. What has happened; is it my father?'

'No, nothing has happened. We're quite safe. The village is so small and remote; he won't think to look for us here. Come and eat, there is some food laid out in my room.'

Anastasia ate a little soup, and drank the wine, but she flinched at every sound: a step on the stairs outside, a horse trotting past, the rumble of a carriage below.

She returned to her room and took off her riding habit, laying it on the chest at the end of the bed, and lay down on top of the covers, ready to flee at a moment's notice. She slept fitfully that night, alert to any noise. Finally, just after dawn, she knocked on Marco's door.

'*Caro*, we should go.'

He was already awake and packed.

'I agree. I'll ask the boy downstairs to fetch the carriage driver, and bring the carriage round straight away.'

They arrived at the villa near Cernobbio late that afternoon. As the sun slid behind the hills, casting an opalescent pink haze over the lake, their carriage rumbled down the driveway towards the Renaissance villa. Formal geometrically shaped flowerbeds led the eye towards the water's edge. Tobias – Marco's cousin – and his wife Caterina stood on the grand stone steps, ready to welcome the young couple.

That evening, they ate dinner overlooking the garden. They chatted amiably about the ceremony the following day and the couple's plans for the future. But there was an undercurrent of anxiety. At each loud noise, or slam of a door, Anastasia started nervously. Marco did his best to reassure her, but she was permanently on edge.

Anastasia slept fitfully that night and woke early. The sun had not yet risen over the grey, imposing mountains, still crowned with snow, on the opposite side of the lake. An early-morning mist hung low over the water; a flock of geese skimmed its surface, vanishing momentarily before reappearing and soaring high over the water. It was such a peaceful scene, and Anastasia began to believe, to hope, that perhaps this would one day be her life. That she too could live in a house on a lake, free from fear. That she might have children, a loving husband; that she would, finally, be allowed to paint and draw.

The sun crested the snow-topped mountains, spilling gold light over the surface of the lake. Anastasia sat at the window watching the changing scene unfold. As the sun rose, the leaden-grey silhouetted mountains took on form and texture. The apricot walls and roofs of little hamlets, sprinkled across the gentle green hills, glowed in the early-morning sunshine. The mist evaporated, revealing fishing boats and little sailing boats bustling between the villages that dotted the lake's shores.

There was a knock on the door. A maid entered with a breakfast tray; behind her was Caterina, carrying a pale yellow silk dress. The silk was embroidered with blue and white flowers across the bodice and the skirt.

'Good morning, Anastasia. I know you had to rush away from Villa di Bozzolo and didn't have time to get a wedding dress. I thought this would suit you well.'

'Oh Caterina, thank you; that is so kind. It is beautiful.'

Caterina laid out the dress on the chaise longue and next to it she placed a bouquet of orange blossom.

'There is a small bouquet for you to carry, and a smaller arrangement for your hair. I hope it brings you luck.'

Caterina's maid helped Anastasia to prepare, dressing her long dark hair with the orange blossom, lacing her into the tight bodice of the dress.

She descended the oak staircase just as the clock in the hall struck twelve. Marco stood at the bottom of the stairs gazing up at her.

'At last, *cara*! You see? All is well.'

The wedding party assembled in the hall. Tobias and Caterina chatted animatedly to the priest. The glass doors leading to the gardens stood open. Anastasia glimpsed the small chapel at the rear of the villa, just a short walk from the house. Marco took Anastasia's hand and led her towards his cousin and the priest. At that moment they heard the clatter of horses' hooves outside. A man was shouting, a girl screaming. Anastasia's heart missed a beat; the voices were all too familiar.

The front door burst open and, pushing past an elderly servant who stood dutifully in the hall, was her father Ludovico, red-faced and sweating with fury. He pulled behind him Anastasia's sister Marietta, who whimpered pathetically. He held her roughly by the elbow and when she attempted to resist, he yanked her arm. She was dishevelled, bruised, with a small bald patch on the side of her head, where her father had clearly ripped out a clump of her chestnut hair.

'Anastasia – get into the carriage now,' he commanded.

Anastasia clutched Marco's hand tightly. He stood between her and her irate father, pressing her against the large armoire in the hall. She looked left and right for an escape route. The front door was blocked by her father. Could she run to the French windows and escape? There was a door on her left that probably led down to the basement; but would it be unlocked? And what would she find on the other side? With luck there would be a door leading to the garden, but it might be a dead end and then she would be trapped. She cursed her own lack of foresight, wishing she had checked the previous day.

Marco's cousin Tobias rushed into the hall and together the two men stood in front of Anastasia, barring Ludovico's way; he retained his fierce grip on Marietta while, at the same time, attempting to grab Anastasia's arm with the other hand.

'Get out of my house!' Tobias said fiercely. 'You are not welcome here.'

'I will not. I am the father and legal guardian of that woman there – a woman you have unlawfully kidnapped. She is betrothed to another; the contract has been signed. I have it here.'

He released his grip on Marietta momentarily, and brought out a rolled-up piece of paper, which he waved in front of Tobias and Marco.

'You are about to break the law,' he continued. 'I warn you, I will not allow it.'

He pushed Marco out of the way, and grabbed Anastasia by the arm. She screamed and attempted to pull away, but Ludovico was far stronger, and before Marco or Tobias had time to react, Ludovico had dragged her to him and held her fast behind him. She kicked him in the calves and attempted to free her arm, but his large hand was wrapped round her elbow.

'It is useless to defy me, girl,' he said, turning his red face so close to hers that she could not avoid inhaling his hot, rank breath. Her stomach lurched and she swallowed hard.

'Please, Marco – don't let him take me,' she pleaded.

Marco and Tobias attempted to pull Anastasia away, but the older man was a match for them. He threw the two girls down the steps of the house where two henchmen stood waiting; they manhandled them into the carriage. Ludovico removed a knife from his belt and stood menacingly in the doorway.

'You come near me,' he said to Marco and Tobias, 'and I'll kill you. Trust me – no court will find for you. Stealing my daughter from me… I am in the right.'

He pushed past the elderly servant once again, down the steps and into the carriage. Within minutes it was over.

Chapter Six

The silkworms were kept in a modern purpose-built shed on one side of the courtyard. It was lined with neat stainless steel racks, over which were suspended white plastic spikes that rotated from a central spindle. It was the third week of May and the silkworm larvae, which had been feeding for four weeks on their diet of mulberry leaves, had arrived at the crucial moment of their life cycle: when they would begin to spin their silk cocoons. Lorenzo explained the lengthy process of gestation to Millie.

'These larvae were hatched almost four weeks ago from eggs that were laid by the queen last autumn. Traditionally, the process begins on the Feast of San Marco – April the twenty-fifth. It's a convenient date to remember, and the climate is perfect at that time. After the eggs are laid, they are kept at a steady low temperature to prevent them developing. Nowadays they are held in specialist refrigerators, but in the old days they sent the eggs up into the mountains to keep cool. They are brought back down in April, into a warmer environment to hatch out. The larvae feed continuously on the leaves of the white mulberry tree *Morus alba*. The variety is very important. I understand that the English tried to rear silkworms back in the seventeenth or eighteenth century and it was a disaster because they used the wrong kind of mulberry tree.'

'So they just lie there munching away on mulberry leaves?' asked Millie as she made notes in her book.

'Yes. Sometimes I come in here late at night just to check everything is OK, and all you can hear is the noise of them eating. It sounds a little like rain on a metal roof, you know? The first time I heard it, in fact, I thought it was rain. I rushed outside and was surprised because it was a clear starry night. It was just the sound of the larvae eating. What did you call it?'

'Munching.' Millie smiled.

'That's a great word for it.'

'That must have been so weird.'

'It's a shame that part of the process is over now, but what comes next is the most exciting stage – they are ready to start spinning their cocoons.'

'How do you know they are ready?' asked Millie.

'Look at this one here…' Lorenzo leaned over the long metal tray and pointed to a little white larva no more than an inch long. It appeared to be almost standing up, waving its head to and fro.

'It's sort of rearing up, do you see?'

Millie nodded.

'That gesture indicates that they are looking for something to attach their silk thread to. In a little while it will find the plastic spokes that we place above the trays. In the old days the farmers used twigs from the mulberry trees suspended over the wooden trays. But these days we try to be a bit more scientific about it – and hygienic. The silkworms find the spindles and start to attach a silken thread to them. There… do you see? One is starting to do it now.'

Millie peered into the tray and saw the larva excreting a silken thread, creating what looked like a random cobweb over the white spindles.

'Soon the larva will begin to spin the thread carefully around its own body. It will take about three days. Hopefully you will still be here when they have finished, but if you have already left by then, I can send you photographs.'

Millie had a momentary sense of disappointment that she might miss this important step in the process. Or was it disappointment at the idea of leaving the villa? She had begun to feel a sense of peace and calm in the short time since she had arrived. Being away from Max, in a different country, away from all the familiar triggers and reminders of their relationship had certainly made their separation easier.

'Within the next few days all the larvae will be completely enclosed in their cocoons,' Lorenzo continued. 'Then we will put them all into these baskets over here and they will go to be spun.'

'How does that work? Do you take the end of the cocoon and sort of unravel it? What about the larva inside? I presume it will have metamorphosed into a butterfly by then?'

'No, no, the larva will be dead.'

'Why? How?'

'We have to kill the larva inside the cocoon before we unravel it.'

Millie stopped taking notes and looked up at Lorenzo in surprise. 'Kill. Really?'

'Yes. It's quite humane; the cocoons are placed in an oven. They are killed fairly instantly. After that, they are unravelled and turned into silk thread. I'll take you to see the unit where that happens if you like – it's not that far away.'

'And what about the poor dead larvae?'

'Oh, they are turned into animal feed, so nothing is wasted.'

'That seems so sad,' said Millie.

'Not really. You must remember that the larvae are destined to die very soon anyway. If you left nature to take its course and allow the larvae to metamorphose into a silk moth, they would break out of their cocoon. The males mate as soon as they can, after which they sleep for twenty-four hours. And then they die. The female lays her eggs, and then she too dies. The silkworm's life is simply about reproduction. They metamorphose, they mate, they die… that is all.'

He smiled encouragingly.

'That's even more sad. One chance at love and it's over.'

'You are a romantic, I think.' Lorenzo smiled at her. 'But farming is a business. We can be humane, but we can't let our hearts rule our heads.'

'I realise that… I'm sorry. But why not wait for them to hatch and then unravel their cocoons?'

'Because the cocoons would be too damaged. The threads would be broken and impossible to spin. They would be completely unusable.'

The visit to the larvae house unsettled Millie. She felt slightly embarrassed by her naivety about the silk-manufacturing process. Lorenzo had been so matter-of-fact about it, and yet it had upset her. The killing of the larvae for the purpose of creating a luxury product that no one really needed seemed a pointless cruelty. They parted on the steps of the barn.

'I've got to go to the village to collect some vegetables for Elena, but I'll see you later?' Lorenzo said cheerily. Millie went back to her room, intending to write up her notes, but she was restless; the room felt airless.

She changed into her bikini and an Indian cotton kaftan, and wandered down to the pool. There were no other guests and she had a choice of sunbeds. She chose one next to an umbrella. She removed the kaftan and lay back on the sunbed, her laptop across her knees, and began to write up her notes.

A message popped into the top right-hand corner of her screen: *Message from Max.*

Her finger hovered over the mouse pad. She considered hitting delete, but finally could not resist opening it.

> *Darling… I miss you. Call me.*

Her palms began to sweat as she considered her options. Should she message him back?

Deciding against it, she returned to her work. A few minutes later, though, the temptation to respond was irresistible.

> *What do you want, Max?*
> *To speak to you… to see you. I'm sorry. This was a mistake.*
> *What was a mistake?*
> *You going; me… I've been an arse. Forgive me?*

She was poised to start typing 'Of course', but something stayed her hand. He had hurt her so badly. He was still married. Nothing had changed.

She began to go through her notes, her heart thumping all the while. Another message arrived.

> *What's happened? Where have you gone? Speak to me.*

She waited a little longer before replying.

> *No, Max… not yet.*

She should have said something definitive like 'It's over – let's leave it at that.' But she couldn't quite bring herself to do that… yet. Baby steps, she told herself. Let him stew a while.

She snapped her laptop shut just as Lorenzo came across the lawn towards the pool.

'Ah, Millie – good – you are here. Enjoying the pool, I hope?'

'Just working really,' said Millie, suddenly embarrassed by her near-nakedness. Blushing slightly, she reached for the kaftan, and hurriedly covered herself up.

'I'm sorry,' he said. 'I've disturbed you; you looked so peaceful.'

'Did I? Well I'm not… not really. And I'm here to work after all, not have a holiday. But the pool was so inviting.'

Lorenzo smiled.

'I'm glad you're enjoying it. I wondered if you would like to visit the silk spinners this afternoon, to see the next stage in the process.'

'Yes, please. That would be great. I'd better go and get changed. Give me ten minutes?'

'Take your time. Make it half an hour; I'll buy you lunch on the way there.'

'I think I should buy *you* lunch,' said Millie, 'but either way it sounds like a lovely idea.'

Lorenzo chose a restaurant ten minutes away from the villa. He and Millie sat on the large terrace of the modern single-storey building overlooking vineyards stretching far into the distance. Lorenzo ordered a glass of prosecco for each of them while they studied the menu.

'I don't normally drink at lunchtime,' said Millie as she sipped the chilled wine.

'Well, it's a local delicacy. This is the home of prosecco, so I thought it was time you tasted it.'

'It's delicious. I'm just glad you're driving and not me,' she said, laughing.

They made conversation about the menu and the restaurant before Millie said: 'She's beautiful, your daughter. It must be hard bringing her up on your own.'

'She is beautiful; she looks so like her mother.' He took a sip of water.

'I'm sorry,' said Millie, 'I didn't mean to pry.'

'No… it's OK. She died four years ago. Cancer.'

'Oh, how terrible,' said Millie. 'You must miss her.'

'Every day,' said Lorenzo.

Millie followed his gaze across the vineyards down towards the river that snaked through the shallow valley.

There was an awkward silence.

'Your English is fantastic… it's perfect, in fact,' Millie said, attempting to change the subject. 'Where did you learn to speak so well?'

'Both Elena and I were sent to school in England. She went to St Mary's Ascot and I was at Ampleforth, in the cold Yorkshire countryside! Elena came back here after school and married a guy called Gianfranco and had the boys, but they divorced a few years ago – it was all rather acrimonious, I'm afraid. But I stayed in England, and went to university there. That's where I met my wife, Caroline. We lived in the UK until she died. I only came back to Italy two years ago, when Bella needed to start school. Elena had been running the villa all by herself since our parents died, and she needed help. I was struggling with a full-time job in London, and looking after Bella. It seemed the obvious solution.'

'I see. And is it working out, living here?'

'Yes and no. Bella has fitted in so well and is happy here – we'd brought her up to be bilingual, fortunately. But Elena and I... we don't always see things the same way, you know? She is my elder sister and likes to be "in charge".'

'Yes, I understand. I have an elder brother – Freddie. He's a surgeon, and like most doctors, he's a bit of a bossyboots too. He's married to another doctor and they live in the countryside with their two perfect children.' She grimaced, laughing. 'He's definitely "Doctor Perfect" – at least as far as my parents are concerned.' She smiled and took a sip of her wine. 'We were both sent away to school too, oddly enough. I went to a Catholic school in Sussex – not quite as posh as St Mary's, but still all nuns and church and hockey.' She smiled, shyly. 'My father was an engineer and my parents lived abroad for years, so Freddie and I learned, early on, to be pretty independent. What did you do in England?'

'I studied economics at university. Then I worked in the City. I was an analyst at one of the big banks. But it was hard work. The hours were very long and it wasn't easy with a small child, juggling nannies and so on. Caroline had always managed our home life. She worked too – but only part-time. She was in marketing for a niche leather business. They were very good to her when she got ill.'

'Oh Lorenzo – you have been through it, haven't you?'

Millie reached out and covered his hand with her own. He didn't pull away.

'And you… I think you have worries too, no?'

'Me… oh, you don't have to worry about me. I'm fine. I've just… broken up with someone. That's all. It wasn't working anyway.'

Millie's reticence to discuss her personal life was a habit acquired early on in her childhood. The physical distance created by her parents' life abroad had meant she rarely discussed relationships with them, particularly if they were going wrong. Even as a child she tried not to worry them: what was the point when they were thousands of miles away? And when she began her affair with Max, she knew instinctively they would disapprove. A married man was not the sort of partner they had envisaged for their only daughter. She had made the mistake of mentioning it to her brother Freddie one night over a curry in Brick Lane, not long after she had bought her flat in Fournier Street. He had been taunting her slightly about the lack of men 'on the horizon' – her mother's irritating phrase – and she had recklessly confessed that there was someone.

'Hallelujah!' he had said, shovelling chicken jalfrezi into his mouth.

'But there are problems.'

'Go on…'

'He's married. But don't tell Ma.'

Freddie took a slurp of his beer. 'How's that working out, then?'

'It's fine, it's good. He's fantastic. We both have time apart. It works well.'

'But he's married.'

'I know. I know…'

'Is he leaving her?'

'It's complicated… there are children.'

'Oh, bloody hell, Millie!'

'You think I should end it?'

'Well, it's not what *I* think, is it? What do *you* think?'

After that, she gave Freddie the impression the relationship was over. And she never told her parents. Now, sitting here in this beautiful valley in the Veronese countryside, with this charming, handsome man, she realised she felt comfortable about opening up to him.

'He's married – the man I'm involved with.'

'Well, I'm sorry. I thought there was something the other night. You seemed upset.'

'That's very… sensitive of you. Yes, I was a bit upset. But you know – onward and upwards, as my mother says.'

On the car journey to the spinners, Lorenzo pointed out places of local interest. There were grand Palladian villas and tumbledown farmhouses; little villages merged into countryside, and on every slope, tucked into each spare pocket of land, were vineyards. Millie felt relaxed with this man, she realised. He felt familiar somehow. His dark hair speckled with grey. His intelligent grey-blue eyes, the strong Roman nose. As they drove through the Veneto countryside it occurred to her that she had not actually thought about Max for several hours.

They drove into the outskirts of a small town and Lorenzo turned the car into a modern industrial estate.

'Is this where the spinners are?' asked Millie. 'I imagined it would be in some rustic old building.'

'Ah yes, I suppose that is the idealised vision that lots of people have. But in fact spinning is a modern industrial process now.'

He drew up outside a gleaming glass and steel building.

'Wow – what is this place?'

'This is the headquarters of an international jewellery business tycoon – Antonio Moretti. He is the man who has, up till now, single-handedly revived the Italian silk business. Come, I'll introduce you and he can explain it all.'

Signor Moretti met Lorenzo and Millie in reception and, after a brief chat, took them down to the basement.

'Here it is – my spinning machine,' said Moretti proudly. 'It's one of the few left in the country. I found this one in a local museum, believe it or not, and had it overhauled. It works fine.'

'How old is it?' asked Millie.

'About fifty years old. This area used to be full of machines like this, producing some of the best silk yarn in the world. Italian silk is top quality because it is so strong; the thread doesn't break, which is a problem with some of the Chinese silk.'

He gestured to a row of machine spools delicately unravelling the silken thread from the cocoons below.

'Each cocoon consists of up to thirteen hundred metres of silk thread. They are tied on to the spools by hand. It's quite a labour-intensive business.'

'What I don't quite understand,' said Millie, 'is why the business came to such a halt fifty years ago. Was it just that the Chinese could produce silk more cheaply than the Italians?'

'No, it's not that simple. When I was a boy every farm round here had a mulberry orchard and reared silkworms. Ninety per cent of the land was covered in mulberry orchards. Twenty thousand people in this area were involved with the silk industry; even my own grandparents were silk farmers. In the spring, all the farmers' wives round here would incubate the eggs inside their bodices.'

'Gosh, really?' gasped Millie, 'next to their skin? That sounds rather revolting.'

'Yes, I know it does sound strange, but the body is the best source of an even heat. When the eggs were ready to hatch, they would be sold. It was a vital source of income – perhaps the only source of income at that time of year – before the wine harvest. But the overuse of pesticides on the vineyards caused a major problem. The silk larvae reacted to the pesticides, and began to overeat, but never made any silk. We simply produced very fat silkworms in enormous cocoons that almost exploded. Ultimately, the business collapsed. It was a tragedy and much of the production moved to Asia – in particular, to China. They were able to undercut our farmers as well. So there were several problems. But my ambition is to bring silk production back here to Veneto. I pay the farmers a good wage for their work. We are starting small – producing just a few thousand metres of silk yarn each month – but it is the best quality in the world.'

He took a skein of shimmering white silk that hung on a hook and handed it to Millie. She stroked it before handing it back to him.

'It's so soft; what's the yarn used for?' she asked, as she made notes.

'I use some of it in my business; my wife makes jewellery with it. That was the start of the business for me really. She had an idea to make jewellery with gold beads and silk thread, and I said – well, if we are going to do this, the thread has to be made in Italy. And so it began. The jewellery is sold all over the world. I am hoping to grow the silk business and am encouraging others to start spinning too. At the moment most Italian mills use Chinese silk; I think it would be better if it were Italian. And silk has many uses beyond fashion. It can be used in cosmetics – shampoo, face cream, soap and so on – and it also has medical applications. I've recently applied for a patent to make prosthetic vascular spare parts out of silk.'

'Wow,' said Millie. 'I had no idea – that's extraordinary.'

Towards the end of their visit, Millie put her notebook back into her bag. Her mobile vibrated silently.

'Thank you so much,' she said to her host. 'It's been fascinating – truly. I'm sure there's a really interesting article here.'

'Well, it's been our pleasure,' said Antonio, 'and if you need anything else do please get in touch with us.'

'I will.'

As they walked back to Lorenzo's car, Millie's phone vibrated again. She climbed into the passenger seat and removed the mobile from her bag. She hardly needed to look at the screen to know who was trying to contact her.

> *Mills – where have you gone? I need to speak to you. Call me – please!*
> *Millie, darling. Don't do this to me. It's torture. Call me as soon as you can.*

She turned the phone off.

Lorenzo glanced at it as she did so.

'Someone you don't want to speak to?' he said, smiling.

'Sort of. Someone who thinks he needs to speak to me.'

'And does he?' asked Lorenzo.

'No, not really. He thinks he does, but he's wrong. He just can't… let go.'

'Can you – let go?'

'Yes, surprisingly. I rather think I can.'

She smiled at Lorenzo and at that moment, sitting in his little Fiat, looking into his clear blue eyes, she meant every word.

Chapter Seven

The Mill Owner's House, Venice
May 1704

The wedding of Anastasia Balzarelli and Anzolo di Zorzi took place at the parish church of San Zan Degolà in the parish of Santa Croce. Afterwards, the wedding party – which consisted of Anastasia, Anzolo and her father – repaired to the large reception room on the first floor of Anzolo's impressive house on the Grand Canal.

'I will go upstairs, if I may, and prepare. The maid will show me the way.' Anastasia noted the look of satisfaction that passed between her new husband and her father when she made this announcement. It was a look that said, 'She has submitted, she is under our control.'

She tried to sound cheerful and positive, so as not to alert either Anzolo or her father that she had no intention of submitting to this marriage.

Throughout the long carriage ride from Lake Como they had stopped only twice – for her father to eat food at a local inn, and to change the horses. Anastasia and Marietta were forbidden to leave the coach on both occasions. Escape during the journey appeared impossible; the two guards her father had employed never took their eyes off either of them.

'I wish to relieve myself,' said Anastasia with as much dignity as she could muster, when they stopped at the coaching house for her father to eat. 'Let me pass. I wish to go into the inn over there.'

'Our orders are to keep you here.'

'That is outrageous,' said Anastasia. 'What do you expect me to do?'

'Do it here,' said the guard, smirking. 'We'll turn our backs if you like.'

When she had finished, her legs stinging from the experience, her eyes smarting with tears of indignation, she climbed back into the carriage.

'I have to escape, Marietta,' she whispered to her sister. 'What *are* we to do?'

'I don't know,' wailed Marietta. 'Maybe Mamma can talk some sense into him when we get home.'

The carriage drew up in front of the Villa di Bozzolo at lunchtime the following day. As Anastasia attempted to follow her sister out of the carriage, she felt the grip of her father's large hand on her arm.

'You will stay here.'

'But I must see Mamma, wash, have something to eat, change my dress. Please, Papa.'

'You are coming with me.'

He banged on the ceiling of the carriage and the horses dutifully took up the trot, round the circular well that stood in front of the villa. Anastasia looked out of the grimy windows and saw her beloved Minou, his head hanging mournfully over the stable door. His ears pricked up as the carriage passed by, his head raised.

'Minou… he's back.'

'Of course,' said her father.

'Can't I even see him to say goodbye?'

Her father hesitated for a moment. Anastasia observed a momentary flicker of sympathy in his eyes before he turned away.

'You'll see him soon enough – when you return here with your husband.'

Anastasia, her eyes burning with tears, looked out through the rear window of the carriage. On the steps of the villa stood her mother and Marietta, clinging to one another.

'Where are you taking me?' implored Anastasia.

'To meet your legal husband.'

'But we cannot be married. I will not marry him, I do not know him.'

'You will know him soon enough.' Her father chuckled. 'You will be wed later today and he will have you legally by tonight. There is no escape for you, Anastasia.'

The ceremony itself was a brief affair, with just her father and one of her new husband's employees as witnesses. Anastasia wept throughout the service; when the priest asked her if she agreed to the marriage, she answered softly, 'I do not.' But the priest, who was legally bound to seek the agreement of both parties, ignored her response and merely said the words she had been dreading:

'I join you together in matrimony.'

As they left the church Anastasia observed her father placing a bag of coins in the priest's hand. Back at the mill owner's large house on the Grand Canal, the bridegroom and Ludovico toasted the business union that had been crystallised by the marriage, and congratulated one another.

Anastasia was in a state of shock and filled with dread over what the next few hours might entail – let alone the prospect of spending the rest of her life with this tall, overbearing grey-haired man. At the culmination of the ceremony, he had kissed her on the lips and she had to fight the need to retch. Just the smell of his skin, the taste of his lips on hers was repulsive to her.

She resolved that if she could stay calm for an hour or so, get away from him for a moment, perhaps she could make her escape – just as she had done a few days before, from her father's house. But this time, she promised herself, she would succeed.

*

A young maid led Anastasia up the wide marble staircase towards Anzolo's bedchamber. She looked at Anastasia with a combination of sympathy and pity as she opened the door.

'Thank you,' said Anastasia, fighting back the tears. 'I'll call for you if I need you.'

The girl nodded and left the room.

A key had been left in the lock: an error of judgement, or a kindness on the maid's part? As she listened to the young girl's footsteps retreating down the corridor, Anastasia turned the key. There was a bolt near the top of the door and she slid that across too. She looked around the bedchamber. There was one other door, painted and decorated with motifs of flowers in bright colours. It led to a large closet that Anzolo clearly used for his ablutions. She peered inside, recoiling at the sight of the half-filled chamber pot on the floor in front of her, and the porcelain basin filled with dirty water, a used towel discarded beside it. She shut the door firmly in disgust. Two large leaded windows looked out over the Grand Canal, and Anastasia stood for a few moments mesmerised by the river traffic that flowed up and down. She had never seen such activity. She caught sight of herself in the long mirror that hung between the windows. Her reflection revealed a young dark-haired woman dressed in a torn, soiled, lemon-yellow dress. This was her wedding day, but there was no joy in her face. She looked exhausted – her skin grey, her eyes dull. She sat down heavily on the bed, pushing aside the heavy, dark-green damask curtains, and tried to make sense of what had happened.

What would Marco be doing now? Was he back on Lake Garda? Might he be planning to rescue her? She clung to these thoughts; the alternative was unthinkable. She heard a heavy step on the marble staircase. Her heart began to race: he was coming. The door handle turned. It held fast. He knocked on the door.

'Now, Anastasia – open up, there's a good girl. I am your husband now and you must do as I say.'

She sat rooted to the spot, unable to move, watching the door handle as it turned ineffectually.

He banged on the door.

'Open up, I say.'

She remained sitting on the bed. He banged once again on the door and shouted: 'Open up! Let me in.'

She stood up, moving towards the wall on the opposite side of the room, leaning against it as if willing it to swallow her up, transfixed by the door as it flexed under his pressure.

'Veronica!' she heard him shout. 'Bring me a spare key to this door. What were you thinking, leaving the key in there?'

She heard the girl mumbling and scuttling away down the corridor. This galvanised Anastasia.

She pushed a wide low clothes chest in front of the door. It was heavy and took all her strength, but finally she had it wedged under the door handle.

'What's going on in there?' bellowed her husband. 'What are you doing? Open this door!'

She dragged a second clothes chest from the end of the bed and placed it in front of the first, then took a chair from the corner of the chamber. It was heavy, but somehow she managed to place it on top of the chest. Soon, there was a mountainous pile of furniture wedged against the door.

She heard him fumbling with the spare key, but the key already in the lock on the bedroom side prevented him getting any purchase. She watched the key anxiously as it wobbled in the lock.

'Damn you, Anastasia – unlock this door! I order you.'

He smashed his fist against the doorframe and it shuddered slightly, but remained impregnable.

'Right… well, you have been warned. Don't think you can get away with this. I will be back. You will have to come out sometime, or you will to starve to death. It's your choice.'

She heard his heavy step on the staircase as he retreated.

She burst into tears. The weeks of planning her escape, the fear and excitement of it, the love she felt for Marco, her terror at being removed by her father so forcibly, this unspeakable marriage – finally overwhelmed her and broke her spirit; she sank down onto the floor and sobbed.

When she woke, the bedchamber was in darkness, but stealing into the alien room came the unfamiliar sounds of river traffic – *gondolieri* calling to one another, seabirds screeching as they flew down the wide canal towards the lagoon. She stood up; her limbs felt stiff. She had pins and needles in her left arm, which had been caught beneath her as she lay. Rubbing her arm, she peered out of the window: it was dark. There was no moon that night, but glimmers of candlelight bounced off the water as the *gondolieri* ferried goods up and down the canal, their way lit by lanterns on the prows of their gondolas. They were going about their lives, perhaps on their way home to their wives and children, while she was imprisoned here. She thought of shouting out to them – asking for help. But what would induce them to rescue a strange woman?

She felt hungry, she realised, and thirsty. She looked around for water. In the closet, she found a jug filled with fresh water next to the ablutions bowl and drank greedily from it. But there was no food. She had not eaten since the night before her aborted wedding to Marco. It seemed a lifetime ago. Her stomach rumbled; there was sharp pain beneath her ribs. The once beautiful yellow silk dress was crumpled and stained. She had no other clothes – although her father had promised to send them on to her the following day. She thought of her sister and mother at home at Villa di Bozzolo and began to weep once again. She was alone, terrified and hungry.

She sat on the edge of the bed and breathed deeply. She needed to stay calm, and think. Her plan, when her father had brought her here, had to been to escape as soon as possible. That was her priority; nothing else mattered. If she could get away from this house, she could somehow make her way back to Villa Limonaia… and to

Marco. She knew escape through the house was impossible – the servants, or Anzolo, would block her way. The only route out of this room was by the window.

As she opened the leaded casement, the room flooded with humid air, bringing with it the faint stench of the canal. The window led onto a small ornate stone balcony. She climbed out onto it, and peered down to the canal below. In the dim light she could just make out a wooden landing station, next to which rocked a gondola – presumably for the use of the mill owner. But it was at least twenty feet below her. Beneath the balcony was just a sheer drop. If she jumped, she would certainly break a leg, or worse. She took another sip of water, determined now to eke it out – she might be here for some time as she developed her plan. She checked the door and the pile of furniture that barred her husband's way. She closed and locked the window. Then, confident the room was impregnable, she lay down on the bed and tried to sleep.

When she woke her hunger had subsided. Early-morning light flooded the room. She took another sip of water from the jug in the closet and splashed a little over her face. She wandered over to the window, and climbed once again onto the balcony. The gondola rocked invitingly far below. She looked left and right and saw that just two feet away to her right was a pipe that carried rainwater down from the roof to the canal below. The previous night had been moonless and in her distress she had not noticed it. If she could reach the pipe, she could surely shin down it and to freedom.

She looked down at the yellow silk dress and began to unlace her corset, removing the silk skirt and long sleeves. She went to her husband's closet and found a pair of breeches and a shirt. They were far too large, but she tied the breeches tightly round her waist with a belt, and tucked the shirt in. Her silk shoes were impractical for such a venture, and his shoes were too large. Standing in her stockinged feet, she surveyed the canal. The water sparkled in the dawn light. The gold-coloured palazzo on the other side of the canal glowed, almost iridescent, in the sunlight. It struck Anastasia as ironic that in other circumstances she might have been content to live in this house, near the water. Everywhere she looked was beauty: some of the buildings had little gardens that ran down to the water's edge. At the centre of the palazzo's garden stood a large lemon tree. Flowerbeds, edged with clipped box, radiated out from the centre. They were filled with a riot of pink and white flowers – roses, Anastasia thought, or tulips. In another life she would have liked to row across to that garden and paint those flowers.

She stepped out onto the stone wall of the balcony and reached across to the pipe. She could just touch it with her fingers. She pushed it; it appeared firm. It was attached to the wall by brackets at intervals; it seemed solidly built and would, she judged, take her weight. She was not reckless, but she was brave and desperate. Besides, she reasoned to herself, what alternative did she have? If she stayed in this house she would either starve to death or be forced to submit to a man she hated.

She launched herself at the pipe, grasping it with both hands. She clung to the pipe for a few seconds, gripping it firmly between her knees. Suddenly she was back in a hornbeam tree that she and Marietta had climbed as children at Villa di Bozzolo. She recalled sitting ten or twelve feet off the ground in a protective network of branches as Marietta cried out below her – begging to be allowed to join her. She would usually comply and drag her smaller sister up into the tree; but at times, she would ignore Marietta's cries and enjoy the sense of solitude up in the boughs of the hornbeam, willing her sister to go back inside and leave her in peace.

She was down on the landing station in a matter of moments. She looked about her; she was alone. She climbed into the gondola and untied the ropes fore and aft. She had never been in a gondola before, but she had watched the *gondolieri* the previous evening and thought she could copy their movements. She clutched the heavy oar in her two small hands and pushed the blade against the side of the jetty; the boat floated towards the centre of the canal. She slipped the oar into the rowlock and dipped the blade into the water, but the gondola would not move.

She lifted up the pole once again, slid the blade firmly into the water ahead of her, and pushed forward with all her might. The gondola slipped silently through the water. Her confidence grew with every stroke, and within minutes the mill owner's house had retreated into the distance.

When it was almost out of sight, she decided to get back onto dry land. She was not, after all, intending to row the length of the Grand Canal. There was a stone landing station to her right with steps leading up from the water. An impressive church stood behind. She steered the gondola to the water's edge and hauled heavily backwards on the oar to prevent a collision and deftly leapt out. She skirted the church and sprinted down a passageway, only stopping when she reached a tiny bridge leading over a narrow canal.

Anastasia had never visited Venice. She was, she realised, completely and utterly lost; she had no points of reference. She had heard once of Venice's great church, San Marco, but had no idea where it was, or what she would do if she found it. She crossed the small canal and turned right into another narrow passageway – it looked much like the first. The buildings were tall – they appeared to go almost to the sky, which was just a ribbon of bright blue beckoning above. There was a smell – waste of some kind, or vomit. A rat scuttled past; it ran over her stockinged feet. She screamed before mumbling: 'It's just a rat, Anastasia…'

The far end of the passage was blocked; it seemed there was no way through. Then she saw a narrow opening, just wide enough for one person. She squeezed through the dark gap, and found herself in a small square. She shielded her eyes against the intensity of the light. An innkeeper was opening his establishment, placing a table and chairs outside. He nodded at the strangely dressed girl. She tried to walk casually past, inhaling the scent of coffee and hot chocolate that escaped from his doorway. Next to the inn stood a baker's shop. As he opened his door, the smell of freshly baked bread floated out. Anastasia's stomach rumbled. She had no money. Perhaps she could offer the baker something in return for a loaf of bread. She looked down at herself – at her soiled feet, her ill-fitting breeches. She had nothing to offer.

At one end of the square was a narrow canal that curved around to the right. The path could take her either left or right. She looked up into the sky and tried to work out if she was facing east or west. It was pointless, as she had no idea in which direction she ought to be walking. Disoriented, she turned right. Once again she found herself in a narrow passageway, indistinguishable from the first. She emerged from the claustrophobic darkness of the alleyway into bright sunshine and found herself on the edge of another small *campo*.

It took just a moment before she realised that she was standing in front of the mill owner's house. In a panic, she turned and ran straight into the arms of the mill owner himself – Anzolo di Zorzi.

'Got you!

He forcibly picked her up and carried her, kicking and screaming, into the house.

He strode up the marble staircase. The door to the bedchamber was wide open. A locksmith had been called and had managed to dislodge the key, but the bolt on the other side of the door was fast and it was still impossible to enter through the door so a servant had been dispatched to climb up the rainwater pipe and enter through the open window.

Anzolo threw Anastasia onto the bed. She tried to move away, but he held her fast. He threw off his coat, and ripped off her breeches. Veronica, who had been cleaning the passageway, stood speechless in the doorway. Anzolo saw her reflected in the mirror.

'Get out!' he shouted. 'And shut the door. Now!'

The girl did as she was told. She heard Anastasia scream. She stood, unable to move, listening to the terrible sounds from her master's bedchamber, tears pouring down her face. She too was just eighteen and had never known a man. And what she heard from her master's bedchamber that morning would remain with her for ever.

Chapter Eight

The Mill Owner's House, Venice
July 1704

Anzolo kept Anastasia a prisoner for the next two months. Her mother continued to write to her daughter each week, but the letters were never delivered. Instead, Anzolo read each one, and then locked them in his desk. Two large chests containing Anastasia's clothes were delivered to the house, as promised, along with a secret letter of love and encouragement from her mother hidden among her daughter's underclothes. Polonia had lived with a controlling man all her adult life, and understood how to avoid detection.

One morning as Anzolo buttoned his long silk waistcoat, two servants, supervised by Veronica, brought the chests into the bedchamber.

'I shall unpack these a little later,' Veronica suggested.

'No – do it now. I should like to see Anastasia's clothing.' Anzolo sat on a chair by the window watching as Veronica removed the shifts, dresses and cloaks.

'That is a pretty gown, Anastasia – wear that later, I'd like to see you in it.'

Anastasia lay in bed, silent and unresponsive. As Veronica picked up a neatly folded pile of nightgowns she noticed the letter nestling in the folds of linen and lace. 'Mistress, perhaps it would be best if we left these nightclothes in the chest – I can move it over there near the bed.'

'Yes… thank you,' said Anastasia weakly. 'Whatever you think is best.'

'Well, I must be off for the day,' said Anzolo cheerfully. 'Enjoy your unpacking, Anastasia – now your things are here you will begin to feel more at home.'

Hearing his footsteps retreating down the stairs, Anastasia began to weep.

'Feel more at home… because of a few dresses. Is he mad?'

'I know, Mistress,' said Veronica soothingly, 'but here is something that might help a little.'

She retrieved the letter and handed it to Anastasia.

My dearest Anastasia,

I hardly know how to begin. Your father has done such a terrible thing in marrying you to that man. I will never forgive him. Your sister has not left your bedchamber since you were taken from us. She is devastated and blames herself for revealing where you went. But I have assured her that you will forgive her. My darling, you must be strong. Somehow, we will survive this, *you* will survive this. You are brave, my dear, and courageous. We must hope that a solution can be found and that somehow you will be able to return to us soon. I love you, my darling daughter.

Your Mamma

In the early days of her imprisonment, Anastasia took great comfort from this one communication. She kept it hidden in the chest, and took it out each day when she was alone. It gave her the strength to survive. She begged Anzolo to release her – both from the marriage and her enforced imprisonment. She asked to be allowed outside, or even to visit her mother and sister. When those requests were refused she suggested they be allowed to visit her. She also wrote to her mother, but Anzolo never sent the letters. Instead they too were locked away in the desk in his study.

'Did my mother receive my letter, Anzolo... did she not respond, or write to me?' Anastasia would ask. Anzolo would merely shrug his shoulders and leave, locking the door behind him.

Eventually, Anastasia began to understand. Her letters would never be delivered, and her mother's letters were also being retained – for she was in no doubt that Polonia would not have abandoned her and would be writing regularly. Her husband was intent, she realised, on breaking her spirit.

At times, it seemed that he had succeeded. There were days when she would throw herself on the bed as soon as he had left the room, and sob into the dark green damask bedcover. But Veronica would come upstairs and knock on the door; she would unlock the bedchamber and bring her mistress a cup of hot chocolate, and comfort her as best she could. Somehow, Anastasia survived by retreating from her physical environment into her imagination. She thought about her beloved dog Bianca and her horse Minou, imagining herself once again riding Minou round the farm. She visualised herself with Marco – walking through the woods, fishing on the lake, lying in his arms. She recalled the moment she had realised that she loved him. She could remember it so clearly. She was just fifteen and he had pulled a chair out for her as she sat down for dinner. He had held his hand on the small of her back as he guided her, and she had trembled at his touch. It had been so hard to spend time together, under the watchful eye of her domineering father. But somehow they had managed snatched afternoons, or fleeting moments hidden in the shadows at family gatherings where they could kiss, unseen. Gradually, over the following few years, their feelings for one another had grown.

'I love you, Anastasia,' he told her one day, after they had raced their horses through the woods around Villa Limonaia. 'I love the way you ride your horse, the fire in your eyes and the sensitivity in your heart.'

'And I love you, Marco Morozoni...'

But she'd had no word from him. No letter, no message. She knew, in her logical moments, that Anzolo would confiscate any communication from his rival. And yet, she hoped each day for some message concealed in her linen, or hidden on a breakfast tray. Increasingly, as the days turned to weeks, she began to fear that perhaps Marco had forgotten her. She thought often of his words to her on their way to Lake Como – 'I am with you now... I will protect you, I promise.' Had he forgotten his promise? Had he abandoned all hope of them ever being together, now that she was married to Anzolo?

As for Anzolo, he knew nothing of Anastasia's true love. He saw nothing of her misery, her loneliness. He was determined to break his young wife's spirit. She would yield to him, in the same way that his employees obeyed his orders unquestioningly. He was not a violent man; he did not abuse her; he had no wish to beat her, or hurt her. He merely insisted that he had a right to her body and was determined that she would bear him a child – hopefully more than one child – to carry on the business. And once she had a child, he would allow her more licence. Until then, she would remain in the bedchamber, taking her meals there, bathing there – her only contact with the outside world her maid Veronica. It became routine for Anzolo to lock his wife in her room each morning while he attended to business at the mill. And each night, when he returned, he would force himself on her.

Anastasia learned to separate herself from the violation of her body. As Anzolo lay on top of her each night, grunting and sweating, his rough chin scraping against her cheek, forcing his way into her, she would imagine herself by the lake with Marco, or that the sensation she felt against her face was the flank of her beloved horse Minou.

Veronica had become Anastasia's only friend, and was her eyes and ears on the world outside.

'I wish I could let you out,' she often told Anastasia when she brought her a cup of hot chocolate or something to eat. 'He's gone to the mill… he'll be away for hours. But the others will know what I have done and he will kill me if he finds that I've helped you.'

'I understand, Veronica, but if you could bring me paper and paints I would find it so much easier to bear my imprisonment.'

Veronica smuggled paper into the bedchamber and with it a pen, stolen from her master's desk.

'I have no money, Mistress, so I cannot buy paints… I'm so sorry.'

Later that night, as Anzolo slept, snoring loudly, Anastasia crept over to his clothes and found the little bag of gold he kept tied to his waist. She took a couple of coins and hid them beneath the long damask curtains that surrounded the bed.

The following morning, when Veronica unlocked the door and brought her breakfast, she gave the coins to her and begged her to buy charcoal, paints and brushes.

As soon as her husband left for the day, Anastasia would arrange her temporary studio. She placed two chairs opposite one another – she would sit on one, and she attached paper to the other. She arranged water and brushes on the windowsill of the room. At the end of the day Veronica would come upstairs and alert Anastasia to Anzolo's return; together they would hide the painting equipment behind a damaged panel beneath the window and return the chairs to their former positions.

It calmed her to draw and paint, and allowed her to retreat completely into her imagination. As her collection of paintings grew, so too did her confidence. Knowing that she would be free to paint as soon as Anzolo left the room gave her hope; something to live for. Her only problem was a practical one – a shortage of subjects. She sketched scenes on the canal, looking through the locked and barred windows: gondolas ferrying their gay, laughing passengers back and forth; galleons heading for the open seas, flags fluttering atop poles; barques, their white sails half-furled as their masters steered them down the canal, preparing to hoist them aloft once out in the windy lagoon. She painted the buildings on the opposite side of the canal too – delicate watercolours of the amber and russet palazzos, their arched windows inspired by Eastern architecture. But her real skills lay in capturing nature and, locked away in a room, her choice was limited. Veronica provided the solution; she would bring her a flower from a vase in the reception room, or an insect that she had found on the floor. Anastasia had a fascination with nature in all its forms and was painstaking as she sketched a beetle, or butterfly, or moth. One day Veronica arrived with a small dish filled with silky white cocoons. Anastasia recognised them instantly: they were the cocoons of silk moths.

'Where did you find them?' she asked the maid.

'Well… there is a garden a little way from here, and they have an old mulberry tree. The owner is a very elderly gentleman… it is said by some that he is already dead, and his servants have embalmed him. He sits all day in the window overlooking the canal. Nobody ever sees him move. The mulberry tree has been there as long as anyone can remember. As I walked past this morning, on my way to the market for the cook, I saw a branch of the tree hanging over the wall and the cocoons were nestling on the underside of the leaf. So I took it and brought them to you. I have the leaves here too.'

Anastasia was delighted with this latest gift and drew the cocoons and the leaves in meticulous detail. She was anxious to capture the emergence of moths as they hatched from the cocoons. Each evening before Anzolo returned she would hide her collection behind the panel under the window, hoping the cocoons would not hatch out in the night and deny her the opportunity to observe the phenomenon.

A few days later, her patience was rewarded. As she sat near the window sketching a rose that Veronica had brought to her on her breakfast tray, she noticed one of the cocoons rocking slightly. This went on for several hours, and before long, all the cocoons were moving perceptibly on the small dish. Veronica brought her lunch and stayed to watch as one of them hatched. A tiny hole appeared at one end of the cocoon. A pale creamy moth wriggled its way into the world, its tiny jointed legs unfolding inelegantly as it did so, its surprisingly large body expanding as it escaped the cocoon's embrace. It was covered in soft down and Anastasia was tempted to stroke it. But instead, she sketched quickly what she had seen. Soon, another moth began to emerge from its cocoon, then a third and a fourth. By the end of the afternoon the little dish was filled with soft downy cream-coloured moths, stretching their wings and relishing their freedom. This then was metamorphosis. The first moth began to excrete a gold-coloured liquid. One of the other moths – a male, Anastasia presumed – shifted its body towards the female, and put his tail end against hers. In a second the mating was over and the male moth soon lay prone on the ground by her feet. A second male mated with another female and the same thing happened. The male lay quite still near the first.

Anastasia smiled up at Veronica.

'Did you see that? Are they sleeping or dead? It would be funny if they were dead – just one time and they must die. If only it was so simple for us…'

The two young women laughed; it was the first time Veronica had ever heard her mistress laugh – and it felt good.

'You'd better go, Veronica. I'll put the moths away soon, I just want to watch what happens next.'

The moths did not disappoint; the following day, as Anastasia opened up the split panel beneath the window, she saw that the

female moth had laid thousands of tiny white eggs on the floor
of the cavity. Anastasia had seen silkworm eggs before, of course.
Her father employed the wives of his tenant farmers to care for
the moth eggs, and when she and Marietta were children, he had
sometimes – in a rare moment of kindness – taken them to see
the eggs being laid. It was common practice in the countryside for
the farmers' wives to take a handful of the eggs and incubate them
inside their bodices, in readiness for them to hatch into larvae, and
the cycle would begin again. The farmers' wives would go into
the mulberry orchards and collect armfuls of fresh young green
mulberry leaves, which they would chop up small and lay out on
trays. The tiny baby larvae would be distributed over the leaves
and would feed there for several days. As the larvae grew larger
and stronger, more and more leaves would be collected; they had
an enormous appetite and the silk 'mothers', as the farmers' wives
were known, had to be constantly vigilant, ensuring there was
enough food for them. By the end of the larvae-growing season,
the mulberry orchards would be entirely stripped of their leaves.

Anastasia found great solace in her observation and painting.
Once Anzolo had left for the day, her bedchamber became both
workroom and studio. It gave her purpose and fed her imagination.
But she often gazed out of the window, searching for fresh subjects
to capture. One morning as Anzolo dressed, he watched her as she
gazed intently out of the heavily barred window.

'You are interested in something out there, Ana?'

'The gardens on the other side of the canal. The flowers in the
palazzo garden, in particular, are so beautiful. I wish I could row
over there and paint them.'

'Paint them? I did not know you painted, your father never
told me.'

'My father did not approve,' said Anastasia.

'Well, quite right. What does a woman in your position want with painting? You should concentrate on having a child… that is your duty.'

Anastasia began to understand that having a child might be her only salvation and, although appalled at the idea of bearing a child with a man she despised, she nevertheless started to hope that she might become pregnant – if only to be allowed out of the room. One evening, when Anzolo came back from the mill, she broached the subject.

'Anzolo – if I were to have a child, would you allow me out of this room, out of the house?'

'Yes, Wife, I would. But you have run away before and I do not trust you. You are wilful – I see that. But when we have a child, part of the bargain I have with your father will be satisfied.'

Anastasia had been ignorant of so much before she married. Her mother had never explained what would happen on her wedding night. Nor did she really understand the process of pregnancy, but she knew enough to realise that her monthly bleed meant that she was not pregnant. Perhaps, she wondered, if her husband *believed* her to be pregnant, he might relinquish his hold on her and allow her some freedom? Might the nightly assaults on her body cease? She recalled a conversation she had had with Caterina, Tobias's wife, on the eve of her planned wedding to Marco.

'I must retire early this evening, Anastasia,' Caterina had said. 'I hope you will forgive me. I am expecting our second child and the early months have taken a toll on me. I am almost over it now – but for the first few weeks I suffered terribly with sickness each morning.'

'How awful,' said Anastasia sympathetically. 'Mamma has never mentioned such a thing to me.'

'It is a secret among us women,' said Caterina, 'and not every woman suffers the same way. I am just unfortunate, I think. But, as

I say, I am much recovered and am beginning to feel stronger, but my doctor insists that I go to my bed as early as possible each day.'

As she sat alone in her bedchamber in the house on the Grand Canal, Anastasia began to form a plan. If she could feign sickness, might she convince Anzolo that she was pregnant? That evening, as they ate supper together in their bedchamber, she laid the foundations.

'I have little appetite this evening, Husband – forgive me. I was very sick this morning and have been feeling unwell all day.'

'Do you wish to lie down?' Anzolo asked.

'Thank you… I will.'

She lay on the bed.

'Have you felt like this before?' he asked.

'Never, although yesterday, now I recall, I felt nausea. It's odd… I know only one cause of such a thing.'

She watched Anzolo's face intently as he took a large gulp of wine.

'What are you suggesting?'

'I suggest nothing; I merely wonder if… perhaps I am with child.'

Her husband leapt to his feet and strode over to the bed where she lay. He put his hand on her forehead.

'You have a slight fever. You must rest. I will send Veronica to you. I will sleep next door tonight and in the morning I shall send for the doctor.'

'Oh, must I see a doctor? Surely, we should wait a while. In case… anything goes wrong.'

'Nothing will go wrong. You are young and healthy. Sleep now. I will see you in the morning.'

As he left her for the night, locking the door behind him, Anastasia felt her heart quicken. She lay on the bed, a solitary candle flickering beside her, casting shadows around the room that formed the boundaries of her world. The light reflected in the myriad of tiny panes of glass in the casement window overlooking the Grand Canal, scattering beams of light, like fireflies, around the room. The iron bars that had been fitted over the windows were a constant reminder of her incarceration. She had been imprisoned in this room in Venice for so long and had endured his nightly assaults – until tonight, when she had set in motion a train of events that, once begun, could not be undone. If she failed, or weakened at any time over the next few days, she feared she would be trapped here, forced to submit to Anzolo, for ever. It was vital that she delayed any visit from a doctor for as long as possible. Locked in her airless bedchamber, she was as helpless as ever. What she needed to do now was persuade her husband that she should be allowed to leave this room.

Then, and only then, would she have a chance to escape.

Chapter Nine

Villa di Bozzolo
May 2017

It was mid-afternoon by the time Millie and Lorenzo returned to the villa from their visit to the jewellery entrepreneur. Lorenzo parked the elderly Fiat in the shade of the barn and Millie felt the heat of the sun on her neck as she walked across the courtyard

'Have supper with me, this evening?' he called after to her. 'Elena is going out and it would be lovely to have your company. Bella will be there, but I hope you won't mind that?'

'No, of course not! I'd love to meet her properly. Thank you.'

'See you at seven.'

Millie spent the rest of the afternoon typing up her notes. She now understood the process of sericulture – the rearing of the silkworm and the spinning of silk. There was a lot of local 'colour', and she had taken photographs of both the villa's silk farm and the silk-spinning machine; one or two were certainly good enough to publish. The rest of the article would focus on the more glamorous side of the silk industry. Lorenzo had offered to take her to Venice to visit one of the oldest silk-weaving businesses, which was famous for its list of wealthy and influential clients. And Millie was keen to speak to one or two of the well-known fashion houses that were now using this top-quality Italian silk. As she sat at the desk in her cool bedroom, with the windows wide open, overlooking the gardens, she speedily wrote the first few paragraphs of her article. The words and phrases came easily to her, almost as if they were being dictated.

During her break-up with Max, she had really struggled to engage with the process of writing. When she sat at her laptop, at home in her flat, or in the office, her mind would be flooded with memories of their time together and she wrestled with ideas and words, unable to achieve any sort of creative flow. But now, here in the villa with its centuries of history, protected by the cool thick stone walls, feeling the polished oak boards beneath her feet, she felt calm and totally immersed in her writing. She reread what she had written and, satisfied with the result, took a quick shower and changed into white jeans and a loose peasant top. The sun was still fierce, burning the tops of her shoulders, as she walked the short distance between the villa and the barn.

She heard them long before she saw them. She followed the sounds of giggling and shouting, and found Lorenzo playing cards with his daughter on the small metal table on the terrace.

'Hi,' she said, sitting down at the table to join them.

'Ah, good evening, Millie. Bella – you remember Millie?'

Bella slapped down a king on her father's card and shouted 'Snap!' delightedly. The pair laughed.

'Come on, Bella, let's put this away now that our guest is here.'

'Oh, don't stop for my sake!' said Millie. 'Can't I play, too?'

Lorenzo smiled at her.

'I tell you what – let me get you a drink and you take over from me. But I warn you – she is a demon.'

Bella was a pretty child with a heart-shaped face and a rosebud mouth. Her brown hair, bleached gold by the sun, matched the colour of her eyes. She watched Millie's face intently as they began to play. She appeared shy at first, placing her cards on the table quietly and deliberately, but soon both of them relaxed and slapped their cards down with gusto. Millie was enchanted by her energy... her joy. Up until that point, her experience of children had been limited to the occasional weekend with her two nephews although theirs was not a world she felt truly able to share; she felt out of her depth with them, unable to find a real connection. But playing Snap with Bella seemed so natural. Both were competitive and neither would yield. Finally, Lorenzo called a halt to their game.

'We have to eat. I've made pasta and if we don't eat now it will be ruined. Can you put those cards away?' he asked Bella.

'Yes, of course,' said Millie. 'Just one more game?' she asked Bella conspiratorially.

'Yes!' cried Bella, slapping down the first card.

Finally Lorenzo swept the cards into his hand and put plates of pasta in front of them both.

'Now, enough – eat.'

'Sorry,' said Millie, laughing. 'It's been a long while since I played Snap. I used to play with my brother's two boys but they're teenagers now and a bit cool for that sort of thing. I'd forgotten how compulsive it can be.'

After dinner the three of them played Cheat until Lorenzo finally called a halt.

'Bella – it's time for bed now. Go and do your teeth and I'll come in a little while and we can read.'

'I'd like Millie to read to me.'

'Me? Really? I'd be delighted. What are you reading?'

'*The Fantastic Mr Fox*,' said Bella.

'OK, great. See you shortly.'

Reading to Bella was both a delight and a surprise. Millie had occasionally been allowed to read to her two nephews, but the boys were obsessed with stories about vehicles: buses, trains and tractors. The books were frankly dull, and she was rather ashamed to admit – even to herself – that she often daydreamed as she read to them, desperate for them to go to sleep.

Bella's room was a symphony of pink and white. She had an old sleigh bed along one wall, covered with a patchwork quilt made of squares of old Liberty Lawn dress fabrics – some with a rich red background covered with sprigs of white flowers, others in pale pink dotted with red daisies, interspersed with squares of pure white, decorated with pale pink rosebuds. The whole quilt was overstitched by hand. A white mosquito net hung over the bed, which added a romantic fairy princess touch to the room. A photograph of the child with her mother hung on the wall opposite her bed. Caroline had certainly been a beautiful woman – tall, fair-haired with intelligent blue eyes. In the photograph, Bella sat on her mother's lap smiling contentedly into the camera.

'That's a beautiful picture,' said Millie.

'Yes… it's my mother.' Bella gazed sadly at the photograph, her little hand fiddling anxiously with the end of the bedstead.

'I thought it must be. How lovely to have her here with you.'

Keen to change the subject, Millie noticed Bella's dolls and teddies, lined up along the edge of the bed, sitting facing out into the room.

'Gosh – you've got a lot of friends there.'

'Shall I tell you their names?'

'I'd love that,' said Millie.

Bella climbed onto the bed and introduced Millie to her toys, holding each one up for her to inspect or cuddle.

'Now, where's that book?' said Millie finally, as she put a toy husky next to Bella's pillow.

Bella reached under the quilt and retrieved the book. Settling herself on the bed, she laid it on her lap. She touched the quilt next to her.

'Will you sit with me here?'

Millie sat on Bella's bed a little awkwardly at first but gradually the little girl put her at her ease. As Millie relaxed, leaning up against the pillows, Bella lay next to her. She crept closer and closer until

Millie could smell the clean scent of shampoo in the child's hair. As Bella turned the pages of the book, she snaked herself around Millie, draping her arm over Millie's stomach, so that by the time the story was finished the child was wrapped around her. Millie closed the book, and realised that Bella had fallen fast asleep.

Lorenzo pushed open the door and stood watching them.

'That is a vote of confidence,' he whispered. 'She doesn't do that for everyone, you know. Here, let me help you.'

He reached over and moved Bella's arm. Millie slipped off the bed and watched him carefully slide Bella beneath the covers. He turned off the nightlight and put the book onto the floor next to her bed.

Together they walked towards the door and both turned to check that Bella was asleep before putting out the overhead light. As he pulled the door closed behind him, Millie looked up at him.

'Thank you for letting me do that. It was lovely.'

'Thank you…' he said. And then he held her face in his hands and kissed her.

Chapter Ten

Villa di Bozzolo
August 1704

Marietta woke early. Ever since her sister had been taken away, she rarely slept peacefully. Her last waking thought each night was of the carriage being driven away from the villa and of her sister's tear-stained face through the rear window; and it was the first thing she thought about each morning. In the middle of the night, alone and lonely without Anastasia sleeping in the bed beside her, the thought of what her sister might be enduring was imagined but no less frightening for that. Her sister might be weeping, or locked in a room somewhere. She had no picture of the man who had taken Anastasia from her, so could not visualise him, but somehow that made the situation worse. In the absence of any concrete facts, she concocted a hideous creature in her mind – misshapen, foul-smelling, devilish. She spoke to her mother of her fears whenever they were alone together.

'Oh Mamma – what kind of man could he be, to take someone against her will?'

'Oh darling… the world is full of wicked people; and your father is as much to blame.' Polonia spoke in a whisper as they sat together in the drawing room of the villa, anxious not to be overheard. 'I will never forgive him. He is a cruel man and has done us ill all our lives, but this is the worst thing he has ever done.'

Marietta reached out and clutched her mother's hand.

'Mamma – do you think he has a similar plan for me?'

'I pray not, Marietta, but quite honestly, he is capable of anything…'

At this Marietta began to weep and her mother whispered into her hair, 'Let us not think of that now, *cara*. Our priority must be how to comfort Ana.'

'Yes, you are right. We must rescue her,' said Marietta desperately.

'My darling – it is impossible. How would we find her? And if we did, where would we take her? We cannot bring her here. And you know that he would find us, wherever we went. I have no answers, I am as desperate as you.' Polonia began to weep.

'But what of Marco?' asked Marietta. 'Might he not help us?'

'How could he? She is married now; it is too late for them. He would not be able to take her as his wife.'

'But he loves her! Surely he would not desert her so easily?'

'Oh Marietta, you are young and romantic. I'm sure he still has feelings for Anastasia, and he might be willing to help us, but how can we even contact him? I cannot write to him. Every letter I write to Anastasia, or anyone else, is read first by your father. And the servants are under orders not to take any letters from either of us, unless first sanctioned by him. We are trapped. He has seen to that. And I fear she is lost.'

Lost… that word reverberated around Marietta's mind for days afterwards. At night, she woke with tears streaming down her face.

'Lost', she repeated out loud to the darkness.

One morning in late August she woke early, bathed in sweat. The previous day had been close and hot. Her mother had declared it the hottest day she had ever known. The household was under strict instructions to keep the shutters of the villa tightly closed all day, to keep the sun at bay. The rooms were stifling and airless, and Marietta – desperate for the slightest hint of a breeze – opened the shutters in her bedroom. The air outside was as hot, humid and still as it was inside. And instead of a refreshing draught of cool air, her skin burned the moment the sun spilled through the open window. She closed the shutters and lay on her bed, fanning herself.

'There must be a storm soon,' her father declared when the family convened for their meal later in the day in the shuttered dining room. 'I have never known such heat.'

In the hour before dawn the storm began to gather. As the column of humid air that hung over the valley rose into the sky, it connected with colder air high up in the atmosphere and triggered violent electrical activity. Marietta opened the shutters of her bedroom and peered outside into the blackness; there was a blinding flash of sheet lightning that illuminated the room. Moments later, she heard a familiar scraping sound – scrabbling, followed by a pathetic whine. It was Bianca, Anastasia's dog, clawing at her door.

As soon as she opened the door the little white dog rushed in and jumped straight onto the bed, where she hid herself beneath the damask counterpane.

'Bianca darling, you're safe here.' Marietta picked her up, cradling the little dog in her arms, nuzzling her cheek against its soft head. She climbed back into bed and placed the dog beneath the damask bed cover, so that she lay alongside Marietta's thigh. She rested her hand on the dog's flank to comfort her, feeling Bianca's racing heart beneath her fingers.

As thunder rumbled across the sky, forks of lightning crackled earthwards. She heard the horses calling out, their whinnying audible even over the noise of the storm. She heard her father shouting in the courtyard outside, waking the groom.

'Get down here, Mario! Help me to calm the horses.'

Marietta crept over to the window and peered over the windowsill to watch the activity below. Her father, draped in a black cloak, pushed the groom towards the stables. The horses reared up, shaking their heads in fear at the storm. It struck her as ironic that her father should show such concern for his horses, when he had so little empathy for his own wife and daughters. She crept back to bed and lay fondling Bianca's soft white fur, considering how she might rescue her sister.

She had written a letter to Marco the previous day, begging him to go to Venice – to find Anastasia and bring her back. She had hidden the letter in the chest where she kept her underclothes, confident that it would remain undiscovered. She could not give it to one of the servants, for they were under strict instructions to inform her father of any letters coming in or out of the house. The only solution was for Marietta to deliver it herself. She was not a strong rider like her sister, but nevertheless had decided to ride over to Lake Garda later that morning. She knew that once her disappearance was discovered, her father would be furious and would doubtless punish her on her return, but at least she would have done what she could to protect her sister. She would have to lie about where she had been; she could pretend that she had merely taken the horse for a ride around the farm and somehow got lost. He would believe that – for he often told her that she was feeble, and stupid. As she lay in bed and listened to the crackle of lightning, and watched forks of bright white light pierce the dark sky, she realised that she would have to delay her trip to Lake Garda. As long as the storm continued, her father would be outside in the stables, keeping a watch on the horses.

Dawn came almost imperceptibly; just a delicate line of pale lemon light lay along the horizon, indicating that the sun had risen, but the sky above it remained as dark as night, lit only intermittently by streaks of lightning. Marietta climbed out of bed and sat in the window of her room observing the scene below. She watched as her father attempted to calm the horses. He opened the stable door of his own beloved chestnut stallion. A fork of lightning crackled out of the blackness, magnetically drawn to the metal weathervane on top of the stable building. There was a spark and within moments fire began to smoulder in the roof of the stables. A fine trail of grey smoke floated up into the dark sky. Sensing danger, the horses became even more agitated.

'Mario – get the men and put that fire out!' shouted her father over the sound of thunder that rolled menacingly across the valley.

The young stable boy ran to the cottages on the far side of the yard and roused the occupants.

'Angelo, Dario! Come quickly – there's a fire in the stable building.'

Marietta watched the scene unfold. It gave her a frisson of pleasure to see her father so discomforted. She loved the horses, of course, but had no doubt that between them the men would pull them all to safety. Besides, the fire appeared insubstantial.

Angelo and Dario ran into the courtyard carrying large wooden buckets and began to haul up water from the well in the centre of the yard. Two more servants emerged from the villa and ran across to help them. Marietta heard her father shouting.

'I will lead the horses out of the stables now, and take them to the barn; they will be safe there.'

Ludovico placed a halter over the stallion's head and pulled the beast out of his stall. He spoke gently to the animal, soothing him, as they crossed the yard to the barn, before returning for a second horse. The fire was beginning to take hold in the attic spaces above the stables and smoke was now billowing out of the front of Minou's stall. Ludovico opened the stable door and then closed it behind him, obviously intending to put on Minou's halter and lead him calmly to safety. At that moment there was a violent clap of thunder and a huge fork of lightning plunged into the yard, illuminating the scene.

Minou reared up. His hooves clattered against the closed stable door as he attempted desperately to escape. He tried to turn round in the stall, kicking out frantically. He was obviously terrified of the thunder and lightning, and sensed the fire close by. Marietta expected to see her father emerge from the stall leading the horse by the halter, but there was no sign of him. The men had formed a line to hand along buckets of water and were fully occupied putting out the growing blaze, which now encompassed most of the roof of the building. Sparks flew down onto the stalls below and ignited the straw bales stored there. Thick black smoke billowed from the top of the stable block.

Polonia ran out of the villa wrapped up in her dark red cloak and Marietta heard her mother's voice, but could not make out what she was saying over the roar of the fire, the rumble of thunder and crackle of lightning. Mario stopped passing buckets and looked across at the stables. He ran across the yard and opened the stable door that housed Anastasia's beloved Minou. The grey horse rushed out, knocking him over. Mario staggered to his feet and called out to the men in the line, who stopped hauling water and instead ran to the stables, opening up the remaining stable doors. Polonia's elderly white mare bolted into the yard, followed by Marietta's little black horse. Four other carriage horses were also released.

The courtyard was now filled with horses running frantically around, rearing up in alarm. Mario caught Minou by his mane and stroked his head in an effort to calm him. Pacified, he was led to the barn; then Mario returned to the yard and took each horse to safety.

The rain that had threatened all night finally came. A deluge of hail and rain descended from the heavens, flooding the yard within minutes. The stable block, which had been ablaze a few moments before, began to hiss and smoke as the rain doused the flames. Only then did Marietta hear her mother shout to Mario.

'Where is the master?'

'I don't know…' Mario was struggling with the last of the horses. 'I last saw him go into Minou's stable.'

'He must still be in there,' shouted Polonia.

Mario ran into the stable. Marietta heard him shouting.

'In here – quick!'

Dario and Angelo followed him and within moments they had hauled Ludovico Balzarelli out of the stable. His face was charred by the smoke, and covered with blood. It took four men to carry his lifeless body into the villa.

'Please God…' prayed Marietta. 'Please God, let him be dead.'

Chapter Eleven

Villa di Bozzolo
May 2017

With Bella safely in bed, Millie and Lorenzo sat together on the terrace, enjoying the warm evening. 'I will turn the lights out in the barn,' he said. 'Sometimes fireflies come into the garden; they hover around that old olive tree there in the corner and dance.'

They sat contentedly together, sipping wine, the garden lit by the moon and stars. Encouraged by Millie, he talked a little about his wife.

'She was a beautiful woman,' said Millie. 'That's a lovely photograph in Bella's room.'

'Yes… she was beautiful and clever. She was my best friend – and that's the hardest thing to deal with. I feel so alone sometimes. My sister is great, but… she's my sister.' He laughed nervously. 'We are a family, but there is something missing – you know? At the heart of it all.'

'I understand,' said Millie. 'In some ways, I feel the same. I've never been married and my last relationship looks like it's over. Even when it was still working, it was dysfunctional… because he's married.'

'That must be very difficult – not being able to be with someone when you need them.'

'That's exactly it. You're very understanding – very non-judgemental.'

'Why would I judge you? You can't help who you fall in love with. There is a proverb – in Italy as well as in England – *in amore e in guerra tutto è lecito* – all is fair in love and war?'

'That saying always sounds so reasonable, but it's not true really, is it? The love bit, I mean. If you're mixed up with a married man, you find ways of justifying it. You tell yourself he's not really happy with her, so that makes it OK. Or, it's me he really loves, not her. But the thing about the man I've been involved with is that he's not just a husband, he's also a father – like you – to two little girls – about Bella's age, actually. So he's not just being unfaithful to his wife, he's being unfaithful to them too. And although I have loved him so much, at the end of the day I have nothing, really. I have a nice flat, but I have no life when he's not with me. I've got some lovely friends, but they're mostly married now, or paired up. And my family all think I'm weird. Whenever I go home, my mother can't resist that inevitable question: "Anyone special on the horizon?" She tries to make it sound casual, but I can hear the panic in her voice. And the truth is, there has been someone special for years now, but I can't tell anyone about him. It has to be secret, for his sake but also for mine. I'm too ashamed to tell people about him. I told my brother once and he was so cross with me – so disapproving.'

'That was unfair of him, but my sister Elena would probably be the same.'

'The real issue is – why do I put up with a second-rate relationship just so I'm not completely alone? It's pathetic. I'm an educated woman with a great job and her own flat, living in this feminist age. Why do I care if I don't have someone? Why do I need a man to define me – to make me feel complete? The answer is that I shouldn't. But I want a companion, just as you do – someone just for me; a best friend. Someone to be there when I've had a bad day, or a good day for that matter. Do you understand?'

He nodded.

'We've discussed him leaving her but he never does. And really, in my heart of hearts, why should he? I mean, he shouldn't – he has responsibilities.'

'That's very moral of you.'

'Once a Catholic… I'm lapsed now, of course. But something must have rubbed off on me. You might argue I should have been a bit more moral and stopped it before it even began. But he was so persuasive. So… passionate; it was intoxicating.' Millie gazed at the fireflies.

'And now?'

'I don't know. *He* broke it off a few weeks ago, when we were in Florence for my birthday. I was devastated at first. I'd had such dreams, you know – of how the relationship might end up. But now I think maybe he was right. Maybe it was the best thing – to end it. The best thing for me, I mean.'

'Because you met me?'

'No, not exactly. Even before I met you, I was already thinking that it would be better if it was over. And then, just as I was coming to terms with that idea, he texts me. He wants me back, he says. But I don't know if I can go there any more. Meeting you has made me realise that there are other paths… other possibilities, you know? My life doesn't need to be defined by him.'

On the other side of the garden the fireflies shimmered in the darkness, like flashing fairy lights hung in the old olive tree.

'Here come real stars to fill the upper skies,
And here on earth come emulating flies,' quoted Millie.

'Who wrote that?'

'Robert Frost. We had to study him at A-level. They're fascinating, aren't they – fireflies?' said Millie. 'What's the point of all that flashing?'

'They are looking for a mate,' said Lorenzo.

'Ah! How appropriate.'

At that moment, the door to the barn slammed shut.

'*Per l'amor di Dio! Perché é buio?*'

Lights streamed out of the kitchen onto the terrace as Elena pushed open the French doors.

'Ah, good evening, Millie, Lorenzo… Why are you sitting in the dark?'

Lorenzo gestured towards the fireflies.

'I wanted Millie to see them properly.'

'Oh… well, I'm sorry, I've spoiled it, haven't I?'

'Not at all,' said Millie, standing up. 'I really ought to be going anyway. Thank you, Lorenzo, for supper and such an interesting day. What time are we going to the silk mill tomorrow?'

'Oh yes… let me just call them in the morning and confirm it's OK. But we'll need to leave early – it will take a couple of hours to get to Venice.'

'Venice! Why do you need to go so far? There are silk mills nearer to us than that, surely?' asked Elena.

'Not like this one. I want to introduce our guest to the Bordignon mill – they are the only mill still using the old technology. It will be fascinating and good for her story, I think.'

'Do you need to go yourself? Millie has a car.'

'Yes, Elena, I do need to take her. It's very hard to find and I would like to introduce her. Perhaps you would be kind enough to collect Bella from school for me tomorrow?'

'I suppose I can. Well, goodnight,' Elena said, brusquely.

Millie's room in the villa was hot and airless. She opened the shutters and flung open the window before lying on the bed. It had been a lovely evening. And a lovely kiss. There was no huge passion there, but it felt natural, familiar. She plugged her phone into its charger and turned it on. Did she really need the complications of another love affair so soon? She hadn't got over Max yet, and she knew she needed time to recover. Perhaps she should put the brakes on a bit with Lorenzo. Get the article finished. Go back to England, back to real life.

The phone sprang back into life, and began buzzing relentlessly. There were several missed calls from Max. She put the phone back down on the chest of drawers. She felt tired and wasn't sure that she wanted to hear what he had to say.

She undressed and brushed her teeth. She sat in front of the mirror and took off her make-up. The phone continued to buzz. Eventually, she weakened and called her voicemail.

> *Darling… please call me. I have some wonderful news. Well – difficult news. I've split up with Katje. You won't believe this, but she's got someone else – only her bloody Pilates instructor. He 'understands' her apparently. Anyway, she wants a divorce. Darling – can't you see? We can be together now. The cottage in Sussex – everything you want. Call me.*

Chapter Twelve

A midwife was sent for. Anzolo, excited at the prospect of finally having a child, was determined to ensure that nothing was amiss. The midwife's name was Juliana di Luna, and she had a reputation for helping women of all ages. At sixty years old she had delivered hundreds, possibly thousands, of babies and had helped as many again avoid, or abort, pregnancies. Her tiny garden was full of sage, rosemary and chasteberry – plants that would bring on a woman's menstruation, or ease their labour – and she saw it as her God-given role to aid the women of Santa Croce whatever their burden. Juliana had known Anzolo's first wife and had comforted her through two miscarriages. She was intrigued at the prospect of meeting his new wife.

As she walked onto the *campo* in front of the mill house, carrying her bag of herbs and potions, Veronica was waiting for her in the alleyway that ran down the side of the house.

'Juliana – *signora* – please come over here.'

Veronica led the midwife down the narrow lane.

'Juliana – forgive me but my mistress sent me to talk to you. There is something you must know before you meet her.'

'I have been summoned by Anzolo di Zorzi to attend his new wife; I should speak with him first.'

'Please, Juliana, this is important – for the sake of my mistress.'

'Well, what do you have to tell me?'

'My mistress has been forced into this marriage. She… she has been raped.'

'How do you know?'

'I have heard her… and I know; she has told me as much. She is so unhappy. He keeps her imprisoned in her room and he takes her against her will – every night.'

'Do her family know how she is treated?'

'Yes… at least her father knows. He arranged the marriage. But her mother and sister know nothing. She has not heard from them; she believes the master is keeping their letters from her.'

'Tell me what you wish me to do.'

'My mistress has told Signor di Zorzi a lie, and you must be part of that lie if she is to survive.'

'Go on.'

'My mistress tried to run away when she was first sent here, ten weeks ago. But Anzolo caught her and now keeps her prisoner in her room. The door is locked, the windows barred. Anzolo wants a child. My mistress believes that if she were pregnant he might allow her to leave her bedchamber, even to leave the house. And so she has created a story that she is pregnant. She is desperate. Please, please do not give her away. He must believe she is pregnant.'

'I understand. She is not the first woman who has been kept prisoner in this way, and will not be the last. I will go to her.'

Juliana ducked out of the alley and strode across the *campo*. She knocked on the great oak doors of the mill house and was admitted by the footman.

'My name is Juliana di Luna. I am here to see Signora di Zorzi.'

'Ah, *signora*…here you are.' Anzolo came striding down the impressive marble staircase and into the entrance hall. 'Come with me. My wife is upstairs.'

Juliana was led into the bedchamber. Anastasia lay on the bed dressed in a simple shift of white linen. The room was filled with a fine haze; there was a pungent, overpowering smell that caught in the back of Juliana's throat.

'See how I care for her,' said Anzolo, pointing towards a brass perfume burner shaped like a bird, with a fine trail of smoke rising from its beak. 'The scent is musk, ambergris and civet, which I am reliably informed, will produce a male child.'

'Ah, yes. Well, let us hope so,' said Juliana, smiling down at her patient. 'If it does not poison us all first,' she muttered conspiratorially to Anastasia.

The young woman looked pale, she thought, her white skin contrasting with her dark hair falling around her shoulders. She looked up at Juliana, her dark eyes pleading.

'So… here you are,' Juliana said kindly, taking her hand and squeezing it. 'Signor di Zorzi – it might be best if I were to examine your wife alone?'

'Yes, yes… I will wait next door. Call me when you are sure?'

'Of course.'

When Anzolo had left the room, Juliana sat down on a small chair next to Anastasia's bed and whispered into her ear.

'Your maid has told me of your trouble. Is it true that he rapes you?'

Anastasia's eyes filled with tears – of shame, of relief. Juliana was the first person she had been allowed to meet apart from Veronica since her imprisonment.

She nodded her head.

'And now – what? You wish to escape?'

Anastasia opened her eyes wide and nodded towards the door.

'He may be listening,' she whispered.

'I will help you,' said Juliana quietly. 'I have helped other women in your situation. Just tell me one thing – are you pregnant?'

Anastasia shook her head.

'Please… Please do not give me away?' she pleaded.

They heard a heavy step in the corridor outside.

Putting her finger to her lips, the midwife lifted Anastasia's shift to expose her belly and pressed down with both her hands, just as Anzolo barged into the room.

She swiftly pulled down the shift to cover Anastasia.

'Well?' he barked impatiently, 'is she with child?'

'It is very early to say, but the symptoms are there. Her sickness, her breasts – they are tender. Her belly shows signs. If you will allow I shall attend her from time to time to ensure that all is well, but I see no reason why she should not be delivered of a healthy child.'

Juliana squeezed Anastasia's hand.

'Well, that is good news. Now you had better leave,' said Anzolo. 'We will call for you when we need you.'

'Just one thing, *signore*, before I leave; your wife, she is very pale. I am a little concerned for the health of the child. I notice the windows are barred. It is so hot in here and the scent from the perfume burner is very strong. May she not have some fresh air?'

'They are barred for her own safety,' said Anzolo brusquely.

'Well, then may I suggest you let her sit in the garden, or walk a little each day? The sunshine would do her good.'

'I have no garden,' said Anzolo hurriedly, 'and she already walks a little each day.'

He was defensive.

'Well, perhaps she needs to walk a little more – to the Rialto and back again. Or a visit with friends.'

'Yes… well, thank you,' said Anzolo, pushing Juliana towards the open door, eager now for her to leave. She turned to Anastasia before she left the room and smiled conspiratorially.

'I will see you again soon, *signora*.'

The following morning, as Anzolo dressed for the day, Anastasia sat up in bed. Earlier that morning she had forced herself to retch into a basin that had been laid by the bed. Anzolo had looked on contented, convinced it was a sign of her pregnancy. He had even shown some concern for her welfare.

'I'm sorry the child makes you so unwell but hopefully it will pass.'

'It will,' said Anastasia, wiping her mouth on a linen cloth. 'Usually it is gone quite soon – and then I am hungry.'

'That is good; you must eat for the health of the child.'

When Veronica brought up a tray of breakfast, she ate greedily.

'Perhaps we should do as Juliana suggested,' said Anzolo as he watched his wife eat. 'A little visit outside might be advisable.'

'Do you mean that I might leave this room?'

'Yes… perhaps you may go down to the drawing room today. Then we will see.'

Over the next few days Anastasia was allowed a little more licence. Once she was dressed, the footman escorted her to the large drawing room on the first floor, where she admired the blue damask chairs and the graceful gilded tables decorated with delicate porcelain figurines. The walls of the drawing room were lined with teal-coloured silk and covered with paintings – scenes of Venice mostly – that delighted her. Her husband, for all his lack of empathy, was clearly a man of wealth and taste. But wherever she went the footman, Tomasso, followed her. It was clear that she was never to be left alone for a moment.

When Anzolo returned from the mill, they ate their meals in the grand dining room. The servants, who had until that time been a mystery to her, became increasingly familiar. In addition to Veronica, there were two maids, Bettina and Filomena, who served at the table and cleaned and tidied downstairs. They smiled at their new mistress, and she wondered how much they knew of her relationship with their master. One afternoon, when her husband went back to the mill after lunch, Anastasia wandered towards the front door of the house, but Tomasso followed her. He was obviously under strict instructions to guard the door.

While her visits to the drawing room and dining room had relieved the tedium of her existence slightly, Anastasia realised that if she were ever to escape the mill owner's house, she must first be allowed outside. Her continued feigned morning sickness had convinced Anzolo of her pregnancy, but now her breasts were tender and she could feel the familiar ache in her womb that presaged her monthly bleed. Time was short, and she resolved to persuade him to allow her to visit the mill as soon as possible.

'I am so impressed by your house, Anzolo,' she said that evening as they ate dinner. 'And by the beautiful furnishings that you have here. They show such grace and taste. The silks – they come, I presume, from your own mill?'

He nodded with a self-satisfied air, and ate a forkful of food.

'I am intrigued by your work,' she continued. 'My family produced raw silk, as you know, but I have never seen it being spun or woven. I cannot imagine what sort of mill could create silk of such beauty. Please, Anzolo, may I visit the mill tomorrow?'

Anzolo poured himself another large glass of wine and studied his wife. She had a little more colour in her cheeks that evening, and was certainly very pretty. He would have her that night, and maybe tomorrow he would be minded to take her to the mill.

Later, as Anzolo plunged into her, Anastasia struggled to hold back her tears and even simulated enjoyment, anxious to reassure her husband that she was a contented wife. But the act revolted her and when it was over, and he lay snoring next to her, she washed herself as she always did, desperate to cleanse herself of his scent and his seed.

The following morning, she once again feigned sickness, anxious to continue the illusion of her pregnancy.

'I should like to take you to the mill today,' said Anzolo as he tied his cravat around his stringy neck. 'We are producing a particularly beautiful fabric at the moment for the Marquis of Lucca. Be ready before midday… if you think you will be well enough?'

'Yes, once I have eaten a little food, I'm sure I will be well.'

When Veronica brought her mistress's breakfast, Anastasia was waiting by the door.

'Put that tray down, Veronica. I am to leave the house today. He has promised; we are to visit the mill. This is my chance to escape, Veronica – my only chance. You must help me, please. If I escape, I shall send for you. I will always be in your debt.'

Dressed in dark red brocade that set off her dark hair and eyes, Anastasia felt genuine waves of nausea mixed with excitement as she studied her reflection in the mirror. She was scared, certainly, but also determined. This was the day that she would escape her tormentor. She was anxious to look her best so as to convince Anzolo that she was a dutiful and happy wife. It was vital that he did not suspect anything.

As he escorted his wife proudly down the staircase, she took his arm and even kissed his cheek. 'Thank you, Anzolo, for this special day. I am so excited to see your beautiful mill.'

The sunlight, as the front door was opened, was almost blinding. She had been inside for so many weeks, and the pale stone of the *campo* and the surrounding buildings reflected the sunlight with such brilliance that she had to shield her eyes with her gloved hand.

'It is too bright?' asked Anzolo.

'No, no…' she said quickly, anxious he should not be discouraged. 'It is wonderful to feel the sun on my face.'

They walked the short distance to the mill. The entrance was an unremarkable oak door that opened onto a long corridor.

'Up these stairs are my offices and I have a room where clients can come to look at our fabrics. We have a sample of every fabric ever produced – each one pinned to a ledger with details of how much was made, and who it was for. Would you like to see it?'

Fearful that she would be trapped upstairs with no means of escape, but anxious not to offend her husband, Anastasia made a suggestion.

'I would love to… but maybe we could see the mill room first?'

The clatter of the looms in the mill room was almost deafening.

Anastasia stood for a moment in genuine amazement, and surveyed the scene. There were five looms, each operated by a single weaver; the bobbins ricocheted backwards and forwards, moved into position by a small child sitting beneath each loom. Completed lengths of fabric were stretched over the looms – dark purple silk brocades, rich red cut velvets – each loom fed by hundreds of reels of brightly coloured silk.

The walls of the mill were lined from floor to ceiling with wooden shelving containing large bobbins of silk and folded pieces of fabric.

'That is beautiful fabric,' Anastasia shouted over the clanking of the loom to a young weaver, scarcely older than herself. 'It's cut velvet, isn't it?'

The young woman nodded.

'How many threads do you have there?'

'Over seven hundred, my lady.'

'And how long does it take you to thread the loom?' Anastasia asked politely.

'Many months. It is a labour of love.'

The young girl glowed as she spoke about her work, her quick fingers guiding the threads and feeding long metal rods into the pile of the velvet, which she cut with a swift action.

'I've worked here for five years,' said the girl, 'and my father before me.'

'It looks very complicated, what you are doing.'

'It is – it's taken me many years to perfect the skill.'

Anastasia bent down and spoke to the young boys and girls who were employed to shift the bobbins from side to side.

'That looks a difficult job. You must be careful not to let the bobbins hit you.'

'Yes, *signora* – we know. It doesn't happen often.'

All the while, as she chatted amiably to the weavers and their assistants, she was looking left and right for a possible means of escape. Veronica had drawn the layout of the mill room that morning. There were only two entrances to the mill – the door through which she had arrived and a window in a small office, off the main mill room where the manager worked. The office overlooked the Grand Canal and this was her only possible escape route. If she could get out onto the pontoon somehow, Veronica would ensure there was a gondolier waiting for her.

'My cousin – Antonio – he will wait for you,' she had promised.

Anzolo scarcely took his eyes from his beautiful wife, and any chance of escape seemed impossible. As she wandered through the mill, her heart racing, the door to the office suddenly opened. The manager walked into the mill room, leaving the door ajar, and through it Anastasia could clearly see the window that Veronica had drawn, and beyond it – gleaming in the sunshine – the Grand Canal. The manager held a large ledger in his hands and as he laid the heavy leather-bound book out on a table to one side of the room, he bowed low in front of Anzolo, and spoke to him. Anastasia could not hear what the manager said over the noise of the looms, but Anzolo was momentarily distracted; he peered down at the ledger, studying what looked like a column of figures. Anastasia took her chance and slipped out of the mill room and into the small office. The window was unlocked and it was a matter of moments before she had opened it and climbed through and out onto the jetty, where a gondola stood ready. The *gondoliere* beckoned to her.

'Veronica sent me. Are you Anastasia?'

'I am.'

'Then jump aboard.'

The *gondoliere* moved his craft swiftly away from the jetty and within seconds had joined the throng of gondolas in the centre of the canal. By the time Anzolo noticed that his wife was no longer by his side, it was too late. He rushed around the mill room searching for her, then saw the open door that led to the small office overlooking the canal. The window was wide open, and as he climbed through it and stood on the jetty all he saw were hundreds of vessels sailing up and down the Grand Canal. His wife was nowhere to be seen.

Chapter Thirteen

Villa di Bozzolo
August 1704

Ludovico Balzarelli lay unconscious in his bedchamber, his wife at his side. The doctor was sent for and diagnosed a violent trauma to the head.

'There is nothing really that we can do, *signora*,' he said. 'I cannot give you much hope. He has suffered terribly. It will be a miracle if he survives.'

'I think my daughter's horse, Minou, must have kicked him,' suggested Polonia.

'That certainly seems to be the case, *signora*. He has injuries to both the legs and body – but it is his skull that has been most damaged. It looks as if the horse trampled on your husband's head once he was on the ground.'

The fire had added to his injuries – Ludovico's hair and the top of his scalp had been badly burned. He had a broken leg and several broken ribs, and the doctor suspected that vital internal organs had been damaged.

Polonia played the part of 'distressed wife' in front of the doctor but when he left, she sat next to Ludovico's lifeless body praying silently, but fervently, that God would liberate her from her tyrannical husband.

The storm had subsided, and a cool fresh breeze blew through the courtyard. The stable roof had collapsed, leaving a tangled mass of charred beams and stones, and the yard was under a foot of storm water. The horses, temporarily stabled in the barn, were calm, bedded down with fresh straw.

Marietta removed the letter she had written to Marco the previous day from her clothes chest, put on her riding habit and a cloak and went to see her mother. Ever fearful that her prone husband might regain consciousness and overhear them, Polonia drew her daughter away from his bedside, her finger to her lips.

'I shall ride now to Lake Garda,' Marietta whispered. 'There is no time to lose. If Father survives, this might be our only chance. And if he dies, then we will be one step closer to helping Anastasia.'

'*Cara* – don't ride. God knows what state the roads will be in after such a storm. Take the carriage.'

'Oh thank you, Mamma. But will Mario, or Dario take me? Papa had given instructions not to allow us to leave the villa.'

'I have told them that their master is not long for this world. They take their instructions from me now. Take the carriage.'

'Yes, Mamma – God bless you.'

The journey to Lake Garda took many hours. In places, the road had been nearly washed away. Large holes had opened up, causing the carriage to judder and vibrate so violently that Marietta was frightened they would lose a wheel. The driver lurched left and right in an attempt to avoid the ruts and potholes. Finally, as they turned off the main road and onto the lane that led through the woods to the villa on the lake, the sun broke through the grey clouds that had hung so menacingly in the sky all morning, and Marietta opened the carriage window and breathed in deep draughts of clear lake air.

The villa stood on a promontory that extended into the lake, so was surrounded by water on three sides. The main path led visitors through the lush gardens, past lemon trees and flowering jasmine scrambling over hedges and walls. The storm that had raged all night and morning disappeared as swiftly as it had arrived and the sky was now brilliant blue, mirrored by the lake. A flock of birds flew low over the water as a fishing boat, moored in the middle of the lake, hauled in its catch. Marietta, exhausted by the journey and the trauma of the fire, sat down for a moment on a stone seat that nestled against the warm wall of a large stone gazebo and closed her eyes. Vicenzo Morozoni emerged from a small cottage that stood a little way from the main villa. He recognised Marietta instantly.

'Marietta my dear, how good to see you. How on earth did you get here after such a terrible storm?'

'I came by carriage,' she said, leaping to her feet.

'Oh good – I'm glad you did not ride on such a morning. Have you come to see Marco?'

'Yes. I am here to beg his help.'

'My dear, he is not here. He left over a week ago. He has been so downcast since… well, since Anastasia was taken from him. He is travelling; he has gone to Tuscany.'

'Oh, but we need his help,' wailed Marietta. 'We have to rescue Anastasia. We have had no word from her since she was abducted. We write to her, of course, but we have no idea if our letters reach her, for she never replies. It is so unlike her. We feel sure that her husband is keeping her letters from us. Mamma is frantic with worry. I have come to ask Marco to go to Venice and bring her home to us.'

'Yes, I see. But your father… surely he will not allow her to come home.'

'My father was in an accident last night. I do not believe he will survive,' Marietta said firmly.

'Oh, I'm sorry to hear that, my dear.' Vicenzo pondered. 'Well, you had better come inside and let us discuss what might be done.'

As Vicenzo poured Marietta a glass of wine, she told him how the fire had started.

'It was a flash of lightning; it hit the roof of the stables and before long there was a terrible fire. The horses panicked, of course, and

Minou – Anastasia's horse – must have kicked my father when he was putting on his halter.'

'How terrible,' said Vicenzo.

'Is it?' replied Marietta. 'I do not think so. I think it is a gift from God.'

Vicenzo looked surprised.

'I know it is a wicked thing to say, but my father is a cruel man. He has given my poor mother nothing but pain all her life. He beats her, and he has often beaten Ana and me. Now he has gone too far – giving Anastasia to this man in Venice. We cannot forgive him. I know it is a sin to say this but I hope he dies.'

'Oh my dear,' said Vicenzo, reaching out and holding Marietta's hand. 'What a terrible time you have all endured. I had not fully realised. I knew Ludovico had a temper, but I had no idea he was capable of such cruelty. Stay here tonight, and tomorrow you can return home. I shall write to Marco in Lucca and explain what has happened. I am sure he will go to Venice as soon as he knows you need his help.'

As the carriage clattered into the yard at Villa di Bozzolo the following day, the sun had done its work and the worst of the floodwater had subsided. The remains of the stable roof had finally collapsed during the night, leaving nothing but a mangled mess of charred timbers, broken stable doors and piles of burnt straw spilling out into the deserted courtyard.

Marietta climbed down from the carriage. 'Mario, Angelo,' she called out. No one answered.

Ludovico's dog Arturo lay in his usual spot on the steps of the villa. As Marietta passed by, he raised his shaggy head and whimpered pathetically. She bent down and scratched his ears.

'What is it, boy?'

The front door was ajar.

'Mamma, Mamma… I am returned,' she called.

She went up the large staircase and along the corridor that led to her parents' room.

Her mother was standing by the window, leaning on the windowsill. She turned and smiled at Marietta as she walked in. It was a smile Marietta had never seen before – of pure joy, of relief.

'Mamma – are you all right? Is Papa…'

'Yes. He is dead. Not more than an hour ago. I have sent for the doctor – he will be here soon.'

Marietta went to her mother and hugged her.

'How did it happen?'

'He never woke up. That is all. It was inevitable, I suppose. After all, the doctor had told us his injuries were serious… ' She turned away from her daughter and went and stood over the body of her husband. She pulled back the sheet to reveal his contorted face. His dark brown eyes were bloodshot, wide open and staring, his mouth apart as if caught in the middle of a cry.

'But his eyes are open,' said Marietta.

Her mother ran her fingers over the staring eyes and forced his lids closed.

'Not any more,' she said. She looked up at Marietta and there was a flicker of understanding between them.

'Mamma – did you… help him?'

Her mother held her finger to her lips. There was the sound of footsteps outside in the corridor and moments later the doctor pushed open the door.

'Ah *signora* – my condolences. I thought it was unlikely he would survive.'

He gave a cursory glance at Ludovico's corpse, then leaned down and listened for a heartbeat. He noted the closed eyes and the cold skin; he pulled the sheet over the man's face.

Ludovico Balzarelli was dead.

Chapter Fourteen

Villa di Bozzolo
May 2017

Millie had a sleepless night. After listening to his voicemail, she resisted calling Max. Instead, she switched her phone off: she needed time to think. She tossed and turned for what felt like hours before falling into a restless sleep. She woke less than an hour later, and turned on the bedside light. The room was airless and stuffy. She climbed out of bed and opened the shutters. From her bedroom window she could see the garden leading down to the vineyards, the river in the distance – a moonlit, silver snake writhing through the darkened landscape. She had a sudden frisson of homesickness. To be back in her cosy flat in Spitalfields, with her own things around her, with Max sitting on the sofa laughing, pouring her a glass of wine, or shouting at something that had annoyed him on the television, suddenly seemed enchanting.

She climbed back into bed and considered calling him. But it was two o'clock in the morning and he might still be living in the house with Katje. It would just complicate things if she were to ring now. She must have finally fallen asleep, for she woke with the early-morning sun reflecting off the mirror in her room, bouncing patterns of light onto the dark furniture. She rolled over and closed her eyes once again, but sleep eluded her.

She got out of bed and ran a deep bath. Sliding under the water, she considered her options. Lorenzo was a lovely man, but how could she turn down Max now, after all that they had meant to one another? It would be absurd. And for what? Lorenzo had kissed her, that was all; they were not in a relationship. They had just met; she hardly knew him. No… she should be sensible. Max was finally offering her everything she had wanted all these years – the chance to be together, buy the cottage in Sussex. Wrapped in a large towel, she sat on her bed and dialled Max's number.

'Darling, at last,' he said. 'I thought you'd forgotten all about me.'

'Don't be silly. I'm sorry. I was… busy. Working. I *have* got a piece to write, you know.'

'I know, darling – is it good? I'm sure you'll do something wonderful with it. So… what do you think? Isn't it marvellous news?'

'Yes. Yes, it is. But are you sure? I mean, is it really over? I couldn't bear… to be disappointed.'

'Darling, it's *so* over. I don't know how we've lasted as long as we have. Katje's not been happy for a long time; and you know I haven't.'

'But what about the kids?'

'What about them? They'll be fine. They'll stay with Katje and I can see them once a week. She's not going to be stupid about that stuff. As long as she gets a nice house to live in and enough money to last her, she'll be a good girl.'

'Oh Max, you sound so cynical.'

'Realistic, darling. I've done this before, remember? Now, when are you coming back? I want to see you.'

'I… I don't know. I'm not finished. I mean, I'll be two or three more days, at least. There are two more places to research and—'

'Well, get on with it and hurry home. Look, I've got to go. Hugo's at the door champing at the bit.'

Hugo was Max's tennis partner.

'Oh, OK. Have a good game.'

'I will, darling. I can't tell you how happy I am. And I can't wait to see you. Have you missed me?'

'What a question,' said Millie. It was odd; she couldn't just say, 'Yes.' Had she missed him?

'Bye, babe,' he said, not waiting for clarification.

And so she had made her decision. She would go back to London, she and Max would move in somewhere together; perhaps she would sell her flat in Spitalfields and they could buy somewhere larger – a big mansion flat, or a house with a garden. Together they would make plans and buy new furniture; she might even get rid of the soulless white china and buy something prettier. Something that would look good on a dresser – the sort of dresser owned by a proper family. And she would be happy. Why was it, then, that she did not quite believe it?

Chapter Fifteen

Lucca, Tuscany
August 1704

Marco received his father's letter while he was staying with his old friend Luigi Agnoli on the outskirts of Lucca. Villa Agnoli stood in extensive grounds and had been redesigned some twenty years earlier for the present incumbent's father. Luigi and Marco were wandering in the gardens when a footman rushed up to Marco and handed him a letter.

'The messenger asked me to tell you that it was a matter of urgency, *signore*,' said the footman.

'Thank you. I should read it at once – if you will forgive me, Luigi.'

'Of course, my dear fellow.'

Marco sat on the low wall surrounding the ornamental pond. The footman had given him two letters; one was from his father – he recognised the handwriting.

> My dearest Marco,
>
> I write with news of our friends from Villa di Bozzolo. Marietta came to visit me today. It seems there has been a terrible fire in the stables at the villa and her father is dangerously ill. More importantly, Marietta and Polonia are increasingly concerned for the welfare of Anastasia; they have received no word from her since she was taken

to Venice. Marietta begs us for help. She asks that we go to Venice, find her beloved sister and return her to the bosom of her family.

I feel duty-bound to offer assistance. She has told me such terrible tales of Ludovico, and of how he has ill-used his wife and daughters for so many years. I had no inkling quite how difficult their lives have been. Did you? We must try to help. Might you go to Venice and see if you can discover Anastasia's whereabouts and if she requires our support, or help? I know it will be hard for you, for I understand what you have felt for her, but I have promised Marietta that we will do what we can.

I have offered to explore any legal means whereby Anastasia might be liberated from her husband. I recall a similar case some years ago in Venice. The priest had been bribed by the father to overlook his daughter's reluctance to marry the man of his choice. Venetian law is very clear on this matter; both parties in any marriage must be willing. And so the lady did eventually obtain a divorce, and it occurs to me that this might be a possibility for Anastasia. Let me see what I can discover about the legal situation.

God speed my boy.

Your loving father

Marietta's letter was short and impassioned.

Dearest Marco,

Please help us. Poor Anastasia has been married, against her will, to a terrible man named Anzolo di Zorzi. He is a wealthy silk mill owner with a large house in Venice. We have heard nothing from her since she was taken from us and I am fearful of what he might be subjecting her to. I cannot go and help her. I beg you – bring her home to us.

Yours ever Marietta

'Luigi,' said Marco, folding up the two letters, 'I must go to Venice, I am needed.'

'Dear boy, of course! Do you require company? I would be honoured to come with you.'

'I am on an errand of mercy, it might be dangerous.'

'All the better – our family are famous for our love of danger. Besides, it is many months since I visited Venice.'

The two men set off early the following morning. The journey by carriage would take two days and nights and, after his initial enthusiasm, it soon dawned on Marco that he had little idea of how he would actually rescue Anastasia. As the carriage rumbled through the countryside towards Venice, he had time to reflect on the tragic events of the past few months. He discussed them at length with Luigi.

'I feel so ashamed, Luigi, that I didn't do more to protect her at the time.'

'From the sound of it, perhaps there was nothing you could do.'

'I keep going over it in my mind. We should have married the day she arrived, in Lake Garda. Or married the moment we arrived on Como.'

'It's easy to say that now you know what happened but you thought you were doing the right thing at the time.'

'The worst of it is that since she was kidnapped, I have been almost paralysed. I should have gone after her straight away.'

'Why didn't you?'

'My cousin Tobias convinced me that we should wait. "Ludovico has right on his side," he told me. "Think, Marco, of the scandal if you were to try to retrieve her now. Her father has a contract with this man." In his opinion there was nothing I could do – and I should try to forget her.'

'And what did your father think?'

'When he returned from his expedition a few days later, he was shocked, of course. But he was also angry that I had run away without telling him. "I had approved the marriage already; I could have spoken to Ludovico. I'm sure we could have come to some agreement," he said. But he didn't know what Ludovico was really like. Anastasia had told me about him, but I had never discussed her fears with my father. If only I had, he would have understood. But instead he thought I was reckless and that, like Tobias, I must just accept the situation. But now, of course, I regret everything. How could I let her be taken from me so cruelly?'

Luigi tried to reassure his friend, but Marco was filled with regret and self-loathing. He dreaded what he would find when he got to Venice, especially after he had shown so much weakness. Why had Anastasia not written to her family? Why had she not written to him and begged him to come and rescue her? He had received no letters and had interpreted that – wrongly, he now realised – as a rejection on her part. He had felt a childish jealousy of her new husband; he imagined that perhaps Anastasia had fallen in love with him. He saw now how absurd that was. How foolish he had been. He was now rightly ashamed of his inaction. He had abandoned her; worse, he had attempted to forget her. But now he had a chance to redeem himself.

*

The two men arrived in Venice late in the afternoon on the second day. Luigi's family owned a small palazzo on the Grand Canal, opposite the Fondaco dei Turchi, the Turkish trading house. As soon as they were settled, Marco suggested they begin their search for Anzolo.

'Let us go together,' replied Luigi. 'I suggest we ask one of the silk merchants here in Venice. They will know him, I am sure. There is a particularly fine shop near the Rialto. Come – we can be there in no time.'

The silk merchant's shop was in the corner of a small *campo* behind Venice's main vegetable market. The entrance hall was filled with a myriad of different-coloured silks. It had the feel of a souk, with damask and cut velvets draped around the walls. The merchant ushered in the two gentlemen.

'*Prego, signori.*'

'*Buongiorno, signore.* We are come from Lucca. You have some wonderful silks on display here. Are they all made here in Venice?'

'Yes, there are several mills here in Venice creating some very fine work. This silk damask here was only recently sold to the Pope. It's top-quality.' He held up a dark-red cut velvet for the two young men to admire.

'I would like to see some brocades,' said Luigi, 'suitable for a waistcoat.'

The merchant scurried away and returned with a bolt of sky-blue silk decorated with green flowers.

'This is a popular design, *signore.*'

'I like it very much. I wonder… do you know a weaver – a mill owner named Anzolo di Zorzi? I hear he does very fine work.'

'Indeed, indeed! Signor di Zorzi produces some wonderful fabrics. I have a damask here that was delivered only last week from the di Zorzi mill.' The shop owner proudly held up a bolt of dark-green silk damask.

'That is beautiful. I will take a length of the damask, and also the blue silk.'

The merchant folded the lengths of fabric.

'Please have it sent over to Palazzo Agnoli, on the Grand Canal.'

'Straight away, *signore*.'

'I would love to visit the mill where this damask was made. Is it close by?'

'Oh yes – in fact it is almost opposite your own palazzo, *signore*. I will write down the address for you,' said the merchant, bowing low.

The two young men walked swiftly to the Rialto Bridge, where they hired a gondola. The late-afternoon sunshine cast long shadows along the Grand Canal as the *gondoliere* steered his craft expertly through the throng of traffic. He dropped them at a set of stone steps leading to a narrow passage.

'The house of di Zorzi is up this alley, on the right. It sits on one side of a small *campo*. You can't miss it,' said the boatman as he dropped the two men off. They walked up the passage until they arrived at the small square, where they hesitated, lurking in the shadows, watching the front of the house.

'I suppose we can't just knock on the door and ask to see her, can we?' asked Luigi.

'No… I suspect we would not receive a welcome here. If her family has not heard from her, I fear she is restrained in some way. Let us wait here, and observe who comes and goes.'

They leaned against the wall, keeping careful watch on the house. As afternoon turned to evening the heat went out of the day. The sun slipped down over the lagoon, and a full silver moon rose high in the sky. No one entered or left the house. The *campo* was deserted. It wasn't until the bells of the nearby church had struck nine that the two spies saw a tall greying man emerge from a doorway on the far side of the *campo*.

'Is that him, do you think?' asked Luigi.

'It must be. But he looks too old to be her husband – even older than her father. My God, I cannot believe what she has had to endure! I must be bold… knock on the door and demand an audience. Let's just have this out here and now.'

'Don't be a fool, Marco – you will never get her back like that. Think. What would be best for Anastasia?' advised Luigi softly. 'Let's take a look around and see what can we can find. We don't even know that she is there.'

The two men walked back towards the water's edge. There was a jetty projecting out in front of the house. They jumped on to it and looked up at the front of the house. It was a fine establishment, certainly. Twelve windows looked out on to the Grand Canal. There was a balcony high up on the top floor, and the windows that led onto it showed the faint glimmer of candlelight. It was the only window that was lit.

'Do you think she might be up there?' asked Marco. 'I could climb that water pipe and look through the window.'

'My dear friend, the pipe won't take your weight. You need to rescue her, and you can't do that if you kill yourself first.'

'No, Luigi, I *can* do it. The pipe fixings look strong enough.' Marco pulled off his short cloak and began to climb the pipe. As he came level with the balcony, he swung across and grabbed hold of the ornate carved stonework. Nimbly he leapt over and stood on the edge of the balcony, from where he could see clearly into the room. It was a bedchamber, with a large bed to one side and various chests, overflowing with clothes. But there was no sign of Anastasia. The door suddenly opened. A young girl came into the room, carrying a candle. She saw Marco at the window and screamed. He leapt from the balcony back onto the pipe and slid down it as fast as he could, lacerating his hands as he did so. Both men retreated from the jetty onto the stone steps at the entrance to the lane.

'My God, that was close,' panted Marco. 'I'm not sure who that girl was, but she certainly wasn't Anastasia.'

As they leaned against the wall, catching their breath, the young girl emerged from the house.

'You… you were at the window.'

'I was, but I wish you no harm,' spluttered Marco.

'Who are you?' asked the girl

'Who are *you*?' he echoed.

'I am Veronica – servant to Signor di Zorzi and his wife.'

'His wife… Anastasia?'

'You know her?'

'I was engaged to be married to her, but she was taken from me.'

'You must be Marco,' said Veronica. 'She spoke to me often of you.'

'Spoke… she is dead?' Marco gripped the girl by the arms.

'No, no – she is well, I assure you.' The maid looked suspiciously around her. 'Can I trust you?'

'Of course,' said Marco.

Veronica drew the two men into a small doorway.

'We must not be seen,' she explained. 'My mistress was kept here against her will – locked in that bedchamber for ten weeks or more. It was terrible. But two days ago, she escaped.'

'Oh, my poor Anastasia! I have been so weak. I should have tried to find her weeks ago. Where has she gone? I am come to take her home.'

'Oh, sir… are you truly her friend?'

'Madam, I am. I wish her no harm. Her sister Marietta sent me. Please believe me.'

'I do believe you, sir. She is in hiding, with the midwife Juliana di Luna.'

'She is with child?' said Marco.

'No, she feigned pregnancy to get out of the house. She pretended she needed fresh air. She was so clever and so brave.'

'That does not surprise me – she is the bravest girl I know,' said Marco. 'Tell me how to find her and I will go to her now.'

Juliana di Luna's house was at one end of a narrow lane off a small *campo* in the heart of the Santa Croce district. In the darkness, with only the bright August moon to light their way, the two young men became hopelessly lost in the warren of narrow alleys. They argued as to the correct route.

'I'm sure we need to go this way,' suggested Luigi.

'No, did she not say we were to turn left after we had crossed the canal?'

Eventually, more by luck than judgement, they found themselves on Calle Orsetti outside the house of Juliana di Luna.

Marco knocked on the door. A metal grille was slid to one side.

'I am here to see Signora di Luna.'

'Who wants her?' asked a disembodied voice.

'My name is Marco Morozoni. I am… I was engaged to be married to a lady who I think is sheltering here – Anastasia Balzarelli.'

The grille snapped shut. Marco could hear murmuring from behind the door and then silence. Moments later, shutters opened above their heads. They looked up. A buxom woman, with wild dark-red hair traced with silver tied loosely on top of her head, her ample breasts scarcely contained by her corset, leaned out of the window.

'I am Juliana di Luna,' she whispered hoarsely. 'Can you prove who you are?'

'If you have Anastasia with you, tell her Marco is here. Tell her I have news from Marietta. Her father Ludovico had an accident. He may not even be alive. Tell her that. She can come home with me, I will protect her – I will never let her be taken away again. And tell her Minou is waiting for her.'

There was silence. The window was snapped shut. Marco heard the sound of muffled conversation coming from upstairs, followed by the creaking of a casement window opening. Anastasia, her pale skin glowing in the moonlight, her dark hair loose and wild around her shoulders, called down to him.

'Marco... Marco – is it you? You have come, at last. Who is there with you?'

Marco found he had no voice: he was transfixed by her, by her luminous beauty. Her voice sounded different – faint, frightened.

'My darling,' he said at last, 'all is well – this is Luigi, he is a good friend.'

Anastasia smiled, revealing her neat, white teeth.

'Thank God... Come up, come up quickly.'

There followed the sound of locks turning, and bolts being slid back, before the door to the street was finally opened. A young maid led the two men up the narrow stairs to Juliana's sitting room. Framed in the window stood Anastasia. She still wore the dark-red damask dress in which she had escaped – it hung loosely on her delicate frame. She looked beautiful, but painfully thin, Marco thought, and her face spoke of sleepless nights, with dark rings encircling her black eyes. Seeing Luigi, she appeared startled, and stood back hesitantly. Juliana tugged at his sleeve.

'Come with me,' she whispered, pulling Luigi out of the sitting room towards the staircase.

Left alone, Marco walked across to Anastasia, his hands outstretched. She took his hands in hers. Tears cascaded down her pale cheeks as he folded her in his arms.

'Don't cry, don't cry! I'm here now... I'm so sorry, Ana. I love you, I love you...'

He buried his face in her wild dark hair and felt her body relax as she curved herself against him.

Her tears of relief turned to sobs as the weeks of fear and revulsion for Anzolo poured out of her.

He led her over to a high-backed chair and sat her down on it, pushing a cushion into the small of her back. She sank back as if exhausted. He knelt beside her, holding her two hands in one of his while wiping her tears away with the other. Then he poured a small glass of amber liquid from a decanter on the table and handed it to her.

'Drink, drink this. It will do you good.'

She sipped the dark wine and felt its warmth seeping through her.

'Thank you for coming, I thought I'd never see you again.'

She began to cry once again.

He moaned and buried his face in her skirts.

'Marco?'

She lifted his face towards her.

'What's the matter?'

'I should have come before. I'm so ashamed. How could I have left you there, suffering heaven knows what indignity.'

'What could you have done? You didn't even know where I was.'

'I should have gone straight to your father – demanded to know where you were. Threatened to kill him if he didn't tell me.'

'He would have laughed in your face. You were powerless… As was I.'

'My father, and Tobias… they convinced me that there was nothing we could do. But all the while you were imprisoned here in Venice, with that awful man.'

He began to weep, and rested his head once again in her lap.

'I understand,' she said stroking his hair, 'really.'

Marco looked up at her. She was staring out of the window, her face glittering in the moonlight. He wiped her tears away once more.

'How did you bear it?'

'Because there was no alternative.'

She looked at him, her eyes dry. He felt her body stiffen slightly. She was defensive again, protecting herself.

'I am staying with my friend Luigi in Venice near the Fondaco dei Turchi,' he said. 'Come back with us there tonight, and tomorrow I will take you home to Villa Limonaia.'

'My father will force me to come back here. It is hopeless,' said Anastasia dejectedly.

'Anastasia, there was a fire in the stables. Your father was badly injured – he may even be dying. Marietta wrote to me, telling me that as he tried to rescue the horses, Minou kicked him.'

Anastasia smiled slightly.

'Did he? What a clever boy… my lovely Minou.'

'But Anastasia – whether Ludovico is alive or dead, my father and I have a plan. He says that Venetian law may allow you to divorce your husband. The marriage was not legal; you were coerced.'

'Worse,' said Juliana di Luna firmly, coming back into the room with Luigi. 'She was raped.'

Anastasia began to cry once again, and hid her face in her hands. 'Oh Juliana, do not say such a thing.'

'But it is true, Anastasia,' retorted the midwife. 'And it must be made public if you are to escape that dreadful man. Venice has many faults, but on this one thing it has right on its side. If a woman is coerced, forced into a marriage against her will, then the contract can be overturned. I will speak on your behalf, Anastasia – I have done it before. The court holds no fear for me. Go with your friend Marco; I see that he will look after you. And when you need me to testify, I will stand up for you, as will Veronica. We will support you.'

Chapter Sixteen

Villa di Bozzolo
May 2017

Lorenzo called Millie at eight o'clock.

'Good morning. Did you sleep well?'

'Yes, absolutely,' she replied. 'Although I've been awake for ages. What time do you want to leave for Venice?'

'As soon as I get back from dropping Bella at school. Can you be ready?'

'Yes. I'll just have a bit of breakfast and I'll see you in the hall.'

There was an atmosphere of tension in the dining room as Millie sat down at her usual corner table. She was the only resident eating breakfast that morning. Elena stalked back and forth through the swing baize door to the service kitchen, dressed in her customary black jeans and shirt.

'Would you like an egg?' she asked, avoiding Millie's gaze and staring instead out of the window.

'No… no, thank you,' said Millie. 'I'll just have some of your fabulous bread and a piece of cake. That will do perfectly.'

Millie found herself in a quandary that morning. The previous evening Elena had discovered her sitting in the dark with her brother on the terrace. She had obviously detected something between them. Perhaps Lorenzo had even told her of his growing affection for Millie. Was Elena now jealous of the developing relationship between Millie and Lorenzo?

And now, as if that wasn't bad enough, Millie was going to have to disappoint him. After her morning phone call with Max, Elena would be entitled to be angry with her. Last night she had kissed her brother, leading him on. This morning, she had promised to return to London and to Max. Elena didn't know about Max, of course, but Millie's own sense of guilt somehow added to the atmosphere of mistrust in the dining room that morning.

She went back to her room to collect her notebook and brush her teeth. On the way back down the grand staircase to the hall, her eye was caught by a portrait hanging in a particularly dark corner of the landing. It was of a young woman, seated at an easel; she was painting what Millie now recognised as a silkmoth, its eggs nestling on a mulberry leaf. Millie wondered why she had not noticed it before.

Once she and Lorenzo were on the road to Venice, she asked him about it.

'The portrait on the landing... oh yes. It's good, isn't it? We ought to hang it in the drawing room really. We don't know who it is. A relative, I suppose...'

'I'm not a huge expert in fashion through the ages, but it looks like about the seventeenth or eighteenth century,' said Millie. 'Is the painting not signed, or marked in any way?'

'No, oddly it's not.'

'She's painting a silkmoth, isn't she? It's exquisitely done; presumably it was painted somewhere here, on the farm?'

'Maybe, yes... although if you look carefully, it's not the farm that you see through the window, it looks more like Venice. It's a bit of a mystery.'

*

As they drove along the monotonous motorway towards Venice, Millie avoided any mention of her confession the previous evening about her relationship with Max. Marco didn't ask if she had decided to go back to him. Nor did he mention the kiss. Instead, they talked about Lorenzo's daughter.

'How was Bella this morning?' Millie was genuinely curious.

'She was well. She told me she enjoyed her story very much.'

'That's good,' said Millie. 'I enjoyed reading to her. She's a sweetie.'

'She asked if you were coming back this evening.'

Millie looked across at Lorenzo; his eyes were determinedly focused on the motorway ahead, but she knew he was aware of her gaze.

'Well, I'd love to read to her again. Let's play it by ear, shall we?'

They parked in Venice's multi-storey car park by the station and boarded a *vaporetto*.

'Do you know Venice?' asked Lorenzo as he guided her to a seat at the front of the waterbus.

'Not really. I came here as a teenager, with my family. But I've not been since, I'm ashamed to say.'

As the *vaporetto* carved its way up the Grand Canal, Marco acted as an informal guide.

'There, on the left, is the Venice Casino. We could take a look later, if we have time. And here, on the right, is the Fondaco dei Turchi; it was the old trading house for Turkish merchants. It's a museum now, I think.'

The *vaporetto* made stops on each side of the Grand Canal; every few hundred yards, locals and tourists battled through the crowds to get on and off the boat. The boatmen called out the names of the stops, expertly manoeuvring the craft next to each pontoon.

At the cry of 'Santa Stae', Lorenzo helped Millie up from her seat. 'This is our stop.' He took her hand and guided her up the narrow gangway and onto the landing station.

'How far away is the mill?' asked Millie.

'Only about ten minutes.'

They walked in single file through the complex maze of narrow streets and lanes, emerging finally in a small *campo*, surrounded on all sides by apricot stucco plaster facades peeling away from ancient brickwork. It had an air of faded elegance.

Lorenzo strode across the *campo* and knocked loudly on what seemed to Millie to be a somewhat unremarkable oak door. Moments later, it was opened by a slim young man, who showed them to a small waiting room. In a large display case were jewelled handbags made of silk, cut velvet shawls and, in pride of place, a silk damask trouser suit.

'This is stunning,' whispered Millie.

Within minutes they were ushered upstairs to meet the owner of the mill – Signor Giovanni Bordignon.

A tall, aristocratic man, he welcomed them warmly into his office.

'Please do sit down. It is hot today; would you like a little water, or a coffee?'

'Water would be fantastic, thank you,' said Millie. 'You speak very good English.'

'I was an academic before I took over the business. I worked at the university here. I taught politics.'

'Gosh – this must be quite a change for you.'

'Yes, indeed. But it is the family business. It has been in our family for well over two hundred and fifty years, and there was a mill on this site long before that. You cannot walk away from a legacy like that. It was my duty to take over, but also my pleasure.' As he talked to them, he laid out lengths of silk on a long table in the centre of the room.

'These are examples of silks that have been in production for decades; some were produced over two hundred years ago.' He went over to a large desk and removed three heavy leather ledgers. He laid them out next to the silk lengths on the table, and opened the first one carefully. 'In these books is a note of every fabric we have ever made. You can see where the clerk has written the name of the fabric, who it was intended for, how much was made and, always, a little piece of the fabric is attached to the page. So if we wish to make it again, we can do so. The patterns are all kept in the mill room downstairs – at least the ones produced since the invention of the Jacquard loom. This fabric here, for example, was originally made for the Tsar of Russia back in the nineteenth century. We have also made vestments for many of the popes. Earlier this year, a famous designer here in Italy ordered several metres of a fabric we first produced in the eighteenth century. He wanted to make a dress for the finale of his fashion show. It cost him over twenty thousand euros.'

'Twenty thousand euros – wow!'

'Yes, it's a lot of money. But it takes such a long time to produce – four months just to set up the loom – all just to make a few metres of fabric. To be honest, the money he paid didn't actually cover the costs.' He laughed. 'Now, would you like to see the looms?'

Stepping into the mill room, Millie felt that she had been transported back in time. The walls were covered from floor to ceiling with wooden shelves filled with coloured bobbins and roll after roll of Jacquard paper patterns. Four large Jacquard looms, made in the early nineteenth century, were in operation. The noise was deafening as the wooden machinery clattered back and forth. Each loom had been set up to make a different fabric – a rich red silk cut velvet on one, a purple silk damask on another.

'The designs are determined by a paper pattern unfolding across the top of the loom,' explained their host. 'Originally, the paper patterns punched with tiny round holes automatically guaranteed that every length of any particular silk, or cut velvet, would be identical to the last. Here you can see each loom set up with hundreds of reels of silk thread, which create the weft pattern on the warp linen background.'

Millie wandered between the looms talking to the weavers. She was surprised to discover that some were art students keen to learn about the traditional weaving system.

'This is part of my postgraduate course,' said one. 'It takes me over five months to create a metre of fabric, but I love it.'

Among the lengths of purple cut velvets, and red and dark-green silks, Millie's eye was caught by one piece in particular.

'That's incredible; it looks like real leopard skin,' she said. 'It's so lifelike. What's it for?'

'A very special client – they want it for a chair in their drawing room,' said Signor Bordignon. 'We can do zebra, or cheetah… any animal really.'

After Millie had made notes and taken photographs, Signor Bordignon invited her through to his opulent office. 'That's the Grand Canal through the window,' said the owner proudly. 'This is where we bring our VIP clients to view our designs.' Giovanni motioned to hundreds of books containing original silk fabrics.

Millie picked up one of the sample books and sat down on a seat to look through it more carefully. As she got up to swap it for another, she looked out of the window onto the Grand Canal.

'You have a wonderful view from here. What a stunning location for an office.'

'It is,' said Signor Bordignon. 'We're very lucky.'

'The view from here… Lorenzo – does it remind you of anything?'

'It's the Grand Canal, Millie. I have seen it a thousand times – in real life, pictures and paintings; I'm not sure what you mean.'

'Isn't it the view in one particular painting?'

He sat down on the bench seat next to her.

'My God, you're right. The portrait on the stairs at our house – that is the view, or at least, something very similar.'

'I'll take a shot on my phone so we can compare it when we get back to the villa.'

At the end of the visit, they thanked Signor Bordignon warmly for his help.

'Could you can send me a jpeg of your logo, and we can link to your Facebook page if you have one, and your Twitter feed?' Millie asked. 'I'll let you know when the article will be published. It will be online, as well as in the newspaper.'

A few yards from the *campo* was a busy little street filled with local shops selling bread and vegetables. Sandwiched between a chemist and ice cream vendor stood a small cafe overlooking a narrow canal.

'Are you hungry?' asked Marco.

'I'm starving,' replied Millie.

'Well, this place is good. I've eaten here before. You won't find any tourists here. They do a fantastic *spaghetti alle vongole*.'

'Well, you were right,' said Millie, as she twirled forkfuls of pasta into her mouth. 'This is utterly delicious. I was really hungry.'

'Did you not have much breakfast this morning?'

'I had enough… it was fabulous, as always,' she said evasively.

After a few minutes, she plucked up the courage to ask Lorenzo about Elena's earlier unfriendliness.

'Your sister… she doesn't like me very much, does she?'

'No, don't think that; she doesn't know you. She is very shy and rather stiff. I'm sorry if you felt any animosity. There is none, I assure you.'

'I just thought, last night, she seemed a bit put out that I was there.'

'Please don't worry. She'd had a long day visiting one of the boys.'

'OK, if you're sure.'

'Yes, of course. Now, would you like dessert, or coffee?'

'Oh, just a coffee would be lovely – thank you.'

Marco ordered two espressos. He smiled at Millie a little nervously.

'So… are you coming back to read to Bella this evening?'

'Lorenzo… about that.' Millie faltered, unsure how to proceed. 'I spoke to Max this morning. It's got a bit complicated.'

'Ah,' he said.

'He's left his wife, or rather she's left him. And he wants us to get together…'

'I see. So, that's good news, isn't it?'

'Yes,' she said weakly. 'Yes, I suppose it is.'

'You don't sound very sure.'

'Do you know… I was this morning, but now – maybe it's not the right thing to do after all. Oh, I'm just a mess.'

'Look…' Marco sipped his coffee. 'I can't advise you – it wouldn't be right. I don't think I can be really objective.' He smiled. 'Why don't we go and look around? You can't come to Venice and not see San Marco, or the Doge's Palace.'

'Oh yes,' said Millie, relieved that the awkward moment had passed, 'let's do that. I'd love that. Thank you.'

They spent the afternoon wandering the streets of Venice. They visited the fish market near the Rialto, and Lorenzo bought a bag of chillies.

'You can only eat a tiny amount – they are fierce – but they're very good. Elena will love them.'

They crossed the Rialto Bridge and wandered down past the expensive designer shops towards the Piazza San Marco. Lorenzo took her to Harry's Bar and bought her a Bellini, which she drank too quickly. He bought another, which she sipped.

'We must go in a gondola,' he suggested as they emerged from the bar.

'But aren't they terribly expensive?'

'They are a little, yes, but come on, let's do it.'

He negotiated a price with the *gondoliere* and held her hand as she stepped aboard.

'I've asked him to take us through some of the smaller canals – to show you the real Venice.'

As the gondola slipped through the water, Lorenzo draped his arm across the back of the seat. Millie found herself resting her head on his shoulder. The Bellinis had relaxed her.

'This is so peaceful. You get a completely different view of the architecture from a gondola, don't you?' she mused.

Max, her job, the silk article's deadline all receded; she was aware only of the beauty of Venice and the scent of the man next to her. As the gondola floated down the narrow canals, Millie had enticing glimpses of other people's lives. A couple embracing in a doorway; a woman sitting alone in a window watching the canal traffic; a child playing hopscotch in a tiny *piazza*, observed by an old woman – his grandmother perhaps. The lives of these people were the same as the lives of people anywhere, in any town, in any country, and yet there was something enchanting about these scenes of normality unfolding in this ancient gem of a city.

As they neared the Grand Canal, the traffic began to increase. Long barges delivering bottles of water squeezed past their gondola. A speedboat filled with glamorous tourists, its engine at low throttle, manoeuvred its way past. The inhabitants blew kisses at Millie and waved. She, slightly embarrassed, waved back, laughing. As the gondola joined the bustle of the Grand Canal, heading back to Piazza San Marco, Millie looked up at Lorenzo. He kissed her then and she kissed him back. And there was passion, real passion. She felt the heat spreading down through her body as he kissed her. All thoughts of Max disappeared in an instant. She was just here, with this beautiful man, in a gondola in Venice… and it was perfect.

Chapter Seventeen

Villa di Bozzolo
October 1704

In the weeks following Anastasia's liberation, Polonia and her daughters formed a tightly knit bond. With the death of the head of the household, the atmosphere at Villa di Bozzolo was undoubtedly happier, but the three women remained constantly vigilant for fear that Anastasia's husband would seize her and take her back to Venice. Polonia insisted that her daughter should never be alone. Whether she was painting, walking in the gardens or visiting the silk farms, a male manservant was ordered to accompany her whenever she was outside the villa.

'It seems I have escaped one form of imprisonment only to have it replaced with another,' reflected Anastasia woefully.

Memories of her incarceration dominated her thoughts night and day. For while she was now physically removed from Anzolo, her experience could not so easily be left behind. The rapes she had suffered at the hands of her husband had left her damaged, not just bodily but emotionally. She wondered sometimes if she would ever be able to let a man near her again – even her beloved Marco.

But he was determined to show her that he understood; that he could be patient and still loved her. Gradually his devotion broke down the barriers. Anastasia had always enjoyed spending time at Lake Limonaia, and now it became a place of solace. When she could persuade her mother to let her visit the villa in the carriage, she relished the time she spent there with Marco. They rode through the woods surrounding the estate, or went fishing on the lake. With their catch safely aboard, Marco would row the boat to the shore and drag it up on the stony beach of one of the tiny villages that dotted the edges of the lake, and together they could wander the streets before taking lunch in a local inn. In the afternoon, they set up their easels ready for an afternoon's painting. Marco was not a talented artist, but he enjoyed seeing Anastasia so absorbed in her work, her mind totally focused on the scene she was painting.

Sitting at her easel, she was completely involved with the subjects that took her interest – the beautiful lake, a magnificent flower, a colourful insect. But when Marco tried to kiss her, she would turn her cheek, unable to offer him the intimacy he so obviously desired. She knew he was confused by her rejection and yet she felt unable to explain. Before she could open herself up to another man, she needed to feel safe again. And part of feeling safe would involve a definitive and formal separation from her husband.

One day in early November, the Balzarelli family visited Vicenzo and Marco at Lake Garda. After lunch, Marco took Anastasia and Marietta riding in the woods, leaving Polonia and Vicenzo in the drawing room.

'Polonia,' began Vicenzo, 'I invited you here today to discuss the possibility of Anastasia divorcing her husband. I know that we have spoken once or twice about this, and I gained the impression that you were unsure how to proceed.'

'I was – I am,' said Polonia. 'Ludovico dealt with all legal matters. Now that he is dead, it is not something I pretend to understand.'

'Well, if you will allow, I have taken the liberty of doing some initial preparation.'

'Thank you, Vicenzo. I am so grateful.'

'Marco and I feel some responsibility. He loves your daughter – I hope you know that. His desire to marry her was sincere; it remains sincere. We would both be honoured to help Anastasia. You understand that it will be important for us to build a proper legal case. While you and your daughter obviously feel that Anastasia has been badly used by both her father and her husband, unfortunately that is not sufficient to seek an end to the marriage. We must find witnesses to the harsh treatment she received at the hands of her husband. Anastasia must be prepared to testify against Anzolo, to speak plainly of the indignities she suffered. And the court may want to hear from you about your own husband's role in this sorry business.'

'I will say whatever Anastasia's case requires,' said Polonia firmly. 'While my husband was alive I was unable to speak freely, but now I am at liberty to tell the truth. Ludovico used us all badly for many, many years. He beat me, and my daughters. He was a cruel, heartless, domineering man. Nobody knew; we kept it from everyone – we were ashamed. But Ludovico had another vice – he was a gambler. Anastasia was offered to Anzolo as payment for a gambling debt. He granted her hand in marriage to that terrible man in return for cancelling the debt. He would rather have given up his own daughter than sell part of the farm, or the vineyard. Can you believe any father could do such a terrible thing?'

Vicenzo reached out and took Polonia's hand in his own.

'I cannot, Polonia. I am shocked, appalled that he could do such a thing.'

'When Anzolo agreed to the idea of taking Anastasia as payment, they realised that between them they could form a successful business partnership – between silk producer and silk manufacturer. Ludovico was always jealous of your success, Vicenzo. He thought this was his opportunity to build a business that would rival your own. And if Anastasia had produced a son, the child, his grandchild, would have become the heir to one of the most successful silk empires in Veneto. That was his motivation. Poor Anastasia was just a pawn in their business dealings.'

'I can see that the complications multiply,' sighed Vicenzo. 'I have taken the liberty of obtaining the services of two legal experts in this area. A lawyer called Zan Jacomo Gradenigo – he will present the case to the court – and a procurator, Giovanni Venier, who will marshal the evidence. He will need to speak to everyone concerned – yourself, Marietta, Anastasia and any independent witnesses who could support Ana's case.'

'Anastasia told me that the maid Veronica was very loyal,' suggested Polonia. 'She has asked me to bring her to the villa; she is concerned that Anzolo might be cruel to her, or punish her in some way for her kindness.'

'Good, well, let us send for her. You can employ her, I presume, at Villa di Bozzolo?'

'Yes, indeed. And there's another potential witness: the midwife.'

'A midwife?' Vicenzo peered at Polonia quizzically over his delicate spectacles. 'Is Anastasia…?'

'No, no – it was all a fabrication,' she replied hurriedly. 'Anastasia pretended to be with child in order to escape her imprisonment. She calculated – rightly as it turned out – that if Anzolo believed her to be with child, he would allow her to take the air outside the house, for her health, and so she could make her escape. The midwife, Juliana di Luna, was part of that deception.'

'Excellent.' Vicenzo leaned forward excitedly. 'We'll tell the procurator where to find her. Once he's collected all the evidence, he'll hand it over to the lawyer, who will determine the best legal case.

'There are several possibilities, I understand. Annulment – although this generally relies on non-consummation. From what we know of poor Anastasia's incarceration, that seems unlikely and would be difficult to prove. But there is also an opportunity to annul if we can prove coercion; in other words, that she was forced into the marriage against her will. That is a distinct possibility, I would have thought.

'The third option is to demonstrate that her life was in peril. I think we can assume that was also indisputable. But nothing is simple with the patriarchal court. Their duty is to uphold marriage, remember. They are not inclined to grant a divorce. The case will be heard and judged by the Patriarch of Venice – a man named Gianalberto Badoaro – and his second-in-command, the Vicar of the Cathedral of San Pietro. Once our lawyer has made a deposition to the court, it is likely that Anzolo will engage his own procurator and try to build the opposing case. We must pray that God and common sense will prevail.'

Over the following weeks, Anastasia, Marietta and Polonia all gave their evidence to the procurator, Giovanni Venier. He went to the church where the marriage had taken place, in the parish of San Zan Degolà, and spoke to the priest who had presided. Anastasia assured Venier she had refused to give her assent to the marriage. Now he accused the priest of overlooking the reluctance of the bride. But the priest brushed the procurator's questions aside. 'She gave her assent – the marriage was perfectly legal,' he assured him. But Venier was not convinced. He spoke at length to the parishioners, all of whom had differing opinions of the priest.

'He is as crooked as a sickle,' said one.

'He is a godly man, who would never do anyone ill,' said another.

As Venier stood outside the church, preparing to leave, a young girl with flame-red hair approached him.

'Sir, may I speak with you?'

'Yes. What do you have to tell me?'

'I am employed to clean the church. I was there the day that Signor di Zorzi married that poor girl. I know him a little because my cousin, Filomena, works for him. I felt sorry for the girl getting married – she was weeping all through the ceremony and she did *not* give her assent, I swear it. At the end, her father gave the priest a bag of gold. He said it was for the collection plate,' said the girl. 'But I never saw Father put the money there. I found it later in his bedchamber in a box he had hidden in the bottom of a chest.'

Venier's two key independent witnesses were the midwife, Juliana, and the maid, Veronica. Venier visited Juliana di Luna at her home in Calle Orsetti and she told him of the terrible cruelty to which Anastasia had been subjected. She was a mature woman, who had spoken in court before. Her testimony would be sound enough, he reckoned. But obtaining Veronica's testimony presented a problem: she was still living in the household of Anzolo di Zorzi, the very man who would be his adversary in court. Anastasia was fearful that Anzolo would punish Veronica if he knew that she had given evidence against him. And so Marco went once again to Venice. He waited in the lane near the house until Anzolo had left for the mill, watching the older man as he crossed the *campo*. He looked bowed, Marco thought; sad even. Could he perhaps, in some twisted way, be missing Anastasia? Had he imagined that his imprisoned wife actually loved him? It seemed unlikely – and yet what could induce a man to behave so wickedly? Knocking on the oak door, Marco was shown into the hall.

'I am sorry to intrude,' he said to the footman, 'but I have been sent by a member of Veronica's family to speak to her on a matter of urgency.'

Tomasso, the footman, looked dubious, but nevertheless sent for Veronica.

She drew Marco to one side, away from Tomasso's prying eyes and ears.

'Speak quietly,' she told him.

'I have come to ask you to speak out for Anastasia in court. It is asking a great deal, I know – for if you speak for Anastasia, you cannot remain here. I fear that Anzolo might punish you.'

'I will be happy to speak for her and to leave this house – if Anastasia will take me in?'

'Yes, of course. Be in no doubt, your future is secure. Now, if you are coming, be quick. Pack your bags and let us leave before Anzolo returns.'

Veronica emerged ten minutes later with a small, embroidered drawstring bag that contained her few possessions and, in her other hand, a roll of paper tied with a ribbon.

'Is that everything?' asked Marco incredulously.

'Yes,' whispered Veronica. 'I don't have much anyway, and I don't want to alert Tomasso.'

'What do you have there?' whispered Marco, pointing to the rolled-up paper.

'These are Signora Balzarelli's drawings. They were hidden in her room; I thought she would like to have them.'

'That was thoughtful; thank you.' He took the drawings from her and slipped them into a leather bag that he carried over his shoulder.

'Where are you going?' challenged Tomasso as they approached the front door. 'The master said nothing to me of you leaving.'

'I'm not leaving, I just have to go on an errand with this gentleman. I won't be long. It has something to do with my mother, and nothing to do with you,' said Veronica assertively. 'Now get out of my way.'

Veronica boldly pushed the footman aside. As soon as she and Marco left the house they walked swiftly across the *campo* and down towards the jetty, where Marco had a *gondoliere* waiting for him.

'Ha…' said Veronica, laughing, 'it will be wonderful to leave this place. I came here first as a girl and have never enjoyed working here. Signor di Zorzi took me on as a kitchen maid at first. Then I became maid to his first wife. She had many miscarriages, poor woman. He was so angry each time she lost a child. He wanted an heir so badly and when she lost one and then another, it was as if he couldn't forgive her. He used to say it was her fault because she insisted on going out into the town and meeting friends. But what he didn't see was that she was broken-hearted too and he never gave any thought to her. She had a terrible life and in the end I think the heartache of losing those children killed her. It will give me nothing but pleasure to speak out against Signor di Zorzi.'

When Marco's carriage clattered into the courtyard at Villa di Bozzolo, Anastasia rushed down the steps to greet Veronica.

'Oh Veronica – welcome to Villa di Bozzolo! Marco, thank you so much for bringing her here. Come, both of you, get out of the carriage. You must be tired. Oh, let me look at you!'

She stood back and looked into Veronica's eyes.

'Anzolo hasn't been cruel to you since I left?'

'No, Mistress. He challenged me about you running away. He asked me over and over, "Did you know what she was planning?" But I just insisted I knew nothing. In the end he gave up. He'll know now, though, won't he?'

'Yes, I imagine he will. Now come inside. We will show you your room and your things can be taken there so you can settle in. Where is your luggage?'

Veronica lifted up the small drawstring bag.

'This is all I have, Mistress. I have very little of my own. And I didn't want to raise suspicion in front of Tomasso. I left my spare dress at the mill house.'

'Well, that was sensible. And we can buy you some new clothes now you are here safely with us.

'Marco,' continued Anastasia, taking his hand in hers and kissing it. 'I am so grateful to you. Once again you have rescued me.'

She gazed deeply into his eyes and squeezed his hand.

Wanting to stay, but realising he should leave, he grazed her hand with his lips as he bowed low.

'It was nothing… I was glad to do it. I shall leave you both now. I should get back to Lake Garda.'

Standing in the grand hall of the villa, Veronica looked around her.

'It's a beautiful house. And the countryside here is so pretty with all the vineyards and orchards everywhere. I've never left Venice before in my whole life. I am not used to seeing fields and farm animals.'

'Oh Veronica! And when I was brought to Venice I had scarcely ever left Villa di Bozzolo. I just hope you will be happier here than I was in Venice.'

'I will, Mistress, I'm sure of that. It will be a fresh start for me. I worked for that man for so long; I went there when I was just ten years old. He was not a cruel man, but harsh, at times, to all his servants. And the way he used you, madam, it was terrible. He was never kind to his first wife, but to lock you in that room for all that time— I just wish I could have done more to help you.'

Her eyes filled with tears, which she blinked away. Anastasia took her hands in her own.

'Veronica, you made life bearable, believe me. Now let's take you to your room and then you must meet my mother and sister.'

And so, with all the evidence safely collected the scene was finally set for the court hearing, which was due to be held on the tenth of January. Anastasia was understandably nervous.

'Oh Mamma – what will happen if the patriarch does not find for me?' she asked one morning as they sat in the dining room overlooking the gardens.

'Anastasia, it's impossible to imagine any other outcome. Your father was so wicked and your marriage so terrible. We have a case on the grounds of coercion alone.'

But Anastasia was not so easily mollified. She slept fitfully at night, disturbed by memories of Anzolo, his face close to hers as he raped her each night. She would wake from these nightmares and weep quietly. Now that their father was gone, the sisters took their little dog, Bianca, to bed with them each night and she would crawl up the bed and nuzzle her mistress as she wept.

'Oh Bianca, help me to sleep and think good thoughts,' Anastasia would whisper.

By day she painted, or visited the silk farms and vineyards – for since their father's death Anastasia had done her best to manage the business. Accompanied at all times by one of the grooms, she relished these rides around the estate on her beloved Minou. But when she returned home at the end of the day, and the candles and lamps were lit, her thoughts often turned to those dark evenings locked in the bedchamber in the mill owner's house, as she waited despairingly for the sound of his footsteps in the corridor, and the turn of the key in the lock.

Polonia sensed her daughter's distress. She had lived with a vicious, controlling man for many years, and could understand much of what Anastasia had endured during her own brief marriage. She too had been taken against her will. In fact, she had never experienced a loving physical relationship with Ludovico. But somehow she had learned to cope with it, to separate her heart and her head from her body. And her daughters had been a huge compensation for all the years of unhappiness.

Now she was determined to both support her daughter and also bring some joy into her life.

'My darling girls,' she said one evening as they sat in the salon playing the card game Trappola, 'I think we should celebrate Christmas with some guests this year. Would you like that?'

'Oh Mamma!' said Marietta, 'that would be wonderful. We were never allowed to entertain properly when Papa was alive.' She smiled at her mother and a look of recognition, of some shared knowledge, passed between them. It did not go unnoticed by Anastasia.

'What do you suggest, Mamma?' she asked.

'I thought we should ask Marco and Vicenzo and perhaps some of our other neighbours. They could come for the feast of Christmas Eve and stay with us until the New Year.'

'But where will they all sleep?' asked Marietta.

'We have space in the attics of the house, remember? Your father never let me invite people to stay, so those rooms have been locked up for many years. But if we air them, and light the fires, they can be brought back to life, and we will have space for everyone.'

And so the preparations for Christmas began.

The three women decorated the family chapel in the grounds of the villa with greenery collected from the farm in readiness for the Mass that would be said on Christmas Day. The main rooms were cleaned and polished; the bedrooms on the third floor made ready for guests – the beds were aired, the fires were lit and bowls of potpourri arranged on chests, bringing a sweet scent to the bedrooms for the first time in decades.

Down in the basement kitchens Angela and Magdalena, the cook and her kitchen maid, were busy preparing festive treats. The aroma of boiling quinces floated up the stone steps and into the hall, as they made *mostarda* – a sauce of quince, sugar, ground mustard seed, candied lemon and orange pieces. It would be served on Christmas Day with *ossocollo* – a Venetian sausage that Angela prepared from the neck of the pig she had ordered from one of the tenant farmers. Marinated with salt and saltpetre, it was then dried, seasoned with pepper and spices and stuffed into the guts of the pig. As the festive season drew nearer, carts carrying produce rattled into the courtyard: baskets of clams for the Christmas Eve *risotto de pevarasse* and an eight-foot eel that required two men to carry it down the basement stairs.

On the morning of Christmas Eve Anastasia and Marietta went out to gather greenery to decorate the salon and the dining room. Once this was done, they spent a happy hour creating a seasonal log – made with fruit, juniper and laurel foliage, which would be set alight in the fireplace of the grand salon at sunset, in front of all their guests. The *Ciocco* – a ceremony to honour renewal – was an ancient ritual, after which the family would sit down to a banquet.

In the afternoon, Anastasia and Marietta went to their bedchamber to change for the early-evening celebrations. Polonia had insisted that they both have new dresses and they had spent many happy hours with the dressmaker from Verona, who brought bolts of silk, damask and velvet in a myriad of different colours. Anastasia had selected a dark-green silk, which set off her dark hair and pale skin. Marietta's dress was the colour of candied oranges.

As they dressed, they heard the distinctive sound of a carriage and four trotting into the courtyard.

'That will be the first of our guests,' cried Marietta excitedly. 'I hope it's Marco and Vicenzo.'

'Let me take a look,' said Anastasia, peering through the window.

A grey-haired man leapt from the carriage and marched up the stone steps to the villa. He banged angrily on the door.

'Oh no!' said Anastasia. 'It's Anzolo.'

'I'll stop him,' cried Marietta. She rushed down the steps into the main hall just as Giuseppe, the footman, approached the door.

'Do not open it!' screamed Marietta. 'It's Anzolo. Bolt the door! Where is Mamma?'

Polonia was in the drawing room and, hearing the commotion, rushed into the entrance hall.

'What is it, Marietta?'

'Anzolo – he is outside.'

'Do not open the door,' Polonia instructed Giuseppe. 'Bolt it. And please ensure all the windows downstairs are locked. Is Anastasia upstairs?' she asked Marietta.

'She is, Mamma.'

'Go back to her. I will send Giuseppe to join you, with your father's pistol.'

The ground floor secured, Polonia went upstairs to her bed-chamber and opened the window. She called out to the strange man below: 'Who is there?'

'Anzolo di Zorzi – husband of your daughter, Anastasia. I know she is here. I demand her return. She is my wife and I have my rights.'

'You have no rights over my child, you are a despicable wretch. My husband is dead and any contract between you is void. Get off my property and never come back!'

Polonia slammed the windows shut and sat down on the bed, shaking with indignation.

Marietta rushed in from her bedroom. She peered through the windows. At that moment a second carriage drew into the courtyard.

'It's Marco,' said Marietta excitedly.

'Get away from the window,' said Polonia. 'Leave this to me.'

She once again opened the window and leaned out.

'You must leave, now,' she shouted to Anzolo. 'There is nothing for you here.'

'I will not leave, not without my wife. She is pregnant with my child.'

'You are a fool,' spat Polonia, 'she is not pregnant. She lied to you.'

Anzolo appeared momentarily stunned. He stumbled back down the steps to the villa and fell into the arms of Marco, who swung him round, gripping him firmly by the shoulders.

'Get out of here, and don't come back again.'

Marco bundled the man into his carriage. As he slammed the door behind him, he shouted through the window.

'You will see Anastasia again, but only in court, when she is granted a divorce!' He hit the flank of the lead horse of the pack and the carriage swung round the central well of the courtyard, out through the grand archway and onto the open road.

Chapter Eighteen

Isolo San Pietro di Castello, Venice
January 1705

The divorce proceedings were heard in the Patriarchal Court of San Pietro di Castello – the principal cathedral in Venice, and the seat of the Patriarch of Venice, Gianalberto Badoaro. The patriarch was fifty-seven years of age and had been a priest since the age of twenty-eight. He was ordained Bishop and Patriarch of Venice by the Senate in 1688, and over the many subsequent years had made rulings on more cases of divorce than he cared to remember.

There had been a cathedral on the Isola di San Pietro, or Olivolo as it was known colloquially, for nearly a thousand years. The building had been renovated thirty years earlier by the architect Francesco Smeraldi, from an original design by Palladio. The white stone facade dominated the tiny island on the far eastern reaches of the district of Castello. Connected to the rest of the district by two land bridges, it had an air of tranquillity which distinguished it from its bustling neighbour. Castello was perhaps best known for its industry and, in particular, boatbuilding, in the area called the Arsenale. Many of the divorce cases Gianalberto had heard over the years featured enraged wives who often worked in and around the Arsenale. Most of the plaintiffs were women who had married too young and were frustrated to be shackled to an older husband incapable of satisfying their needs, or had in some cases been married against their will to husbands chosen for them by their fathers. The phrase 'I said yes with my voice but not with my heart' was commonly cited by these women as justification for their divorce.

As a priest, Gianalberto Badoaro had never enjoyed the married state himself but he understood the complexities of personal relationships, having been secretly involved with a married woman named Lucrezia Aguiari, a parishioner in his diocese, for several years. In spite of this rather obvious breach of the priestly code, he nevertheless took his role as patriarch – and the ultimate arbiter of disputes between married couples – very seriously. It was his duty to encourage couples to remain together. That was what the Church expected of him. He was required by law to accede, where possible, to the defender in the case – usually the husband. *'Il favor matrimonii'* was his dominant principle. The Council of Trent, over a hundred years earlier, had complicated matters by insisting both parties consented to the marriage. Until this time, it had been common practice for a father to arrange his daughter's marriage ignoring her wishes but the Catholic Church had decided that some form of consent was essential to a happy marriage and priests were required to ensure both parties were willing. In spite of the clear rules, many priests still allowed fathers to control the proceedings and it was not uncommon for them to overlook a bride's reluctance in return for a little pecuniary reward. Gianalberto tried, where possible, to disregard these misdemeanours, much as he disregarded his own transgression when he took his mistress, the beautiful Lucrezia, to his bed. The life of a priest was a lonely one and he understood temptation.

In spite of the patriarch's inclination to preserve marriage at any costs, if a procurator had done his work properly and could produce evidence of coercion – or, worse, danger to life and limb of the wife – then the patriarch would generally approve the separation, although it gave him no pleasure to do so. He was aware that, on occasion, the women who came before him were capable of devious behaviour. They would lie and bend the truth to suit their case. To ensure that he was not outwitted or manipulated, Gianalberto would often interview witnesses himself. The procurator would supply all the evidence, but Gianalberto was aware that a good procurator was also capable of coaching or guiding the witnesses to tell an expedient version of the truth in their written testimonies. Gianalberto took a certain pride in his ability to cut through the procurator's meddling and get to the heart of the matter. To search the souls of the witnesses, and try to discover who was fabricating evidence and who had a genuine grievance.

In the weeks leading up to Christmas he had overseen a case in which the wife – Camilla – sought an annulment from her husband Gasparo due to non-consummation. Gianalberto had read her testimony, but he nevertheless asked her to explain, in court, what exactly she meant by non-consummation.

'After the first night Gasparo tried to have sex, but he couldn't put his penis into my vagina. He spilled his seed outside of me, and on those first nights in the first months, and more than one time each night, he tried the same way, and he was never able to know me carnally. He always spilled his seed outside. When my husband's penis became erect, he was only able to sustain it for a few moments.'

Anxious to test Camilla's evidence, the patriarch had asked her if she had rejected her husband's advances in any way.

'I did not push him away with my hands. The truth is his penis was erect but not such that it convinced me he could consummate the marriage, because when his member touched me, it did not have the force needed to enter. I am a virgin.'

Midwives were called to testify on Camilla's behalf and swore that having examined her they were convinced she was still a virgin: *'There was no sign that Camilla had had sexual relations with a man, for her vagina was closed and the passage was very narrow,'* declared one.

'As a midwife, and having seen women with similar conditions, Camilla has not had sex, nor is her hymen broken. Her opening is closed,' confirmed another.

Gasparo had had his day in court too, and was forced to endure relentless questioning from both the patriarch and his second-in-command, the vicar. Gasparo insisted that he had entered his wife on numerous occasions, but that her *'passage is blocked and thus my penis cannot enter far enough so that the seed can be received into the womb'.*

The vicar demonstrated a commendable knowledge of carnal relations in his next question:

'Having said that you put your penis into the woman and spilled your seed is different from saying the woman's passage is blocked. And that is evidence of poor aptitude that your penis could not enter and spill seed, because as everyone knows, when the penis is potent and erect and tears the first cloisters of the vagina, it enters and spills seed.'

But in spite of the vicar's tough and, at times, embarrassing questioning, Gasparo produced some winning evidence when he called on several women who were willing to testify that he had been perfectly able to have sex with them, and in a couple of cases even succeeded in impregnating them.

In the patriarch's summing-up of the case, the couple were *not* granted a divorce, but were instead persuaded to make an effort to persevere with their marriage for one more year, on the grounds that Gasparo was clearly capable of the act of love.

Gianalberto went back to his official residence that evening certain in the knowledge that he had done God's work that day and protected the sanctity of the marriage bond.

The Balzarelli vs di Zorzi case he was due to start hearing after Christmas was a different matter altogether. He had read the testimony provided by both parties, and it was clear that he was dealing with a far more serious breach of the marital contract.

A young wife – of an undoubtedly good family – had, it appeared, been coerced into a marriage by her father. Her husband – a gentleman considerably older than his bride – had, according to the witness testimonies, taken his young wife against her will and kept her forcibly in a room in his house. On the face of it, it was a terrible story and he was inclined to sympathise with the young woman. But his duty demanded that he test the evidence before him. Besides which, the husband in the case denied the accusations most hotly, protesting that his wife was a willing participant in the ceremony and an enthusiastic bride who relished their nightly sexual encounters. She had even thought herself pregnant just three months after the ceremony. And as everyone knew, pregnancy was only possible if the woman had enjoyed an orgasm.

The court sat in the cathedral on the Isola di San Pietro. In the middle of January, with a chill east wind blowing in off the lagoon, it was an inhospitable setting for such an occasion. Anastasia and her mother and sister arrived early, accompanied by Marco, Vicenzo and Veronica. With them were their legal team – lawyer Zan Jacomo Gradenigo and the procurator Giovanni Venier.

As the party crossed the footbridge onto the island a rainstorm blew in over the sea. In the freezing atmosphere, the rain soon turned to hail and then snow, falling on Anastasia's dark hair. She pulled up the hood of her cloak and tucked her icy hands into her muff.

Inside the cathedral it was no warmer. The vast space simply absorbed the cold wind and air and amplified it. The family assembled on one side of the cathedral. Anzolo and his team sat on the other.

As the patriarch and vicar processed down the aisle, the court rose. Anastasia felt her legs buckle beneath her. Marco caught her, helping her to her seat once again.

After the patriarch had made his opening pronouncements, he called for Anastasia as the chief litigant to give her testimony. He had read the witness statements provided by the procurator, but he wished to question her further. Anastasia walked unsteadily to her place in front of the patriarch's wooden throne.

'I would like you to describe your wedding,' he said. 'Were you a willing participant?'

'I was not. I was kidnapped by my father and brought to the ceremony against my will. I was to marry another gentleman and my father found me and took me away just as that ceremony was about to begin. He took me straight to Venice; for two days we travelled and I was not allowed food or water, or any change of clothing. I was taken straight away to the church of San Zan Degolà for the ceremony.'

'And did the priest ask if you gave your assent?' asked the patriarch.

'He did, and I told him I did not. I could not. I had never even met this man who was to be my husband. How could I be expected to marry him?'

'And after the ceremony, was the marriage consummated?'

'No, not the first night. I locked myself in the bedchamber... I was so terrified of him. I was... I was a virgin and could not bear the idea of him touching me. I had no idea what to expect.'

Polonia began to weep and murmured, 'Oh Ana, Ana, what did I do to you? Why could I not protect you?'

'Silence in the court,' said the vicar. 'You will have your chance to speak.'

'Once you were in the bedchamber, what did you intend to do?'

'I had only one thought – to escape. I climbed out of the window... I was so desperate. But I became disoriented and lost; I had never before been to Venice, and I ended up back at the mill house. He caught me and took me upstairs...'

Anastasia ground to a halt, seemingly unable to continue. Her throat tightened, and her eyes filled with tears as she saw the horrified reaction of her family sitting in the front pews of this great cathedral. How could she really describe, here in this holy place, what that man had done to her? She looked over briefly at Anzolo and saw that he was smiling at her. Was he amused? Did he relish the idea of her describing their first sexual encounter?

'And what happened when he took you upstairs?' asked the patriarch. 'Were you a willing participant as a bride should be? Did he approach you delicately, kissing you and fondling you as he is supposed to do?'

'No!' Anastasia almost shouted. 'He did not. He ripped off my breeches – I had worn some of his in order to climb down the drainpipe – and he took me, like an animal. I was a virgin and he took me roughly and cruelly. And it hurt. I bled afterwards and he seemed pleased. Then I wept. I always cried afterwards. He took me in the same way every night. He would just force his way into me, even if I turned my back or tried to hide in the closet from him. He would grab me, throw me down and—' Anastasia began to weep, her resolve to be strong evaporating with every word she spoke.

'You may sit down,' said the patriarch gently. He called next for Polonia Balzarelli.

'Your daughter suggests that her father arranged the match without her knowledge. Is that true?'

'It is true.'

'Was he a good father?'

'No! He abused us terribly. He often beat me, and his daughters. We meant nothing to him.'

'How did he choose a husband for his daughter?'

'He lost her to that man in a card game.' She pointed accusingly at Anzolo di Zorzi, who merely smiled in return.

The court gasped, and the patriarch looked surprised.

'In a card game?'

'Yes, a game of Basset.'

'I am not familiar with it,' said the patriarch truthfully.

'It is a high-stakes game of cards. My husband met this man, Anzolo di Zorzi, in the casino here in Venice. As the game proceeded, Ludovico, my husband, kept losing. Instead of just leaving and cutting his losses, he continued to play until he owed that man so much that he faced financial ruin. He offered Anastasia to Anzolo in payment of the debt.'

'Is this true, *signore?*' asked the patriarch during his cross-examination of Anzolo. 'That this girl was the stake in a game of cards?'

'No, that is nonsense,' protested Anzolo. 'I had known Signor Balzarelli for some time, and we determined to unite our two families. I am one of the biggest silk producers in Venice. He owned numerous silk farms. It was a good match. I admit that I had not met Anastasia before the wedding, but she gave her assent in the ceremony. And she was an enthusiastic participant in bed each night. She had orgasms, I know she did. I was married before and I understand how to pleasure a woman.'

The patriarch turned next to the two independent witnesses. Veronica was called first. As she stood anxiously in front of the patriarch, she felt Anzolo's black eyes boring into her.

The patriarch asked her to describe what she had heard on the defendant's wedding night.

'I had never heard such a terrible thing. She screamed and cried. But it was not the sound that a woman makes when she is happy, or content, sir. And it happened every night after that.'

'And what was her life like? You were her maid, you must have known her better than most,' said the patriarch.

'She was kept a prisoner in her room. The door locked; the windows barred. Even in the hottest weather at the end of the summer – do you remember how hot it was last summer? Even then, she was kept in that room in the heat. I felt sure she would become ill, or die.'

'Was she fed and clothed adequately?' asked the patriarch.

'She was, I saw to that. I brought her food each day and her mother sent her clothes. But she was so sad, sir, so terrified that she often could not eat.'

Juliana di Luna, the midwife, was called next and declared Anastasia was covered in bruises when she examined her.

'Can you confirm that she was not a virgin?' asked the patriarch, somewhat superfluously.

'Of course she was not a virgin, that is not the issue. But surely to be taken by force is not how married love should be consummated,' said Juliana grandly.

Anzolo's legal team did their best to rebut these accusations. His loyal mill manager, who had been his witness at the wedding, was called to the stand and swore that Anastasia had given her assent during the ceremony.

'I heard her with my own ears,' he declared with conviction.

The footman, Tomasso, was called to the stand and testified that Anastasia was not a prisoner; she had been allowed out of the bedchamber regularly.

'She ate lunch and dinner in the dining room with the master.'

'Every day that she lived at the house?' asked the patriarch.

'Not every day, no…' Tomasso replied uncertainly, '…at the start, the Master said that she was shy and preferred to keep her own company in her room.'

'Did she ever go outside the house?' persisted the vicar.

The footman faltered before responding. 'I do not remember, I imagine so.'

*

Anastasia's final witness was the young girl who cleaned the church of San Zan Degolà. Her name was Maria Teresa Pinottini.

'You clean the church, I understand, and were there polishing the silver on the day of the wedding?' asked the patriarch.

'I was – I go there every day after lunch and clean the church.'

'And what did you see that day?'

'I saw a young girl – that young woman there in the green dress. She was weeping and wailing and was dragged in by her father. Her dress was filthy and her hair a mess. She did not look like a bride to me.'

'I am not interested in your views on her state of dress. What did you see of the ceremony? Did she give her assent?'

'No, she did not. The priest, Father Cavazza, he asked her if she gave her assent and she said loud and clear "I do not give my assent." Father Cavazza just ignored her and declared them married. Then her father – who I do not see in the court here today – he gave the priest a little bag of coins; I heard them clinking. It was a bribe, you can be sure of that. Father Cavazza has done it before.'

'The priest will not take kindly to your disloyalty, *signorina*,' observed the patriarch.

'I do not care. I've seen too many young women married against their will in that church. It's time to take a stand,' said Maria Teresa, tossing her red curls and smiling broadly at Anastasia.

'Do you know the plaintiff?' asked the patriarch, observing Maria Teresa's smile.

'What do you mean?'

'Do you know Signora Balzarelli? Or did you know her before her marriage?'

'I do not, and I did not – I have never met her. But when Signor Venier, her procurator, asked me what I had seen in the church that day, I had to speak up for what is right. I will lose my job, but I can find another.'

Tears poured down Anastasia's face as she mouthed 'Thank you' to the flame-haired girl.

During the weeks of the trial, the family stayed at the palazzo belonging to Marco's friend, Luigi Agnoli. Each evening, as they sat in the comfortable salon overlooking the Grand Canal, they discussed the day's proceedings.

'His mill manager was very convincing,' complained Polonia. 'Even I believed him – and I know he was lying.'

'Maria Teresa rebutted everything he said,' soothed Vicenzo. 'I cannot believe they will do anything but find for Anastasia.'

'What if they insist that they remain together and try to see if she can learn to love him?' asked Polonia. 'I've heard they do that sometimes.'

'Surely not after all that we've heard of the rapes, and how Ludovico traded her so disgracefully in a card game. No… I feel sure Ana will be vindicated.'

For her part, Anastasia found the incessant conversation about the case unbearable. She retreated to her bedroom in the palazzo to paint or draw, to calm her nerves. She often took her supper in her room too, unable to cope with the combined anxieties of her family. Alone with an easel, paint and paper, she was calm and in control. She would paint a moth trapped in the web of a greedy spider, or a beetle upturned and wriggling on the wooden floor. As she studied the jointed legs or delicate wings of an insect, she was able to disassociate herself from her body and her anxieties. She mixed ultramarine with lampblack to capture the iridescent blue-black of a beetle's carapace; and used the finest sable brush to accurately paint the tiny downy hairs on the legs of a moth. In the failing light, as the candles sputtered their last, she would paint or draw until her eyes were weary with the strain. Only then would she try to sleep. But she would always wake before dawn, her thoughts crowded with worries of what the next day would bring and what lies Anzolo would tell in order to keep her tied to him for ever.

The day of the final judgment came in early February. The family assembled on Isola di San Pietro for what they hoped would be the last time. The skies above the patriarchal court threatened snow as they crossed the bridge onto the island. The vivid green lawns surrounding the cathedral were covered with snowdrops. Anastasia stopped to pick some of the tiny white flowers as they walked towards the court. Her posy assembled, she tucked it into the bodice of her dress before covering herself with her warm velvet cloak. With luck the flowers would survive until she returned to the Palazzo, where she would be able to paint them. Whatever happened, she told herself, she would never return to Anzolo.

Inside the cathedral, it was as cold as ever. The patriarch and the vicar arrived amid great pomp and asked the assembled company to stand for their decision.

Anastasia's heart raced as she felt herself disassociating from her body. It was almost as if she were floating above herself, looking down on the group standing in the court. Her mother Polonia, her pale face pinched with the cold and anxiety. Marietta, her natural effervescence kept in check as she stood holding her mother's hand. Marco, tall, handsome, stoic. Vicenzo, his gentle face a picture of optimism. He was even smiling. And there was Anastasia herself– a tall lonely girl with a sad pale face, framed by long dark hair. The posy of snowdrops she had picked earlier that day stood out against the dark green of her dress. The sensation of floating faded, as the patriarch began to speak.

'This has been a difficult case, with differing opinions on both sides. The litigant believes her marriage to be unlawful due to coercion on the part of her father and husband. The defendant rejects this and seeks to prove that she was a willing participant and presented witnesses to support his claim…'

Marietta's grip on her mother's hand tightened.

'But I find that the evidence presented by the defendant was acquired through bribery or undue influence. Both witnesses had much to gain from supporting the defendant. My judgment is that there has been coercion in this marriage. The litigant, Anastasia Balzarelli, was not a willing participant and on those grounds I annul the marriage.'

Anastasia sank down onto the wooden pew and held her head in her hands.

'In addition,' continued the patriarch, 'I find that the treatment of this young woman was sufficient to suggest a risk to life and limb. This is a very serious matter, and in consequence, I deem any dowry or marriage contract between her now deceased father and Signor di Zorzi to be null and void. He therefore has no rights over any property belonging to the Balzarelli family.'

Anzolo stood up and began to protest, but the patriarch stopped him.

'You will sit down, *signore*. This is my final decision, and you are lucky that I do not seek to prosecute you for the harm that you did to your wife while you had her incarcerated in your house.'

The patriarch and the vicar were the first to leave the court, followed by Anastasia's family, who filed out of the pews and up the aisle of the church. Her mother chatted animatedly to Vicenzo, while Marietta threw her arms round Marco.

'Oh Marco! It's over,' she said, 'now everything can go back to how it was before.'

Anastasia caught Marco's eye as he hugged her younger sister. They smiled at one another – it was a smile of recognition, of understanding. Both knew that life could never go back to the way it was: there had been a shift, a perceptible change. Her experiences, their experiences, had altered them for ever.

Veronica took Anastasia's arm and whispered, 'I knew it would be all right.'

Anastasia simply said, 'Thank you.'

As she got to the door of the great cathedral, snow began to fall. The green lawns had turned a glistening white as Anastasia turned to look back at Anzolo. She expected to see him remonstrating with his legal team, arguing or shouting. But instead he sat with his head in his hands and sobbed – loud, desperate cries of pain, as if he had lost his most precious possession.

Part Two

Metamorphosis

'In that part of the book of my memory there is a
heading which says

"Here begins a new life"'

Dante Alighieri

Chapter Nineteen

Villa di Bozzolo
April 1705

In the months following her divorce, Anastasia often rose before dawn, let herself out of the villa and took Minou for an early-morning ride, trotting down to the river that snaked its way through the valley to watch the sun rise over the vineyards. There, as she surveyed the landscape, feeling the sun on her face as she stroked Minou's mane, feeling him warm and damp beneath her gloved hand, she would tell herself that she was fortunate to live in this beautiful place, to be alive, to be free. But in spite of the beauty she could see all around her – the mist rising on the river, the dark grapes glistening in the morning dew, the shadows rippling through the woods – there were days when she felt her good fortune was being squeezed out by an all-pervasive blackness.

She managed the farms for her mother, she visited Marco and Vicenzo, she socialised with their few friends, but it was clear to everyone that she was diminished, unable to truly relish her new-found freedom.

'In my opinion, she needs to get far away from here,' Vicenzo said one day to Polonia. 'I see in her a woman in pain. I know she has told Marco that she cannot forget what she went through in Venice, she can only be truly happy when she paints. She is a talented artist, but she needs inspiration. She would benefit from the opportunity to learn more about art. She has a special gift that has never been nurtured, and I believe that if she is given a chance to study it may help her to overcome her troubled past.'

'Where do you suggest she goes?' asked Polonia.

'I have business in Amsterdam. I could take her there.'

'Amsterdam! Why so far?'

'There is someone I would like her to meet – an artist – who I believe would inspire her.'

'But what of Marco? Could he bear to lose her once again? What will become of them both?'

'I fear, Polonia, these are questions we cannot answer at present. I believe Marco and Ana do love one another. But after everything Anastasia has endured, she needs to make a fresh start. Marco understands that.'

'So, Marco will not accompany you?'

'No… I think it best if she goes without him. Besides, Marco needs to remain at Villa Limonaia to manage the estate. But when Ana and I return, I'm sure you will find that she is much improved and, hopefully, they can be properly reunited.'

And so the trip was agreed. Anastasia would require a maid and companion, and chose Veronica to accompany her. Vicenzo's loyal valet Andrea made up the party. Anastasia and Vicenzo pored over maps of Europe, at the villa on Lake Garda, laid out on the floor of his study.

'We will go west across the mountains.'

'Can one cross the mountains?' asked Anastasia, wide-eyed.

'Indeed so. In the winter it is virtually impassable, but now that the spring has come we will be able to make the journey. But it will be hard. The coach will have to be dismantled and taken over the pass on mules. We will continue our journey on a sedan chair carried by porters. If there is still snow on the route we will have to transfer to a sled on the way down. It's an exhilarating experience.'

'It sounds terrifying! And once we are down from the top of the mountain?'

'They will rebuild the carriage and we will continue our journey, travelling up the Rhône Valley to Lyon. It is a beautiful city, Anastasia, at the confluence of two great rivers flowing through France – the Saône and the Rhône. It is an artistic centre; a meeting point for painters from both the Netherlands and Italy. You will like it there. They also make wonderful silk. The silk makers of France are very talented. There will be much to divert us.'

'And after that?' asked Anastasia excitedly.

'North – through the towns of Mâcon, Dijon, Langres.' Vicenzo traced his finger along their route on the large map. 'We might make a diversion and go to Reims – to see the cathedral. It is a wonderful creation. Then, on to Brussels and finally… Amsterdam. I have some business there and we can stay for a few weeks, perhaps longer. I have a friend – an acquaintance really – whom I met on my last visit there. She is a talented botanical artist and I believe you could learn a great deal from her. You must take some of your paintings to show her. I believe she takes students to study with her. Her own daughters work with her, and are about your age, maybe a little older. I think you would find it most interesting to meet her.'

'What is her name?' asked Anastasia.

'Her name? Maria Sibylla Merian. She… is also divorced.'

'Really?' asked Anastasia. 'It is possible in the Netherlands too?'

'Yes. Although she and her husband married and divorced when she was still living in Germany. Her husband was an artist too, but they were not happy together. She lives and works now in Amsterdam and returned recently from a lengthy expedition to Suriname.'

'Suriname? Where is that?'

'It is in South America. She went on an expedition to study animals and plants in the area. In her last letter to me she mentioned that she will soon publish a new book about it. She is a most interesting person.'

'She travelled there alone?' asked Anastasia.

'No, with one of her daughters, Dorothea. But it was remarkable – two ladies, unaccompanied. She is indomitable, fearless, with great inner spirit. They only returned because poor Maria Sibylla developed malaria; she is still not in the best of health, but continues to work hard. I have a collection of her drawings here somewhere.'

Vicenzo rummaged through his extensive bookshelves before pulling out a large book, which he opened carefully on the library table.

'Here it is! *Neues Blumenbuch* – "The New Book of Flowers". Take a look at the paintings, Anastasia; they are extraordinarily accurate. Every leaf, every petal, is so detailed and yet is painted with such verve, such vitality. She published it in 1675 when she was twenty-eight years old.'

'Just ten years older than me,' said Anastasia, carefully turning the pages of the book.

'I believe the pictures are often used as patterns for embroidery,' said Vicenzo.

'The flowers are so lifelike. I feel I could touch them, smell them.'

'Yes – she is hugely gifted. Her latest works are more to do with the insects she discovered on her travels – in particular moths and butterflies. She is fascinated by the process of metamorphosis.'

'As am I!' declared Anastasia. 'When I was...' She faltered, feeling the now familiar sense of panic rising in her chest as she recalled her incarceration in Venice.

'Go on, my dear. Breathe deeply and carry on. Tell me.'

'When I was in... that room... I painted. It was my only comfort. I had to do it in secret, you understand. But Veronica smuggled paper and paints into my room, hidden under my breakfast tray, or bundled up with my linen. One day she brought me some little eggs on the back of a mulberry leaf. I recognised them instantly as silkworm eggs. I painted them and watched them develop and metamorphose into moths. It kept me sane. At night I would hide them behind a panel beneath the window.'

Vicenzo reached out and held Anastasia's hand.

'My dear, you have endured such a great deal. I feel sure that you and Maria Sibylla are destined to be friends.'

As the day of their departure drew nearer, Anastasia and Veronica spent a great deal of time together. Veronica had moved many of Anastasia's possessions up to one of the rooms in the attic. Here she could lay clothes out on the bed and help Anastasia decide what she wanted to take on the journey. Eventually Ana's clothes, painting equipment, books and notebooks would be carefully stowed in leather trunks that were arranged around the edges of the room.

Anastasia had ordered new clothes to be made for Veronica – several new dresses, new underclothes and a warm woollen cloak. The young maid was excited at the prospect of travelling.

'I had never left Venice before I came here to you, and now I am to visit France and even the Netherlands. I am the luckiest girl,' said Veronica as she folded Anastasia's nightclothes and laid them carefully in the trunk.

'And I am lucky to have you with me, Veronica. You became like a sister to me when we were in the mill owner's house. I will never be able to thank you enough for all that you did for me.'

Outside on the landing Marietta stood listening at the door. Ever since Anastasia's return to the villa and Veronica's arrival, she had been aware of a growing distance between herself and her sister. She had always considered herself to be Anastasia's only, and best, companion. She had been loyal and cared for her all her life. They had been interdependent. All the years they had spent surviving their father's tyranny had drawn them together. Now she felt dejected and abandoned: her sister was leaving her and taking Veronica with her, while she was to be left behind.

*

Towards the end of April, as narcissi bloomed in the large urns that lined the terrace at Villa di Bozzolo, the day of Anastasia's departure finally arrived.

'Goodbye, Mamma,' Anastasia said, holding her mother tightly to her. 'I will miss you so much.'

'Goodbye, my darling Anastasia. I will miss you too. But I feel sure that this journey is just what you need. And you will be in the very best hands with Veronica looking after you. And I know Vicenzo will take good care of you both.'

'He has become such a good friend, Mamma. I've always liked him, but over the last few months we have become so close. He is almost like a…' She faltered momentarily.

'Like a father?' asked her mother.

'Yes, in a way. The father I never had, wished I had…'

Marietta looked on resentfully.

'Marietta,' said Anastasia, hugging her. 'Don't be sad, I will miss you too.'

'Take me with you then?' her sister entreated, her eyes lighting up enthusiastically.

'Take you with me? But this has not been discussed.' Anastasia was confused, and looked to her mother for an explanation.

'Now, Marietta,' said Polonia, 'we had agreed.'

'Agreed what?' Anastasia looked from one to the other, bewildered.

'That this was *your* opportunity, Anastasia. Marietta asked if she could come with you a few weeks ago, but I discouraged it.'

'Why?' asked Ana.

'Would you have liked her to come?' said Polonia.

'I don't know…'

'Exactly. I felt, after all that you have endured, it was better for you to be alone – with Vicenzo, of course. Besides, I would be so lonely with both of you gone.'

'I just feel,' said Marietta, twisting a silk handkerchief in her hands, her brown eyes filling with tears of self-pity, 'that I am always left out.'

'Oh Marietta!' exclaimed their mother. 'We have discussed this. Your time will come, I assure you. But you must let your sister have this opportunity now.'

'Marietta,' said Anastasia, looking deeply into her sister's eyes. 'Look after Mamma and I promise that if it's possible, I will send for you. But Mamma is right. I need just to get away – from everything.'

'Even from Marco?' asked Marietta. 'The man who loves you so much. You'd leave him behind too?'

'Marco understands better than you think. If we are meant to be together then we will be. But now, I need to go on this journey, alone.'

Anastasia kissed her sister on both cheeks. Marietta stood stiffly, refusing to return her embrace. Ana bent down to kiss her little dog, Bianca, on the head, and stroked her soft fur.

'Bianca, look after my sister.'

She looked up at Marietta as the dog licked her hand contentedly.

'You will take care of her, won't you?'

'Yes, yes, of course,' said Marietta bitterly. 'As usual, I will take care of her and Mamma.'

'Mamma, just one further thing before I go…' Anastasia went over to Giuseppe, the footman, and whispered in his ear.

'I have asked Giuseppe to bring something down here that I have been working on over the past few weeks…'

The footman returned to the hall carrying a canvas, which he leaned up against the back of the damask sofa. It was a painting of a young dark-haired woman seated at an easel, wearing a pale lemon dress, her hair falling onto her creamy shoulders. In her hand she held a paintbrush and was turning towards the viewer as if she had just been interrupted in her work. The painting on her easel was of a cream silkmoth, next to which had been placed a little basket of newly laid silkmoth eggs. The room in which the painting was set was dark and panelled, the only illumination coming from a latticed window through which could be seen the Grand Canal in Venice. A second silkmoth flew through a small casement window.

'Oh!' said Polonia. 'It is a painting of you, dear Ana. It's wonderful. Who painted it?'

'I did! It's a self-portrait. I started it after the divorce and have been painting it ever since. I hope you like it. I thought it would be a comfort to you, Mamma, while I am gone.'

'Oh my dear…' Polonia kissed Anastasia. 'It is – it will be. That room, is that where you…?'

'Where I was kept? Yes. Painting it has made it somehow… less important, less real. Now, it's just the background for a painting. That was the dress Marco's cousin lent me before the wedding that never took place. It seemed appropriate to be wearing it in the picture. And it's almost the colour of a silkmoth, pale and creamy. The moth flying through the window is me, escaping at last. Of course, I know silkmoths can't fly – they are trapped for ever, weighed down by their duty to reproduce. But I like to think that this moth laid her eggs and then flew away. It's a metaphor for what happened to me, I suppose. I've called the painting *Metamorphosis*. And this journey to Amsterdam with Vicenzo… Mamma, Marietta, this will be *my* metamorphosis. When I return, I will no longer be the frightened girl in a lemon-yellow dress who was kidnapped and married against her will, imprisoned in that room. I will be Anastasia Balzarelli – strong, brave and capable, a free woman, flying through the window. And with luck, a better artist too.'

Anastasia hugged her mother and sister one last time as her luggage was loaded into the family carriage. She and Veronica were to leave that afternoon and travel first to Villa Limonaia, where they would stay for one night, before leaving finally for Amsterdam the following morning. As the carriage circled the well in the centre of the courtyard at Villa di Bozzolo that afternoon, Anastasia looked out through the rear window and waved at her mother and sister, who stood on the steps to the villa. Her mother waved cheerfully, while Marietta stood sullenly by her side. Anastasia thought back to the last time she had seen them through the carriage window – on the day her father kidnapped her and took her to Venice. So much had changed since then.

As the coach rumbled through the Veneto countryside on its way to Villa Limonaia, Anastasia thought about Marietta's reaction to her departure. Her sister's anger at what she perceived to be Anastasia's good fortune she found most hurtful. Marietta had seemed so supportive of her throughout the divorce; had been so anxious for them all to return to Villa di Bozzolo and live a happy life together. It seemed churlish for her to be so envious of this opportunity that Vicenzo Morozoni had given Anastasia.

Veronica observed her mistress as she looked anxiously out of the carriage window.

'You look troubled, Mistress.'

'Me? Oh no! I was just thinking about Marietta. She's just being so childish. She's young, I suppose; she doesn't understand.'

Veronica smiled encouragingly. She had a fleeting sense of guilt that she perhaps had caused the rift between these sisters. After all she was accompanying Anastasia on a trip Marietta would have enjoyed.

'Oh, there is nothing to be done,' Anastasia said eventually, 'and besides, I have other things to worry about.'

'Mistress?'

'Marco… May I talk to you about him?'

'Of course.'

'I feel so confused. I loved him so much before… Anzolo. When we were planning our own marriage, I was so happy. I adored him. He was everything I could have wanted in a husband.

And I still believe that. And yet, I find it so hard to show him my feelings. It's as if I am trapped by what has happened to me, unable to explain.'

'I'm sure he understands. He seems such a kind gentleman.'

'He is; he's like his father. They are peas in a pod. When I'm with Vicenzo, I can see the man Marco will become – thoughtful, intelligent, sensitive. But I know Marco struggles to understand why I have not already rushed to marry him.'

'Perhaps you will, one day.'

'I would like to think so. If he can wait for me…'

They arrived at Villa Limonaia in time for dinner. As they sat in the dining room overlooking the lake, Marco was polite and kind, but conversation was stilted, as if there was something he felt unable to say.

'I shall miss you so much,' he finally admitted, once his father had left the room to finish supervising his packing upstairs.

'I know, and I shall miss you too,' said Anastasia earnestly. 'I do still love you, Marco – do you believe me?'

She walked round the table and knelt beside him. She held his hands in her own and kissed his fingers, one by one. She looked up into his dark brown eyes. Her fingers traced his mouth.

'Then why are you leaving me?' He stood up and pulled her up next to him. He wrapped his arms around her waist. She felt a sensation of longing – something that she thought had disappeared for ever.

'It's something I need to do… for myself. Your father understands.'

'My father is taking you away from me.'

'No, Marco! He is trying to put me back together. For the first time since the awful day I was married to Anzolo, I am excited about something – looking forward and not back. With luck, it is a sensation that will remain with me when I return. I really believe we can continue with our lives, just give me a little time.'

Later that night as Marco sat in his father's bedchamber, surrounded by leather trunks, he voiced his concerns.

'I fear she will forget me. Please don't keep her away too long?'

'My dear boy, the time will pass swiftly. She will not forget you, she loves you – and when we return, I hope that you and Anastasia will once again be able to return to the relationship you had before, and marry. That is my dearest wish.'

The following morning, as Marco kissed Anastasia's hand, he said simply, 'Goodbye, darling Anastasia. I wish you happiness and joy. And I hope your journey brings peace to your heart.'

'Goodbye, my dearest Marco,' Anastasia said, holding him to her. 'You have been so understanding of all that I have endured. I know that this will be hard for us both, but I honestly believe we will be stronger at the end of our separation. And hopefully when I return we will be able to find in one another all that we thought we had lost.'

As she climbed into the carriage Vicenzo took her hand and squeezed it tightly. She waved at Marco as the coach trundled up the steep driveway, through the wooded gardens. He stood on the driveway in the early-morning sunshine, the lake glistening behind him, until the carriage was completely out of sight.

From Lake Garda, Vicenzo and Anastasia travelled west to the Italian lakes of Como and Maggiore. Every village they passed reminded Anastasia of that fateful journey with Marco when they had set off, filled with excitement, at the prospect of their marriage. Vicenzo had arranged for them to stay with Tobias and his wife Caterina on Lake Como. He was keen to see his nephew but was concerned that Anastasia might find the memories it brought back too painful.

'If you feel unable to return there, after all that happened, we could stay in a small inn I know nearby. I realise their house might bring back terrible memories for you—'

'No,' she said bravely. 'That would be unfair; you wish to see Tobias and I should also like to see them again. No, it will be good for me – to begin to put the memories behind me.'

The coach turned off the main road, onto the drive leading to the Renaissance villa. The formal flowerbeds that led down to the shores of the lake were filled with daffodils and tulips. Her memory of the house had been so clouded by the awful arrival of her father, of her fear at being taken away against her will, that she had recollected it as a dark place. But now as they approached the villa, the sun bathing the pale apricot walls with warmth and light, she saw how beautiful it was.

Caterina, holding a baby in her arms, stood with Tobias at the door to greet them.

'My dear Anastasia,' said Caterina as she kissed her, 'I cannot tell you how happy we are to see you again – and looking so well. We are delighted that you felt able to return here to us.'

As they entered the grand hall, the scene of Ana's violent kidnapping just a year before, the couple's young son Giacomo galloped happily astride his hobby horse, banishing Anastasia's memories.

Anastasia's room at the villa overlooked the gardens at the rear of the house; it was thoughtful of Caterina, Ana thought, not to give her the same room as before. After dinner, as the men sat at the table nursing cigars and little glasses of amber-coloured amaretto, Anastasia took the opportunity to sit with Caterina in the drawing room overlooking Lake Como.

'My dear, I cannot imagine what you have been through. We were so very sorry,' said Caterina.

'I know,' said Anastasia. 'It has been a terrible experience. But I am free now. I have you partly to thank.'

'Me?' said Caterina. 'Why?'

'When I was imprisoned by that awful man, I realised that I might only escape if he believed I was pregnant with his child. I recalled a conversation you and I had the night before…'

'The night before you and Marco were supposed to marry?'

'Yes,' said Anastasia, wiping a tear with the back of her hand. 'You told me that you felt nauseous because you were expecting another child – your beautiful new baby Alessandra. I remembered that, and I was able to convince him that *I* was pregnant. I made myself sick every morning.'

'That was very ingenious, Anastasia. I cannot imagine how frightening it was for you. And what of Marco – do you still intend to marry?'

'I don't know. He is willing. He still loves me, and I do still love him. But something is wrong – I am frightened of letting him get close to me. Of letting anyone get close to me. I can hear what people say and see everything around me, but every colour is muted. Every sound is muffled; it's as if I am trapped inside a cocoon – another prison of sorts. Vicenzo thought I needed to get away and offered to take me with him on his travels. It seemed a solution of sorts.'

'You are running away?'

'No, not running away, exactly. But having some time to reflect. To get a sense of myself. To rid myself of the demons that fill my thoughts…'

Caterina reached out and held Anastasia's hand.

'Oh Anastasia, I'm so sorry.'

The following morning, as Veronica and Andrea loaded luggage into the carriage, Anastasia and Vicenzo took their leave of Tobias and Caterina.

'Thank you for your hospitality. Perhaps we can return on our way back from Amsterdam?'

'You will be welcome, Anastasia – at any time.' Tobias put his arm around his wife's shoulders as they waved them goodbye.

Leaving Lake Como, they travelled through Turin, arriving towards the end of the day at the village of Susa. It nestled at the foothills of the precarious pass of Moncenisio, which had recently been opened after the long harsh winter. The summits of the snow-capped mountains glistened in the late spring sunshine and pockets of snow and ice clung to the shady crevices as the coach approached the pass. Moncenisio was the most direct and, arguably, the most scenic route between northern Italy and France. There was an alternative – to travel by sea from Genoa to Marseille – but it was hazardous; Barbary pirates operated along that stretch of the Ligurian coast. The mountain pass was considered an uncomfortable but safer option.

Vicenzo and his coachman negotiated with the porters known locally as *marrons*. His coach could not be driven over the mountain, and so had to be dismantled and carried in pieces over the pass by mule. He and Anastasia were to be carried individually in an 'Alps machine' – effectively a flimsy sedan chair attached to ropes and poles carried by two *marrons*. Veronica and Andrea would accompany the luggage on mules.

On their first night in the foothills of the Alps, they stayed at a small inn. Over a simple supper, Vicenzo explained the likely rigours of their journey.

'We must wait here until the *marrons* deem that it is safe to cross the mountains. They will watch the weather closely and only when any fear of storms, or snow, or low cloud is past, will they attempt the journey. Hopefully we will not have to wait too long, given the quality of food at this inn.'

'And we must leave the coach behind, you say?' asked Anastasia.

'No, the horses must remain here but the coach comes with us – it will be dismantled and strapped to some sturdy mules, which will take it over the pass. You and I will travel in the Alps machine. It is not comfortable, my dear Anastasia, but the *marrons* are experts and will not let us fall. In fact, they are so used to it that they run most of the way. The route will be rocky and difficult at times and occasionally you may be forced to walk. If it is very snowy when we near the summit we may have to transfer to a sled for the downward journey.'

'A sled? I haven't been on one of those since I was a child,' said Anastasia. 'But then it was just on little hills near the villa. Can we really sled all the way down a steep mountain?'

'I agree, it sounds risky – and it is – but the *marrons* will be with you, one in front and one behind, and are experts at steering; they will keep us on the path.'

The following morning Anastasia woke early. As she looked out of her window she could see the summit of Moncenisio, shimmering in the pink dawn light. There was not a cloud in sight. Moments later, Vicenzo knocked on her door.

'Anastasia – the *marrons* say we should prepare to leave shortly. The weather is with us. Get ready, my dear – wear your warmest travel clothes and bring a cloak and muff for the high pass – it will be cold up there. Breakfast is ready downstairs.'

Anastasia greedily ate the bread and hot chocolate that had been laid out in the small dining room, aware that it would be their only meal that day. She felt excited and nervous about the journey. By that evening, if all went well, they would be in France.

The sedan chair swayed and rocked as the porters nimbly negotiated the rocky paths and tracks that zigzagged their way up the mountain. Veronica, on her mule, clung bravely to the reins, but she had never ridden before and was clearly struggling just to stay in the saddle.

'Veronica,' Anastasia called down to her, 'let me take the mule – I am an experienced rider. Take my place in the Alps machine.'

But Veronica demurred.

'I cannot, Mistress. It would not be right.'

As they approached the summit, the rocky paths disappeared under a layer of snow. The sure-footed *marrons* and the mules took it in their stride. As they weaved their way around the mountain, they came to a shaded crevasse, where the winter snow and ice had no chance to thaw; the mules disappeared up to their girths in deep snow. The *marrons* called a halt and shovelled a way through, creating a clear path. They sang as they worked – joyful Alpine songs that amused their party greatly. Anastasia was grateful for her thick cloak and fur muff and, in an effort to remain warm, paced up and down on the cleared track with Veronica as the men dug energetically. They were soon on their way and when they finally arrived near the summit, Vicenzo suggested they pause for a moment to look at the view. The party clustered together, gazing back at the Piedmont plain beneath them.

'It looks so beautiful and green!' marvelled Anastasia.

'The Po Valley stretching away as far as the eye can see,' said Vicenzo, 'all the way to the sea.'

'Farewell beloved Italia,' said Anastasia.

The *marrons* were determined that the group should keep moving. The sun was high in the sky, but it would be dark by the early evening and they had only a few hours of daylight in which to make their descent.

On two occasions, when the snow was too deep, they had to transfer to sleds. As they sped down the mountain, Anastasia felt the cold air rushing against her face, felt a thrill as her body hurtled down the slopes – the *marrons* in front and behind, steering the sled with skill and expertise. When they reached the snowline, the party transferred again to mules and the sedans.

'Veronica, I insist that I take the mule for this part of the journey. I've ridden mules before on the farm,' Anastasia said firmly.

Anastasia's mule was a stubborn beast; he knew the route he was to take and she was amused by his determination to follow some predetermined path at a steady pace that she was unable to affect. As they descended, the temperature rose and the vegetation became increasingly verdant. Before long they had left the grey rocks behind and found themselves in the foothills, trotting through lush meadows filled with wild flowers. As the sun began to slip behind the summit, the party finally arrived at the base of the pass. They were taken to a small inn in the village of Lanebourg, where they were to spend the night while their carriage was rebuilt, and in the morning they set off on the next stage of their journey – to Lyon.

Chapter Twenty

Villa di Bozzolo
May 2017

Millie reached across the bed, her hand sweeping the soft white sheet. She was alone. Lorenzo must have left early and gone back to the barn. Sharp shafts of light forced their way round the frames of the window shutters. She peered at her watch on the bedside table – half past seven. He would be getting Bella ready for school.

She opened the shutters, and light flooded the bedroom. The sky was a cloudless, brilliant blue. She climbed back into bed and reflected on the evening she had spent with Lorenzo. The gondola, the kissing, the sun slipping behind the arcade on Piazza San Marco casting an apricot glow on the cathedral; it had been so romantic. As they walked hand in hand through the busy lanes, Lorenzo had suggested they stop for supper at a restaurant he knew.

'But shouldn't we be getting back to Villa di Bozzolo?' asked Millie.

'Let's eat first. Or we could stay somewhere here overnight and go back in the morning?'

'Stay here? Really? But we haven't booked anywhere… and besides, what about Bella?'

'Why are you being so sensible?' he asked, gazing at her across the table. 'She's *my* daughter; let me worry about her. Besides, Elena will look after her.'

'But you'd have to call her and explain. She won't like it.'

'Millie, you're unbelievable! OK. We'll eat and go home – but it's a bit of a wasted opportunity, I think.'

'I don't need a glass of wine,' said Millie as they ordered dinner. 'If you're driving you can't drink, so I won't have any either.'

'That's very thoughtful, but I insist you have a little. I'll order.'

After dinner they walked to the Rialto Bridge, where they boarded the *vaporetto* for the station. In the car park, as he opened the car door, Lorenzo kissed her.

They held hands on the drive back to Villa di Bozzolo. When Lorenzo needed to change gear he let her hand slip away, but their fingers soon intertwined again. Gradually the monotony of the motorway lights lulled Millie to sleep. She woke up as they drove under the tall stone archway into the yard of Villa di Bozzolo.

'Here we are – home,' said Lorenzo, waking her with a kiss.

'Oh, well done. We made it. I'm sorry I fell asleep. You must be tired,' said Millie.

'Not *that* tired,' said Lorenzo, kissing her again, passionately.

She laughed, nervously, her heart pounding. Only that morning she had been determined to go back to Max. And now, here she was, kissing Marco. She was torn, she realised, between the two.

'So…' He gazed lovingly into her eyes, 'may I… come up with you?'

'I suppose so,' she said blushing, then, 'Yes, that would be lovely.' She kissed his cheek.

He kissed her mouth, her eyes, her forehead…

'You don't sound very sure?' he murmured into her ear.

'I am…' she said hesitantly

'I ought to check on Bella first. I'll come up in a moment – OK?'

As Millie brushed her teeth, waiting for Lorenzo to arrive, she looked at herself in the bathroom mirror.

'What are you doing?' she said out loud.

Could she really spend the night with Lorenzo? She gripped the edges of the washbasin and looked at herself. She was taking a risk – she knew that. And yet… it had been a wonderful day. He was handsome, sexy – It felt right somehow. There was a knock on the door…

The sex was tender, sensitive, loving. Her first time with Max had been so passionate they could hardly wait to get onto the bed. But with Lorenzo it was totally relaxed – almost as if they had been lovers for ever. Afterwards, they fell asleep in one another's arms. He smelt of something comforting. Warm croissants… was her last conscious thought before she drifted into a deep sleep.

As she reached for her phone, she was surprised to see it was already eight o'clock. Propping herself up in bed against the pillows, she heard Lorenzo's voice through the open window. He must be outside in the yard. She pulled on a T-shirt and walked over to the open window.

He looked up, as if sensing her presence.

'Good morning,' he called up to her. 'You are looking wonderful.'

'Good morning,' she said, shading her eyes slightly against the glare of the day, 'so are you.'

'I'm just taking Bella to school – I'll pop up when I'm back. OK?'

'Sure. Bye, Bella.'

'Bye,' called the little girl. 'Will you come and see me later?'

'Yes… yes, of course. I'd love to.'

She ran a bath, and filled it with sweet-smelling oil. Lying in the warm water, she had an uneasy sensation, something she had not felt before. It was guilt. She felt guilty, she realised, about the night she had just spent with Lorenzo. She had – in effect – been unfaithful to Max. It surprised her. She had felt so ambivalent about him since he'd broken up with her. Her emotions had ranged from anger to sadness, to a sense that perhaps it was all for the best that it was over. But his phone call the previous day, telling her that his marriage was over, had changed something fundamental. Instead of feeling relaxed and happy that she had begun a new relationship, she was more confused than ever. She got out of the bath and, wrapped in a large bath towel, moisturised her legs and brushed her hair. She cleansed her face – something that had been overlooked the previous night – and put on a simple sundress. She sat down at her desk and opened the lid of her laptop to check her emails. But she was unable to concentrate. All she could think of was Lorenzo and the fact that he would be coming back soon. Would they make love again? *Should* they? Perhaps she ought to talk to him honestly about it; he would understand. She was startled by a knock on her bedroom door.

'That was quick,' she called out as she crossed over to the door. 'Come in,' she said seductively, opening it.

There stood Max. He was carrying an overnight bag; he looked tired, a little older, his grey hair swept back off his high forehead.

'I certainly will come in, you gorgeous creature,' he said, dropping his bag on the floor and pulling her towards him. He kissed her fiercely on the mouth.

'What are you doing here?' she said when he finally released her.

'Surprising you, my darling – and who was being "quick"?'

'What do you mean?'

'You said, through the door, "That was quick".'

'Oh, it was the maid. I asked for a… another pillow.'

'Oh… well, here I am!' he said, throwing himself down on to the unmade bed. 'God, it's hot, isn't it?'

'Yes, it is. Max, I'm slightly confused – I mean, it's lovely to see you of course, but why did you come? I thought we'd agreed that I would see you in London, when I've finished this silk industry story.'

'Well, you sounded a bit anxious when I phoned you a couple of days ago, so I decided to come here and keep you company. I knew where you were staying, obviously, as Sonia booked it all. Just got on the first flight I could. You look ravishing, by the way – come back to bed.' He held his hand out towards her.

'No… No! Max, I have a meeting shortly. I was about to go and have breakfast. Um… why don't you come too? You must be starving. What time did you leave this morning?'

'God, don't ask! I got a flight from City airport in the middle of the night. You're right – I am starving actually. Come on then.'

Max chose a table by a window in the dining room, and sat down proprietorially. Millie collected a selection of bread and croissants for them to share, keeping an anxious eye on the green baize door to the kitchen. Had Lorenzo told his sister about their 'date'? And if so, how would Millie explain Max's appearance at the hotel that morning?

The baize door swung open and Elena walked into the dining room carrying a large china dish filled with slices of cake. She went from table to table, taking tea and coffee orders. When she arrived at Millie's table, she looked down her aristocratic nose at Max.

'I wasn't expecting another guest. Would either of you like tea or coffee?'

Millie was about to respond, explaining that Max was her boss, when he interjected.

'I'm a surprise visitor,' drawled Max. 'I'm Millie's other half. Could we have a couple of coffees, do you think? I'm gasping.'

Millie looked down at the table, blushing.

'Latte or cappuccino?' replied Elena coolly.

'Two lattes, please,' said Millie sweetly.

'Eggs?' asked Elena, staring pointedly at Millie.

'Not for me. Max – a boiled egg? Elena does them wonderfully.'

'Why not?' said Max, gazing out of the window. 'Never had an Italian boiled egg before.'

As Elena disappeared again through the green door, Millie whispered, 'Please stop being so…'

'What?'

'So bloody rude! Elena is a very upper-crust Italian lady, you shouldn't treat her like a servant.'

'Ooh, sorry!' said Max sarcastically, leaning back in his chair. 'So, what's this meeting you've got, then?'

'It's with Elena's brother; he's runs the silk farm here. We're going to visit a couple of his contacts for the story.'

'I'll tag along,' said Max.

'No, Max, I don't think that's a good idea. Why don't you spend the day here – have a bath, rest, swim in the pool? It's lovely. And tonight we can go out for dinner and have a chat.'

'Why go out? Won't madam here cook us something?'

'No, Max – she only does breakfast. I'll take you to a local restaurant.'

'Let's go to bed first,' said Max lasciviously, as Elena put their coffees on the table. Her black eyes flashed as she looked across at Millie.

'Thank you, Elena,' said Millie, blushing deeply. 'Can I ask, is Lorenzo around?'

'He took Bella to school, but I thought you'd have known that,' Elena said sharply.

'Yes… of course. Thanks.'

Somehow Millie got through breakfast; each time Elena came into the dining room she threw furious looks in her direction. At last, Millie persuaded Max to go back to the room.

'I need to go and make some arrangements with Lorenzo. You settle in upstairs, and I'll be back later.'

She ran across to the barn, desperate to explain the situation before Elena returned from the villa's kitchen.

'Lorenzo, thank goodness, you're here.'

'I am.' He looked away awkwardly, picking up a mug of coffee from the worktop.

'I'm so sorry,' she said, touching his arm. 'I had no idea he was coming. He just turned up – out of the blue.'

'I see. Well, that must be a nice surprise for you.'

'No, it's not nice… not really. In fact, it's a bit of a nightmare. I had no idea he was coming.'

'Maybe it's for the best he turned up when he did – perhaps just in time.' Lorenzo looked at her wistfully. 'I was beginning to fall in love with you.'

Millie sank down on one of the rush-seat chairs at the kitchen table and put her head in her hands.

'I'm so sorry. I had a wonderful time last night and yesterday. It was romantic, you're wonderful, Venice is fantastic. I was… swept away by it all. I have no regrets about what we did – honestly. But… well, you know the history between Max and me. It was wrong of me. It was unfair to you, and unfair to him. But him just turning up like that this morning – I can't pretend it wasn't a shock.'

'I understand,' said Lorenzo, sipping his coffee.

'Do you? You really are the most understanding, kind man I've ever met. Do you want me to go? I could move to another hotel,' Millie continued, pacing the kitchen. 'I'll try to get Max to go back home as soon as possible. Apart from anything else, I'm working and he's just a distraction. I've already told him that you and I have a couple of meetings planned for today… if you can still face it?'

'Of course – you're here to work, we need the publicity. Of course we must continue. I think I can manage to control myself.'

He smiled at her. She felt a twinge of regret. What would their day have been like if Max had never turned up? Would she and Lorenzo have spent it happily together? Would they have slept together again that night? If they had, would she now be even more torn?

'Of course… well, thank you for that. I do so appreciate it. And you know, don't you? That if there was no Max, it would be so different… I would be falling in love with you too.'

Chapter Twenty-One

A manor house outside Lyon
May 1705

André Arnaud was a man of great wealth. At fifty-two, he was one of Vicenzo's oldest friends. They had studied together many years earlier in Florence and had remained close ever since. He was a silk merchant and took great pride in supplying the court of Louis XIV. His impressive manor house, surrounded by landscaped gardens, stood in the countryside just outside Lyon. Built thirty years earlier of local limestone by his father, the house was André's pride and joy. The grounds had been laid out with neat box parterres filled with sweet-smelling lavender. The interior of the house was decorated in the latest style. The main rooms downstairs had high ceilings with intricately designed parquet floors. The walls were panelled; gilded mirrors hung above mantelpieces. The bedchambers featured newly installed bed 'niches' that created recessed beds enclosed on three sides between carved and gilded panels.

The main salon was lined with sky-blue silk and covered from floor to ceiling with paintings. English, French and Italian artists were all represented, but Anastasia was intrigued to see that André Arnaud also had a passion for paintings by Dutch and Flemish artists: Rembrandt, Aert van der Neer and Hans Bollongier took pride of place.

After lunch he offered to take Anastasia and Vicenzo on a tour of the house.

'André – it seems you love the work of Dutch artists,' Anastasia noted as she surveyed the densely covered walls.

'I do, my dear.'

'André has a good eye for beauty *and* a good investment,' interjected Vicenzo. 'He appreciates the clarity of the Dutch artist's vision.'

'You are right, Vicenzo. In many ways the Dutch have dominated the art world for the last hundred years or so. But I do so appreciate the workmanship. Anastasia, look at these tulips painted by Bollongier. They are exquisite, no?'

'They are…' Anastasia studied the painting. 'There is a little snail crawling across the table. It's perfect in every detail, isn't it? As if he has just captured it in a moment. I wish I could paint like that.'

'You paint very well indeed, Ana,' encouraged Vicenzo. 'Practice is all that's required. Now,' he went on, pausing before a painting of a young dark-haired woman. 'Here is a painting you should take a look at.'

It was of a woman in an emerald-green silk dress, holding a brush in her right hand and an artist's palette in the other. Her head was cocked to one side, as if musing on where next to place her brush.

'Who is she?' asked Anastasia.

'The artist Artemisia Gentileschi.'

'It is a self-portrait?'

'Yes. She was Italian, and very successful. She painted in the court of the English king, Charles I, and was the first woman to ever be admitted to the Accademia delle Arti del Disegno in Florence.'

'I had no idea a woman would be given such an honour. I am ashamed to admit that I have never heard of her,' said Anastasia.

'She died fifty years ago, and was never properly recognised for her genius during her life. But I am so glad that you could see this painting today. I hope it will bring you a little inspiration.'

André Arnaud was a man of considerable sensitivity and wisdom. His family had acquired their fortune through the silk industry. He owned several silk mills in Lyon and took great pride in his royal customers but he was also interested in politics and philosophy. He read widely – particularly the new wave of philosophy that sought to challenge the absolute authority of both the monarchy and the Catholic Church. He was a free-thinking man, in many ways like his old friend Vicenzo, and Anastasia enjoyed their long conversations after dinner about art, religion and politics.

'I know your family are involved in the silk industry, Anastasia. Here in Lyon – as you probably know – we have a thriving silk industry. But it has been damaged by the loss of many of our Huguenot silk weavers.'

'What happened to them?' asked Anastasia.

'They have been persecuted and many driven out of France, or worse. There has long been conflict between the King and the Protestants, but twenty years ago he went further: he revoked the Edict of Nantes – a law that gave rights to Protestants in France to worship freely. Since that time terrible things have happened. I am no Protestant, you understand. Our family has always been Catholic, but I do not agree with the persecution of such people. They have suffered terribly. They have been tortured, sent to the gallows, their women put into nunneries, their children murdered, their churches burned to the ground – sometimes with the congregation still inside. Many have fled already for the Netherlands, Switzerland and England. We have lost literally hundreds of thousands of good, hard-working people from our country.'

'That's awful,' said Anastasia.

'It is a disgrace. But if you persecute people for their religion, you just drive it underground. Even now there is a rebellion going on, in the mountains of the Cevennes south-west of here; thousands of Huguenots, living in the mountains and fighting for their faith against the King's dragoons. There are bloody battles almost every day. I don't know how it will end.'

'You say there were Huguenots here, in Lyon?' asked Anastasia.

'Yes. There was a big Huguenot settlement. Many worked in the silk industry and were very talented, but when the persecution threatened to engulf them they fled. Some went west, others north, heading for the sea – desperate for their lives. Many were killed, I heard, on the beaches before they could escape; but thousands managed to get away. One of our best weavers – Pierre Leman – got to London. He writes to me now and again. He originally went to Canterbury, but has settled in Spitalfields and is running a successful business there. I am glad he escaped, but it is a tragedy for our industry here. Now his skills, and the skills of many of his faith, are being recognised and made use of in other countries. And we have lost something very important.'

Vicenzo and Anastasia stayed with André for three days before continuing their journey. They travelled through Mâcon, Dijon and the hilltop town of Langres, where Anastasia wandered the cobbled streets and admired the pale-gold stone buildings. From there they journeyed to Brussels and then on, finally, to Amsterdam.

Rain drizzled from a pewter-coloured sky as the coach travelled north across the flat plains that lay to the south of Amsterdam. Anastasia slept fitfully, her head lolling against the collar of her velvet cloak. When she woke, she gazed out of the mud-spattered windows of the coach onto wide open fields filled with flowers, interrupted at intervals by irrigation dykes and lines of poplars arching over in the wind. This monotonous landscape was relieved by simple half-timbered farm buildings, and pockets of dense woodland where pigs grazed the undergrowth. Peasants worked the land, much as they did in Veneto. But here there were no vineyards, no mulberry orchards. As the sun broke through the leaden skies, dappled sunlight filtered through the trees; groups of children played in the streams that ran through the woods.

Vicenzo looked up from his book and smiled at her.

'Ah, you are awake at last.'

'Have I been asleep long?'

'Since we left Leiden. We will soon be in Amsterdam. We should be there before nightfall.'

Anastasia was excited that they would soon arrive at their destination.

'Where will we stay?' she asked.

'I have taken a house on one of the canals. Once we have settled in, we will visit my friend Maria Sibylla.'

'I cannot wait. I have longed to meet her ever since you told me about her.'

'I know. But you must understand that she is not in the best of health. I hope she will be able to show us her new work and perhaps allow you to study with her for a week or two. I will enjoy spending as much as a few weeks here if you wish. So there will be time for you to get to know the city and also Maria.'

As the coach trundled north, Anastasia reflected on their long journey from Lake Garda. They had been travelling for nearly thirteen weeks. In that time, she realised, she had rarely thought of Marco. That surprised her, and yet perhaps it told her something. Was he really the man she was destined to spend her life with? More importantly, she had scarcely thought of Anzolo. When she first returned from Venice she had suffered night terrors. They began as dreams, and somewhere between sleep and wakefulness it would begin – a shortness of breath, a vivid, almost physical sensation of being overwhelmed by her tormentor. Eventually she would drag herself gratefully from sleep and tell herself: 'It's over, it's over.' But since they had crossed the pass of Moncenisio, since she had left Italy in fact, the nightmares had faded.

Her days had been filled with such interest. She had seen so much and learned a great deal, and through it all she had kept a diary, and made pen and ink sketches of everything she had seen on their journey: the glistening summit of Moncenisio; the stubborn mule; the bizarre Alps machine and the nimble *marrons* running so energetically up the mountain paths. She had made sketches at André Arnaud's house too, and of points of interest in Mâcon and Langres. She had drawn the magnificent cathedral of Reims and the Grande Place in Brussels. Had these novel experiences banished Anzolo from her mind? Or was it simply time working its magic?

Now she was about to meet Maria Sibylla Merian. She had resolved to learn all she could from this remarkable woman. She would study her technique, listen to her philosophy, benefit from her wisdom and experience. This, she hoped, would be the beginning of her transformation from young amateur to professional artist. This, then, was the dawn of her metamorphosis.

Chapter Twenty-Two

Amsterdam
August 1705

Maria Sibylla Merian felt stiff, and her hips ached as she negotiated the steep staircase from her bedroom on the second floor of the 'Rose House' on Kerkstraat.

Since her last episode of malaria, an illness she had contracted on her visit to Suriname and which had left her weakened, she allowed her daughter to get up first and open up the shop.

'Dorothea, Dorothea!' she called down to her daughter.

'Yes, Mama.'

'Have you set the engraving plates up for me?'

'In a moment, Mama.'

'Well, we have a lot to do, if we are to finish the engravings for the book. I am anxious to get on with them today.'

Her next publication – *Metamorphosis Insectorum Surinamensium* – would feature the insects and animals of the tropical rainforests of Suriname. There would be sixty coloured plates in all and she still had half a dozen left to complete.

A bell jangled, indicating the arrival of someone in the shop. Maria Sibylla paused on the landing. She would let her daughter deal with the customer, while she rested for a moment in the sitting room on the first floor. If she went downstairs she would only get drawn into conversation with someone keen to buy one of the myriad of insect and animal specimens they had collected on their travels.

*

The shop was filled with glass display cases containing geckos, turtles and snakes; butterflies and moths covered the walls, and glass-domed jars covered every surface, protecting naturalistic arrangements of butterflies and moths carefully positioned, as if *in situ*, on pieces of twigs and bark. There was the brilliant aqua blue of the *Achilles Morpho* butterfly, the pale and intricately decorated White Witch moth; the extraordinary Vine Sphinx moth with its flashes of turquoise across delicate pale grey wings. These exotic collections appealed to the growing middle class of Amsterdam who, through the influence of the Dutch East India Company and its exotic imports, liked to decorate their homes with an eclectic mix of art and nature.

The voice in the shop below sounded familiar: there was an Italian lilt to it. Curious now as to its owner, she was about to investigate when she heard Dorothea calling up to her.

'Mama, Mama… you will never guess who is here!'

'Well no, how can I guess? Shall I come down?'

'No, no! We will come up,' said the familiar Italian voice.

Vicenzo appeared in the drawing room moments later, followed by Anastasia and Dorothea.

'My dear old friend, how are you?' he said, taking Maria Sibylla's hand and kissing it.

'Always such a gentleman; I survive, thank you. And who is your young companion?'

Standing shyly behind Vicenzo was Anastasia, her dark hair tumbling around her shoulders, wearing a deep-red velvet cloak.

'Ah, may I introduce my dear friend Anastasia Balzarelli? I have known her since she was a little girl. I have brought her to meet you, Maria Sibylla. She is a talented artist.'

The girl blushed.

'Oh Vicenzo, that is not true,' she said. 'Madam Merian, it is a huge pleasure – no, an honour – to meet you.'

The young woman held out her hand. There was a pleasing sincerity about her that Maria appreciated.

'An honour! Well, well, well… I don't know about that. Is he right – my old friend here – that you have talent?'

'Not at all; I am not talented in the least, *signora*, but I love to paint and draw and am eager to learn.'

'We wondered,' interjected Vicenzo, 'if Anastasia here might be allowed to take a few lessons with you, Maria Sibylla – to learn at the feet of the master, as it were.'

'Lessons! Well, I suppose it could be arranged. I am busy these days preparing the last few engraving plates for my next publication, but if she does not mind helping me with that, I could find time to teach her a little of what I know.'

'We will pay, of course,' said Vicenzo. 'Anastasia does not expect any favours.'

'Well, I will not deny that extra income is always welcome. Many of my old pupils left me while I was in Suriname. I think we can manage to take on another. What do you say, Dorothea?'

Her daughter nodded.

'Well, let us sit. Would you like some tea, or chocolate perhaps and then we can talk a little and I can find out more about you?'

Maria settled herself in a high-backed chair near a carved fireplace, decorated with tiny classical figurines. On a table next to her chair was an orchid in a carved bowl, to which had been attached two preserved turquoise butterflies. The walls of the drawing room were lined with pea-green striped wool and covered with paintings of flowers and insects, interspersed with the occasional landscape. The room was filled with natural light filtering through the half-glazed door from the landing and the tall windows overlooking the canal. Two painted shelves hung on either side of the wooden fireplace and were decorated with delicate pieces of blue and white Chinese porcelain. Sconces on either side of the door displayed a collection of blue and white tea bowls in decreasing sizes; and set out between the arrangement of high-backed chairs, covering the wooden floor, was a Turkish carpet in shades of blue, red and green. A globe sat in one corner of the room and leaning up against the wall beneath the windows were paintings in various stages of completion; pictures of shells in myriad different shades of pink, apricot and cream, and botanical paintings, as well as pictures of crocodiles and iguanas – strange creatures the like of which Anastasia had never seen before.

Maria Sibylla was a woman in late middle age. Her once-dark hair was greying and, although not beautiful, she had grace and elegance. She wore a dark-blue silk dress, edged in white linen around the neckline. She had delicate hands with long tapered fingers and her dark eyes scrutinised her young companion.

'So, Anastasia, tell me a little about yourself.'

Dorothea reappeared with a tray of hot chocolate that she set down on the table between them.

Anastasia began falteringly.

'I come from a farm near Verona. We have a vineyard and also a silk farm.'

'A silk farm,' said Maria, sitting forward enthusiastically. 'So you have observed, as an artist, the metamorphosis of the silkworm?'

'I have, *signora*,' replied Anastasia eagerly. 'As well as growing up on the silk farm, I recently spent time in Venice and had the chance to observe as the silk cocoons hatched out into little pale creamy moths. It's a fascinating process, as you know, and I recorded it in my paintings.'

'I should like to see those paintings. Did you bring them with you?'

'She did,' said Vicenzo. 'They are in the house we have taken on Keizersgracht. If you would like to see any of her work, I shall arrange for the pictures to be brought over here. They are very good.'

'I should like that very much,' said Maria. 'And what took you to Venice, my dear?'

Anastasia looked down, anxiously, at her hands; her eyes filled with tears.

'You do not need to tell me,' said Maria sympathetically.

'No, I would like to. I was married to someone who lived there, against my will. I was forcibly kept in a room.'

'Oh, my dear.' Maria Sibylla leaned forward and took Anastasia's hand.

'It was when I was imprisoned that my maid Veronica brought me the silk cocoons. Their metamorphosis was, in some ways, my salvation.'

'I am glad; the observation and recording of these transformations has been my salvation over the years, too. And may I ask, how did you escape?'

'With the help of my maid, and a little deception.'

'And now?'

'I obtained a divorce, and am free.'

Maria Sibylla squeezed her hand.

'Then we have several things in common. A love of painting, a fascination with nature, and it may surprise you to know that I, too, am divorced.'

Anastasia looked knowingly at Vicenzo, who smiled.

'And so, I understand a little of what you have been through,' continued Maria. 'Vicenzo – could you send Anastasia's work over to me today? I shall take a look at it and if I like what I see, I shall take you on. We shall start at half past nine in the morning. Does that suit you?'

'Thank you, *signora,*' said Anastasia. 'It suits me very well.'

Chapter Twenty-Three

Amsterdam
September 1705

Vicenzo had taken a corner house on the intersection of Keizers-gracht and Leidsestraat, which was just five minutes' walk away from Maria Sibylla's house, and a few doors down from a Walloon church that had welcomed a large influx of Huguenots from France; over fifty thousand had arrived in Amsterdam during the previous twenty years and they now formed a quarter of the city's population.

Sitting in the window seat of her first-floor bedroom, Anastasia could watch the canal traffic as it ferried goods between the town centre and the docks. With the graceful houses on either side of the water, it reminded her of Venice. But whereas in Venice the view from her window came to represent her incarceration, here the life she observed from her bedroom was liberating.

Anastasia quickly grew to love Amsterdam, in particular the way the water intertwined with the city's streets. Birds squawked their way up the canals, heading towards the North Sea, and swans floated in stately fashion, diving beneath the water for food. Having spent much of her young life in the relative tranquillity of the Italian countryside, she relished the bustling streets, lined on either side with shops selling clothing, fabric, books, antiquities and curios. There was always something delightful to look at, or an interesting shopkeeper to talk to.

The only aspect of life in Amsterdam that Anastasia struggled to cope with was the cold wind. Chilly, salty breezes whistled up the canals from the North Sea as she crossed a bridge, or turned a corner, and she soon learned never to leave the house without a cape and a pair of gloves.

The highlight of her day was the four or five hours she spent with Maria Sibylla. Maria was a fine teacher and Anastasia worked hard to be a dutiful and deserving pupil. Each morning, as she entered the shop, there was a strong scent of coffee, wax polish and printer's ink – a dark scent of turpentine, oil and soot that caught in the back of her throat. As the shop bell announced her arrival, she would hear Maria Sibylla calling her.

'Is my pupil here? Come into the workroom, dear – let us get started.'

On her first morning with Maria Sibylla, they discussed Anastasia's previous work.

'These are very good, Anastasia,' Maria said, as she studied Ana's paintings of silkmoths. 'I like the way you have painted the moths in their natural habitat, with mulberry leaves. That is my way too – to accurately reflect their lives. We all sometimes need to make use of a dead insect or animal in our work, but far better to paint the creature while it lives – to observe its life cycle. To watch it eat, shed its cocoon, mate and so on. My first paintings were all of silkmoths. When I was a little girl aged just thirteen in my home town of Frankfurt am Main, my stepfather's brother was in the silk trade, so we had access to the cocoons, caterpillars and so on. I became fascinated then by the process of metamorphosis.'

Over the next few weeks, they studied insects, plants and shells. Maria demonstrated how to dissect an animal to explore what lurked beneath the surface. She taught Anastasia the importance of observation and the care of her subjects.

'They will not mate, or perform for us, if they are not happy; and the best way to keep an animal happy is to feed it its favourite food,' she said, dropping strands of grass and clover into a glass case containing woolly bear caterpillars.

Anastasia was already familiar with many watercolour techniques, but Maria showed her how to prepare *carta non nata* – a special vellum made from the delicate skin of naturally aborted lambs – with a coat of white paint.

'This material is very costly, but it's worth every penny,' said Maria. 'It holds the colour from your brush like nothing else.'

She demonstrated the use of gouache, as well as watercolour.

'They are very different, but are ideal mediums for our kind of work.'

'Do you ever work in oil?' asked Anastasia.

'No… Women artists are forbidden to use oil paints here in Amsterdam; it is the ruling of the local guild. It's ridiculous, of course, but I don't let it worry me.'

As well as lessons in painting technique and engraving, Maria broadened Anastasia's horizons and showed her how her art could be applied to other mediums.

'Over twenty years ago now, I perfected the process of painting directly onto silk. That can be very effective. And my work is often used by embroiderers – they take the paintings and copy them in wools and silks. Here I have an example, on this chair…' and she handed Anastasia a small cushion decorated with a pineapple that rose majestically over spiky green leaves.

Every day was the same routine. They worked solidly for three and a half hours and then, at one o'clock, they would hear Maria's maid struggling up the stairs from the basement kitchen, carrying a tray with their lunch.

Maria Sibylla observed the glances Anastasia gave the dark-skinned maid as she set out their food. 'Thank you, Elizabeth,' said Maria. 'We'll help ourselves.' Elizabeth smiled and left the room.

'I met Elizabeth when we were in Paramaribo, in South America,' explained Maria as she ladled *snert* – a thick pea soup – into bowls. 'She was a slave working on one of the plantations. I liked her and offered to bring her back here with me as my maid. She now has her freedom, of course; she could leave at any time. But she stays with us. We pay her well and she cares for us well in return. She is a marvellous cook. Eat your soup – it's good. Not too heavy in the middle of the day and I find it's the best thing to eat when one is working.'

After lunch, Maria Sibylla would usually take a nap, during which time Anastasia was free to return to the house on Keizersgracht. Sometimes, if the weather was good, she would take a walk. One afternoon she wandered along Herengracht, ending up in a little cafe, where she ordered hot chocolate. Settling at a corner table, from where she had an excellent view of both the canal and the street outside, she took out a book of poems – one of the large collection of books that she had acquired since arriving in Amsterdam.

As her chocolate was set on the table, she noticed a tall young man enter the cafe and take a seat at a table in the window. He wore a dark brown velvet coat over a simple white shirt and, unusually for that time, he wore no wig – his fair hair was cut closely cropped to his head. As he ordered coffee, she noted his French accent. He looked around the cafe and smiled at Anastasia, revealing neat white teeth and gentle pale blue eyes. Like Anastasia, he had a book with him, and both proceeded to read intently. When Anastasia rose to leave the young man looked up and smiled again. It seemed for a moment that he might be about to stand, but he remained at his table and returned to his book.

The following afternoon Anastasia returned to the cafe and, once again, the young man arrived within minutes, smiled at her, sat at the same table as before, ordered coffee and read his book. He smiled again when she stood to leave. The next day, it was exactly the same. Anastasia felt a sensation she had not felt for many weeks – since she had left Italy – an anxiety, a fear, almost, of this young man who seemed intent on following her. That night she dreamed of Anzolo for the first time since she had left Venice. She woke almost struggling for breath, the sense of panic once again rising in her chest.

The following morning as she worked with Maria Sibylla, painting a black and white caterpillar, she struggled to capture the detail of the tiny hairs that emerged in little regular clumps from its belly.

'It's impossible; I cannot paint anything so delicate, madam,' she said, depositing her brush firmly into the pot of water at her side.

Maria looked at the painting and then at Anastasia.

'I agree, it is difficult work – but you are more than capable. I think, perhaps, that something is troubling you this morning. Let us stop for a while and talk.'

'I do not need to talk. I am just clumsy and have no ability. I can paint a pretty picture of a flower, or a vineyard, or a moth. But I do not have your skill. It is hopeless.'

Anastasia rose from her chair and stood looking out of the window at the long narrow garden at the rear of Maria's house.

'Anastasia, you told me on the day I met you a little of what you went through when you were married. And you know that I, too, have been unhappy in a marriage. Mine was not filled with suffering as yours was, but it was a poor, joyless thing.'

'Is that why you left him?' asked Anastasia, turning from her place by the window and sitting back in her chair.

'Yes. I simply did not love him – that's the truth. I do not think I ever truly loved him. I was eighteen when we married – just like you. He was ten years my senior – an artist and someone I thought I had a connection with. But over time it changed. There is ten years between my two girls; that should tell you something about our marriage. I couldn't bear to have him near me towards the end.'

'How did you leave him? Did you have to escape, too?'

'No, nothing so extreme. But I went away, a long way away in fact, both metaphorically and physically. My work has always been, in some small way, a representation of God's power in the world. The more I study these little creatures that fascinate me, the more I see His hand in nature. My job, such as it is, is to present God's miracles in my paintings. But I do not seek praise for it; in fact, I would prefer that those who buy my books or paintings glorify God as a consequence. At one point, during my marriage, I read the words of Jean de Labadie, who said, "Everything we hear or see announces God or figures Him. The song of a bird, the bleating of a lamb, the voice of a man. The sight of heaven and its stars, the air and its birds, the sea and its fish, the land and its plants and animals. Everything tells of God, everything represents Him, but few ears and eyes try to hear or see Him."'

Maria Sibylla touched the delicate petals of a pale-yellow orchid that sat on her desk.

'This philosophy made sense to me. It was what I already believed. And there were other matters that led to my moving away from my home and from my marriage. My beloved stepfather, who taught me all I know as a painter, died, and his affairs were in a terrible mess. There were huge debts; he left my mother with nothing, effectively. We, my mother and I, were forced to bring a lawsuit against my stepfather's natural daughter, Sara, from his first marriage. It was all most unfortunate but we won in the end. But something had changed inside me. It was all so distasteful and unpleasant; I simply couldn't bear it. I moved with my mother and daughters to Friesland and we joined a Labadist community. My stepbrother was already there and he encouraged me. It was what I needed at the time – to embrace a simple, spiritual life. To share with others in Christian fellowship.'

'To withdraw from the world?' asked Anastasia.

'Yes, to a degree. The Labadists believed that the time of Jesus Christ was at hand and for a while we lived very happily in the community. We grew our own food, we worshipped together and it provided a security of sorts. People came from everywhere to join us – from France, Germany, the Netherlands, even England – and from all walks of life. We were taught to detach from worldly things, from property, pride in our work and elegant clothes. We shed them like an ill-fitting cocoon.'

'It sounds wonderful,' said Anastasia dreamily. 'Why did you leave?'

'I began to resent the lack of intellectual freedom. I went there to explore new ideas and found that in reality, limitations were put on us all as to what we were allowed to read and discuss. I realised that my daughters would suffer in that environment. It's one thing to give up your own intellectual curiosity, especially if you are already widely read, as I was, but quite another to have it denied to you as a young person. I could not bear the thought of my daughters growing up in the world without a proper under-standing of independent thought. And so I left, and came here to Amsterdam. I have never regretted it.'

'My father refused to allow us to explore any intellectual activ-ity,' Anastasia said. 'It's one of the many things I love about living here – my freedom to buy books whenever I like.'

Maria Sibylla nodded.

'And what happened to your husband? Did he join you in your search?' asked Anastasia.

'After I left him and went to join the Labadist community, he was desperate to join us in Friesland, but he never shared my faith, and I did not see how it could work. Perhaps that was an excuse. Either way, he stayed for a few months, living outside the community, and begged to be allowed to join me. Finally he gave up. We were divorced and I came to Amsterdam. I shall tell you something, Anastasia, that I do not often share with people. For many years after I left my husband, I could not admit to being divorced. I would tell my pupils and customers that my husband was dead, whereas in reality he was still very much alive, and married to another woman, with a child. Why did I do that? Shame. Fear. Embarrassment.'

'I understand – it *is* a shameful thing. I feel it, too. Your husband married again but what of you – were you never tempted?' said Anastasia.

'No. I was thirty-nine when we divorced; I had my two daughters and didn't need that sort of… intimacy. And what of you, my dear? Do you wish to marry again?'

Anastasia looked down at her hands, fiddling with the lace on the edge of her sleeve.

'I cannot. I cannot bear the thought of anyone… touching me. Do you understand?'

'Yes, I do, completely. Although I worry that you are very young to make such an important decision. You have never experienced the joy of children. I would hope that, one day, those feelings of fear, of revulsion, would recede. That love would overcome such feelings. Vicenzo tells me that you were to marry his son – what of him?'

'Oh Maria, I don't know! I did love him so much, but part of me cannot forgive him for not fighting hard enough to prevent my father taking me away. I know that is unfair. What could he have done, after all? But on the day he let go of my hand, and allowed my father to kidnap me, it is as if the thread that bound us together was broken.'

Maria Sibylla smiled.

'You may not always feel that way. One day, you might forgive him. Or perhaps you will meet someone else?'

'But I find it so hard to trust anyone – men, I mean. I am frightened.'

'I cannot tell you what to feel, Anastasia, or what to do. But I know this. If you are an artist, you must keep your heart, as well as your eyes, open. You must allow the sun's rays to enter your soul every day and warm your body and your mind. If you cannot see clearly, you cannot paint. If you cannot feel deeply, you cannot paint anything of consequence, Anastasia; and if you cannot love, you will not be able to transform yourself into the artist I know you are capable of being. Open your heart, my dear, and banish your fear, and learn to trust.'

Anastasia thought about Maria's words on her way back home that afternoon. It made sense intellectually, and yet she was unable to put her mentor's advice into action. If anything, she retreated from social encounters; she avoided the cafe on the Herengracht, and thus any potential encounter with the young man who, she feared, was attracted to her. After her morning lesson, she either returned home or, if the weather was sunny, she walked in the Botanical Gardens.

Vicenzo was also an enthusiastic visitor to the Botanical Gardens. He had a long-standing association with the head plantsman, and spent much of his time discussing new varieties that would grow in the microclimate of Lake Garda. One afternoon as he and Anastasia sat in the herb garden, sketching the rare plants that filled the neat parterres, she noticed the young man from the cafe. He was sitting on a bench on the other side of the garden. He raised his hand briefly in greeting.

Vicenzo looked up from his sketch.

'Who is that?'

'I don't know… I have seen him once or twice in a cafe I go to on Herengracht.'

'He is very forward. Have you been introduced?'

Anastasia shook her head.

'I did not invite his attentions,' she assured him. 'I think he has been following me. I find it quite upsetting.'

'I shall go and speak to him,' said Vicenzo protectively. He walked purposefully towards the young man. After a few moments, Anastasia noticed how Vicenzo's initial hostility relaxed and softened, until the two men were laughing together. He brought the young man across to meet her.

'Anastasia, let me introduce the son of an old acquaintance of mine – Sébastien Benoît. His father, Jean-Antoine, was a colleague of Peter Leman, the silk weaver. Do you remember we discussed him with André Arnaud in Lyon?'

Anastasia nodded; she looked up shyly at Sébastien.

'I had not realised that Jean-Antoine had brought his family to Amsterdam, so I have invited them to dine with us tomorrow at our house. He tells me that he often goes to the cafe – he has been visiting it since he arrived in Amsterdam.'

Sébastien blushed.

'Forgive me if I alarmed you,' he said to Anastasia. 'I meant no harm. I like that cafe very much – the view of the canal is excellent, and the coffee is good. I have missed you these last few days.'

'I have been busy with my studies,' said Anastasia coyly.

Vicenzo slapped the young man on the back.

'It will be good to see your father again; it must be ten years at least since we last met. You were just a boy.'

'My father will be equally delighted, I am sure, sir; thank you. We will look forward to tomorrow evening very much.'

As Sébastien loped off, he turned when he got to the entrance to the garden and waved once again at Vicenzo and Anastasia. Ana raised her hand fleetingly, before returning once again to her sketchbook.

Chapter Twenty-Four

Millie's final days at Villa di Bozzolo were a nightmare of diplomacy, verging on farce. She persuaded Max that he should only stay for a couple of days, to allow her to finish the story in peace. His presence at the villa made her uncomfortable. The place had become associated in her mind with Lorenzo and she lived in dread of the two men encountering one another in the hall or dining room. The best plan, she decided, was to take Max out during the day.

'I need to see the area – to get some local colour,' she said one morning over breakfast. 'Lorenzo has been kind and introduced me to the silk farm, spinners, weavers and so on, but it would be good to get a sense of the landscape and I've not even been to Verona yet. Shall we go together?'

Delighted to be involved, Max threw himself into the task with abandon and suggested they sit by the pool with her laptop and plan their day together.

'It's such a shame that we're too early to see one of the operas – they don't start for a month. I'd love to take you to see *Aïda* – I've heard it's stunning.'

'Well, we could still look at the amphitheatre – it's first-century, isn't it?'

'And there's Juliet's House,' Max said enthusiastically, 'I gather it's a bit of a tourist trap – but it might be interesting.'

'Sure,' said Millie, 'whatever you fancy. We'd better get going if we're going to fit all that in.'

She was jumpy – she felt awkward sitting next to the pool with Max, the barn just a few metres away. Once or twice she heard the familiar voices of Lorenzo and Bella, who were hidden by the hedge that marked the edge of the barn's garden. Her heart began to race a little, with a complicated mixture of emotions. She felt excitement at hearing Lorenzo's voice, mixed with a slight sense of disappointment that she couldn't call out to him, push through the break in the hedge, sit with him and Bella on their terrace and chat easily as she had become so used to doing.

She felt relieved when she and Max finally drove away from the villa.

Over lunch in a small trattoria in Verona, he was affectionate and romantic; he opened up about his break-up with Katje.

'Looking back, she was never interested in anything that I was involved in. Her whole existence was centred on perfecting her lifestyle – having the best house, the greatest figure, the most exciting garden designer… It was pretty vacuous. I began to realise I was just a chequebook as far as she was concerned.'

'Oh Max, I'm sure that's not true,' comforted Millie.

'Oh, it was… and will continue to be so, I suspect. I don't imagine the divorce will be either reasonable or fair. She's employed a shit-hot set of lawyers who will screw me into the ground.'

'Did you tell her about us?'

'No, it seemed easier. Dishonest, obviously, but I'd rather leave her with the impression that she is the only guilty party, with her sordid little affair with the Pilates instructor. I mean – God… Honestly. Pilates! I presume he is extremely toned…'

He laughed.

'Aren't you upset?'

'Now that would be ridiculous. I may not be telling her the whole truth about us for legal reasons, but I have no leg to stand on when it comes to feeling distressed or betrayed, do I? No, I'm not upset. I'm relieved, to be honest. The marriage has been struggling for years. I don't think I should ever have married her.'

'Why did you? Something must have attracted you.'

'You've never seen her, have you?'

Millie blushed, remembering the episode in the cafe in Notting Hill Gate.

'No…' she lied.

'She's pretty cute. And my first wife was a nightmare, always tired and grumpy, and Katje was just so available, and blonde and sexy.'

'Max!' Millie laughed. 'You're impossible.'

'I know. One is not supposed to say these things any more. But you understand, don't you? You always understand. And you're beautiful, and auburn-haired, and sexy – *and* you're ferociously intelligent, you never annoy me, you have talent and you have a career. *You* are the woman I should have been with all my life.'

He took her hand across the table, and kissed it.

As they lay in bed that night after making love, Max suggested they should invite Elena and Lorenzo out for supper the following day to thank them for their hospitality. At the mention of Lorenzo's name, Millie flushed. She turned away from Max, pretending to look for her phone.

'I don't think that's a good idea. I mean, they've been really sweet to me, but they won't expect it. We'll give them a good bit of PR in the piece. Besides, they seem awfully busy.'

The thought of sitting between Lorenzo and Max with Elena's disapproving gaze trained on her all evening was unbearable.

*

Max and Millie's final day together was spent at a modern fabric mill, which was using some of the newly produced Italian silk. Millie had been intending to make the visit with Lorenzo, but she couldn't face the prospect of a two-hour car journey with her erstwhile lover, with Max making polite conversation from the back seat of the Fiat.

'Will you be able to communicate properly with them?' asked Max sensibly. 'Surely better to take Lorenzo, if he's willing to give up the time.'

'I'm sure we can manage – my schoolgirl Italian has improved hugely while I've been here.'

Fortunately, the manager of the mill spoke broken English, and between them Max and Millie managed to communicate.

'This wool is for Max Mara's winter collection,' the mill manager said proudly as they wandered through the huge purpose-built factory filled with state-of-the-art stainless steel machinery, so at odds with the Jacquard looms Millie had seen in Venice.

The machines were operated with impressive precision by young women in overalls, their hair covered with caps to prevent stray tresses getting caught in the machinery. It was interesting, she thought, that weaving had always been a feminine skill.

When they got back to the villa she booked a local restaurant for dinner. Max suggested they should have a glass of wine on the terrace before heading off.

'Let's go and look at the view. We can have a glass of Villa di Bozzolo Prosecco – I gather they produce it here.'

Millie hoped fervently that Lorenzo wouldn't choose that moment to wander through his garden. She found Elena's son Lino in the villa kitchen.

'Lino – how are you? I wonder… Could we have a couple of glasses of your prosecco, do you think? We're sitting on the terrace.'

As they sipped their wine, Bella, wearing her pink swimsuit, appeared through the hedge that ran along the boundary of the swimming pool. When she saw Millie, she ran towards her.

'Can you come and read to me tonight?'

'I can't today, Bella, my friend is here,' said Millie nervously, indicating Max. 'Maybe tomorrow?'

The child accepted this explanation and, throwing her towel over her shoulder, ran off towards the barn.

'She seems friendly. Is that the dragon's daughter?' (The 'dragon' was Max's nickname for Elena.)

'No!' hissed Millie. 'It's her brother Lorenzo's little girl.'

'Ah yes… the tall, handsome Italian brother. Odd that I've never met him.'

Millie sipped her wine and gazed at the view.

'So you've been over there – to their house, have you?' he continued, glancing quizzically over his Ray-Bans. 'Sounds cosy.'

'Yes, I've been there. Before you came out, Elena was nice enough to invite me for supper once or twice.'

'Oh, so she does cook dinner, then? I thought you said she only did breakfast.'

'Generally, yes. But as I was writing a piece about them, it seemed sensible for me to interview them over dinner. And I was on my own – she was just being nice.'

The following morning, when Max left to go back to London, Millie waved him off with a combination of regret and relief. Surprisingly, she'd enjoyed their time together, but before she too left the villa, she was anxious to have a proper conversation with Lorenzo: there was unfinished business. As soon as Max's taxi disappeared through the archway onto the open road, she went over to the barn and found Lorenzo on the terrace, working on his laptop.

'Oh, good! You're here. Is Elena around?' she asked.

'No, she's gone to Verona.'

'Can we talk?' asked Millie, sitting down to join him.

'Of course. How's Max?'

'Gone back to London.'

'So soon... I didn't get a chance to meet him.'

'Funny that; he said the same thing about you. Bella came over yesterday evening – we were having a glass of your prosecco on the terrace, and she asked when I was coming over to read to her... Max gave me a very funny look, I can tell you.'

'Do you think he guessed?'

'I don't think so. And if he did, he's too sophisticated to mention it. He's a pragmatist. As far as he is concerned, we are together now, and that's all he cares about.'

'And are you... together?'

'Yes... I think we are.' Millie found herself unable to catch Lorenzo's gaze. She looked instead at the garden. 'I wanted to come over and say sorry.' As soon as she said the word 'sorry' she regretted it. It was so inadequate. It was the word you use when you bump into someone in the street, or spill a glass of water. You don't begin to fall in love, to bind yourself with someone's life, and then walk away and just say 'sorry'.

'What for?'

'If you feel I led you on... I meant all the things I said. I loved our time together.' She couldn't find the right words. These were platitudes – they didn't explain her feelings, perhaps because she couldn't really understand how she felt.

'No, you never did that – led me on, I mean,' Lorenzo said with characteristic generosity. 'You were honest from the start about Max. I can't pretend I didn't hope you would fall hopelessly in love with me, and leave him...' He smiled, but his blue eyes told a different story. 'Millie – seriously, you have nothing to reproach yourself with. We met, we were attracted, but it's not to be.'

He got up, suddenly, from the table and turned away from her.

'Do you want a coffee?' he asked over his shoulder as he headed to the kitchen. She watched him brush his face with the back of his hand.

'Yes, thank you.' She followed him into the kitchen, where he busied himself filling the filter with dark espresso. He put the pot on the stove and turned on the gas.

'So… it's that simple?' she asked. 'We met, we were attracted and that's it.'

'Do you think it's more complicated?'

'No, I suppose not. But, Lorenzo, I do love being with you. And I want you to know that if Max hadn't split up with his wife, I would have been very tempted to stay here, to carry on with our relationship. Oh, that sounds awful, but do you understand?'

'I do, but think about it, Millie. Could you really give up your work? Your job? Your flat? For me – a middle-aged Italian you hardly know, with a little girl in tow, a crumbling house and an overbearing sister?' He laughed gently, pouring dark viscous coffee into two little maiolica cups. He slid a cup towards her and their fingers touched. She picked it up and sipped it, leaning back against the aged marble worktop.

'Well, put like that, it doesn't sound that appealing.' She smiled bravely, grateful for the coffee, aware tears were close. 'Except that you're not just a middle-aged Italian, you're a wonderful man, with an adorable daughter, living in a stunning house. And I think your sister is quite right to be a bit grumpy with me.'

Lorenzo smiled; he looked deeply into her eyes. He reached out and covered her hand with his.

'We'll miss you – Bella and me. And if things don't work out with Max… don't forget about us.'

Millie threw her arms around his neck and buried her face in his shoulder.

'I'll never forget about you,' she said through her tears.

Chapter Twenty-Five

Amsterdam
September 1705

Vicenzo's house on Keizersgracht was a hive of activity as the household prepared for the dinner party. He had hired a cook, Amelia, for the duration of his stay, and her job had until now been relatively simple: to prepare meals for just two guests in the dining room each day and feed the small staff in the kitchens. A dinner party for five was a more ambitious task, and Amelia was determined it would be memorable. She had asked for Veronica's help.

'I went to the fish market this morning, and then ordered the vegetables. Amelia is preparing a feast down there in the kitchens,' said Veronica cheerfully as she laid out Anastasia's dark-green silk dress.

'Oh, thank you, Veronica; that was kind of you. I'm sure Vicenzo could bring in an extra kitchen maid if we need one,' said Anastasia.

'No, I'm happy to do it. I enjoy working for you, *signora*, but I like to keep busy. And I am used to kitchen work; that's how I started. Besides, I get to taste everything as she's cooking it.' Veronica laughed.

'You seem thoughtful, *signora*,' she added as she dressed Anastasia's hair. 'Is all well with you?'

'It is, Veronica. Thank you. My work with Madam Merian has been very enlightening – in more ways than one.'

'In good ways, I hope, my lady?' said Veronica, tightening the laces of Anastasia's bodice.

'Yes… and thought-provoking too. We talk about so many things – yesterday, of her own marriage and divorce. I have found it difficult to talk to anyone about what happened to me with Anzolo. I try hard not to think about it at all; it's easier to bury it. But her advice is to let the light in.'

'And can you?'

'I don't know. I must try. She believes I need to learn to love again.'

'Well, you have loved in the past, and maybe you still do?'

'Yes, possibly. I do still think of Marco, really I do. I picture his sweet face as I fall asleep at night, and remember the happy times we had together. But I am so fulfilled by my work here… Maria has made me see my future may not involve love at all. She has given me ambition, Veronica. She is an independent woman, with no husband in her life. She supports herself through her work. I find that a compelling idea. The time has come, I think, to make some serious decisions about my future.'

Sébastien and his parents – Jean-Antoine and Angelique – arrived just after seven o'clock. As they sat in the drawing room overlooking the gardens, Anastasia sensed Sébastien's gaze following her around the room. Whenever she looked at him, he looked away, but it was clear that he felt a strong attraction towards her. Sébastien appeared to be a cultured young man; he played the lute and the spinet. He was already involved in his father's silk business, but confessed to Anastasia that his secret ambition was to be a musician.

'I have written a number of pieces for the spinet and perform them from time to time. I dream of travelling, with my lute, to London, or even Italy one day, and playing in Venice, or Florence… or Verona, where you come from. But, in the meantime, I must help my father with his business.'

Anastasia warmed to him. He appeared sincere. He was sensitive and courteous; he was certainly handsome, and he made her laugh.

After the guests had left, Vicenzo and Anastasia stood for a few moments in the hall.

'He is an attractive young man, that Sébastien,' said Vicenzo.

'Is he? Yes, I suppose he is. I hadn't really noticed,' said Anastasia, blushing.

'Mmm, well, I think he has noticed you.' Vicenzo kissed her on the forehead.

'Oh Vicenzo, don't be so silly.' Anastasia walked upstairs. On the landing she turned and said: 'Thank you for this evening.'

'Goodnight, my dear.'

Over the following few weeks, Anastasia and Vicenzo frequently met with the Benoît family. They visited the Botanical Gardens, or met to play cards and enjoy meals together. Anastasia grew fond of Sébastien, and they enjoyed discussing poetry, literature and music.

'I am a poor musician,' she confessed one evening, when Jean-Antoine asked her to play for them after dinner. 'Let Sébastien entertain us, he has a real talent for music.'

'He loves to play,' Angelique said proudly. 'Ever since he was a little boy it has been his passion. But his father, sadly, doesn't encourage him.'

'He must work for the family business, not waste his time with music,' said Jean-Antoine.

'Artistic endeavours can never be a waste of time, surely,' said Anastasia defensively. 'I love to paint; is that a waste of my time?'

'You are a woman,' said Jean-Antoine, pragmatically. 'Women should be encouraged to develop their artistic ability. It is an attractive quality.'

'You talk about it as if it is just a delightful pastime whereas I believe that nurturing my artistic ability, such as it is, might one day help me to run my family business. My father is dead, as you know, and there is no son to take over. I have that responsibility now. And this visit to Amsterdam with Vicenzo has shown me a way in which I can really make a difference to that business.'

'Well, I stand corrected,' said Jean-Antoine. 'I had no idea you had such ambition.'

'It is an ambition that has developed slowly over the last few months. I initially came here merely to study with Maria Sibylla – just hoping to become a better artist. To be allowed to paint and draw was enough; my father disapproved of women being involved in any artistic or cultural activity, sadly. But what Maria has demonstrated is that it is possible for a woman to survive independently through her artistic endeavours. I may not have a great artistic talent like Maria Sibylla, but she has shown me that there are other ways to adapt my skills. She has suggested I design silks, for example. Her paintings are often used as inspiration for embroidery, so why not for silk design? I have begun to see a different future – one that could combine my artistic nature with the business I will have to run.'

'You are an unusual girl, Anastasia,' said Jean-Antoine. 'My son could learn a great deal from you.' He slapped his son affectionately on the back.

'She has always had spirit,' said Vicenzo proudly. 'You should see her on a horse, she is fearless.'

During the weeks they spent in Amsterdam, Anastasia insisted that no one, apart from Maria Sibylla, should know anything of her divorce.

'I would rather keep it private. People can be very unforgiving. They are liable to judge me, Vicenzo – do you understand? I have already alarmed Jean-Antoine, I think, with my ambitions to run the family business.'

'Of course, my dear,' reassured Vicenzo. 'I would not dream of revealing anything that made you uncomfortable. Have you told Sébastien nothing of your past?'

'No,' said Anastasia. 'He knows nothing of Marco, or Anzolo. He is a sweet, innocent boy, and I think he cares for me; but Vicenzo, I do not love him. He is a good friend, and I enjoy his company – that's all.'

One morning, Anastasia was assisting Maria Sibylla, inking an engraving plate for her new publication, when Andrea, Vicenzo's manservant, rushed breathlessly into the workroom.

'*Signora*, can you please come with me? The master has received some news from home and is anxious to share it with you.'

'Of course, Andrea,' said Anastasia, 'if you can spare me, Maria?'

'Yes, Dorothea can help me. You'd better go.'

Anastasia found Vicenzo in his study.

'My dear, you are here. Sit down,' he said, gesturing towards a chair.

'What is the matter, Vicenzo? Is it bad news?'

'I hardly know what to say; how to tell you.'

'Is it my mother? Is she all right?'

'Yes – yes, oh yes, it's nothing like that. Everyone is quite well.'

Anastasia relaxed and sank back into her chair.

'It is about Marco.'

'He is well?'

'Oh yes. My dear, it seems that Marco is anxious to discover if you still care for him; and whether you still feel bound to him. The truth is, Anastasia, he has expressed his desire to be married. He writes to me asking for my advice.'

Anastasia was stunned, unable momentarily to speak.

'Who does he wish to marry?'

'I hardly know how to tell you.'

'Please, Vicenzo.'

'He wishes to marry… your sister.'

'My sister!' Anastasia rose from her chair and began to pace the room. 'Marietta?'

'Yes, my dear. Oh Anastasia, I am so sorry. He has sent a letter for you – here, read it.'

My dear Anastasia,

I hope all goes well with you in Amsterdam. My father wrote to me a little of your remarkable journey and your stay in Lyon. I imagine you are enjoying your studies with Mme Merian? My father has always spoken very highly of her.

I had hoped you would write to me, my dear, but as each day passes with no news from you, I feel I must conclude that you no longer feel bound to me. Am I correct in my assumptions? If you have decided that our engagement is at an end, then please know that I understand. If, however, our time apart has caused you to wish to rekindle our love then please write and tell me as a matter of urgency.

Anastasia, I must tell you that I have become most fond of your sister Marietta, and she of me. But if you are soon to return to Italy and wish to try to go back to what we had, then I shall cease my friendship with Marietta. You have the prior claim and I do not seek to overturn that in any way. I still care for you; love you. And please know, my dearest Anastasia, that you were my first love and will always have a special place in my heart.

I await your letter.

Yours always,
Marco

Anastasia let the letter slip to the floor. Vicenzo leaned across and picked it up.

'May I?'

'Yes,' she answered distractedly.

Vicenzo scanned the letter.

'This is a most peculiar state of events, Anastasia.' He folded the letter, and reached across to take her hand. 'I hardly know what to say.'

'I wonder why Mamma did not write to me of it herself.'

'She must be very distressed by it all – as am I! You know I had always hoped that you and Marco would one day be together.'

'Oh, this is my fault, Vicenzo – all my fault.' Anastasia got up and paced the room agitatedly. 'I have expected too much of Marco, leaving him alone for so long, expecting him to simply wait for me to return. I have not written to him once – I have been so absorbed in my work. Marco is right to ask for some clarification. I cannot keep him waiting for ever. And perhaps if I truly loved him, I would never have left Italy. Marietta told me as much, on the day I left.'

'You needed time to heal. Marco understood that.'

Anastasia gazed out at the canal; an elderly black horse pulling a *trekschuit*, a horse-drawn boat filled with passengers, stumbled on the towpath. The driver whipped it fiercely. Anastasia flinched, thinking of her faithful Minou, and began to cry silently.

'Oh my dear girl,' said Vicenzo, putting his arms around her. 'We must write straight away to Marco, and then return to Italy. If we leave now, we should be back before Christmas. If we leave it much later, Moncenisio will be closed for the winter.'

'No, Vicenzo.' Anastasia dried her eyes. 'I will write to him; but I cannot go home yet. I feel I have come so far – both literally and figuratively. But there is much more I wish to do. Do you remember the other day, when we had supper with the Benoît family, that I said I would like to learn how to apply my skills to silk design?'

Vicenzo nodded.

'Sébastien suggested something to me a few days ago. I should have discussed it with you before, but I hadn't quite made up my mind. Sébastien and his family are travelling to London in the next few weeks. Jean-Antoine is keen to develop his silk business there. They have suggested that, if I am serious about learning to be a silk designer, I might travel with them. They are staying with friends in London, in Spitalfields, who are silk designers and weavers – the Leman family.'

'London! You cannot go to London on your own. And I must return to Italy before they close the pass for the winter.'

'But I won't be alone. I will be with Jean-Antoine, and Angelique and Sébastien. They will look after me. And I will have Veronica with me, of course.'

'But what of Marco and Marietta?'

'I will write to him, explaining how I feel – that I need to continue my journey a little longer. Perhaps you will take the letter for me?'

Vicenzo nodded and sat down in front of the fire, despondently.

'I know you think I should go back, Vicenzo, and part of me wants to do that; to rush back to Marco and beg him to take me back. But if Marco seriously cares for Marietta, what will I gain by returning? I could not bear to be rejected. Whereas if I stay, and go on to London, I will learn a skill that could help me to transform my father's business.'

'But you could do that in Italy – we could find people in Verona or Venice to teach you.'

'But these designers in London are among the best in the world, so Sébastien says. It would be exciting and challenging and I could learn so much. There is no one else to run the business now that my father is dead. My mother does her best with the farms, but she has no real interest in it, or head for figures, come to that. The business won't grow under her stewardship. And Marietta is a child, with a child's temperament. She has demonstrated that very clearly. By pursuing Marco – and be sure, that is what has happened – she has shown me that she thinks more of herself than her duty to the family. My father wanted nothing more than a strong son to take on his business. He never had a son, but he did have me. Now that he is gone, I will be the one to transform his silk farms. I will turn the Balzarelli family into a major silk producer. One day, we will make the best silk in Italy, and I will design it. So let Marco and Marietta marry, if he truly loves her. Perhaps I am not destined to do so.'

Anastasia knelt down by Vicenzo and took his hand in hers.

'I cannot thank you enough for all that you have done for me. Bringing me here, showing me a new path for my life. I think you do not quite know how important this journey has been. How transformative. I am on the verge of something life-changing, and I am filled with excitement, Vicenzo. The metamorphosis has begun.'

Chapter Twenty-Six

London
May 2017

Drizzle spattered against the windows of Millie's plane as it touched down at Heathrow.

London seemed to be submerged beneath a grey blanket of cloud. She had the familiar sense of disappointment that she always felt on returning to England. The long queues at passport control, the subterranean baggage claim – all conspired to create within her a quiet despair. On the Tube back into London, she took the seat nearest to the door and wedged her small suitcase beneath her knees. She took out her phone and glanced at her messages before the signal was swallowed up in the tunnel.

Can't wait to see you. Meet me at the office? Mx

And further down:

Bella sends her love. She asks if you will come back soon? Lxx

The Tube filled up as the train neared London; Millie's legs were uncomfortably pinned against the sharp edges of her suitcase. She squeezed out of the train with relief at Green Park and transferred to the Jubilee Line. She had just sat down at her desk at the office, and taken her laptop out of her bag, when Max emerged from behind a partition.

'Darling, you're back. I'm so glad.'

He pulled her up from her chair and kissed her passionately.

'Max!' she said, pulling away. 'What are you doing?' She looked around anxiously in case anyone had observed them, but the offices were relatively empty and those who were there were staring intently at their screens.

'Darling – who cares who knows about us now? We've come out! I've mentioned to a few people that I'm divorcing Katje; we don't have to hide in corners any more. Get yourself settled and then we're going out to lunch.'

'Max, I really ought to get this piece finished. I thought Sonia wanted it by the end of the week.'

'Darling, don't worry about that. Lunch – today of all days – is more important.'

The restaurant Max had chosen was top-end, Michelin-starred and filled with pseudo celebrities and bankers. To Millie, wearing jeans and a T-shirt, it seemed inappropriate and pretentious.

'Max, I'm not dressed for somewhere like this. I've just got off a plane, for God's sake. I left the villa at five o'clock this morning for an eight o'clock flight. I'm tired and I feel a bit grubby. Couldn't we have done this later, when I've had a chance to have a shower and sort myself out?'

'Oh darling, you look fine, gorgeous. I wanted us to celebrate. Don't spoil it.'

He ordered vintage champagne.

'God, Max – it's over three hundred pounds a bottle!' said Millie, peering at the wine list.

'This is a big day, darling – and you're worth it.'

The champagne was undoubtedly delicious, but Millie couldn't help but remember the simple prosecco she had enjoyed with Lorenzo on her first day at the villa. She looked through the overpriced menu and suggested a simple bowl of pasta, but instead Max ordered the restaurant's full tasting menu.

'Max, I can't eat all that. I had a disgusting panini on the plane, I'm not even hungry.'

'Nonsense,' he declared.

He was like a child, she realised, overexcited to have her back. He was full of plans for their future together and batted away any problems.

'We'll live in your flat to begin with. I know it's small, but we'll be cosy together. And besides, we'll soon be able to sell it and move on. Where would you like to live?'

Before she had a chance to reply, he continued: 'Somewhere near the office would be good, and near the children, I suppose. A mews house perhaps. I've always wanted one of those…'

Millie was finding it hard to get involved, to share his excitement. Perhaps it was the early start, or the champagne; it always made her feel deflated after the initial thrill of the first glass. What was it Churchill had said? 'A single glass of champagne imparts a feeling of exhilaration. A bottle produces a contrary effect.' Occasionally she drifted away, imagining herself back in the apricot-coloured villa, wandering through the vineyards with Lorenzo, playing cards with Bella, reading her a bedtime story.

Don't you think so, Millie? A mews house – wouldn't it be great?'

'What? Sorry… yes, I'm sure it would be fabulous. Look, I'm tired, Max – this is lovely, but can't we head back home now? I'm dying for a shower.'

Reluctantly, he paid the bill and hailed a taxi.

Back at her flat in Fournier Street, she took a shower, unpacked her bags, put her laptop onto the small desk in the window. The flat felt small and cramped after her week in the stately rooms of the villa. Outside the weather was gloomy. She had got used, she realised, to constant sunshine, the sound of splashing from the swimming pool, the hum of the mowers as Lino or Angelo tended the lawns. The fridge was empty and she thought back ruefully to Elena's delicious cakes and pastries.

'I'll have to dash out to the corner shop and get some bread and milk,' she said. Max didn't demur. Exhausted, she hauled on some leggings and a fresh T-shirt and ran down Fournier Street towards the grocers. Back in the flat she unpacked her unappetising shopping. Max was sprawled elegantly on her sofa, flicking through channels on the TV. He followed her into her tiny bedroom – 'bijou', as the estate agent had originally described it. Now, it seemed absurdly crowded with the tall, languorous Max installed in it. Her 'compact' wardrobe and chest of drawers were already filled to capacity with her own clothes.

'I've no idea where we're going to put your stuff,' she said anxiously, peering into already overstuffed drawers.

'Don't worry, darling. I'll use that hall cupboard – besides, we'll be moving on soon, if we can find somewhere nice.'

She fell asleep almost the moment her head touched the pillow – much to Max's irritation – and woke early with the pale dawn London light trickling through the grubby window.

She slid out of bed, leaving Max sprawled across her queen-size mattress, and padded through to the sitting room. Opening up her laptop, she began to write up her story for the paper. It poured out of her.

> Nestling in a gentle valley, in the heart of the countryside just outside Verona, lies Villa di Bozzolo, owned by brother and sister Lorenzo and Elena Manzoni. The villa, along with its vineyards and tenanted farms, has been occupied by the same family since it was built over four hundred years ago. Rich, fruity Valpolicella and crisp

sparkling prosecco have long been part of the financial sustainability of this farm, and the Manzoni family are rightly proud of their heritage.

But there is another arm to the villa's financial success – silk. Their villa's name means 'House of the Cocoon', and it comes as no surprise when you arrive at this ancient place to find that the barns surrounding the stunning courtyard are filled with not just cases of wine, but metal crates lined with mulberry leaves on which feast millions of silkworms.

Silk has also played a vital part in the history of the Veronese area. The great architect Palladio designed and built over four thousand villas back in the seventeenth century, for clients who had made their wealth through silk. This is the untold story of Verona – not Romeo and Juliet's doomed love affair, not even the millions of gallons of Valpolicella and prosecco that pour from the rich soil each year, but the hundreds of thousands of small farms that – for as long as anyone can remember – have produced raw silk of such quality that the kings and queens of Europe, tsars of Russia, and successive popes, have considered it the best in the world.

Until the middle of the twentieth century, that is…

The story – she thought as she wrote it up – was interesting, but it needed something extra; added glamour, a bit of mystery. She downloaded the photos she had taken on her phone. Shots of the silkworms spinning their cocoons, pictures taken at the magnate's state-of-the-art premises, where his 1950s spinning machine unravelled the thread, turning it into long skeins of white silk. There were photos of the Bordignon mill in Venice, with its Jacquard looms, creating fabulous damasks; the ancient ledger containing a sample of every fabric ever produced. And finally, a shot she had taken of the portrait of the young woman in a room overlooking the Grand Canal. How did this picture fit into the piece?

She placed the photograph of the portrait alongside a shot she had taken from the Bordignon showroom: it was definitely the same view. The buildings beyond the latticed window appeared not to have changed in four hundred years. Who was this woman whose portrait hung on the landing at Villa di Bozzolo and why was she seated in a room at the Bordignon mill? What was the connection?

She made herself a cup of tea, and stared out of the window at the grey, rain-soaked London dawn. She wondered what Lorenzo and Bella would be doing. They were an hour ahead; it would be a quarter to seven. Might they be up, getting Bella ready for school?

She was keen to discuss the photograph with Lorenzo. With Max's arrival at the villa, it had slipped her mind while she was there. It was too early to call. She would email him and attach the two photographs.

Dearest Lorenzo,

I am back. It is raining; this is London as you probably remember it – dirty, crowded and depressing! The flat seems cramped, but empty somehow. I am writing up my piece now and was reminded of the portrait hanging on the landing. Take a look at it next to the shot I took from Bordignon's showroom. The views are identical, don't you think? Why is a picture of a woman who worked or lived at that mill hanging on your wall? It would make a wonderful ending to my piece if we were able to find out. Perhaps Signor Bordignon knows more. I am kicking myself that I did not pursue it while I was there; somehow everything got so complicated and muddled. I will email him about it from here and see what he knows.

Much love,
Millie.

PS Please tell Bella that I will be back to read to her soon – very soon xx

Chapter Twenty-Seven

The coach journey from Amsterdam to Ostend had been difficult. The roads were heavily rutted and the weather had turned wet and cold, causing the coach to get stuck in the mud. Ostend was full of travellers, and the Benoît family, along with Anastasia and Veronica, had been forced to spend the night in a small inn next to the docks, with flea-infested beds and almost inedible food.

'I would move us if I could,' said Jean-Antoine as he pushed the unappetising *boudin* and cabbage around his plate that night, 'but there is no room anywhere else.'

They left at first light and boarded the packet ship to Dover, which set sail on the first tide. The crossing was far from comfortable; it took over twelve hours in rough seas. As the white cliffs of Dover loomed into view on that overcast night, they were required to moor for several hours outside the harbour, waiting for the tide to rise sufficiently to make a safe landing. It was either that or transfer to a small rowing boat, which would take them to the shore. They opted to wait on the larger ship, but the swell was excessive and Anastasia suffered terribly from seasickness. Veronica did her best to ease her discomfort, but as the boat rocked and rolled on the seas there was little that could be done. They finally arrived in

Dover, exhausted, just after midnight, and were taken by cart to the White Horse Inn next to St James's Church.

'The stagecoach to London sets off from here. Once we arrive I shall ensure we are booked onto the next scheduled departure,' promised Jean-Antoine.

Too tired to eat, they retired to bed as soon as they arrived at the inn. The following morning Anastasia woke to find the sun streaming through the small cottage window of her bedroom. Her room was at the back of the inn; it was clean and simply furnished, and as she peered out of the leaded window she had a panoramic view of the medieval fortress – Dover Castle. The party assembled in the dining room of the inn for a mid-morning meal. Fresh bread was laid out with cooked mutton and a game pie wrapped in a thick suet crust. The food was plain, but tasty, and they ate enthusiastically.

After breakfast Anastasia and Sébastien decided to go for a walk.

'Shall we go and explore the castle?' suggested Anastasia.

A chill wind whistled up Castle Hill road as they walked around the perimeter of the fortress. It was garrisoned with soldiers and so they were unable to enter; instead they sat on a wooden bench overlooking the English Channel below.

'The sea is so calm today – I wish it had been like that for us yesterday,' said Anastasia, inhaling the strong salty air. 'I feel much better today; it was a relief just to have a proper night's sleep.'

'My father thinks that the coach will be leaving for London tomorrow,' said Sébastien, 'so just one more night and we can be off.'

'I am excited at the prospect of going to London, aren't you?' said Anastasia. 'It is so good of Jean-Antoine to bring me with you. And it will be wonderful to meet Peter and his son James. Your father tells me that Peter has great talent.'

'He does… he is only eighteen, but he has been designing for several years already. We shall stay with them at their home in London.'

As they walked behind the castle, Anastasia took Sébastien's arm. He had become a good friend to her since Vicenzo had left Amsterdam, but he could never be a true confidante. There was so much of her life that he could never understand – her marriage, her relationship with Marco, her sister Marietta's betrayal.

She thought wistfully of Vicenzo now, as she walked back towards the inn. She hoped he was not lonely travelling without her – they had been such good travelling companions. She had thought of him as a father figure. And he had hoped she would one day be his daughter-in-law. They had shared so much and had so much in common. Before Vicenzo left Amsterdam, she had given him two letters to take back to Italy. One was addressed to Marco; the other was for her mother. As he put them carefully in his leather attaché case, he asked: 'Do you forgive Marco, in your letter? And do you ask him to wait for you?'

'I forgive Marco, yes. As for whether I can forgive Marietta… I am not so sure. I always thought we were best friends. We protected each other throughout our childhood. We defended each other against our father. He was our foe and we united in that task. But perhaps with his death, we have lost our common enemy and now, with nothing to fight against, we have turned on one another.'

'You did not turn on her.'

'I did not bring her with me to Amsterdam. She wanted to come and I left her behind. She was hurt and angry, and this is her revenge.'

'Revenge?' Vicenzo looked concerned.

'I believe so. I hope that she truly cares for Marco, but I fear her reasons for pursuing him are complicated. Please talk to him before they marry and do your best to ensure that their feelings for one another are genuine. I could not bear for him to be unhappy in his marriage. He does not deserve it.'

*

Now, as she and Sébastien Benoît wound their way around the perimeter of the castle, she wondered what Marco would be doing that day. Was he fishing in the lake with Marietta? Did they ride together in the woods near the villa, as she and Marco had done? She had a momentary pang of jealousy that brought tears to her eyes.

'Anastasia,' said Sébastien, as he saw her dabbing at her eyes with a handkerchief, 'are you all right?'

'It's just the cold wind, making my eyes water.'

'Here, take my arm again. We are nearly back at the inn. In just a few short hours we will be off to London. And a new adventure.'

'A new adventure. Yes, indeed.'

As the chill wind blew in off the English Channel, clouds began to gather above Dover. Anastasia pulled her cloak around her shoulders as she and Sébastien hurried back to the White Horse Inn.

Chapter Twenty-Eight

Villa Limonaia
January 1706

Low cloud had descended on Lake Garda overnight and now lay like a thick blanket over the surface of the water. The view from the drawing room at Villa Limonaia was quite obscured and as darkness fell, added to the sense of melancholy that January afternoon.

A fire roared in the grate, throwing sparks onto the Turkish carpet. Vicenzo, who had finally returned that morning from Amsterdam, sat exhausted in a chair, warming his feet and hands, sipping a cup of hot chocolate.

Marco, who had been out riding when his father arrived, rushed into the drawing room when he saw Vicenzo's trunks laid out in the hall.

'Papa, you are returned at last! I am so pleased to see you.'

Vicenzo leapt to his feet.

'My boy! I am glad to be here. I feared we had left it too late to get across Moncenisio before the snows came. But we were lucky. How are you, dear boy?'

'I am well – but is Anastasia not with you?'

'No, but I have a letter for you. I think before we discuss the matter further, you should read it.'

Marco sat down by the fire opposite his father and opened the letter.

Keizersgracht,
Amsterdam,
6 September 1705

My dearest Marco,

I write this letter with a mixture of emotions. I am happy for you – if you believe that you have found love with someone who loves you in return. We did once love one another so much. But my experience in Venice changed something between us and perhaps nothing can be done. I cannot pretend that I do not feel regret that it should end between us. Some of my happiest memories are of the time we spent together on the lake, fishing, painting and walking together. You will always have a place in my heart.

Yours ever,
Anastasia

Marco stood up and walked over to the window; he pulled the curtains closed against the darkening cloud outside. Vicenzo poured him a small glass of port.

'Come back and sit by the fire. I have not read the letter, and do not know its contents. Is she happy for you?' he asked.

'She says so… but I am not so sure.'

'May I read it?'

His son handed him the letter.

'When she writes of our time together,' said Marco, 'all the old feelings come rushing back. It is as if I have been in a dream since she left and went to Amsterdam. Father, I don't know what to do.'

'If you are unsure, it would be wrong to marry,' said Vicenzo. 'I feel certain that Anastasia still loves you and she will return to us here before long.'

'But she does not say that in her letter.'

'I think she is trying to protect herself. If she declares herself to you, and then you reject her, how would she be able to bear it?'

'She still loves me, then?'

'I am sure of it,' said Vicenzo, standing up with his back to the fire.

'But why did she not come back with you?'

'She is determined to finish what she has begun – to learn what she can in England. I think, perhaps, she is testing you…'

Marco gazed into the flames.

'When I rescued her from the midwife's house I felt all the old love, the passion. She felt it too, I know. But it was too soon after all she had been through. I see that now.'

'Just give her a little more time,' advised Vicenzo. 'Be patient a few months longer.'

'And what do I tell Marietta?'

'Have you actually asked her to marry you?'

'Not in so many words, no. We discussed it once or twice, but I have not spoken to her mother about it. I was waiting to hear from Anastasia. And although in her letter she gives her blessing, from what you have said she does, I think, still love me.'

'I believe so. I believe too that Marietta will survive. Anastasia believes she has acted out of base motives – some sort of revenge against her sister.'

'But she has been so attentive while you have been away. I have often stayed with her and her mother at Villa di Bozzolo. She is a very affectionate girl.'

'I'm sure she is. She is young and pretty and alone. And you are here, while her sister is away. But Marco – do you love her, as you loved Anastasia?'

'No.'

'Then you have your answer. Trust in Anastasia. Go away for a while, stay with Luigi in Lucca. While you are there, you can do a little business for me – visit our merchants. Give yourself time to consider, Marco. Do not rush into an ill-considered marriage with someone who may not truly love you.'

At Villa di Bozzolo, heavy rain had turned to snow overnight. As Marietta looked out at the white carpet of snow that led down to the frozen river in the valley, she thought of Marco and the ride they had taken a few days earlier in the woods near Villa Limonaia. He had not actually asked her to marry him, but he had asked her if she wished to marry soon. Before she had left the villa, he had kissed her on both cheeks and told her that he was 'very fond' of her. It was not the declaration of love that she had been hoping for, but it was certainly a sign.

Her mother, Polonia, had the ledgers for the farm laid out on the large desk in an alcove next to the fire. She sighed as she tried to reconcile the expenditure of the farms against the income from the wine and silk. But her workings were covered with crossings-out, and her head ached.

'If Anastasia does not return soon, I think I must appoint a proper farm manager. I struggle with these figures. And I cannot get out to visit the farms as often as I would like, especially now the bad weather is upon us. Why have we not heard from her? It is so unlike her to be so—'

'Thoughtless?' Marietta interjected.

Giuseppe the footman knocked on the drawing room door.

'I have two letters for you, my lady,' he said, proffering a silver tray.

'This one is from Anastasia!' said Polonia, excitedly. 'I recognise the writing.'

She tore open the envelope.

Dearest Mamma,

I hope you are well and managing with the farm without me. I fear it is quite a burden for you, but trust that you are receiving the support you need from the tenants. They are all good men and will do their best, I am sure.

If you are reading this letter, then dear Vicenzo has returned safely to Villa Limonaia. I gave him my letter to have delivered to you, because I intend to remain in Amsterdam. I hope you will forgive me, but there is still so much to do; so much to learn.

I now intend to go to London with a delightful family of Huguenot silk merchants who I met in Amsterdam. Jean-Antoine Benoît and his wife Angelique are old friends of Vicenzo's. They have a son called Sébastien who is almost my age. We will stay with friends of theirs in London who are successful silk weavers and designers, and I am very excited at the prospect of meeting them, and learning how to adapt my artistic ability to the silk industry.

Marco wrote to Vicenzo asking his advice. It seems that he and Marietta have become close while I have been away. He is even considering marriage. This came as a surprise, as I'm sure you can imagine. Did you know about it, Mamma? I cannot believe you knew and did not write to me. Or perhaps you thought it was a flirtation that would come to nothing. I hope that Marietta has true feelings for Marco. He does not deserve to be used ill. I do still care for him – very much – but I am not ready to return to Italy. If he cannot wait, then he makes my decision to remain here easier. By the time you read this letter, I should already be in London and will write to you from there.

Kiss Bianca and Minou for me. I miss them so.

Your loving daughter,
Anastasia

Marietta picked up a book that she had abandoned earlier and sat by the fire, where she started to read.

'Are you not interested in what your sister has to say?' Polonia asked her.

'Yes, of course. What does she say?'

'I think, Marietta, it is more a question of what she has to say about you.'

Marietta put her book down and looked quizzically at her mother.

'I read in your sister's letter,' continued Polonia, 'that you have formed an attachment for Marco. Is that true?'

'We have formed an attachment for one another.'

'But he is engaged to Anastasia.'

'Don't be ridiculous,' said Marietta agitatedly. 'She has left him. What on earth is he to do, wait for her for ever?'

'They had an understanding.'

'An understanding; she just thinks she can have everything. She wants to keep him for herself, even if she is not here. What about me? Who am I to marry? She has already been married once and now she wants Marco too.'

'Her first marriage was nothing but torture for her. Have you forgotten already what she went through? I thought you loved her?'

'I did! I do. But she has left us, Mamma. And I am here alone, and so is Marco. Why should we not find comfort in one another?'

'You are a wicked girl – or a stupid one. You are meddling in things that you do not understand. Marco is a good man and honourable. What must Vicenzo think of us – of you? I see he has written to me. I insist you cease this relationship – now.'

'Why? Why should I have to wait for Anastasia to make up her mind? Why does everything revolve around her?'

'Marietta, do not ask me to choose between you and Anastasia. I love you both. Together we have endured so much. Now your father has gone, we must care for one another. But this liaison with Marco must stop. We will find another husband for you, someone of your own.'

'So, you side with her once again,' said Marietta, throwing her book onto the chair as she stood up to leave. She paused at the door. 'But she does not know what I know.'

'What do you mean?'

'What you did to Papa.'

'Marietta, what I did was for all of us.'

'Well, I wonder what Vicenzo and your beloved Anastasia would think if they knew what you had done – smothering your own husband.'

Marietta slammed the heavy door behind her as she left the drawing room. A maid who was polishing a table nearby scurried away, down the stairs towards the kitchen. The oak doors in the great hall had been left open, and a chill wind blew in from the courtyard. Marietta slammed the doors shut, just as Bianca crawled out from her basket beneath the table. She trotted happily over to Marietta and jumped at her, pawing at the hem of her dress with her sharp claws. Marietta kicked her aside and went upstairs. The little dog whimpered and crawled back to her basket, where she licked her sore belly for a while before finally falling asleep.

Chapter Twenty-Nine

Fournier Street, Spitalfields
May 2017

Millie's silk story had been put on hold until she had the solution to her 'mystery' ending.

'Darling, don't worry about it,' said Sonia at their weekly meeting, 'let's hold it back for a while. It would sit well in September; we could link it with London Fashion Week. Try to find a London link perhaps – a designer who is showing in London who has used Italian silk, that sort of thing. In the meantime, I've got a piece for you about sham holiday lets. The silly season is almost upon us and we need this by the beginning of June. Can you manage that?'

'Yes, of course.'

'And how's it going with Max? He seems over the moon.'

'Yes, he is, oddly.'

'Why oddly?'

'Well… going through another divorce, all the disruption for the kids; selling the house… It's like water off a duck's back to him, apparently.'

'Don't you know him at all? That's Max all over, darling. Don't look back, don't worry about what's ahead, live for now. Isn't that why we all love him?'

'Yes,' said Millie, 'I suppose it is… Well, I'd better get on.'

*

Sonia was right, of course: Max did live for the moment. And now that he was living in Millie's tiny flat, she was more aware of that than ever. He leapt out of bed each morning and commandeered her kitchen, spilling freshly ground coffee on the worktops and cooking scrambled eggs; in the evening, he arrived carrying cases of wine that he piled up on the small table, or with bags of groceries with which he proceeded to create elaborate dinners. He complained about her under-equipped kitchen and ordered expensive gadgets, which were delivered almost daily.

'What's this, Max?' she had said one evening, as they opened another large box.

'A coffee machine, darling. I can't live without a good espresso.'

'What's wrong with my little stove-top coffee maker?'

'Well, it makes terrible coffee for a start. No, this is state-of-the-art. Italian. Stainless steel. Makes a stunning coffee and froths milk all at the same time.'

'But it's huge, Max. Where am I going to put it?'

'Clear out some of that junk there,' said Max, pointing to a set of old French biscuit tins that she had found on an antique stall the previous weekend at Spitalfields Market.

'But I've just bought them. They're pretty.'

These petty squabbles raged back and forth on a daily basis. They argued about the correct technique when making risotto, about where to have dinner, about what television programmes to watch. Max was like a caged animal, she sometimes thought – a man of boundless energy with no outlet.

'Can't you start playing tennis again?' she asked one morning as he sprayed espresso all over her kitchen worktops.

'Where, for God's sake? There are no courts round here. Darling, I've been thinking; we need to get on with our move – and soon. Let's go back to Kensington.'

'And live round the corner from Katje? I don't think so, Max.'

'Well, it wouldn't be so bad. I could play tennis and see the kids.'

*

Max's children, twins Charlotte and Tabatha, had also become a bone of contention. Katje had suggested that Max take them for one evening each week and one day at the weekend. Millie had done her best to embrace the situation, but neither of the children appeared to like her. At their first meeting together, Max had collected them from home and had suggested they all go out for supper at the Pizza Express in Notting Hill Gate. Millie had arrived from work, slightly harassed and a little tired, to find the two girls staring glumly out of the restaurant window, with Max reading emails on his phone.

'Well, you two, how lovely to meet you,' she had said as cheerfully as she could. The children remained silent.

'Max, have you ordered?' He looked up from his phone absent-mindedly. 'Ordered… oh no, I was waiting for you.'

'Well, we'd better get on with it. What's your favourite pizza, Charlotte?'

'I'm Tabatha,' said the child sulkily.

'Oh of course, how silly of me. OK – Tabatha?'

'I don't like pizza. Mummy says they're bad for you, they make you fat.'

'Oh! Well, not at your age.'

'Mummy says you can never start too early to watch your figure.'

'I'm not totally sure I agree with that,' said Millie seriously. 'How old are you?'

'Eight,' said Tabatha.

'Well, I think you could allow yourself a little pizza, or lasagna?'

'I hate lasagna!' said Charlotte fiercely.

'Right,' said Millie, as cheerfully as she could. 'Max, would you like to order for the girls?'

'Sure,' he said after a pause. 'What's it to be, girls – goat's cheese salad?'

*

Their first weekend together was even worse. Katje made it quite clear that she expected the girls to be collected by ten o'clock in the morning and not be returned until the following day.

Max appeared to have no interest in his daughters; after he had deposited them in the flat, he announced that he had finally managed to get a tennis game together with Hugo and would be back later that afternoon. Faced with an entire day in which to entertain two disgruntled children, Millie was filled with understandable anxiety.

The flat had one small spare bedroom, into which she had managed to squeeze a small put-up bed next to the existing single bed. That triggered the first argument of the day as the girls squabbled over who slept where.

'The beds are almost identical,' declared Millie.

'No, they're not. One is comfortable and the other is just a camp bed,' said Tabatha.

'I used to love camping when I was little,' said Millie cheerfully. 'We could make a tent in there, if you like. I'm sure I've got some old sheets and things that we could use.'

'No, thank you,' said Charlotte, 'we don't like camping.'

'Oh…' said Millie. 'Well, what are we going to do today?'

'We normally watch television on Saturday mornings. We've already missed our favourite programme coming over here,' said Tabby gloomily.

'Oh well, perhaps we can watch it on catchup TV?' said Millie brightly. She turned on CBeebies for the girls.

'Don't you have Sky?' asked Charlotte.

'No, I'm afraid I don't.'

The twins raised their eyes heavenward and looked at one another conspiratorially, united at last in their mutual loathing of their unsatisfactory babysitter.

*

Millie made herself a cup of coffee with the large, noisy espresso machine and opened her laptop, searching for inspiration as to how to spend the afternoon with two grumpy little girls.

'Let's go to London Zoo,' she suggested brightly, handing them a plate of sandwiches.

'We don't like sandwiches,' said Tabby predictably. 'And we don't like zoos,' declared Charlotte, absent-mindedly eating a tuna sandwich.

'Well,' said Millie cheerfully, 'it's a beautiful day and I *do* like zoos, so I think we should go.'

She turned off the television and removed the plate of sandwiches. She found the girls' coats and shepherded them down the narrow stairs of the communal hall of the house in Fournier Street.

Outside, she frogmarched them to the Tube station and, keeping a firm grip on both their hands, finally arrived with them at the entrance to the zoo.

'Come on then, you two, let's go and look at the aquarium.'

The girls, predictably, disagreed throughout the trip on where they should go next and what they wanted to do. One liked the big cats, but the other preferred monkeys. Charlotte was fascinated by insects, but Tabby declared they 'made her feel sick'. Millie spent the following twenty minutes darting between the two children, as one sat gloomily at the entrance to the insect house while the other gazed fascinated into each glass exhibit. But slowly, their resistance evaporated and they began to run from enclosure to enclosure, displaying something resembling normal childish enthusiasm. At three o'clock Millie stopped for a well-earned cup of tea at the restaurant. She bought milkshakes and cake and laid out them out on the table with a flourish.

'These look delicious, don't they?'

The children had reverted to their previous mode of 'non-cooperation' and said nothing.

'Right,' said Millie cheerfully, 'you both sit here for a moment and eat your cake. I just need to use the loo. Unless either of you needs to come?'

The girls both shook their heads.

'Well, eat your cake and I'll be back in just a second.'

The queue for the ladies' loos was twelve-people deep. Millie stood anxiously in the line, bobbing out of the queue from time to time to check on the girls. They sat at the table, sullenly eating their cake, staring at their separate phones.

When she finally returned to the restaurant they were nowhere to be seen. She rushed back to the loos to check if they had gone in there, but peering underneath the cubicle doors produced nothing more than shocked stares from the other customers.

'I'm looking for two little girls – pink coats, about eight,' she explained apologetically.

A sharp knot of panic gripped her stomach as she scoured the restaurant. They were definitely not in there. She went outside. Children's entertainers roamed the area outside the restaurant, creating zoo animals out of balloons, juggling and performing magic tricks. They were surrounded by clutches of giggling children, wearing pink, blue and green coats, but Tabby and Lottie were not among them. In full panic mode now, Millie studied the map of the zoo outside the restaurant. Perhaps they had gone to the shop? They were the kind of children who would expect to be bought something on a trip to the zoo. But they were not in there either.

There was an information kiosk near the restaurant and she ran towards it. An American couple were making laborious enquiries about the penguin enclosure.

'I'm so sorry,' she blurted out, 'would you mind if I just pushed in front of you? I've lost two little girls and it's urgent.'

They stood back politely. 'Please, go ahead.'

'Is there a tannoy to put out an announcement?' she asked the girl behind the desk, who looked blankly at Millie.

'I've lost two children. I need to make an announcement,' explained Millie firmly.

'I'll have to check,' said the girl.

Millie waited anxiously at the desk, tapping her fingers on the kiosk's countertop, while the girl phoned her manager. Then, in the distance, she spotted them – two little girls in pink coats, giggling together and peering out from behind a tree near the butterfly house. She rushed over to them and grabbed them both by their coat hoods.

'Where have you been? I've been frantic. I thought I told you not to leave the restaurant.'

The girls smirked. 'We'll tell our daddy what you did, leaving us alone like that,' said Tabatha.

'You know as well as I do that I just went to the loo and all you had to do was stay at the table.'

'We were bored,' said Charlotte.

'Well, bad luck! We're not finished yet. You're coming with me while I go and get my coat and then we're going to look at the butterfly house.'

The butterfly exhibit was entered via a large inflatable caterpillar; it was warm and humid inside, and planted with a wide range of trees and plants to represent different ecosystems around the world. Fluttering high up in the steamy polytunnel, and landing on banana plants and palm trees, was a bewildering array of butterflies and moths. Within moments, a butterfly with almost translucent blue wings landed on Tabby's shoulder. She screamed, 'Get it off, get it off!' But a young zoo attendant wandered calmly over to her.

He gently guided the butterfly onto his hand. 'It won't hurt you,' he said. 'It's a beautiful Glasswing. Do you see it has see-through wings – that's how they got their name. He's interested in your pretty pink jacket, he thinks you're a flower.'

Tabby looked dubious.

'Can I have it?' asked Charlotte. He placed the butterfly on her outspread hand and she looked up at Millie with genuine delight. He caught another one; it fluttered its bright-green wings languorously as he transferred it to the back of his hand. He held it out for Tabby to study. 'This one is called a Bramble. Why do you think it's called that?'

'Because it's the colour of an apple?' asked Tabby nervously.

'That's right! Would you like to hold it?'

The butterfly stretched its green wings languorously.

Tabby put her hand out gingerly, and the zoo attendant nudged the butterfly onto the back of her hand. Millie knelt down next to her.

'Well done, Tabby, that's really brave.'

Tabby looked up at her and smiled.

'I held it,' she said delightedly.

The Bramble fluttered its wings and flew off into the steamy undergrowth.

Millie guided them towards a display of silkmoths.

'These are interesting. I've just come back from Italy and seen how silk is made. One cocoon can be unravelled and produces thirteen hundred metres of silk thread. Can you believe that?'

The girls stood in rapt attention as she explained the process.

When, finally, just before five o'clock, Millie suggested they go home, they both cried: 'Oh, don't let's go yet… there's so much more to see.'

'We'll come another time, OK? But we'd better get going. The zoo will be closing soon, and Daddy will be wondering what's happened to us all.'

'He won't notice if we're not there,' said Tabby, as they pushed through the turnstile onto Regent's Park Road.

'I'm sure that's not true,' said Millie, although she wasn't entirely convinced.

They arrived back at the flat just before six o'clock. Max was lying on the sofa, fast asleep. The girls squeezed together on a small armchair and took out their phones.

'Oh good, you're back,' said Max, pulling himself up from the sofa. 'Where did you get to? Have you had a nice time?'

'We went to the zoo,' said Charlotte.

'I held a butterfly,' interjected Tabby.

'Well done, Mills. Was it fun?' He leapt to his feet and, standing behind Millie, wrapped his arms around her, kissing her neck.

'We had a good time, didn't we, girls?' said Millie, extricating herself from Max. 'But we ought to get some supper going. What's it to be? Pasta? Takeaway?'

'Could we have Chinese, please?' asked Tabatha politely.

'Yes, Tabby, we could. Max can go and get it. I'm having a glass of wine and a well-deserved sit-down.'

Later that night, as Millie tucked the girls up in their makeshift beds, Charlotte said, 'I'm sorry we ran away, it wasn't fair of us.'

'Well, no harm done. I was just scared what might have happened to you.'

'It's been a nice day, today,' said Tabby.

'Yes, it has, Tabby. Sleep tight.'

Later that night, lying wide awake as Max slept peacefully beside her, Millie thought back over the day. It appeared she had won the girls over – a victory of sorts. Perhaps they were just in need of a little attention, something she feared they rarely got from their self-absorbed parents. She thought wistfully of the harmonious relationship she had developed with Bella. Would she ever feel so 'easy' with Tabby and Lottie? It was unlikely. Bella was, in some way, in search of a mother and Millie knew that in the short time they had known one another they had developed a close relationship – a bond almost. But the twins already had a mother; Millie could only ever be a temporary diversion. At best a one-day-a-week mother, at worst just a babysitter, a caretaker.

She checked her phone as she turned out the bedside light. There was an email from Lorenzo.

Dear Millie,

Thanks for your email. I'm sorry London seems disappointing now that you are back home. I do remember the dirt, and the crowds – you're right, although Caroline and I lived in a mansion block flat with large windows that let in the light – it helped to raise the spirits.

Thanks for sending the photos. The similarities in the backgrounds are indeed remarkable. I will ring or email Signor Bordignon and see if we can find out a little more. I'll let you know as soon as he gets back to me. Perhaps you might need to come out again… to do a little more research?

Take care of yourself. We miss you… Bella and I.

With love,
Lorenzo.

PS Bella asked me tonight if you will come back to read to her soon?

Chapter Thirty

Anastasia and the Benoît family were installed in Peter Leman's house in Steward Street. Peter was a master weaver of Huguenot descent, who had lived initially in Canterbury before finally moving to Spitalfields, the centre of the English silk industry. His eldest son, James Leman, had been apprenticed to his father for four years, and had already shown a prodigious talent for silk design.

Anastasia, Sébastien and James soon became good friends. With their backgrounds in the silk industry, and being of similar age, they had much in common. At eighteen, James was tall, good-looking and ambitious. He was delighted to have a young woman of Anastasia's intellect and beauty in the household, and could not deny that he was attracted to her. But he observed early in their friendship that he had a rival for her affections. He noted Sébastien's eyes following her around a room, how he blushed when she came down for dinner in the evening, how his hands trembled slightly as he handed her a cup of coffee at breakfast. Sébastien admitted as much one evening, as he and James sat alone in the dining room after dinner.

'I love her, James. That is the truth. I have loved her since the day we first met in a cafe on the Herengracht. But I do not know if she truly cares for me.'

'Have you asked her?' asked James logically.

'No, I dare not. There is something so distant about her, as if she is behind glass. I am unable to get close to her.'

'Like one of the butterflies she loves so much,' James said with a laugh. But, seeing that his new friend was downcast, he went on: 'Surely, Sébastien, it would be better to declare yourself. Discover if she loves you. If she does, all will be well. If not, it would be as well to know, surely?'

Anastasia was aware of Sébastien's feelings towards her. She suspected he had loved her since they had met in Amsterdam. But the truth was, she did not return his feelings. She cared for him, and she liked him, but she knew she could never love him. She had no wish to hurt him, and she was quite clear that the purpose of her visit to London was to learn as much as she could about the art of silk design, and nothing more. She enjoyed the company of her hosts, and James in particular was amusing and attractive, but she was determined not to be distracted by love.

Two or three days after the family had arrived in Steward Street, Anastasia asked Peter Leman if it would be possible to visit their mill and watch the weavers at work.

'I am keen to learn the process of silk design. My own family produce raw silk in Italy, and I would like to think that when I returned, I could turn my new skills to some use.'

To Sébastien's irritation, Peter suggested that James accompany Anastasia to the mill the following day. Sébastien wanted to go with them, but his father, Jean-Antoine, interjected.

'No, no, dear boy, I'd like you to come with me. I have appointments tomorrow with various silk merchants, and it's important that you meet them, too. I am considering opening a London office and you need to be with me when I make new connections.'

Sébastien watched enviously the following morning as James took Anastasia's arm to cross the road towards the mill. He noted how she laughed at a comment James made. She threw her head back, revealing her long white throat, her dark hair falling around her shoulders. As they reached the corner of the street, she looked back at the house. Sébastien was still standing in the window. She raised her hand and waved to him.

Once at the mill, Anastasia was relieved to find that the noise, and the activity of the weavers, brought back no bad memories of her time in Venice. She really did feel, for the first time in many, many months, free of all her old anxieties. James took time to speak to all the weavers; he discussed the technical difficulties of a particular cloth, and offered to adapt designs where necessary.

'You know a great deal about the weaving process, James,' said Anastasia admiringly, 'you are obviously more than a designer.'

'My father is a master weaver, as well as a pattern designer; he has taught me everything. I joined the business at fourteen and learned to weave – and my God, that's hard work, I can tell you. But I was drawn to design from the beginning. Since I was a child, I have been able to draw and paint.'

Anastasia admired a bolt of cloth hanging over a table in the workroom.

'This is beautiful; I love the gold and silver threads running through it. Even on a dull day like today, it gleams in the light. Did you design it?'

'I did. It's an order for someone in the Queen's household – they want it for a waistcoat.'

'And how do you manage, working alongside your father?'

'I am fortunate that while my father is an excellent weaver, he has never had quite the same passion for design as me. And so he is in charge of the weavers, and I the design. We have a good partnership.'

'I too have always loved to paint,' said Anastasia, fingering the silk designs pinned along the walls of the mill. 'My father did not approve, so I had to hide it from him. But now that he is gone, I feel liberated!'

That afternoon James took Anastasia into his small study in the attics of the house. The room was not quite as Anastasia had expected; she had thought it would be filled with bolts of cloth and paper and watercolours. But instead, the walls were lined with shelves filled with strange collections of reptiles, and insects preserved in alcohol; they reminded her of her time with Maria Sibylla.

'You are interested in studying animals in nature?' she asked as she wandered around his study, running her hand along the shelf.

'Oh yes, it's a preoccupation of mine. Obviously, most of my silk designs are based around flowers. I'm not sure that a lady would be so keen to have an exotic reptile on her bodice. But maybe one day…'

He laughed as he rummaged among the papers on his desk before bringing out a sheaf of designs that he laid out for Anastasia to study. The colours of his designs leapt off the page; with bright backgrounds, decorated with flowers and leaves, they were both orderly and energetic.

'These are wonderful,' she said. 'They are very similar to the botanical paintings by Maria Sibylla Merian. Do you know her work?'

'My father has shown me a copy of her flower book… what is it called?'

'*Neues Blumenbuch* – "The New Book of Flowers". You have much of the same clarity and accuracy; particularly this design here with the leaves. They remind me very much of several of her paintings.'

She held up a picture decorated with brilliant orange, scarlet and blue flowers, linked by pale green stems and leaves. 'How do you think of them? They are all so different. They are magical in some way – realistic, and yet not realistic.'

'The starting point is a real flower, or leaf, and then I let my imagination take over. But really, the business is more orderly than that. When a painter – like Maria Merian, for example – paints a flower, or butterfly, she simply paints what she sees. But I have to consider how a design will work on a tight bodice, or a man's waistcoat. How it will fold itself around the body. And in order for the weaver to follow my design I have to conform to a process, of course. Here, I'll show you.'

He brought out a set of black and white designs drawn on graph paper.

'The initial design must be very accurate, so the weavers can follow it exactly. Once the design is finalised, I paint them with watercolour to indicate the colours I want. These bright oranges and yellows here – they will be highlighted with gold thread, so they gleam, come alive almost, in the candlelight. Like that fabric at the mill that you admired earlier.'

'Where do you get your inspiration?' asked Anastasia.

'I am influenced by many things – textiles from the Far East, decorative objects that have been brought to Europe from the East Indies, China and India. When my father left France many years ago, this style was just beginning. As I said before, it's not just about making an accurate representation of a flower or plant. We distort it in some way – stretch it perhaps to enhance the design, to flatter the body wearing it. And I am keen to explore what we could do with other design elements. My friend, the silk designer Christopher Baudouin, has recently created a wonderful design that uses architectural motifs. My father is not so keen, but I like it.'

He pulled out a black and white pattern incorporating an arch and a pergola mixed with exotic flowers.

'This is stunning,' said Anastasia. 'And you think this will be popular?'

'Yes, absolutely. I've already had an order for it.'

'What garment would you use such a fabric for?' asked Anastasia.

'Well, the order was for a man's waistcoat – men love this sort of design. But it would also work well with women's gowns. It's ideal for a mantua because there are so few seams to break the design's flow.'

'Will you teach me how to design? I can paint – Maria Merian taught me so much – but I have no idea how to translate it.'

'Of course! I have a meeting tomorrow with Joseph Dandridge. He is a freelance silk designer my father has brought in to join us. Come with me?'

Joseph Dandridge had recently moved to a village outside London called Stoke Newington. As the carriage drove north through the parishes of Islington and Hackney, Anastasia noted the large elegant houses, newly built, that stood incongruously between old half-timbered cottages.

'More and more people are moving up here from London,' said James. 'There is a large Quaker community. But many people – even those working regularly in London, like merchants and lawyers – have chosen to move here, where they can be closer to the countryside, and keep horses and so on.'

The carriage turned off Church Street and left the village behind. They drove down Green Lanes and crossed a small bridge over a river before swinging round onto a farm track that led to a small cottage surrounded by fields. Joseph Dandridge came out to meet them. He was older than James – in his early forties, Anastasia thought. He had dark brown hair, silvering at the sides, and neat spectacles perched on the end of his nose.

'Welcome, friends – come in, come in. There's a fire in the sitting room.'

The house was old, low-beamed, with small rooms that led off a central hall and staircase.

'Come into my study first, then you can meet my wife Martha, and the children.'

Joseph had a small study at the rear of the house overlooking fields. He was obviously a keen entomologist – the walls of the study were lined with glass cases filled with insects and butterflies.

'I feel as if I am back in Maria Sibylla's showroom,' Anastasia said as she wandered between the displays.

'Madam Merian – have you met her?' asked Joseph, admiringly.

'I have… I studied with her in Amsterdam for three months. She taught me a great deal. Not just how to paint, but how to observe. I too love butterflies and moths. The first insect I painted was a silkmoth. My family own a silk farm in Italy, so it was the first insect I became familiar with.'

Over the following few weeks Joseph took Anastasia under his wing and she travelled to Stoke Newington two or three times a week. She grew fond of his wife Martha and their three children – James, Elizabeth and Mary – who were almost her age. She would work with Joseph in the mornings and, after lunch, would walk in the woods and fields around the cottage with Mary or Elizabeth.

James also introduced her to Christopher Baudouin, and they often worked together at James's house. Between them, the three designers taught Anastasia how to translate her designs to graph paper. They encouraged her to experiment with bold colours, how to 'invent' flowers.

'Observation is, of course, vital,' said Joseph one day, as she sat with him in his study, attempting a design. 'But this is fabric, not a formal study of a flower or plant. Let your imagination get to work. You are allowed to invent, to create – that's what design is. Maria Sibylla taught you how to observe accurately. Now you need to hone that skill and take flight – like a butterfly.'

They taught her how to use metallic threads to make the fabrics 'live'.

'Use a *pail red* here,' advised Christopher. 'It's a metallic pale gold and will create a delicate glowing yellow on that petal there. And here, I think you need frost gold – it's a brilliant metallic orange shade. And on the blue of this petal, use frost silver; it will emphasise the delicacy of the blue. Once you have completed your design, write the instructions for the threads on the back. Then the weaver will know what to set up on the loom.'

Eventually, Anastasia had a silk design that she was happy with and one evening she came shyly into the drawing room, where James and his father Peter were drinking Madeira in front of the fire.

'I've finished my design,' she said, holding the paper behind her back. 'Can I show you?'

'Of course,' said Peter.

She laid it out on the small card table. The curtains were closed against the dark January evening. Rain hammered against the windows and the fire hissed in the grate. Anastasia stood awkwardly in front of the fire, waiting for their verdict on her first completed design.

'I like it very much,' said James. 'It has great energy. What do you think, Father?'

'It's good – it's very good,' said Peter as he poured Anastasia a glass of Madeira.

'Congratulations!' said James, 'here's to your first fabric,' and he clinked his glass against hers.

'I'll set up the loom first thing tomorrow,' said Peter.

'The loom?' Anastasia was confused. 'Why do we need the loom?'

'To weave it, of course,' said Peter, refilling his glass. 'We are always keen to acquire new designs and this is perfect for a woman's gown. It will take several weeks to set up the loom – and that costs money, of course. So I can assure you I wouldn't do it unless I could sell it.'

That evening over dinner, James and Peter toasted Anastasia's success. She in turn thanked them for their help and support.

'I could never have done it without you, James – or your friends, Christopher and Joseph. They have been so generous with their knowledge and their time. And Peter – thanks to you too. I am so grateful that you believe in the fabric sufficiently to make it a reality.'

Sébastien looked on a little enviously. Since they had arrived in London, he had spent less and less time with Anastasia. His father Jean-Antoine was preoccupied with developing good relationships with customers in London and took him with him wherever he went. He had discussed only that day the prospect of Sébastien remaining in London to manage the business.

'I know that music is something you live for, Sébastien. But it is hard to make your way as a musician without a patron. Work for me, boy. Help me here in London. Together we could build a fine business between Amsterdam and London. Look at young James, he has so much talent, so much energy – you could learn a lot from him.'

'Papa, I will do what you wish of me, of course. But I fear I can never rival James. He is an unusual, remarkable man.'

'Perhaps you… and Anastasia might remain here together?' suggested his father, as they travelled towards St James's in a carriage.

'Anastasia? I don't know what you mean.'

'Come on, boy, don't think we have not noticed how you follow her around. I am right, am I not? That you love her?'

Sébastien blushed.

'I don't blame you,' his father continued. 'She is a beautiful girl and a fine one. Hard-working, intelligent… A little high-spirited and perhaps too independent, but—'

'She is all of those things, and more. But I fear she does not return my love.'

'Perhaps if you offer her a place here in London, where she seems so content, she might change her mind?'

It was true that Anastasia was content in London. Here she had finally found her niche. She was happy and fulfilled. She had told them nothing of her previous life in Venice, they knew nothing of her marriage or divorce; it was as if these experiences had never taken place. Her entire being was now centred on her desire to school herself to become a skilled silk designer.

The day Anastasia's silk design emerged from the loom it was as if her dreams had finally become a reality. The silken fabric was decorated with a rich mix of scarlet lilies, blue daisies and surreal poppies; she had incorporated a chinoiserie motif into the design too, copied from a piece of blue and white Chinese porcelain in the Lemans' drawing room. The flowers branched out from a long snaking green stem – an impossibility in nature, but quite permissible, she now understood, in silk design. And on the edge of a leaf, repeated at intervals in the design, was a brilliant turquoise butterfly.

It would be several weeks before the finished length was complete, but James insisted they should celebrate such a significant day.

'Let's go to the theatre after dinner,' he suggested when they arrived home. Sébastien was sitting alone in the drawing room.

'You'll come, won't you, Sébastien – to celebrate Ana's first length of silk?'

'Of course. Perhaps something with some music,' Sébastien suggested.

'There's a performance of *Il Trionfo di Camilla* at the Queen's Theatre on Haymarket,' suggested James's mother. 'It's a beautiful theatre, Anastasia – you ought to see it while you're in London. It was designed only last year by Sir John Vanbrugh.'

'I'd love to,' said Anastasia.

As the three young people settled down in the box at the Queen's Theatre, James poured each of them a glass of champagne. Anastasia read the short description of the opera in the programme.

'It was written by the Italian composer Giovanni Bononcini. Have you seen any of his work, Sébastien?'

'Once or twice,' said Sébastien.

'Do you know the story?'

'It tells of Apollo's unrequited love for Daphne.'

He looked pointedly at James, who smiled sympathetically and sipped his wine.

'Oh, that sounds sad,' said Anastasia.

'Eros, the god of love,' continued Sébastien, 'shoots Apollo with a gold arrow, which causes him to fall hopelessly in love with Daphne, the wood nymph. But Daphne doesn't want love. She prefers to roam the forest and remain a virgin for ever.'

James laughed, and snorted into his champagne glass as the theatre grew dark and the opera began.

In the final act Anastasia leaned forward in her seat as Daphne begged her father, Peneus, to protect her from Apollo.

> 'Help me, Peneus!' she sang. 'Open the earth to enclose me, or change my form, which has brought me into this danger! Let me be free of this man from this moment forward.'

As the group travelled back to Spitalfields in the carriage that night, Anastasia was in reflective mood.

'Sébastien, I don't quite understand what happened at the end of the opera.'

'Daphne begs her father for help.'

'Yes, but what happens to her?'

'He turned her into a tree.'

'Oh… so she was no longer human?'

'No.'

'And what of poor Apollo?'

'He continued to love her, for ever. He used his powers to turn her evergreen, so she would never lose her leaves.'

'He must have loved her very much,' said Anastasia.

'I think so… he never left her side.'

'But while I am sad for Apollo, I am sympathetic to the nymph, and her desire to remain free.'

She watched Sébastien's face carefully.

'But did Apollo not deserve her love?' he retorted.

'She wanted nothing more than to pursue her own dreams, to live in the forest, and love was never part of that. His love for her was touching, but she was not responsible for it.'

James Leman shifted uneasily in his seat. The undercurrent of the conversation made him feel awkward.

'So when are we going to hear your first opera, Sébastien?' he asked cheerfully. 'We know you have a musical talent – isn't it time you exposed it to the world?'

'I don't know,' Sébastien said gloomily. 'My father expects me to work with him in his business. He doesn't believe I can survive as a musician.'

'I'm sorry,' said Anastasia sympathetically, taking his hand.

The street lamps flickered in the darkness as the three climbed out of the carriage and up the stone stairs to the front door of the house on Steward Street. Inside, the footman took their coats and hats and James suggested they go up to the drawing room on the first floor for a final drink.

'You both go,' said Anastasia, 'I'm tired, I'm going up to bed. Thank you both for a wonderful evening.'

As Veronica helped to unlace her gown, Anastasia took her into her confidence.

'I am at a loss, Veronica, and I need advice. I fear that dear Sébastien has developed feelings for me.'

'It's been obvious for a long while,' said Veronica as she laid Anastasia's bodice on the bed.

'Has it? I suppose it has, since we were in Amsterdam together. I have tried to love him. He is charming, and kind, and sweet.'

'And handsome,' said Veronica.

'And handsome. But I do not love him. Do you know what I thought as I watched the opera this evening?'

'No, *signora*.'

'If I were the nymph who was turned into a tree because she is so frightened of love, then my Apollo is not Sébastien – dear kind Sébastien – but Marco. He is the man who deserves my love... I think the time has come for us to finally return to Italy.'

Part Three

Regeneration

'If you give people light, they will find their own way.'

Dante Alighieri

Chapter Thirty-One

For all her determination to return home, Anastasia was sad to say goodbye to the Leman and Benoît families. They hosted a farewell dinner the evening before her departure. Jean-Antoine Benoît gave a brief speech in which he thanked Anastasia for her delightful company and wished her well.

'I feel sure that you have a great career ahead of you. I have rarely seen someone, and a woman in particular, take so naturally to the art of silk design.'

'You are too kind,' she said in return. 'And I would like to thank you all so much for your hospitality. You have all been so good to me.'

'Don't leave yet,' called out James cheerfully. 'You still have so much to learn, Anastasia, and I have so much I can teach you. Besides, you are very talented; that silk you designed has been very popular. Stay here and work for me. Together we will make a fortune.'

Anastasia laughed. 'You are very kind, James, but I don't want to work for someone else – even someone as talented and entertaining as you. I have my own business back in Italy, remember, and my duty lies there. But I will always be grateful to you – and Joseph and Christopher – for teaching me so much.'

'It was easy,' said Joseph, 'you were the perfect pupil.'

*

James and Joseph may have been sad to see her go, but none felt it so keenly as Sébastien. She took him aside after dinner and spoke to him alone in the Lemans' elegant drawing room.

'Dear Sébastien – I will miss you. You have been such a good friend to me since we met in Amsterdam, all those months ago. In many ways, I feel as if I have known you all my life.'

'Don't go,' he said. 'Stay here with me. Marry me.'

'Oh, Sébastien, if only life were that simple. I can't marry you.'

'Why not? I adore you. I love you. And I think you like me, don't you?'

'I am very fond of you, really. But there is something I must tell you. Something I have kept from you since we met. Out of shame, I suppose... or embarrassment.'

He looked perplexed. 'What could you possibly have to be ashamed about?'

'Sit down – it's quite a long story. When I was eighteen, my father, the silk farmer, lost me in a card game.'

Sébastien sank onto the blue damask chair.

'Lost you? I don't understand.'

'No... how could you? Your father and mother love you and would never do anything to hurt you. But my father was a cruel, vindictive man. He beat my mother and me, and my sister. Our childhood was dominated by fear mixed with occasional moments of happiness when he was away. Well, as I said, he lost me in a game of cards – to a silk weaver in Venice. I was the stake. I was forced to marry this man against my will. He was much older than me, and while not physically violent, he was cruel. He knew I was a not a willing participant in the marriage and so he kept me imprisoned and... used me as his wife.'

'What a beast!' said Sébastien. 'You poor girl, how terrible it must have been for you.'

'I escaped eventually, with the help of Veronica, and divorced him. I left Italy soon afterwards. I needed to get away – to recover. That's why I came to Amsterdam.'

'I understand. But I don't care that you have been married, or divorced.'

'But your father might care, Sébastien. He wants you to manage an important part of his business here. He needs you to put down roots. You should marry some good French or English girl, with no past. Someone he could be proud of, who wants children and who would support you.'

'But I love *you*,' said Sébastien desperately.

'I know. And I am sorry for it. But there is more to my story. Before I was married, I was engaged to another man – Vicenzo's son, Marco. He loved me very much and I loved him. I ran away to marry him, but my father found us and took me to Venice. Instead of marrying Marco – a man I loved – I was forced to marry an old man, who I hated. And so, I am leaving London now for two reasons. Firstly, I have learned so much and I must go back and help my mother run the business and make use of all the skills I have acquired. But, just as importantly, I must go back to find out if Marco still loves me. I have been away too long.'

Sébastien put his head in his hands. Anastasia crouched down next to him.

'So you see, dear Sébastien, I cannot marry you. I do not love you as I should. Manage your father's business here, visit the opera house whenever you can, and write your music. And one day, come to see me in Verona and play for me there.'

When Anastasia set off in a carriage heading for Dover the following day, Sébastien hung back from the rest of the group standing on the steps of the house. She leaned out of the carriage window and called out to them all.

'Goodbye! I will never forget you all.'

'Send us your designs,' shouted James, 'I'll sell them for you.'

'I will.'

'Safe journey,' called out Joseph.

As the carriage got to the corner of Steward Street, Anastasia could see that Sébastien had already gone inside.

'I feel so sad about Sébastien,' she said to Veronica as the carriage headed out of London towards the Dover Road. 'I never intended to hurt him.'

'You cannot be responsible for someone else's heartache,' said Veronica wisely.

Anastasia was determined to travel back to Italy as quickly as possible. She was anxious to see Marco, and tell him that she still loved him. She had written him a letter before she left, begging him to wait for her return. But her fear was that he would already have abandoned her and married Marietta.

There were to be no lengthy stopovers in Amsterdam, Brussels or Lyon. In Dover they stayed once again at the White Horse Inn before crossing the Channel to Calais. From there they journeyed south through France, stopping each night in small village inns. The days were long and tedious and they arrived at their destination each evening stiff, tired and hungry. To pass the interminable hours of coach travel, Anastasia drew and sketched, or read, sometimes out loud to Veronica. They talked of their respective childhoods, of their hopes and dreams for the future. But most of all, Anastasia shared her fears about Marco.

'What if I am too late, Veronica? I have been away so long. What if he has abandoned me and married Marietta? I could not blame him if he had, but I will find it very hard to bear.'

As her carriage finally swept through the archway into the courtyard of Villa di Bozzolo, Anastasia experienced a surge of excitement mixed with relief. Hearing the carriage, Giuseppe opened the great oak door.

'*Signora!*' he called out, 'you are back. Welcome home.'

As he unloaded their luggage, Anastasia stood in the courtyard. She held her face up to the midday sun and breathed deeply. She felt disoriented, dazed almost, to be back at the villa again.

'Where is my mother?'

'She has gone out to visit the farms, *signora*. She should be back in a little while.'

'And my sister?'

'She is not here, *signora*.'

Anastasia stretched her tired limbs. The sun was warm on her back as she walked across the dusty courtyard towards the stables. She smelt the familiar scent of freshly mown hay and straw. She called out 'Minou!' and as she got closer, she heard a familiar sound – Minou's hooves clattering on the cobbles as he manoeuvred himself towards the stable door, over which he hung his noble grey head.

'Oh Minou, Minou,' she said stroking his long nose. He exhaled happily from his pink nostrils.

She put her arms around his neck and kissed the side of his head, breathing in the familiar scent, feeling his soft grey fur beneath her lips. She opened his stable door and pushed him gently to one side.

'Good boy, good boy. I just want to look at you.'

She stroked his back, and patted his flank. She picked up his hooves one by one, inspecting them for stones, stroking his fetlocks as she put each leg carefully back down. She ran her hands down his spine, checking to see if he had any sores, or pain anywhere.

'You've been well looked after,' she said, kissing his neck.

Mario the stable boy appeared.

'*Signora*, how wonderful – you are back!'

'Yes – at last. Thank you for caring for Minou so well. He looks good.'

'He is a good boy,' said Mario. 'I ride him most days. It is always a pleasure. But he will be glad to see you back.'

Anastasia leaned against the side of the stable, one hand on her beloved horse, and looked towards the villa. The memory of her father on the day she had tried to escape, standing on the steps, looking straight at the stables, was pin-sharp. But the fear she had felt then, as she cowered in the corner of the stable, was gone. Now there was just the warmth of the sun, the gentle breathing of her horse and the chatter of the servants as they unloaded the luggage. She patted Minou's side once again, and whispered in his ear, 'I will be back soon. We will go for a ride.' She kissed him on the side of his head and closed the stable door behind her. He shook his head at her and pawed the ground. 'Not now – but soon,' she promised him.

Standing in the hall of the villa, she looked at the frescoes on the walls and gazed through the glass doors leading down to the gardens, the vineyards and the river beyond. She heard the clanking of the range in the basement kitchens and Giuseppe giving orders for her luggage to be taken upstairs. As she removed her gloves, she was aware of the sound of tiny claws pattering across the marble floor. She turned and saw Bianca, her little dog, trotting towards her. She swept her up and held her to her chest.

'Oh Bianca… *Cara* Bianca. You are here!'

She kissed the dog's head and stroked her. She carried her into the drawing room, which was deserted. The farm's ledgers stood on the desk and she cast an eye over them. Her mother's usually careful handwriting had changed. The letters and figures were imprecise, as if her hand had been shaking when she wrote them. Anastasia went into the dining room, where the maid Julia was setting the table for dinner.

'Ah Julia, how are you?'

'Oh *signora*, you are back! I am well, thank you.'

Anastasia noted the table set for one.

'Is my mother dining alone this evening?'

'I believe so, *signora*.'

'Well, please lay it for the two of us. Thank you.'

She climbed the marble stairs and along the corridor to the bedroom she had shared with Marietta. She could see no trace of her sister. Her clothes had been removed; the box where she kept her jewels and letters was gone.

'My sister, Marietta, is she not here?' she asked Veronica.

'It seems not, *signora*.'

She wandered down the corridor to her mother's room. A cloak lay discarded on the bed. She would not have needed it on such a warm day, thought Anastasia. Her riding crop stood against the wall. She must have taken the carriage to visit the farms that day. In the corner of the room was an easel on which stood the self-portrait Anastasia had left for her mother. She studied the picture and then looked at her own reflection in the mirror on her mother's dressing table. She had changed: she was no longer that fearful girl, with a tear-stained face and a torn dress.

Tired and anxious, she went back downstairs, carrying Bianca in her arms.

'Giuseppe, could I have some coffee in the garden, please?'

'Yes, of course, *signora*.'

She sat on the curved wooden bench overlooking the gardens. Bianca sat down happily next to her and Anastasia, her hand resting on the dog's side, fell into a deep sleep.

When she woke, the sun had slipped behind the trees and all that was left was a shimmering red glow on the horizon. The pot of coffee was stone cold. Her neck was stiff and Bianca was no longer at her side. She stretched and stood up, then wandered back into the house. The candles had been lit in the sconces in the hall. The light flickered against the walls, casting shadows on the frescoes.

There was a familiar scent coming from the kitchens. What was it? Pigeon, or poussin maybe. Her stomach rumbled. She had not eaten since the early morning. There was a light coming from the small salon off the hall.

She pushed open the door; the candles flickered. Polonia looked up from her book.

'Mamma!' Anastasia ran to her.

'Oh Ana, Ana, you are home. I couldn't believe it when Giuseppe told me. I returned from visiting the farms an hour or two ago, but you were fast asleep. I so wanted to wake you and talk to you, but Veronica said you had had a long journey, so I left you. Come and sit by me, darling. How are you?'

'I am very well. Tired, but well. And you, Mamma – how are you?'

'I am tired too. But glad to see you.'

'You look pale, Mamma; are you really well?'

'I have a pain, my darling – here.' She pointed to her stomach. 'But now that you have returned, I'm sure it will get better.'

Anastasia sat at her mother's feet and laid her head in her lap.

'You must get better, Mamma – please promise me.'

'I promise.'

'Tell me, Mamma – what news of Marco and Marietta?'

Polonia held her daughter's hands in hers. She felt her tremble, the sweat gathering on her palms.

'Marietta is married.'

Anastasia let go of her mother's hand and fell to the floor. She began to weep. 'I have been so foolish, so foolish.'

'What do you mean? What is the matter?'

'I am too late… She has married Marco, and I am too late.'

'Oh darling, no, not Marco! She has married a young man from Verona – Amando del Corso. His family are farmers near here. It's all been rather sudden. He is a good man and I believe he cares for Marietta. They have been married for just a month. It was a struggle to find the dowry, but I managed it.'

'And… Marco?'

'As far as I know he is at Villa Limonaia with Vicenzo.' Polonia stroked her daughter's dark hair and smiled. 'Come, my darling – let us go and eat and celebrate a little. You are home now.'

'And I will not leave again, Mamma. You can be sure of that.'

Chapter Thirty-Two

Fournier Street, Spitalfields
July 2017

Max left Fournier Street early for a breakfast meeting. The previous evening, he and Millie had discussed the possibility of moving to a large flat he had seen that day in Holland Park.

'It would be ideal, darling. It's not the mews we had talked about, but it's a fabulous place. Plenty of room for the girls, access to a communal garden, and only a few minutes' walk from the house I'm buying for Katje.'

It sounded perfect, Millie had to admit. She should have been excited. Just a few months earlier, it would have been everything she had hoped for. But now the prospect of moving in permanently with Max filled her with dismay. What had changed? Somehow, the reality of living with her lover was so different to the fantasies she had nurtured over the years. He was fun to be with, certainly, and loud and exciting; but he was also impatient, intolerant, demanding and imperious. In fact, he behaved at home exactly as he did in the office. It shouldn't really have come as a surprise. She thought back to the scene in the coffee shop she had witnessed between him and Katje the day they came in to buy a cake. She remembered how Katje had snapped at him. She had been imperious too. Perhaps, Millie reflected, in spite of Max's protestations to the contrary, Katje was exactly the kind of woman he needed. Millie had always thought of herself as strong-minded and brave, tough even. But somehow, when she was with Max she put all her energy into trying to please him, pandering to him. And if she was honest, it had become exhausting.

She had introduced him to her friends; they had gone out for simple dinners, or met in pubs dotted around the capital. But he seemed out of place in their company, in their choice of venue. He was not comfortable with a hipster bar in Shoreditch or Hackney. His patch was Kensington and Chelsea. It was not just that he was older than her contemporaries, his world experience was different to theirs. He had been successful, and rich, and well connected for so long that he had apparently forgotten how to communicate with those less fortunate than himself. People who were just starting out, just about managing to afford a tiny flat, or a crumbling house miles out of town, were a mystery to him. Millie found herself increasingly uncomfortable when she tried to bring these two sides of her life together and gradually she started to avoid such confrontations – making excuses for why they couldn't make someone's birthday, or meet an old friend for coffee. Max's wealth, his certainty about life – all of which had initially been so appealing, intoxicating even – now felt restrictive.

At home he was equally intolerant. He'd had nannies and housekeepers for so long that he struggled in Millie's tiny flat with what he considered to be her inadequate culinary and ironing skills. But most importantly, she realised – to her huge disappointment – that she simply did not consider him her best friend any more. The relationship was too one-sided. He seemed uninterested in her emotional wellbeing. Rather, he expected her to be cheerful, well turned out and capable. He required that she entertain and amuse him. If she demonstrated any weakness, or vulnerability, he became impatient. If they disagreed about what to watch on television, or cook for supper, he sulked, pacing the flat like a caged animal. When she suggested introducing him to her family – something she had yearned to do for years – he looked pained. His own parents were dead; he had no siblings. As far as he was concerned, he had no need for an extra family. So, in spite of him telling her that he loved her, that she was the woman he should have married all along, she had begun to realise that in fact he and Katje were probably perfectly matched. Both were selfish, demanding and wilful. And she feared that if she stayed with him she would be consumed by him – overwhelmed by his strength and certainty that he was always right.

Looking at the details of the large Holland Park flat that he had left on the kitchen worktop, she tried to imagine herself living there. The vast kitchen leading to a high-ceilinged sitting room filled with trendy furniture. The two bedrooms – both en suite – a dressing room with fitted cupboards; a place for everything. It was stunning. And yet… she realised with total certainty that she could never be happy there.

She moved the flat details to one side and made herself a cup of green tea. With Max gone for the day, the flat was quiet and peaceful. She sat down at the small kitchen table and scanned her phone for emails. There had been no word from Lorenzo for days. He had promised to get in touch with Signor Bordignon, but she had not heard back from him. She had deliberately refrained from emailing or calling him, anxious to give her relationship with Max a chance and to give Lorenzo a chance to get over her. But now, alone at last in the flat, she realised that she wanted nothing more than to speak to Lorenzo. She looked at her watch: it was ten minutes past eight. He would be back in the barn, having dropped Bella at school.

She dialled his number.

'Pronto.'

'Lorenzo… it's me – Millie.'

'Millie!' He sounded genuinely delighted to hear from her. 'Oh Millie, I'm so pleased you rang. I've been thinking of you.'

'And I of you, Lorenzo. Do you have time to talk?'

'Of course. Bella isn't going to school today – she has a cold.'

'Oh, I'm sorry. Give her a hug from me.'

'I will. So what do you have to tell me?'

'Not a lot, really. Max has moved in here with me. That's about it.'

'I see. And how's it going?'

'Well… OK. Although somehow, living with him is not quite what I'd thought it would be.'

'Go on.'

'He wants us to buy somewhere together – a larger flat in Holland Park.'

'I know it. It's lovely there – expensive.'

'Yes. Oh yes, massively expensive.'

'So that's all good…'

Millie began to cry.

Lorenzo listened helplessly at the other end of the phone. After a few minutes he interjected.

'Millie – Millie…' he said softly, 'what's the matter?'

'I can't move in with him. I just don't think I love him enough. I should feel excited at the idea of living in a beautiful flat with him, seeing his daughters once a week. It's everything I had hoped for a few months ago. But now it's the last thing in the world I want to do. I'd rather be alone than live with him.'

'Why, what's happened?'

'Nothing specific. It's just that he's not the man I thought he was. Or perhaps he is exactly what he's always been, but I just didn't see it before. We don't have the sort of relationship that I really want. Seeing someone once a week is just not the same as living with them.'

'So, what are you going to do?'

'I'm going to tell him, when he gets back this evening, that I think he needs to move out, to get his life sorted with the girls and his ex-wife.'

'Are you leaving him?'

'I suppose I am. I can hardly believe I'm saying it. But somehow, now I'm faced with the prospect of living with him properly – for ever – I just don't think he and I can go on together.'

Lorenzo was silent.

'Say something?' she asked.

'I don't know what to say…'

'I might regret asking this, but before I left Italy, you told me that you were beginning to fall in love with me. Do you still feel that way?'

There was silence.

'Lorenzo?'

'Yes… I do still feel the same way. But Millie – don't give up everything for me. We hardly know each other. And I have a child; I am responsible for Bella. She was very fond of you – don't break her heart along with mine.'

'I know… I'm very aware of that. I want to suggest something. I didn't know I was going to say this when I rang you this morning – I just wanted to hear your voice – but how would you feel if I came out to see you this weekend? I really want to see you and Bella. And, as it happens, I also need to do some research on the woman in the picture. I think it would add the necessary bit of mystery to the end of the article I'm writing. But more importantly, it would give us a chance to spend some time together.'

'I would love it, if you're sure. But how would Max feel about it?'

'It's none of his business really, is it? I'm going to end it with him. It won't be easy after all this time, but I'm certain it's the right thing to do.'

'If you're sure?'

'I am. I'll email Signor Bordignon and try to arrange a meeting with him early next week, if he's around. Would you have time to come with me?'

'Of course.'

'And I'll talk to Max tonight, and book a flight.'

'Let me know what time, and I'll pick you up from the airport.'

Millie was on the first plane from London to Verona on Saturday morning. Lorenzo was waiting for her at the barrier.

'I can't believe I'm here,' she said, throwing her arms around his neck.

'Neither can I. Come on, let's get you home.'

As they drove under the archway into the courtyard at Villa di Bozzolo, it really did feel like coming home. White doves were lined up in pairs on the barn roof, as if they were waiting for her to arrive. As Lorenzo unloaded her bag from the Fiat she stood for a moment, spellbound, listening to the billing and cooing. He started to walk towards the barn.

'Oh…I'm not staying in the villa, then?' she asked.

'No, it's full of guests, I'm afraid.'

'That's good, isn't it?'

'Yes, but Elena is in a bad mood – lots of cooking and so on. Come on, you're staying with me.'

Elena's son Angelo was playing with Bella when they walked into the barn. The living room floor was covered with her dolls and teddies, arranged around a toy tea party.

'Millie!' shouted Bella as she rushed across the room and threw herself into Millie's arms. 'You came back.'

'I did, darling. How could I keep away?'

'You must be hungry,' said Lorenzo.

'I am rather – I left the flat at five o'clock this morning.'

Together they prepared a simple lunch of pasta and salad. Millie was reminded briefly of the last meal she had made with Max; they had argued, throughout, about the best way to prepare a paella. As she sat at the table with Lorenzo, Angelo and Bella, she raised her glass to them all.

'Here's to you all – it's lovely to be back here again.'

That afternoon Millie and Lorenzo went for a long walk around the estate. In the afternoon sunshine, they lay down among the wild flowers that had been left to grow in the mulberry orchards. Protected by a low hedge from the rest of the estate, they felt cut off from the world. They kissed and made love, a light breeze brushing against their naked skin. Afterwards they wandered, hand in hand, back to the barn.

'Let's have a swim,' Lorenzo suggested. 'The pool is almost empty – the guests are all out for the day.'

They took Bella to the pool and as she jumped happily into the water, Millie lay on a sunbed, watching as Lorenzo played with his daughter. She felt relaxed for the first time in weeks, she realised.

As the sun went down behind the vineyards, they gathered up their towels and went back to the barn. Millie took a shower and unpacked her clothes. It felt strange to place her underwear, her T-shirts in Lorenzo's chest of drawers – and yet, he had cleared a drawer specially for her.

'I know you'll need more space, but hopefully it will do for now,' he said, kissing her.

As the heat of the day began to fade, they sat together on the terrace, drinking cool white wine.

'So tell me – how is business going?' asked Millie.

'It's going well, actually. We had a good crop of mulberry leaves and produced a big harvest of silk this year. Our jewellery friend is very happy with the quality. The initiative really seems to be working. He's hoping to get another five or ten farms involved by next year.'

'So the regeneration has been a success?'

'Yes, very much so. It's small but it has great potential. We think we ought to expand our production next year. I'm going to plant more mulberry orchards. We have a field that's doing nothing at the moment.'

'And the vineyard?'

'Well, the part nearest the house looks like it's going to be a great crop. And we lease some other land, on the other side of the valley, and that's looking good too.'

'I emailed Signor Bordignon, by the way – about the portrait – and I've arranged to visit him on Monday. I hope that works for you?'

'Of course. If Elena's busy, I'm sure Angelo can help with Bella. We've just taken on some extra help with the silk farm, which has given us all a bit more time.'

'Did you have any further thoughts about the portrait? Any clues here in the house, about her identity?'

'I've made a start on that. I went up to the attics a day or so ago, and I found a huge trunk filled with old papers. Deeds of title for small farms that we don't own any more – that sort of thing. Most of them were from the last century when the villa was going through a massive upheaval during the World Wars. This region was a major battlefront and we lost a lot of land then; either it was bombed, or we couldn't afford the upkeep. My grandfather just about managed to hang on to the house back in the 1950s – which, as you know, was when the mulberry crops went wrong and we Italians wrecked our own silk business. But it's hard to find much information about the previous centuries. I dragged the whole box down to the barn, much to Elena's irritation. We could go through it, if you like?'

'The crucial thing to understand is why the woman in the portrait was in Venice,' said Millie. 'And if she lived there, why is her portrait here in your house? Did you ever have property there?'

'I don't know. But let's go and plough through the old papers, and see if we can find out – if you really want to?'

'I'd love to. A glass of wine and a pile of old papers, and I'll be a happy woman.'

'One thing we haven't discussed…'

'What's that?'

'Max. How did he take it – you leaving him?'

'Do you really want to know?'

'Yes, of course.'

'It wasn't easy. He appeared to be completely surprised. I thought he would have picked up on my negativity but he hadn't. He didn't make a scene, though. One thing you can say for Max – he's very cool about that sort of thing. He tried to persuade me but finally he gave up, and moved out the next day; he went to stay with his friend Hugo. He wasn't surprised that I was coming out here to see you.'

'You told him about us?'

'No, not in so many words. I just said I was going back to the villa to do some research. And he said, "To see the handsome Italian."'

'And what did you say?'

'I just said, "Yes… to see the handsome Italian."'

She leaned forward and kissed him.

Chapter Thirty-Three

Villa Limonaia
June 1706

The day after Anastasia's return to Villa di Bozzolo, she and her mother drove over to Villa Limonaia in the carriage. Anastasia would have preferred to make her own way and give Minou some exercise, but Polonia seemed a little unwell, and was not up to riding her own horse such a distance, so the carriage was ordered.

Over lunch Vicenzo and Anastasia regaled Marco and Polonia with stories of their journey – the perilous Moncenisio Pass, their time in France and Amsterdam. Vicenzo was tempted to ask Anastasia about her stay in London too, but was sensitive to Marco's desire to be left alone with her after so long a separation.

'Come, Polonia,' he urged, 'let's go and sit overlooking the lake, and later, perhaps, Anastasia will tell us more of her adventures.'

'Shall we walk in the gardens?' Marco suggested. Dappled sunlight filtered through the trees as they roamed through the woods. Anastasia slipped her arm through his as they stood for a long time gazing out at the lake.

'I've missed this view,' she said. 'London was so busy and dirty. It was exciting though. I'll tell you about it later. But sometimes at night, I fell asleep just imagining myself here, on this spot, looking at the fishing boats, the sun on the water, the geese flying low, skimming the surface, hunting for fish.'

'So you came back for the view and not for me?' Marco squeezed her hand and smiled.

'You know that's not true.' She turned to face him and he leaned down and kissed her. She put her arms around his neck and pulled him towards her, bending her body into his.

'I still cannot really believe you came back,' he whispered in her ear.

He took off his jacket and spread it out on the ground. They lay down next to one another, holding hands, staring up at the sharp zingy green of the early summer canopy of trees.

'Marco,' she said dreamily, 'I am so sorry for all that I've put you through. I've been away too long – thank you for waiting.'

He leaned over and kissed her again.

'I should never have doubted you.'

'Well, I didn't make it easy. I knew in my heart that I didn't intend to leave for ever. But I was so confused after all that had happened with Anzolo. I wanted so desperately to be able to love you again, but I couldn't bear the thought of *anyone* getting close to me – even you.'

'I tried to understand,' he said, 'I did understand.'

'You nearly gave up…'

'Marietta, you mean.'

Anastasia nodded.

'I was weak, and lonely, and she was so attentive and kind.'

'She wanted to hurt me.'

'Really? Was that her only reason?'

'No, of course not. She had always liked you and I suspect she was jealous when we became engaged. She decided that you were to be her consolation when I went to Amsterdam without her.'

'Thank God my father came back when he did. I discussed it all with him, and I realised I didn't really love her, not as I love you. It was difficult telling her. She was hurt, and angry. But finally, I think she understood. Then she met the farmer's son and within weeks, it seemed, they were to be married.'

'I'm sure she will be far happier now that she has someone of her own. I'm glad for her. I will go and see her soon and make my peace with her.'

She sat up and wrapped her arms around her knees.

'I met someone too, in Amsterdam. I travelled with his family to London; they were very kind to me.'

'Did you love him?' Marco asked nervously.

'No, but I was very fond of him. He was a good friend. Unfortunately, he fell in love with me, and in the end it was his declaration of love, his proposal of marriage, in fact, that made me realise that it was *you* I loved. So you see, in many ways we have been on the same journey. And neither one of us should feel guilty about anything.'

She turned round and smiled at him. He laughed.

'So you might have stayed in London and married an Englishman.' Marco stroked her back.

'He was French, in fact, a Huguenot. Very charming. And no… I don't think I could have stayed in London. As I said, it is very crowded and busy – fascinating, and I learned so much there, but there are so many people. There is no stillness anywhere, unless you get out into the countryside.'

'What did you learn?' said Marco.

Anastasia lay with her head in his lap.

'How to observe, how to draw and paint, how to design… I worked with so many talented people. Maria Merian in Amsterdam – she taught me so much. Then in London, James Leman and his friend Joseph taught me how to design, how to translate my ideas into designs.'

'You have changed so much – you seem so content in yourself. I'm so proud of you.' He kissed the top of her head.

'I *have* changed. When I left, I was full of fear. I was almost paralysed by it. But my time away has enabled me to grow, mature, to shake that fear. I know now what I really desire. I believe I have some small talent – certainly James Leman believed I did. I would like to work as a silk designer; to transform my father's silk farms into a proper silk business.'

'That is a noble ambition and I have no doubt you will achieve it. But what of yourself, Ana – can you live with what happened to you, back in Venice?'

'Yes. I've learned that the memories that so distressed me of my time in Venice can be supplanted. New experiences can take the place of the old, painful ones. It's not that I cannot remember what happened, but simply that it no longer hurts me. Perhaps if it had never happened, I would never have gone away. And then I would never have learned to paint and design in the way that I have. But most importantly, Marco, if I had never left, I might never have learned how much I love you.'

She reached up and pulled his face close to hers and kissed him.

'And shall we marry, at last?' he asked.

'If you will have me, yes.'

The wedding was to be held in the chapel at Villa di Bozzolo. After being apart for so long, Marco and Anastasia were keen to marry as soon as possible.

'We see no point in waiting, Mamma,' said Anastasia that evening as they drove home from Villa Limonaia.

'Then we must begin the preparations immediately,' said Polonia.

The dressmaker from Verona arrived a few days later, with a selection of fabrics – brocades, cut velvets and silks. Anastasia chose a pale-grey damask.

'That colour suits you well, Ana,' said Polonia proudly. 'It sets off your pale skin, it will look beautiful.'

'I would have liked to design a fabric for myself but there is no time. As long as the dress is not yellow, I will be happy.' Anastasia smiled knowingly at her mother.

The dressmaker suggested the bodice should be embroidered with silver thread. 'It will gleam in the candlelight,' she said. 'And we will edge the sleeves and neckline in lace.'

Down in the basement kitchens Angela and Magdalena prepared the wedding feast. A wedding cake, filled with fruit, pomegranate seeds and pine nuts to symbolise fertility, was assembled and covered with sugar.

A few days before her wedding Anastasia decided to visit her sister.

'It is time for me make my peace with Marietta, Mamma,' she said over breakfast. 'I will ride over there today. I would like her and her new husband to come to the wedding.'

As she rode into the yard of the large stucco villa on the outskirts of Verona, a tall young man with a mass of dark curls and smiling brown eyes came out to meet her; he helped her down from her horse.

'Thank you. I am Anastasia – Marietta's sister.'

'I am so pleased to meet you at last. I am her husband, Amando del Corso. Marietta has told me a great deal about you. Come inside. I will call Marietta – she was just resting upstairs.'

He showed her into a small salon overlooking the gardens. Anastasia stood patiently, looking out of the window. Marietta silently entered the room and Amando bustled in, behind his wife; he put his arm around her.

'Here she is – your sister.'

Anastasia turned, framed by the window. The two women observed one another.

'Will you not kiss your sister, Marietta – and tell her your good news?'

'What good news is this?' asked Anastasia gently.

'That Marietta is expecting our first child!' Amando kissed his wife affectionately on the cheek.

Anastasia walked towards her sister, her hands outstretched.

'I am happy for you, Marietta.'

Marietta took her hands; she had tears in her eyes. She glanced down nervously.

'I am so sorry, Ana… for everything.'

Amando looked surprised.

'Sorry for what?'

'It's nothing important,' said Anastasia. 'Come, Marietta – show me the gardens of this lovely house.'

'He seems a lovely man,' Anastasia said, linking her arm through Marietta's, once they were alone.

'He is… he wants nothing more than to ride his horse and shoot a pigeon for supper. He is gentle and kind and he loves me completely.'

'Then you are blessed. To find the love of a good and kind man is not easy.'

They sat on a bench and the scent of musk roses filled the air.

'And a new baby – Mamma will be so pleased.'

'I hope so. And yes, he is a good man. Oh Ana, can you forgive me for what I did?'

'I can, and I do. I see now that you felt abandoned by me. We had always been so close – looking after one another all the time Papa was alive. And then, after what happened to me, I shut you out – you and Marco. I was in so much pain, I couldn't bear to be loved, or love in return.'

'And now?'

'When I heard that Marco and you were spending time together, that he had even discussed marriage – it made me realise that I couldn't bear to lose him.'

'He would never have married me. I see that now. He never actually asked me. I was deluding myself – I think I just wanted to hurt you. And I convinced myself that I loved him. But I was wrong – he has only ever loved you. I am so glad that you are back together where you belong.'

After the wedding, Anastasia and Marco spent a few days in a small cottage on the estate at Villa Limonaia. When they returned to Villa di Bozzolo they brought Vicenzo with them.

'We would like to discuss how we might unite our two businesses, Papa,' Marco said to his father as they sat together in the main salon.

'Our marriage gives us the opportunity to create one large and more significant business.'

'In London,' interjected Anastasia, enthusiastically, 'the Huguenot weavers taught me that they could manage every stage of production, from design through to finished product. That is how they increased their profits. I would like to add one more element – the manufacture of the raw material.'

She turned to Vicenzo. 'With our silk farm we can provide the spun silk for your weavers, Vicenzo. We can control the whole process from the cocoon to the final garment. The only issue we have is that your mills make mostly plain silk. I want to design the sort of silk I discovered in London – interesting, complex designs. We may have to find a mill that can help us with that.'

Anastasia and Marco decided they would live at Villa di Bozzolo after their marriage.

'I do not want to leave Mamma alone,' said Anastasia, 'and if we stay here we can manage the silk farms.'

After being spun locally, the silk thread was taken to Vicenzo's family mills in Venice and Lake Como. Anastasia designed a small collection of silk fabrics, which Marco persuaded his uncles to produce in one of their silk mills. They were reluctant at first, but as the designs became popular with the merchants of Verona and Venice, and word of the talented designer Anastasia Balzarelli began to spread, they became more enthusiastic.

There was personal happiness too. Anastasia woke one morning feeling sick. After Marco had left for the day, Veronica brought in a tray of breakfast for her.

'I feel queasy, I don't want any breakfast today.'

'Queasy, you say,' said Veronica. 'Well, *signora*, I think you must know what is "wrong" with you?'

Anastasia looked at her in genuine amazement.

'Oh… do you think that I might be?'

'I do, *signora*. What else could it be?'

Two months before the baby was due to be born, in early May, Polonia was taken ill. Anastasia was going upstairs to rest one afternoon when she found her mother in the corridor outside her bedroom, doubled up in pain.

'Mamma – what is wrong?'

'My stomach, it is very painful.'

Anastasia helped her mother to bed and the doctor was sent for. She and Marco waited anxiously downstairs in the small sitting room. As soon as the doctor entered the room, they both leapt to their feet.

'Do you know what is wrong?' asked Anastasia.

'Yes. I fear your mother is very unwell. She must rest.'

'Is there nothing that can be done?' asked Anastasia.

'Good nursing may ease her discomfort – simple food, little and often. And prayer, *signora*.'

Veronica and Julia, the maid, took it in turns to nurse Polonia. Marietta visited her mother every other day. The sisters grew close once again, and they took some small comfort from the pleasure Marietta's new baby son, Antonio, gave their mother.

As the weeks went by, Anastasia spent as much time at her mother's bedside as she could. When Polonia was awake, Ana tried to entertain her with stories of the farm, or by reading passages from novels or poems. Occasionally she would show her a new silk design she had created, eager for her mother's approval. But Polonia was frequently gripped by pain, often waking from a deep sleep, crying out in distress. At these times, Veronica, or Julia would give her a soothing tisane to drink, but there was little that could be done.

One afternoon as Anastasia sat, as usual, by the bed, her mother stirred in her sleep, and slowly opened her eyes.

'You are here, Ana… good.'

'Yes, Mamma – I am here.'

'Something is troubling me. Can you ask the priest to come here? I wish to make my confession.'

The priest was summoned, and arrived within the hour and was shown upstairs.

Anastasia sat outside in the corridor and listened to him praying over Polonia. She could not make out what he said, but when the priest emerged sometime later, he said simply, 'Your mother will be at peace now.'

The curtains of her mother's room were closed, and it felt hot and airless.

'Shall I open the windows, Mamma?'

Her mother opened her eyes.

'No, come and sit by me. There is something I need to tell you.'

Polonia's skeletal fingers clutched Anastasia's hand.

'Your father—' she began.

'You don't need to speak of him. He's gone and we can forget him.'

'No, you don't understand. Minou kicked him—'

'During the fire. Yes, I know.'

'We thought the horse had killed him,' said Polonia.

'Well, he did, didn't he?'

'No… your father did not die straight away. He lay here on this bed, and the doctor came and said he was badly injured and that he might die. I prayed, Anastasia, so hard, that God would take him that afternoon. He lay quite still for many hours, and I began to believe my prayers had been answered. I was standing there by the window, looking out at the courtyard. And then I heard him. He called out to me, his voice quite strong – "Come here, woman."

'I went over to him and he whispered under his breath, "Kill that horse, Minou. He's a bad one. Take my gun and shoot him now."'

Anastasia gripped her mother's frail hand.

'I stood up to do as I was told. I got as far as the door and I looked back at him, on the bed; I hated him more than I had ever hated him before. He was injured, yes, and weakened, but still alive. I thought: I have been given one chance. If I do nothing now and he survives, what will happen to Anastasia, abandoned in Venice? Marietta had gone that day to fetch Marco and he was going to rescue you at last. Your father would never have allowed it. He would have sent you back.'

'Mamma… what did you do?'

'I went back to his bedside; I picked up a pillow… and held it over his face. He fought me; he was so strong, even then. I sat astride him and I held him down with my hands. I used all my strength. Finally, he began to weaken; he stopped struggling. But I kept the pillow there. I heard the maid knocking on the door and I called out, "Don't come in. The master is not well."

'I thought if I let go, he will recover and then he will kill me. So I stayed there for a long time, until my arms ached and I had no strength left. Finally, I removed the pillow. I leapt from the bed and ran to the corner of the room. I was afraid that he would come back to life. I stood there for a very long time, until Marietta came in and found me.'

'Did she know... what you had done?'

'She did – she could see in his face. But we closed his eyes, before the doctor came. He was a stupid man, he didn't realise what I had done. It was a terrible sin, Anastasia – but I did it for you.'

'Oh Mamma, Mamma – thank you, Mamma – thank you. God forgive you, God bless you.'

Anastasia held her mother's frail body close to her. When she finally pulled away, Polonia lay quite still. Her eyes were still open, but it was clear for anyone to see that she was dead.

Chapter Thirty-Four

Villa di Bozzolo
July 1707

Anastasia sat with Marietta's baby Antonio on her lap in the salon at the villa. A few hours earlier, the sisters had laid Polonia to rest in the family's crypt. Marco and Amando chatted with Vicenzo as the servants moved silently around the room, offering the funeral guests little glasses of Madeira.

'I wanted to tell you something that Mamma spoke about before she died,' Anastasia said quietly to her sister. The baby began to grizzle, chewing the edge of his lace shawl.

Marietta took him from Anastasia and rocked him in her arms. 'I was so sorry I couldn't be here.'

'I know, Marietta, but it happened so suddenly. At least we were able to send for the priest before the end.'

Marietta soothed her child, putting him over her shoulder. 'I'm glad to know she was blessed when she died.'

Anastasia looked around her, at the guests, at their husbands and her father-in-law. She dropped her voice to a whisper.

'She told me about Papa – what she had done.'

Marietta looked up at her sister, alarmed. The baby began to cry gustily. Marietta called to her husband.

'Amando, *caro*, take the baby, please?'

Amando walked over and took Antonio, bouncing him in his arms.

'Come, let's go outside for a moment.' Marietta drew her sister away from the other guests and out into the garden, where they sat on a bench on the large terrace.

'I had always suspected that Papa's death was not quite as I had been led to believe. Before her death, she told me what she had done. She confessed everything to the priest. She carried that dark secret for so long; I feel so guilty – I know she did it for me.'

'She did it for all of us, Ana. Don't feel guilty. It's true that she was desperate for Marco to rescue you from Venice. If Papa had survived, he would have insisted you went back to Anzolo – and she couldn't bear that. I think she looked ahead to the future with him, and she knew that she had to do something – for all of us. It was her only chance.'

'I never really thanked you for your part in my rescue. If you had not been brave enough to go for Marco that day I don't know what I would have done.'

'You had already escaped – somehow you would have found a way to get back to us.'

'But you took a great risk going for Marco. When you left here that day, Papa was still alive. If he had survived, he would have punished you – and Mamma.'

She kissed Marietta on the cheek.

'You would have done the same for me,' said Marietta, squeezing her hand.

The sound of Antonio crying – little anguished sobs – preceded Amando, who joined them on the terrace.

'*Cara*, Antonio is tired.'

'Yes… we must go.'

She stood up and kissed her sister on both cheeks.

'Stay well, and try not to distress yourself, for the baby you are carrying,' she whispered in Anastasia's ear. 'What Mamma did that day was for both of us. She would have been so happy that we have both found happiness.'

*

In the weeks leading up to her confinement, Anastasia suggested to Marco that she would like Juliana di Luna to be her midwife.

'But she is in Venice, *cara*. Surely it would be more sensible to use a local woman.'

'I know it would be more sensible but I would like Juliana. Mamma has gone, Marietta is busy with her own child – I need someone I can trust. Please, Marco. Could you not send for her?'

'Of course, *cara*. I will fetch her myself.'

Marco returned with Juliana di Luna the following day.

'She is here. She came without a moment's hesitation,' said Marco, 'but I warn you – she has aged a great deal since we last met with her. Her health is poor, I think.'

When Anastasia had first met Juliana she had been a vital woman in her sixties, with a mop of unruly dark red hair streaked with grey, and dark flashing eyes. Straight-backed and strong-armed, she was a woman who had experienced life and was afraid of nothing. Just three years later, she stooped, her once-strong hands were swollen at the joints and she shuffled slightly, as if the act of walking caused her pain.

'Dear Signora di Luna, thank you for coming all this way. You must be tired after your journey – please sit.'

Anastasia indicated a chair opposite hers. Juliana sat down heavily.

'I am so grateful to you for coming to help me with my baby. My mother died just four weeks ago, and I felt anxious about the birth, knowing I had no one I could trust to help me. I hope I will not be taking you away from too many other patients?'

'No, no... I work much less these days. I have a young associate who goes to many of the deliveries. I still do several each week, but not as many as I was wont to do, so no one will suffer if I am away for a few days. Now, how are you, *signora*?'

'Very well, thank you. But nervous about the birth.'

'And still busy painting, I see.'

'Oh yes, always painting. I became a silk designer after… what happened. These are some designs I'm working on.'

She indicated an easel set up in the sitting room, covered with graph paper and complex designs.

'Mmm… they look very clever,' murmured Juliana approvingly.

'Let us have some tea – or would you prefer some chocolate perhaps, or something to eat? You must be hungry after your journey.'

'Let us first get you upstairs and make sure all is well with the baby, and then I will eat.'

Anastasia opened the shutters in her bedchamber and lay down on the bed. She felt the comforting sensation of her child kicking as she settled herself for Juliana's examination.

'It is a fine big baby,' said Juliana approvingly. 'I can feel the head down here already. He is keen to be born, it won't be long now.'

Anastasia's labour began a few days later. She woke in the middle of the night with a nagging pain in her abdomen. She stood up and wandered around the bedchamber, feeling an unfamiliar clenching sensation in her belly. Marco stirred in his sleep and hauled himself up in bed.

'Ana – are you in pain?'

'No, not pain. But I think something is happening.'

'I shall fetch Juliana,' said Marco, leaping out of bed.

'No, wait a little. Let her sleep. She is an old lady and I'm not so bad yet. She has told me what to expect and I think this is just the start. Wait until dawn.'

Marco dozed as Anastasia paced the room until the sun began to creep around the edges of the shutters. Pulling them apart, she opened the window and breathed in the cool early-morning air. Doves fluttered in and out of the dovecot on top of the old barn. The horses stood peacefully in their stables, Minou's handsome grey head hanging, as was his habit, over his door. The pale apricot glow on the horizon grew steadily more intense, much like the pain in her abdomen.

As the sun rose, glinting over the rooftops, she woke Marco.

'Get Juliana now...'

Moments later, Juliana di Luna bustled into the room, with Veronica at her side.

'I shall attend her,' she said firmly to Marco. 'It would be best for you to leave, this is no place for a man.'

Marco kissed his wife on the forehead.

'I will be just outside if you need me.'

'She will be fine. Go now! Veronica, stoke the fire.'

'But it is already so hot,' protested Anastasia.

'Trust me, we will need the fire; you must not get a chill. And close that window, Veronica, and the shutters, and light the candles.'

The following seven or eight hours went by in a haze of heat and pain. Anastasia paced the room for as long as possible, but finally was in such agony that she was forced to rest on the bed.

'You would be better standing, or kneeling, *signora*.'

'I cannot, Juliana. I am exhausted.'

'The baby is strong, he won't let you rest yet.'

For Marco, the wait was unbearable. Unable to settle, he wandered from room to room. From time to time, he would climb the marble staircase and listen at the door to his wife's bedchamber. He stood there, half-paralysed with indecision, torn between the urge to comfort Ana and his awareness of Juliana's instructions to stay away.

Finally, as the sun dropped behind the vineyards, colouring the sky fiery orange tinged with violet, Marco heard the cry of a baby. He ran upstairs two at a time and entered the bedchamber just as the tiny child was finally expelled.

'A fine strong girl!' said Juliana di Luna. 'I pride myself that I can tell whether it is to be a boy or a girl, and I was convinced this child was a boy, so strong were the contractions. Perhaps I am losing my touch!'

Anastasia lay, bathed in sweat, smiling broadly.

'Not at all… Perhaps it is simply that she is as strong as a boy, and as brave as a boy. Can I see her?'

'In a moment; let Veronica wrap her up first.'

Juliana di Luna pressed down on Anastasia's belly to help expel the afterbirth.

'Ah, that is why the contractions were so strong. There is another baby.'

'Another one?'

'Yes. I cannot understand why I did not feel it before – it must have been the way they were lying. I am getting old; I am sorry. Rest a little, but I think it won't be too long.'

'But I'm tired,' protested Anastasia. 'I don't think I can do that again.'

'Yes, you can,' encouraged Juliana. 'And you must. It won't be long now and the second one usually comes more easily than the first.'

Anastasia's second contractions came like a solid wave of pain.

'Push, *signora*, push now!' shouted Juliana, as she peered intently between Anastasia's thighs. Anastasia screamed as, moments later, the second child, a boy, was delivered.

Marco, who had been rooted to the spot throughout, was handed his daughter as their son was born. He gazed at his tiny daughter – at her mop of dark hair and inquisitive dark-blue eyes.

'She is so beautiful,' he murmured.

Veronica wrapped their son in a cloth and handed him to Anastasia. He, too, had a full head of dark hair. Anastasia gazed up at Marco, who laid their daughter in the crook of her other arm.

'Two children… you are so clever,' said Marco, kissing her.

'They are wonderful, aren't they?' said Anastasia, weeping, 'and both perfect.'

'As are you, *cara,*' said Marco.

Chapter Thirty-Five

Villa di Bozzolo
September 2017

Lorenzo sat with his sister Elena on the terrace of the barn. The breakfast service at the villa was over and Elena was grateful for the chance to sit down.

'Where's Millie?' she asked, pouring coffee into two small cups and passing one to Lorenzo.

'She's taken Bella for a swim in the pool.'

'Good. I need to talk to you about her. Please don't tell me you love her, Lorenzo,' she said, stubbing out one of the rare cigarettes she allowed herself. 'You hardly know her. And she has another man, for goodness' sake. Have you no pride?'

'She's finished with the other man. And she never kept it secret – I've always known about him. She went back to London in the summer – to give their relationship another chance – but she finally broke up with him this week. I think it's always been a difficult relationship and being together every day proved that it couldn't work.'

'So now she comes back to Italy, and has decided to move in here?' Elena said sarcastically. She sipped her black coffee and lit another cigarette.

'I don't know – it's early days. We are just going to enjoy one another's company for now. She came over to do some work on the article about us – it's not finished yet and she wants to find out more about the painting on our landing.'

'So she says… I think it was just an excuse to come and see you. Lorenzo, I just don't want you or Bella to be hurt. It seems to me that she is not suitable. To have a relationship with a married man, and then instantly start another – she sounds… unstable.'

'She's not unstable, she's lovely, and you can see how much Bella adores her.'

'And you would trust your heart, and the heart of your daughter, to a woman who has affairs with married men.' Elena refilled their coffee cups.

'Not married men! *One* married man. Oh admit it, Elena, you just don't like her.'

'Have you forgotten what Gianfranco did to me? How he carried on behind my back all those years? And you tell me that you want to spend your life with a woman who – for how long, six years? – has been someone's mistress.'

'You make it sound so… sordid. She fell in love with the wrong person. She is very moral really – she feels guilty about it.'

'Huh!' Elena snorted. 'That's not my definition of morality. You are a fool, Lorenzo, and you deserve better than some silly English journalist who is too old to have children, and has no moral compass at all.'

'She is not too old to have children!'

'She's forty if she's a day.'

'She's thirty-eight. I'm sure she could have children if she wanted. She'd make a wonderful mother.'

'Well, you think long and hard about it. We cannot afford another divorce in this family. My divorce from Gianfranco nearly cost us the farm. Have you forgotten all the land we had to sell? Some woman demanding her "share" a few years down the line would destroy us. You should get a… what do they call it? A prenup – if you are going ahead with it.'

'Oh Elena, stop! No one mentioned marriage. We're just taking it day by day.'

There was a rustling on the boundary hedge and Bella pushed through, carrying her towel over her shoulder.

'Where's Millie?' asked Lorenzo.

'She's coming,' Bella said over her shoulder as she ran into the barn.

Elena stubbed out her cigarette irritably and put the coffee cups onto a tray, which she took back into the kitchen.

Millie emerged through the gap in the hedge, her hair wet, her shoulders a little burnt by the sun, her towel clinging to her damp swimsuit.

'Millie!' said Lorenzo, rising to his feet and embracing her, 'You're wet.'

'I'll soon dry.'

She sat down on the terrace and glanced towards the barn.

'I couldn't help overhearing what Elena said.'

'Oh, take no notice.' Lorenzo leaned across the table and squeezed her hand.

'No… she has a point. I look like a bad bet. I've made poor choices in the past, I probably am unstable. Maybe I ought to leave—'

'Millie! Don't you dare! Look, I'm not saying that it will be plain sailing. Let's just take it easy, OK? Get to know each other properly. There's no rush, is there?'

She shook her head, ruefully.

'You'll have to go back to the UK to work, I'll have to stay here, but we can see each other as often as possible. The season slows down around now and by October there will be hardly anyone staying here. I can get over to London.'

'But if Elena hates me so—'

'She doesn't hate you. She's scared of losing me, and it brings back memories of her own divorce. She needs to see that you make me happy, that you care for Bella.'

'Oh I do, I really do.'

'I know that – you don't have to convince me. Do you want some coffee?'

She nodded.

'Then we should look at some of those papers we brought down from the attic. We're going to the mill first thing tomorrow, so we ought to be prepared.'

The trunk was filled to the brim with a muddled mixture of receipts, wills, birth certificates and title deeds.

'Goodness,' said Millie, 'it's chaos – how should we start?'

'How about we make piles – receipts, wills, title deeds and so on?'

'Or we could put them into date order?' Millie suggested.

'Maybe both…'

Millie began with the more significant-looking documents.

'My goodness – here's a marriage certificate dated 1890. It's between a Caterina Manzoni and a man named… Dario Manocci. So that was your great-grandmother?'

'Maybe, or a great-aunt or something – we really need to do a family tree, don't we? Perhaps I ought to make notes as we go along. Put it here, with this birth certificate I found – it's for my father's brother, so nothing very exciting,' said Lorenzo.

Disappointingly, most of the papers that Lorenzo's grandfather had kept in the trunk appeared to be a jumble of receipts for pieces of farm machinery, or bills of sale for parcels of land.

'He seems to have sold a lot of land,' said Millie.

'Yes, it's a shame. We owned a huge amount, or so he always told us.'

Finally, at about midnight, Lorenzo suggested they went to bed.

'Let's call it a day. Sadly, I don't think we're going to find any clues as to the name of that woman in the picture.'

*

Millie and Lorenzo arrived at the Bordignon mill just after twelve o'clock the following day. They knocked on the double oak doors and were shown into the waiting room on the ground floor. Giovanni Bordignon, the owner, arrived a few minutes later.

'Ah good, you are here. Come up to my private office; it's on the top floor. I have something rather exciting to show you.'

The sound of the clattering looms retreated into the distance as they walked up the stone staircase.

The office had windows overlooking the *campo*, and was filled with light. The walls were painted white and it was decorated with an eclectic mix of modern and ancient furniture. A brand-new computer stood on a glass desk. An antique table filled the middle of the room. And at one end was a small upright sofa upholstered in bright-pink cut velvet.

'What a wonderful room,' Millie said admiringly. 'I love the velvet on that sofa.'

'Ah yes – one of our latest colour runs. It's rather good, isn't it?'

'Thank you for seeing us again,' said Lorenzo. 'I believe Millie emailed the picture over to you that we have in our villa. It seems so odd that the view from the window in that picture is the view from this mill – we wondered if you could throw any light on it.'

'I think perhaps I can – anyway, a little,' said Giovanni.

He sat down at his desk and clicked on the keyboard. The girl in the lemon-yellow dress gazed out at them from the computer screen.

'Now…' said Giovanni, leaning back and opening his filing cabinet, 'I have another drawing – one that has been in our family for years.' He brought out a small charcoal sketch, which he laid on his desk.

'They look like the same woman!' said Millie.

'I thought so,' said Giovanni. 'They are very alike anyway.'

'But who is she?' asked Millie.

'I can tell you that. The picture is signed, as you see, by the artist, Dorothea Merian. But I removed the picture from the frame yesterday and on the back I found this.'

He turned the drawing over, and read out the inscription.

'*A study of Anastasia Balzarelli – artist.*'

'It's wonderful to have a name,' said Millie. 'And such a beautiful name too – Anastasia Balzarelli. It has a real ring to it. But we still don't know what the connection is with Lorenzo's family and why her painting is in your house.'

'Well,' continued Giovanni, 'I think I can begin to explain. We have a huge archive of papers from the eighteenth and nineteenth centuries, starting from the day we bought the mill. When Millie sent me that portrait, I knew I had seen the face before... somewhere among our old documents. So yesterday, I dug out the picture. But – like you – I still could see no connection with you or your family, Lorenzo. Then you emailed me yesterday, and I noticed your email address for the first time – Lorenzo@villabozzolo.'

'Yes... what of it?'

'Well, in among the papers, I found the title deeds of the mill – here, take a look.'

Lorenzo looked at it. 'It's rather archaic Italian, I'm not quite sure I understand it.'

'Let me,' said Signor Bordignon, 'I read a lot of such things when I was an academic.'

He read aloud:

> '*I Anastasia Balzarelli, widow of Marco Morozoni, of Villa di Limonaia, Lake Garda, hereby transfer the deeds to the Bozzolo mill to Rafaele Bordignon on the twenty-first of July 1732.*'

'There's a lot more obviously, but those are the key points.'

'OK,' said Millie excitedly, 'let's break this down a little. So Anastasia was married to Morozoni. They didn't live in Villa di Bozzolo but in another villa on Lake Garda.'

'But it was called the "Bozzolo" Mill!' said Lorenzo. 'Could that just be coincidence? Bozzolo – meaning cocoon; I suppose it's a logical name for a silk mill.'

'It could be a coincidence, I suppose. But it's unlikely. Why was your house called Villa di Bozzolo?'

'Because it's always been a silk farm,' explained Lorenzo.

'I am pretty sure that your family must have been the owners of the mill before we bought it in 1732.'

'But there are still so many unanswered questions.' Millie paced the room. 'Anastasia's husband was Morozoni, not Manzoni. They didn't live in Villa di Bozzolo but on Lake Garda. Oh, it's so frustrating! We seem unable to connect her to your house.'

'I agree – but somewhere there is a document that will explain it,' said Giovanni. 'I have one other thing I'd like to show you – it will explain a little more about Anastasia. You remember I told you we kept ledgers of all the silks ever made here?'

He led them to the table in the centre of the room. A ledger was turned to the first page, on which had been pinned a small piece of a coloured floral silk. It had a yellow background and, attached to a green stem, were red and blue flowers, next to a turquoise butterfly.

The entry next to the sample was dated 5 April 1707. It read simply: 'Designer – Anastasia Balzarelli'.

'It's beautiful,' said Millie, admiringly, 'So, she was an artist and also designed silk?'

'Yes,' said Giovanni. 'I have found several more examples of her work in the ledgers – she had real talent.'

Millie and Lorenzo drove back to the villa in relative silence, each wrapped up in their separate thoughts. When they arrived back it was almost dark. Bella was in her pyjamas and watching television in the living room of the barn as Elena stirred a saucepan in the kitchen.

'Ah, you're back at last.'

'Yes,' said Millie, 'I'm sorry we're a bit late; the traffic was terrible.'

'Bella and I ate earlier,' said Elena, ladling pasta into two bowls. 'I kept some for you but it's probably a bit overcooked now.'

'Oh, don't worry,' said Millie gratefully, 'anything is wonderful. Thank you so much – we're starving.'

She placed the two bowls on the kitchen table, while Lorenzo poured them all a glass of wine.

'So was it worth it – the trip?' Elena sat down at the table, sipping her wine.

'I thought so,' said Millie. 'Did you, Lorenzo? It was fascinating, wasn't it?'

'Yes, it was interesting. But it raised a lot more questions than it answered. We now know a lot more about the woman in our painting upstairs; her name is Anastasia Balzarelli and she once owned a silk mill in Venice.'

'Really!' said Elena. 'Are you sure?'

'Yes,' said Millie, 'Signor Bordignon showed us the title deeds of the mill. The Bordignon family bought it from Anastasia Balzarelli and a man called Marco Morozoni – presumably her husband.'

'Did he also explain how they were connected to our house?'

'No – that's the last part of the mystery really. Frustratingly, they gave their address as a house on Lake Garda, and not here.' Millie ate a forkful of food and sipped her wine. 'This is delicious, by the way.'

Elena waved the compliment away with a dismissive gesture.

'Have you considered that the name Morozoni might have changed over time to Manzoni?' Elena took a sip of her wine and wandered over to the open French windows, where she lit a cigarette.

'There's a winery near here – Bortolomiol,' she continued. 'I was looking at their website the other day as they are a competitor of ours. Their ancestor was a man called Bartolomeo, and that's the name they use for their wine. But their family name is Bortolomiol. Different, but close.'

'So you think your family name could once have been Moro-zoni?' asked Millie.

Elena smiled enigmatically, exhaling cigarette smoke into the night air.

'As it happens, I went through another box of those papers from the attic. And I found something that I think you should see.'

'But I brought them all down,' said Lorenzo. 'There was nothing left.'

'There was one more box hidden behind the water tank. I was up there earlier today because I thought there was a leak in one of the bedrooms – in fact it was coming from some guttering that we are going to have to replace – yet another thing to pay for.' Elena raised her eyes heavenward. 'But I saw the box, shoved behind the tank, so I brought it down. Everything's in a mess in there. I had always thought Grandpapa was so organised, but it's as if he just took all the papers from his desk or whatever and threw them randomly into different boxes. Maybe during the war – things were so chaotic.' She inhaled deeply on her cigarette.

'What did you find?' asked Lorenzo excitedly.

'The papers were all mixed up with grocery bills from the 1930s and notes from Papa's school in England; letters Grandpapa wrote his own mother. I even found Grandpapa's will, and his own parents' marriage certificate. There were several other odd birth certificates, and several transfers of ownership of various things – farms and so on.'

Elena stubbed out her cigarette on the terrace and turned back towards Lorenzo and Millie. She wandered over to the coffee table and picked up a folded sheet of parchment tied with a ribbon. She placed it on the kitchen table, with a flourish.

'What is it?' asked Lorenzo.

'Read it.'

Lorenzo undid the ribbon and skimmed the document.

'It's a title deed for a farm near here. There's a map – look.'

He laid the deed and the hand-drawn map out on the kitchen table. A neat line had been drawn around the parcel of fields and woodland. A river had been drawn snaking through the fields.

'That's Raffaele's place, isn't it? He's part of our cooperative,' he explained to Millie. 'Let me see if I can read the deed – it's rather formal Italian.'

Elena took it from him.

'It says that Anastasia Balzarelli and Marco Morozoni, of Villa di Bozzolo, agree to purchase the farm of Luigi Agricola on 29 October 1706.'

'Villa di Bozzolo – they did live here! Oh Elena,' said Millie, throwing her arms around Elena and kissing her on the cheek, 'you're so clever.'

Elena smiled for the first time that evening. 'Well, I have my uses. I had hoped we might find Anastasia or Marco's will. Maybe we shall one day. I'm sure they're somewhere in this house.'

Later that night, as Millie lay with her head on Lorenzo's chest, she murmured into his ear, 'I hate the idea of going back to London. I never want to leave you again, or Bella.'

'I know… I feel the same. But you need to go back to England and perhaps I can come over in a few weeks and stay with you?'

'Of course – anytime. If you think Elena won't mind taking care of Bella?'

He shook his head. 'She won't mind.'

'I thought she seemed a little less hostile to me this evening?' said Millie.

'Yes… I think she was rather pleased with herself for finding that document. I'm glad – it makes her part of it. Up till now it's been something only you and I were interested in but now it's a mystery the whole family can be part of.'

'And at last, I have the ending to my story. Anastasia lived in this house, she was a silk designer; she owned farms and vineyards. And I, for one, can't wait to find out more about her.'

Chapter Thirty-Six

Villa di Bozzolo
November 1707

Anastasia rested for a month after the birth of her children, as was the custom. Her daughter was christened Polonia, in honour of Ana's mother, and her son was named Vicenzo after Marco's father. Juliana di Luna remained with the family for a week before returning to Venice. As she pottered around Anastasia's room, helping her to adjust to motherhood, they had the opportunity to talk about Ana's first marriage and the divorce.

'Juliana, I don't think I ever had a chance to thank you properly for what you did for me at the divorce hearing. Your testimony convinced the patriarch. I am so grateful to you.'

Juliana handed baby Vicenzo to her. 'Think nothing of it – here, take the baby, he is hungry – feed him first and then we will feed Polonia. I have found you a wet nurse – she will arrive tomorrow or the next day.'

Anastasia held her son to her breast. He fed greedily, pawing her breast rhythmically with his tiny fists.

'He is a greedy one!' said Juliana. 'He will be a fine big boy, I think.' She picked up Polonia and rocked her in her arms. 'I am just glad that you have found love with a good man.'

Anastasia gazed into her son's dreamy eyes as he fed.

'I have been fortunate. It was over a year after I left Anzolo before I could bear the idea of being near a man.'

'It was wrong, what he did to you. I knew his first wife, you know. She lost three children and died giving birth to the last one. I think that explained his obsession with keeping you locked away – I don't believe he wanted to hurt you. I think, in some odd way, he believed he was keeping you safe.'

'I wish I could believe that.'

'He was a broken man after the divorce. I saw him once or twice in the street. It aged him; and his business suffered, I heard.'

'I cannot feel sorry for him,' said Anastasia as she laid her son over her shoulder.

'And nor should you,' said Juliana, taking the baby and winding him, 'but I heard that he regretted the way he had treated you.'

When the day finally came for Juliana to leave Villa di Bozzolo, Anastasia clasped the midwife's hands in hers.

'Thank you, Juliana – for everything you have done for me.'

'Call on me for your next delivery, *signora*. I have enjoyed my time away from Venice. A couple of weeks in the Veneto countryside and some good Valpolicella has done my old bones good. And next time – if you have twins, I will not miss it!'

Slowly Anastasia regained her strength and, two months after the children's birth, she resumed her design work. Marco was busy. He ran the silk farms surrounding Villa di Bozzolo, and the vineyards too. They had bought up parcels of land as they came up for sale, building up their ownership of the surrounding land. In many cases, they were farms that Anastasia's father had been forced to sell years before to pay gambling debts. But in addition to his responsibilities at Villa di Bozzolo, Marco also had to oversee the estate at Lake Garda and the Morozonis' own extensive tracts of land. His own father was not in the best of health and his two uncles – Giancarlo and Alessandro – had made it clear that they expected him to manage Vicenzo's estate single-handed.

'We are managing the silk mills, Marco; we cannot deal with Vicenzo's estate and the farms as well.'

He left the villa early in the morning and was often away overnight. When he returned, he was tired and pale. Concerned for his health, Anastasia insisted one morning over breakfast that Marco spend the day quietly at home.

'You are out so early every day, riding around the countryside, back and forth between here and Lake Garda. I think you should stay there more often, and attend to your father's needs. I will be fine here alone, with the children and Veronica. Or maybe the time has come for us to move to Villa Limonaia; I have always wanted to live there.'

'But what of the silk farms, the land we've bought and the vineyards?'

'We could employ an overseer, someone who could report to us in Lake Garda. We can afford it now, Marco. A proper manager. With Mamma gone, there is no real need to stay here.'

'I know my father would like it very much. He misses us both.'

'Well, go and see him and discuss it. If we can find a manager, and your uncles can continue to deal with the silk mills, I see no real reason why it could not work well.'

There was a knock at the door.

'A letter has come for you, *signora*.'

'Thank you, Giuseppe. Open it for me, Marco, would you?'

Marco scanned the letter's contents.

'It's from a notary in Venice.'

'How strange.'

'It seems you have been made a beneficiary of someone's will.'

'We don't know anyone in Venice apart from the merchants we deal with, and none of them have passed away recently, have they?'

'It is someone from your past, Ana…'

Anastasia's heart began to race; there was a tightening in her chest.
'What does the letter say? Show it to me.'

'Just that he has died, and left you a bequest. You need to go to Venice for the reading of the will, next week… at the mill house.'

Marco handed the letter to Ana.

'I'm not going. I'm not interested in what he has left me, I need nothing from him.'

'*Cara*, I will come with you. I think you should attend. It will be a way to prove to yourself that he means nothing to you, that he cannot hurt you any more. You have the children, your work, me…'

Anastasia finally agreed, but over the following days her nightmares returned. She was trapped in the mill owner's bedchamber, or standing on the balcony of the house in Venice, looking down at the dark waters of the Grand Canal. Behind her stood Anzolo, reaching towards her, calling for her. In desperation, she threw herself into the black water below. When she woke, bathed in sweat, with the familiar sensation of claustrophobia, unable to breathe, Marco comforted and reassured her as best he could, but the night terrors distressed them both.

'Perhaps you are right,' he admitted one morning. 'Maybe we should not attend. I think it's too much for you.'

'No, I must do this. And see it through. This will be the end of it – at last.'

The day before the will was to be read, Anastasia and Marco were taken by carriage to Venice. Marco had arranged to stay at the palazzo belonging to his old friend Luigi Agnoli. Arriving late in the afternoon, Ana suggested they visit the cathedral of San Pietro di Castello.

'I should like to go back. My new life began the day the patriarch granted my divorce in that cathedral.'

It was dusk when they crossed the footbridge onto the tiny island of Olivolo. Storm clouds gathered over the roof of the cathedral, and the bells of the campanile tolled as monks carrying flaming torches processed towards the building, led by the patriarch himself, Gianalberto Badoaro.

'That's the bishop who granted my divorce,' Anastasia whispered to Marco. 'Shall we attend the service? It will be vespers.'

As the service drew to a close, the patriarch gave his final blessing and the air was filled with the scent of incense. The patriarch processed down the central aisle of the cathedral. He stopped as he reached the back of the church and looked intently at Anastasia; she smiled at him and bowed her head reverently. A flicker of recognition crossed his face.

'Bless you, my child,' he said, making the sign of the cross.

Sleet was beginning to fall onto the green lawns outside as Anastasia and Marco emerged from the cathedral. Pulling the hood of her cloak over her dark hair, Ana looked back into the marble interior of the church. The last time she had stood in this doorway Anzolo had been sobbing in the front pew – an old man, pathetic and deluded. Perhaps he had loved her, in his own way.

The following day, Anastasia woke early. She stood at the window of the palazzo looking across the Grand Canal. The outline of the mill house was just visible before the canal curved away, out towards the lagoon. Seeing the house now, she realised it held no fears for her: it was simply a building.

A gondola dropped them at Santa Stae and they walked the ten minutes through the narrow alleyways to the mill owner's house. A cold wind blew across the *campo*, and Marco put a protective arm around his wife as they knocked on the great doors. Tomasso, the footman, opened the door. He looked embarrassed to see Anastasia.

She and Marco were shown into the drawing room overlooking the canal. They sat, nervously, in the high-backed blue damask chairs. Just the distant sounds of the canal traffic outside infiltrated the silence. A door slammed somewhere in the house and quick footsteps crossing the marble floors announced the arrival of the notary, carrying a leather bag, his wig slightly askew.

'Ah, good, *signora*, you are here. I see you have made yourselves comfortable. Good. Then we can begin.'

'Are we not waiting for others to arrive?' asked Anastasia.

'Others? No… Oh no. I'm sorry, I should perhaps have made that clear. No – only yourself. There are one or two small bequests for the staff, which I shall deal with myself, but no, you are the only significant beneficiary.'

'Are you sure?' asked Anastasia.

'I am quite sure, *signora*. Signor di Zorzi made a new will only last week – he was quite clear as to his intentions. I have a copy of it here, I will read it to you.'

> I Anzolo di Zorzi of the parish of Santa Croce in the City of Venice, being weak and sickly of body but of sound mind and memory, praise be God. Yet considering the mortality of my weak body and for the satisfying of my friends and relations after my death do make and declare this my Last Will and Testament in manner and form following. First and principally I commit & commend my soul unto the hands of Almighty God my maker & Creator and to Jesus Christ my Redeemer. And my body to return to its primitive dust from whence it was taken to be decently interred at the discretion of my executor, revoking and disannulling all other Wills and Testaments. As touching my temporal goods that God

hath endowed me withal I give & bequeath them in manner & form following. Imprimi I give & bequeath to my wife Anastasia Balzarelli my silk mill and mill house and all my goods moveable and unmoveable in the parish of Santa Croce. Lastly, I constitute and appoint my notary Raffaele Bertucci to be my sole Executor of this my Last Will & Testament – In witness whereof I have hereunto set to my hand and seal the twenty-seventh day of November Anno Domini 1707.

'I don't understand,' said Anastasia. 'He calls me his wife, and yet we divorced over three years ago. I am married again – to this man here. We have children…'

'Until his dying day, he considered you to be his wife,' said the notary, removing a rolled-up sheet of vellum from his leather bag. 'I have a letter for you also.'

My dear Anastasia,

Many years have elapsed since that terrible winter's day when we were ripped asunder by the patriarchal court. I have never forgotten it. Just as I have never forgotten the few precious months we spent together. When we married, I had no foreknowledge of you. It was a business arrangement between me and your father. But when you entered the church of San Zan Degolà on our wedding day, and I saw you for the first time, I knew that I would love you for ever.

Be assured, Anastasia, that I truly loved you. But I was a lonely man, with no family and few friends. You were like a beautiful butterfly caught in my empty house. I am sorry I kept you against your will, but I was so afraid that you would leave.

I have heard that you have now become a fine designer
of silk. You deserve your success and I hope the mill can
be part of that.

Until we meet again.

Your husband,
Anzolo.

'I am confused,' said Anastasia. 'He has left me everything? This
house... the mill next door?'

'He has.' The notary nodded. 'Signor di Zorzi learned of your
success. He had seen some of your silk designs sold by merchants
here in Venice. Your reputation has preceded you, *signora*. This
house is yours to do with as you please. The mill too. The weavers
have long been dismissed; Signor di Zorzi had been ill for some
time and so was unable to maintain the business. But the looms
are intact, and the building is in good order.'

'I'd like to look around the house, if I may?'

'*Signora* – of course. Here is my card. Do please write to me,
or visit at any time if you require further clarification.'

The notary bowed low as he left the drawing room.

Anastasia's heart began to race as she climbed the marble staircase
to the first floor. The long corridor that led to the bedchamber was
somehow both familiar and strange. She remembered the first time
she had seen the door leading to that room; she had felt such a
sense of terror and desperation that day. She stood outside for a
moment, her hand on the door handle.

'Do you want to go inside?' asked Marco.

'Yes... I think I must.'

The room was quite unchanged. The bed was covered in the same
dark-green damask as during her imprisonment. She caught sight

of herself in the mirror between the two long windows overlooking the canal. How different she was from the poor wretch who had been dragged there that day – her yellow silk dress torn and stained; her face pale with terror. Now the woman she saw in the mirror was a healthy-looking, even prosperous figure in an elegant dark-claret silk dress and cloak. Draped over a chair in the corner was the lemon-yellow dress, not torn as it had been that day, but cleaned and mended. It was as if its owner had just stepped outside the bedchamber for a moment before putting it on.

Anastasia opened the closet. Alongside Anzolo's coats and waistcoats hung the dresses her mother had sent her. By the bed stood her clothes chest. It was still filled with her nightclothes and undergarments, interleaved with sheaves of lavender. She picked a nightdress up and held it to her face, inhaling the sweet scent.

'It's as if Anzolo believed that by keeping my clothes here, I was, in some way, here too. What other reason could there be for preserving everything just as it was when I was imprisoned here?'

She opened the long windows that led onto the balcony and stood there for a moment, looking down at the canal. Gondoliers were battling against the choppy wintry waters. A young couple sat together in a gondola, swathed in cloaks and fur, their arms around each other.

Turning back to the room, she sat on a chair near the broken panel beneath the window. It came away easily in her hand. Behind it was her discarded painting equipment – dried-up brushes and paint, rolled-up sheets of unused vellum and scattered over the floorboards, the brown flaky remnants of dried mulberry leaves.

'This was where I hid my silkmoth eggs… I watched them as they grew and metamorphosed. This was the secret place that kept me sane.'

Marco crouched down next to her and put his arms around her. 'Come, *cara*, you've seen enough.'

As they stood in the hall, preparing to leave, Tomasso, the footman, bowed low to Anastasia and handed her a collection of letters, tied up with a ribbon.

'For you, *signora*.'

'What are these?' asked Anastasia.

'Letters for you. They were in the master's desk.'

'Thank you, Tomasso. Signor Bertucci will tell you what I intend to do with the house,' she said.

The notary had given Marco a set of keys to the mill, and he struggled to find the right one to open the oak double doors. Finally the lock gave way and the doors opened on to the familiar long corridor. Anastasia's head began to spin, and she felt as if she was floating. She put out a hand to steady herself against the cold plaster wall.

'Shall we leave?' Marco asked anxiously.

'No… I want to see it all. It just brings it back, how frightened I was that day. It was my only chance.'

The mill room lay eerily silent, the looms at rest, like sleeping long-legged insects. Sunlight filtered through the dust from the skylights in the roof. Lengths of silk lay abandoned on the looms, folded up neatly, as if their weavers had just left for the day.

'It looks so sad,' said Anastasia, picking up a length of emerald green cut velvet. 'So much beauty – forgotten, and unwanted.'

They walked through the mill towards the office overlooking the canal.

'This is the window I escaped through,' said Anastasia. 'I came in here; Veronica had told me it was the only way out. The manager had gone to speak to Anzolo about something, and for a brief moment I was alone. The window was unlocked – I think now perhaps Veronica arranged it. I opened it and slipped out onto the pontoon there. A gondola was waiting for me. In a moment I was gone, it took just a few seconds.'

'Shall we go upstairs?' Marco asked.

'Yes, I never got the chance to go up there before I escaped.'

They returned to the dark hallway and climbed the stone stairs. They passed the first floor, which seemed to consist only of storerooms filled from floor to ceiling with lengths of silk. They continued to climb. The floor above had two rooms – a small office at the rear was lined with wooden shelving filled with ledgers. The second room was clearly intended for meetings with clients; there was a small sofa, chairs surrounding a table on which were laid out sample books, filled with clippings of fabrics, and notes on who had bought what fabric and in what quantity.

There was one further office on the floor above. The door was locked, and once again Marco had to rifle among the keys.

'This must have been his private office,' he said as they entered.

There was a dark wooden desk and chair at one end. A large table stood in the centre of the room, covered with lengths of colourful silk. Anastasia examined it.

'It is *my* silk!' she cried. The design was unmistakable – a yellow background, red and blue flowers climbing up a dark-green stem and a turquoise butterfly, about to take flight.

'It's the design I created for James Leman in London,' she added. 'There is so much of it – many, many lengths – it must be as much as James could ever have produced.'

'Ana – look over there.' Marco pointed to a tiny portrait hanging on the far wall. 'That picture – it looks like you.'

It was a charcoal drawing of a young girl, her dark hair tumbled around her shoulders. She wore a velvet dress draped with a silk shawl.

'It *is* me! I remember, Dorothea did it – Maria Sibylla's daughter in Amsterdam. I left for London before it was finished. She often sketched me as I painted in her mother's studio. How did Anzolo acquire it?'

'It seems he has been following you since the day you ran away.'

As they left the mill, locking the door behind them, Marco asked: 'Shall we keep the mill or sell it?'

'We must keep it,' said Anastasia decisively. 'Your uncles have never been confident producing my designs, the looms here are perfect – the weavers in Venice have the experience we need. We must try to find the old weavers and rehire them if we can. It's a fine mill, Marco, with a good reputation – Anzolo had a long list of clients. And there is so much fabric still to be sold. No, we must keep it – it would be madness to let it go.'

'And the house?'

'Sell it. I could never live there again.'

Chapter Thirty-Seven

Fournier Street, Spitalfields
September 2017

Millie trudged up the stairs to her flat in Fournier Street. Opening the door from the cramped communal landing, she thought how cold and empty the flat felt – it was so at odds with the golden weekend she had just spent in the villa near Verona. She dumped her bag in the tiny hall, switched on the television in the living room and wandered through to the kitchen. Opening the fridge, she discovered it was empty apart from some sour milk and a piece of Cheddar that had seen better days. She filled the kettle and rummaged in the cupboards for tea bags. Sitting at the kitchen table, sipping a mug of green tea, she began to cry.

The last few months had taken their toll; she was emotionally exhausted. She had gone from mistress, to girlfriend, to singleton – all in the space of a few weeks. The long-anticipated relationship with Max had been such a disappointment – the end of years of dreaming. And now her new love, the man she instinctively felt could really be the love of her life, was hundreds of miles away in Italy.

She dialled her friend Kitty.

'Hi there… it's me, Millie.' She could feel her voice breaking.

'Hi! How's it going?'

Millie sobbed unintelligibly down the phone.

'Millie – what's the matter? You're not making any sense…'

She continued sobbing.

'I'll come over.'

Half an hour later, Kitty was buzzing at the communal door.

Millie let her in and retreated to the sofa where she had been lying, prone and weepy, a box of tissues by her side.

'What's up? What's happened? Where's Max?'

The story of her break-up with Max, her new lover – it all poured out.

'Whoa… hold up there,' said Kitty, 'let me catch up! So let me get this right. After years of yearning to be with Max – who incidentally you hid from me and your other friends until just recently, which was pretty unforgivable – you finally move in together, he offers to spend the rest of his life with you, buy you a stunning flat in Holland Park, and then… you turn him down! Oh, and then you pop over to Italy, where you have a romantic weekend with a handsome widower who you've just met…'

'That's about it,' said Millie tearfully, blowing her nose.

'God, it makes my love life look like a scene from *Miss Marple*, without the interesting murdery bits! I've not had a boyfriend for eighteen months – and you've got *two* on the go!'

'I've broken up with Max – it was no good.'

'But we all met in the pub two weeks ago – it seemed OK then.'

'I know, but it wasn't… not really. He didn't really like my friends.'

'Oh thanks!' said Kitty with not quite mock sarcasm.

'It was nothing personal – it wasn't you, or anyone really – he was just older than us, and used to a different lifestyle. He was a bit elitist, if I'm honest.'

'But you loved him?'

'I did… I thought I did. But in the end, the reality of living with him was just not what I'd thought it was going to be.'

'Fine. I suppose these things happen – particularly with relationships that start out in secret. It's not real, is it?'

Millie blew her nose.

'But you've met someone else?

She nodded.

'And do you love him?'

She nodded again.

'So why are you crying?'

'Because I miss him.' She began to cry again.

Kitty put her arm around Millie and gave her a squeeze. She kissed the top of her head.

'I just want to be there with him, not here,' Millie mumbled into her friend's neck.

'I know. Just one thing, Millie…' Kitty pulled away from Millie and put her hands on her shoulders. She looked into her eyes. 'I suspect you used to cry because you missed Max. Are you sure there's not a pattern emerging here?'

'What do you mean?' Millie wiped her eyes with a tissue.

'I mean, that you fall in love with a guy who's unavailable. You spend months, years, longing for him; and then when he is available, you don't want him.'

'I can see why you'd say that,' said Millie. 'But honestly, Kitty – this time it's different. I never loved Max in the way I love Lorenzo.'

'Does Lorenzo feel the same way?'

'I think so – yes. But he's got a little girl and we need to be sure it's right. Neither of us wants to hurt her.'

'Need I point out the one final flaw in this new relationship – he lives in Italy! How on earth are you going to see him?'

Millie began to cry again; Kitty went to the kitchen, found a bottle of Pinot Grigio and poured them both a glass.

'Here, drink this… It might cheer you up.'

Millie downed half the glass in one gulp.

'He's coming over soon, he said in a few weeks.'

'Well, that's all right then, isn't it?' Kitty said encouragingly. 'Although judging by the state of you, I think he'd better come a bit sooner than that, don't you?'

*

After Kitty had gone, Millie took a bath. She spoke to herself in the mirror.

'Get a grip, Millie. Kitty was right. I'm lucky to have found Lorenzo... and he will come and see me soon.'

Then she made herself an omelette and closed the curtains. She sat on the sofa with a rug over her knees and, after she'd eaten her supper, opened her laptop. Her phone bleeped. It was Lorenzo messaging her.

Hi Millie... I miss you already.

I miss you too, she replied.

Google Anastasia. I did it today – you'll find lots of references. They even have a collection at the V&A in London... could you go and take a look?

She typed Anastasia's name into a search engine.

You're right! Yes, of course. I'll call the curator tomorrow. How exciting!

Let me know how you get on.

I will... and come over – soon.

I will – promise.

The following morning she went back to work. Max was not in his corner office. She dropped into Sonia's pod.

'Morning,' she said, as cheerfully as she could.

'Hi!' said Sonia equally cheerfully. 'You're back – again.'

'Yes... I had to go back to Italy, and do a bit more research – I'm chasing up an interesting lead for the end of the story.'

'Oh good! We are going to need that story pretty soon. Have you got anywhere with the London Fashion Week angle?'

'No, but I will. I'll get on with it now.'

Back at her desk, Millie emailed the curator at the V&A and was delighted when she suggested an appointment that afternoon. It gave Millie a chance to get away from the office, an environment she found increasingly unnerving. Max was everywhere she looked: the corridors were lined with photographs of him meeting the great and the good – laughing conspiratorially with successive prime ministers, dining with minor royals, or celebrities.

Millie met the curator in charge of eighteenth-century silk in the grand main hall of the Victoria & Albert Museum.

'I'm Joanna, how do you do?' the curator said cheerfully. 'Come this way.' She led Millie through the maze of rooms taking visitors through the ages of fashion.

'Here is our section on eighteenth-century silk. We're lucky to have the work of many talented silk designers. I understand you are looking for a particular female designer, is that right?'

Millie nodded. Joanna stopped in front of a large glass display case.

'Here is some of the work of perhaps Britain's most famous female silk designer – Anna Maria Garthwaite. She lived in Spitalfields in the middle of the eighteenth century. Spitalfields at that time was the centre of the English silk industry, as I'm sure you know.'

'Yes. In fact, I live in Spitalfields myself. What road did she live on – do we know?'

'Yes. She lived on Princelet Street.'

'That's literally just round the corner from me; I'm in Fournier Street.'

'What a coincidence!' said Joanna, moving down the line of display cases.

'And here is the work of James Leman, a second-generation French Huguenot who worked at the turn of the eighteenth century. He also lived in Spitalfields, in Steward Street – right behind what is now Spitalfields Market. He was famous for what was dubbed, in the twentieth century, "bizarre silk", where the design is contorted in some way.'

Millie looked at the display. There were black and white designs on graph paper and designs painted with watercolours, as well as examples of the finished silks. There were waistcoats, court dresses and frock coats.

'The silks are so beautiful – I had no idea they used so many different colours and designs,' said Millie. 'Is that real silver and gold thread?'

'Oh yes. Leman's work was very highly sought after – he sold to the royal household, and all the best people in society. Now, this is the lady I think you are looking for – Anastasia Balzarelli.'

'Yes! That's her.' Millie gazed at the small collection.

'We don't have a huge amount of her work, I'm afraid, but it's very charming. There is a suggestion that she was trained by James Leman – many people have noted the similarity in their styles. It could just be that was the fashion, or a coincidence, but it's quite possible that she worked with him.'

'She ended up owning a mill in Venice,' said Millie.

'Really!' said Joanna. 'I had no idea.'

'I was in Venice last week and saw examples of her work, still preserved in the mill she owned back in the eighteenth century.'

'Do you have any photographs? Perhaps you'd be able send me something by email.'

'I have one or two, and I could ask a friend to take a few more. Hopefully I'll be going over there myself soon.'

Millie had a momentary pang of anxiety. Would she see Lorenzo soon? When would she be going back?

'Whenever it's convenient, there's no hurry.'

'I had no idea,' said Millie, 'that women were so prominent as artists back then. One imagines them always to be the wife of the designer, or artist, rather than an artist in their own right.'

'Yes, that is a common misconception. And of course, it was never easy for women in the past to excel in the arts. But some did manage it, and it's up to us to make sure that people know about it.'

Back at the office, Millie wrote up her notes and started researching London Fashion Week. She spoke to the PR office handling the shows.

'I'm looking for an Italian designer using silk manufactured in Italy,' she explained. The young press officer knew nobody. She then tried contacting the jewellery designer near Verona – Antonio Moretti. 'Could you recommend an Italian designer, showing in London, who is using your silk?' she emailed.

As she pressed 'send', she became aware of someone watching her. She swung round in her chair. Max stood in the doorway.

'Hello there,' he said quietly.

'Oh… hi!'

'Busy?'

'Yes, just trying to tie up the loose ends on the silk piece. It's long overdue, I need to get it finished.'

'Fancy a drink?'

She knew she should say no, but what was waiting for her at home? An empty fridge and an evening spent alone with the television.

'Yes, OK – that would be nice. Give me five minutes?'

They went to a bar near the office. He chose a corner table, away from prying eyes, and ordered a bottle of white burgundy.

'Drink up – you look like you could do with it.' He chinked her glass with his.

'Cheers. I'm fine!'

'How's the handsome Italian?'

'He's fine too, thank you.'

'I was slightly surprised to see you in the office – I wondered if you might decide to stay out there.'

'Don't be ridiculous!' It was curious that Max could always read her mind. 'I only went for the weekend and it was for work, really. As it happens, we found some interesting links with the past; it turns out one of the handsome Italian's ancestors was a famous silk designer. I went to the V&A today and saw her work. She was rather talented and it will make a fantastic ending to the piece.'

He was gazing at her.

'You're just as clever as ever, and still beautiful. I miss you.'

'Max, don't! It's hard enough.'

'Is it? Then don't leave me. Come back. We don't need to live together – not straight away. Let's adjust to being a proper couple first. I think I rushed it all too much. Living in your tiny flat – it was too much for you. I know I'm a blunderbuss. I'm larger than life, difficult, demanding – but that's why you love me, isn't it? And you know I love you—'

'Max, please. Don't!'

'Why shouldn't I? I want you back and I don't understand why we're not together.'

'It just wasn't working. I don't think, in the end, that we were right for each other. Our friends didn't get along, we argued constantly, and you seemed so irritable all the time.'

'So what? It doesn't mean I don't love you. I mean, honestly, Millie – do you want to live in Italy? Does the Italian want you? For heaven's sake, if you thought it was hard moving in with me, how much harder to leave your flat, your job, your boring friends, and go and live in Italy with a widower and his brat, and his witch of a sister? Really! Is that what you want?'

'No one mentioned anyone moving in. It's too soon. But as it happens, I can imagine living there. I know it sounds crazy; you're right, I hardly know him. But his daughter is not a brat – she's a darling. And his sister can be tricky, but she only has his best interests at heart. More importantly, we're right together. We both know it. So, it's not going to be easy, but I do believe we can make it work.'

'Well, if that's your decision.' Max drained his glass suddenly. 'But if you change your mind, just let me know.' He stood up, bent over and kissed her on the lips.

'See you around, baby.'

Left alone, in the bar, she knew there was just one person she wanted to speak to. She took out her phone and dialled Lorenzo.

'*Pronto.*'

'Lorenzo, it's me.'

'Millie!'

He sounded, as always, delighted to hear her voice.

'Darling, I've been thinking,' she began, nervously, 'this is mad – me being here in London, you being there. I know it sounds crazy, but I just don't think I can stay here alone without you.'

She paused, waiting for his response. Had she said too much too soon?

'Well, that's rather funny, because I was thinking the same thing. I was going to email you tonight. I'd like to come and see you soon. I was thinking tomorrow.'

'Tomorrow – really?'

'Mmmm. Elena will look after Bella and I can get a flight tomorrow lunchtime. Shall I book it?'

'Yes – yes, please.'

'I should be with you by five or six o'clock, if that's OK?'

'Oh Lorenzo, I'm so happy – thank you! I'd better go and buy some food – there's nothing in the flat. Shall I come and meet you? Where are you coming in?'

'Heathrow – but no, don't do that. I can take the Tube from the airport, just text me your address.'

'I'll do it now. See you tomorrow!'

*

Millie struggled to concentrate at work the following day. She finished the section of her article about Anastasia and followed up some leads to an Italian silk designer. There was a scarf designer, based in Florence, who was now using Italian silk. They sent emails back and forth. His work wouldn't be shown in London the following week, but he would be showing in Milan. He sent photographs of beautiful silk scarves, which she could use in the article. It would make a great ending.

She glimpsed Max once or twice during the day, on his way to various meetings. He studiously avoided her section of the open-plan office. But in the afternoon she was forced to walk past his glass partition to speak to the picture editor. Max looked up from his desk; she expected him to smile, and she half-raised her hand in salutation, but instead, he swung his chair deliberately away.

She left work a little early and picked up a few groceries from the shop on the corner. She bought some flowers from the stall near the Tube station and arranged them in a recycled green glass vase that caught the light. She tidied the flat, changed the sheets on the bed, and laid a tray with a bottle of prosecco and two glasses, alongside a little dish of olives.

When the buzzer went, she nearly dropped the tray in her excitement.

She stood at the top of the narrow stairs listening to his footsteps making their way up to the third floor.

'Are you OK?' she called down. 'Shall I come and help?'

'No, I'm fine.'

'Just one more flight…' she called out encouragingly.

And then he was there – tall and slightly gangly, his dark hair flopping into his eyes. He wore a tan suede jacket and blue jeans and carried an in-flight bag.

They kissed on the cramped landing.

'Hello…' he said, stepping back and looking at her. He brushed her auburn hair away from her face. 'You look beautiful.'

'So do you.' She stroked his cheek. 'Come in, come in.'

She led him by the hand into the flat. The sun broke through the clouds outside, filling the compact white space with light.

'I've got a bottle of prosecco ready.' She indicated the tray.

He picked up the bottle and opened it, deftly twisting the cork silently out of the bottle.

She held out their two glasses.

'Cheers,' she said.

'*Salute!*' He kissed her again.

They chatted about his flight, his journey, Bella… But as they drained their second glass of wine, he kissed her, then put her glass down on the tray and pulled her to her feet.

'Let's go to bed,' he whispered in her ear.

She led him by the hand into her tiny bedroom. He removed her sweater, kissing her neck, her face. She slipped off her jeans and unbuttoned his shirt and his belt. She lay back on the bed, wriggling out of her underwear, aching for him.

Afterwards, they slept. When she woke, it was dark outside. She lay silently watching him sleep, his smooth olive skin and dark hair swept off his high forehead. He opened his eyes and smiled.

'Hello…'

'Hello…' She kissed him. 'Are you hungry? I can cook something—'

'Only for you.'

He pushed her over onto her back and kissed her again. She laughed. 'I love you.' She stroked his high forehead with her cool hand.

'And I love you. Oh – and I have something rather exciting to tell you.'

'Really?' She sat up in bed, expectantly.

'I've left it in my bag in the sitting room.'

'Come on,' she said, pulling on her silk dressing gown. 'Here, you can wear this.'

She threw a man's shirt onto the bed that had been hanging behind the door.

'Whose is this?' he asked.

'My dad's. I use it when I'm decorating – it should fit.'

She poured them another glass of wine as he unzipped his bag; he brought out a document in a brown envelope.

'What is it?'

'It's a birth certificate for a child called Stefano – he was born in 1815. His father was Alberto Morozoni. But next to the child's name, the registrar has made a mistake: he's written Stefano Manzoni.'

'Where did you find it?'

'It was in the box that Elena found, mixed up with lots of other stuff. We nearly missed it, but a couple of nights ago, we just laid everything out on the floor of the barn – literally everything. We were all there searching – Elena, the boys, me and Bella. I said we had to look for anything that had both Manzoni and Morozoni. Bella found it.'

'Good for Bella! All those games of Snap, you see – sharpened up her visual skills.'

'So that's how the name was changed – a simple registration error. Until that time, births were not really registered formally, so this was a new thing. And I found another certificate from 1860 – and by then the name was Manzoni…'

They finished the prosecco.

'What shall I cook?' asked Millie. 'I've got pasta, some chicken…'

'No, we can cook tomorrow. Tonight I want to take you out to dinner.'

While Lorenzo unpacked his few clothes, Millie made a reservation at a tiny brasserie round the corner from the flat. It was dark, intimate and romantic and served simple French food. Significantly, she had never gone there with Max.

'I'm not eating there,' he'd said dismissively. 'It's too provincial – it looks as if it belongs in Beaconsfield, back in the 1990s.'

The waiter found them a table in a dark corner and they ordered pâté and steak, but when the food came, although it was delicious they ate sparingly, moving their food aimlessly around their plates, their eyes locked on one another.

'I don't know why we bothered to come out,' she said, gesturing to their plates. 'Neither of us has eaten much – don't you like it?'

'It's delicious – I am ashamed to say that I just don't have much appetite – at least not for food.' He stroked her cheek. 'I love you, Millie. I never want to be apart from you again.'

'Me neither.'

'It's crazy – we hardly know each other, but I feel as if I've known you all my life.'

'I know – I feel the same.'

'So what shall we do?' He sipped his wine. 'I can't leave Italy. I can't leave Elena, or the business. And Bella is so happy there.'

'I know.'

'Could you leave London, leave your job?'

Millie looked into his eyes.

'Yes… I think I could. I could rent out the flat, so I'd have some income. And I could work freelance.'

'Could you really? I mean you're an award-winning journalist. Wouldn't you miss it?'

'Yes, and no. I've been doing it for sixteen years. I've done well; I'm proud of what I've achieved, but there is more to life. You've shown me that. No, it's time. Besides, I'm sure I could be helpful with the villa – I've got lots of ideas about how you could promote the wine, and the silk.'

'It's a risk for you. Putting your eggs in one basket – isn't that what they say?'

'But it's a lovely basket.'

She reached across the table and squeezed his hand.

*

The following morning, Millie took a decisive step: she resigned from her job. Sonia was surprised and called her as soon as she got Millie's email.

'Millie – why?'

'You know why. Max and I have split up, it wasn't working. It's not going to be possible to be around him any more. And more importantly, I'm in love with someone else, who just happens to live in Italy.'

'Wow… You've kept that quiet! OK, well, we'll miss you – but good luck. I think you've got quite a lot of leave due, so you won't need to work out your notice.'

'Thanks, Sonia – and I'll send the last piece over, obviously, before I go. It's quite good, I think – I hope you and Max agree.'

'I'm sure it will be up to your usual standard. And send me any ideas you have from Italy – I'd be happy to take a look if you decide to go freelance.'

Millie called a couple of letting agents and asked them to come round and assess the flat. With a bit of paint here and there, they felt it would be easy enough to rent out. A date was fixed – it would go on the market in three weeks' time.

Lorenzo was anxious to begin helping her to sort out her belongings.

'We need to work out what you're bringing to Italy and what stays here,' he suggested.

'I can do that when you've gone back. There's a load of stuff that needs to be chucked and so on. It's easier if I just get on with it. Besides, I don't want to waste time while you're here. We've only got a couple of days before you have to go back.'

'I could change my ticket,' he suggested.

'No, go back to Bella and Elena – and warn her that I'm coming.' She laughed.

'I'll come back in a couple of weeks with a car and we can load everything up and take you home.'

'That sounds nice.'

'What?'

'"Home".' She kissed him. 'But there *is* one thing that I ought to do before you go back.'

'What's that?'

'Tell my family about you.'

'Of course! I thought perhaps you already had.'

'No, I think I mentioned ages ago, I don't have a particularly close relationship with my parents – it's always been a little distant. Besides, I wasn't sure what was happening with us. But now, if I'm coming back to Italy with you, they ought to know.'

'Well then, you must call them tonight,' he insisted.

As Lorenzo cooked supper in her tiny kitchen, Millie poured herself a large glass of wine and rang her parents' number.

'Hi Mum, it's Millie.'

'Hello darling,' said Marion, her mother. 'Hang on, I'll call Dad – he won't want to miss a call from you.'

'I'm sorry, I've been hopeless about calling recently.'

'I know you're busy, darling. You've been travelling, haven't you? How's the job?'

'Oh… a few changes there actually; I'm going freelance.'

'Really? Is that a good idea, with a mortgage and everything?'

'Yes, it'll be fine.'

'And… anyone on the horizon?'

There it was – the question. But for once, it didn't grate. Millie grinned.

'Actually – yes, there is. He's an Italian called Lorenzo Manzoni.'

'Oh! How lovely,' said her mother, as if Millie were describing a pretty dress she intended to buy. 'David, David! Do come here, darling. It's Millie on the phone; she's got a new chap – an Italian called Lorenzo.'

Millie's father came on the extension.

'An Italian. Where from?'

'The countryside, near Verona. He owns a villa with his sister – it's been in the family for four hundred years, or thereabouts. They have a vineyard and make silk and run a big B&B – rather top-end.'

'So, a bit of a long-distance relationship then?' said her father.

'Not really,' said Millie. 'I've decided to leave London, and move down there to live with him.'

There was a stunned silence on the other end of the phone.

'Gosh!' said her mother eventually. 'Are you sure, darling? This is all a bit sudden, isn't it?'

'Perhaps. But we met in the summer when I went there to write a story for the paper, and we fell in love. He's a widower – in his mid-forties, with a lovely, lovely little girl called Bella. She's only eight and we just all get on.'

Lorenzo grinned at her from the other side of the kitchen.

'Well, that's wonderful,' said her mother, 'but what about your flat?'

'I'm going to rent it out. I've had two agents round today and chosen one. It'll go on the market in three weeks' time – there's a lot of demand for flats like mine.'

'And are we going to get a chance to meet him?'

'Oh yes, of course. He's over here now, in fact, but he's going back tomorrow. But he'll be back in three weeks to help me move.'

'Could we meet, then – for supper or lunch?'

'Yes, but I'm not sure we have time to come up to Berkshire.'

'Oh, don't worry about that. We'll come to you, won't we, David?'

'Of course, Marion,' said her father, finally getting a chance to interject. 'Shall we come to the flat, Millie?'

'Well, it'll be a bit of a mess by then – I'll be packing everything up into boxes.'

'How about meeting at Fortnum's?' suggested her mother. 'They do a lovely lunch there. We'll book it, won't we, David?'

'OK, sounds good. I'll be in touch, Mum, so we can arrange a date. And I'll try to come up to Berkshire on my own in the next week or two. I've left my job, so I've got time.'

'That would be lovely, darling,' said her mother. 'And Millie – you do really love him?'

'Oh yes, Mum. I know it sounds like a bit of a whirlwind, and it has been, but… well, we both just felt it from the beginning, really. I came back here for a couple of months, to see if I missed him. And I did. It's the right thing, I know it is.'

The next few weeks flew by. Millie decorated and cleaned the flat. She packed away her clothes and precious possessions in boxes ready to take to Italy and made numerous visits to the charity shop. On the day Lorenzo was due to arrive, she was finalising her article at the kitchen table when she heard a loud tooting of a car horn. Peering down into the street, she saw him, climbing out of an ancient Volvo. He wore jeans, deck shoes and a dark-blue cashmere sweater. He looked around and then wandered over to the parking signs. Millie banged on the window and he looked up, grinning.

She ran down the three flights of stairs and hurled herself at him in the street.

'You're here! Oh darling, you're here! Now, you can't park there, you'll get a ticket. We'll have to go round the corner to the car park. It'll cost a fortune, but hopefully we'll be out of here in a couple of days. Where's the Fiat?'

'I left it in Italy; it was too small for all your stuff. This is Elena's car.'

'Oh, that was kind of her. Is she OK about me coming back with you?'

'She is resigned.'

'That sounds awful.'

'But Bella is ecstatic, so I think that will make up for it.'

*

Lunch at Fortnum & Mason with Millie's parents was booked for the following day. Millie and Lorenzo arrived early and wandered around the elegant food hall, admiring the decorative displays of tea, coffee and wine.

'I'd like to think we could be selling Villa di Bozzolo wine here one day,' Millie said.

After the initial introductions, and much discussion of what they were going to eat, the conversation between the four flowed easily. Lorenzo delighted Millie's father with his apparently boundless knowledge of Lucca and Florence. Millie's mother, sitting next to her at the table, squeezed her daughter's hand encouragingly from time to time.

Halfway through lunch, her mother dragged Millie to the ladies' room for a private conversation.

'Oh Millie, well done, darling! He's delightful. Educated at Ampleforth, followed by a good university, *and* a City background. His house – the villa – sounds stunning.'

'It's not a test, Mum, like he's ticked all the boxes. I just love him. His education is irrelevant.'

'A good education is never irrelevant, Millie.'

'And the villa is jolly hard work. Running an upmarket B&B is not easy and the vineyard and silk business are like any farming – dicey and dependent on the weather. But I think I can be useful with marketing and PR.'

'And where will you live? I didn't like to ask over lunch.'

'In the barn, with his sister.'

'What about the villa?'

'They just use that for guests.'

'Difficult living with someone else,' her mother warned.

'It'll be fine, Mum.'

'Well, I'm sure Dad will put his hand in his pocket and help a bit if you wanted to buy somewhere—'

'He doesn't need to, Mum.'

'I know, darling. But we'd like to – a wedding present.'

'Who mentioned weddings?'

'Oh Millie, don't be ridiculous! He's an *Italian*. Of course you'll get married.'

'Thanks for being so nice,' Millie said, when they got back to the flat later that afternoon.

'They were delightful,' said Lorenzo, flopping down on the sofa beside her. 'We must invite them to the villa.'

'Yes, of course… when we're settled. Cup of tea?'

'Yes, please. Why don't they come out for Christmas?'

'She was banging on about marriage,' said Millie, putting on the kettle. She took the half-dozen white china mugs out of the cupboard and poured tea into two of them before packing up the rest, along with her stove-top coffee pot, into a cardboard box.

'And why not?' said Lorenzo. 'She's your mother, of course she wants you to get married.'

'Well, it's not up to her, is it? It's up to us.'

She turned round with the box in her hands to find Lorenzo on his knees on her kitchen floor. He handed her a piece of string tied in a little loop.

'Camilla Caparelli, will you do me the honour of marrying me?'

In her surprise, and delight, she dropped the box; there was the sound of soulless white china breaking into pieces.

*

Later that evening, after supper in the tiny brasserie round the corner to celebrate their engagement, they sat together, surrounded by boxes, on the sofa.

'I've been thinking,' said Lorenzo, 'about where we should live.'

'In the barn, of course!'

'To begin with, yes. But there are several old buildings around the courtyard that we could convert into a house. We'd still be near Elena and the boys, but we'd have space for ourselves too.'

'Could we? I mean, can you afford it?'

'I think so… it won't be grand, but we could do something quite interesting. I have some money put aside from my time here.'

'Won't Elena expect you to put any money you have into the business?'

'No, I've always made it clear that I wouldn't do that. It's for Bella and me, and now you.'

As Lorenzo loaded the final boxes into the car the following morning, Millie sent an email to Max.

Dear Max,

I saw my article in the paper yesterday. I hope you liked it. I thought it sat well alongside all the pieces you're running on London Fashion Week.

I leave for Italy today. The flat is let; a tenant moves in next week. It's a big step, but the right one. Sonia offered me some freelance work – I hope you approve? I'm sure I'll be able to dig up half a dozen stories each year that might be worth running.

I'll miss you. You're the best editor I've ever had. Be happy… Say hi to the twins for me?

Much love,
Millie

Chapter Thirty-Eight

From the moment she moved to Italy, Millie knew she had made the right decision. Within the first few weeks, she had begun to establish herself, writing several pieces for English newspapers and magazines about life in Italy and garnering a good list of local contacts. She developed a new illustrated website for the villa with a section about the family's famous ancestor, Anastasia Balzarelli. She also revisited the Bordignon mill in Venice and took photographs of all the silk fabrics Anastasia had designed over the years. Each snippet of fabric was labelled and stored on her computer so she had a complete record of the Anastasia Balzarelli archive. She didn't forget her promise to Joanna, curator at the Victoria & Albert Museum, either.

'I'm so delighted, thank you,' Joanna emailed back.

One morning, Signor Bordignon rang her from the mill.

'I mentioned to you on your last visit that I was keen to revive one or two of Anastasia's silk designs, but I needed to find a customer first as it would cost so much to set up the loom. Well, I think I have an Italian fashion designer who would like to use one of Anastasia's silks in his couture collection. He believes it would make a fantastic corset for the finale of his next show.'

'Which one did he like?'

'The one with the yellow background, and the turquoise butterfly – do you remember?'

'Oh yes! I love that one, too.'

'He'll put it with a yellow silk skirt or something. He's shown me the initial designs and I think it will look amazing. If you are happy, I'll start lacing up the loom and we'll begin weaving next spring.'

'Happy? I'm thrilled! Thank you so much. Obviously, I'll market it as much as I can. I can write a piece about it – I've got good contacts at *Vogue* and *Harper's* now. I'm sure one of them will want a story like that. And perhaps, Giovanni, one day we might go into partnership and create a special line of Balzarelli silks…'

She told Lorenzo about it that evening, when he brought Bella home from school.

'I think we ought to tell our jewellery magnate, Antonio, don't you? I know he's planning an exhibition to celebrate the resurgence of the industry. How about a display on Anastasia?'

'Sure… if you think so,' said Lorenzo, hanging up Bella's coat. 'And maybe we could tie it in with the villa and get some publicity.'

Elena, though reluctant at first, began to have a grudging admiration for Millie's boundless enthusiasm. She saw how keen she was to be involved in the family business and, more importantly, how happy she made Lorenzo and Bella. She said as much to her brother one afternoon in the kitchens of the villa when he was delivering a crate of groceries.

'Are these all right here?' he asked as he pushed the crate beneath the long table in the middle of the kitchen.

'Thank you, Lorenzo, they're fine. How's Millie? I've not seen her today.'

'She's OK. She's got a meeting with the website designers. And she's getting a new label designed for our wine next year – using that yellow flowered silk of Balzarelli's. It looks fantastic.'

'She's a good girl, your Millie.'

'Yes, I think so.'

'And she makes you happy?'

'Happier than I've ever been.'

'Then I'm glad for you. You'd better get on with restoring that little barn early in the New Year.'

'You won't mind us moving out?'

'No, why on earth would I? I'll be glad not to have to cook for you all any more! Go on, get out of my kitchen.'

A week before Christmas, the whole family moved back into Villa di Bozzolo for the festive season.

'We have no guests now until early February so it's a sort of treat for us to live back here,' explained Lorenzo.

'I can't wait,' said Millie. 'It will be wonderful to really live in these elegant rooms, rather than just dashing in and out, arranging flowers for the guests' benefit, or taking photos for the website.'

The villa was a hive of activity. Millie's parents, her brother Freddie, his wife and their sons were due to arrive on 23 December. Lorenzo had also invited Bella's English grandparents. Elena assumed overall command of the operation, carrying around a long list of *cosa da fare* – things to be done – and marching from room to room, issuing orders to anyone within earshot.

'We need to air all the bedrooms, particularly on the top floor. Lorenzo, could you light a fire in each of the rooms to dry them out a bit? They're very damp. All the beds need making, and the furniture needs dusting.'

'I'll do that, Elena,' said Millie, 'I can be in charge of bedrooms. Then you can just concentrate on food – although I'd love to help with anything in the kitchen too.'

*

A couple of weeks before Christmas, Millie made a shopping trip to Verona with Lorenzo to buy presents for her parents and Bella. On the way back to the villa she asked him what Elena might like.

'She's very difficult to buy for. Nothing is ever quite good enough for her.'

'I was thinking… how about we get that portrait of Anastasia reframed? In a style she'd really like. We could get it cleaned up at the same time.'

'Well, that's not such a bad idea. Yes – OK,' said Lorenzo.

'We'll give it to her on Christmas Eve. But I hope she won't hang it back on the landing, where no one will be able to see it.'

'I think it should go in the main hall – between the two sets of French windows leading to the garden and the vineyard. Then every time people go outside, they will see it.'

The restorer delivered the painting a few days before Christmas. He brought it into the small salon to show to Millie; unwrapping it carefully, he stood it up on the small sofa.

'It has come up very well,' he said, smiling. 'I'm very pleased with it. You can really see the buildings in Venice in the background now and the colour of her dress – such a gentle yellow. There's a little basket of silk cocoons too, which now stands out much more. But the most exciting part is that I found a signature on the bottom of the picture; it was hidden behind so much grime, it had completely disappeared. Look!'

'It says Anastasia Balzarelli,' said Millie. 'But that's the name of the sitter, not the artist.'

'Yes, she *is* the sitter, but she's also the artist,' said the restorer. 'It's a self-portrait. I thought it was; the composition suggested it. Artists often paint themselves at work, particularly women artists. It's a way of saying publicly, "This is what I do".'

'Oh, I see.' Millie turned the picture to face the light. 'It's rather good, isn't it?'

'Yes. She's not the greatest portrait artist, but it's not bad at all.'

'Well, I'm delighted with it. I just hope my soon-to-be sister-in-law will like it, too; I'm giving it to her for Christmas.'

'I'm sure she will love it. Shall I wrap it up again?'

'Please do. I'd hate to spoil the surprise.'

Millie hid the painting in her bedroom. She and Lorenzo had taken the room she had slept in when she first arrived at Villa di Bozzolo nearly nine months earlier, as a single journalist looking for a story and escaping an unhappy love affair. As she leaned the painting against the wall and looked around her it seemed incredible that this ancient house, with all its mysteries and history, was now her home. Her life had been completely transformed by the house and the family who lived in it. She had metamorphosed from a single woman with a good career and an unsatisfactory love life into someone with a family, whose working life would now revolve around the people she loved.

Back in the villa kitchen, Elena was baking and cooking. The main meal of the Christmas festivities would be served on Christmas Eve and it was to be a grand affair. Millie wisely kept out of her way, but offered to help decorate the dining room.

'I'll go out and get some greenery and wild flowers, if there are any around,' she said.

Lorenzo arrived that afternoon with a tall Christmas tree, which they stood in the main hall. He went up to the attics and brought down boxes of old decorations.

'These are fantastic,' said Millie. 'Some of them must be Victorian.'

'Yes, I think they are. But be careful with them – Elena is very protective.'

'You could do a fantastic, atmospheric Christmas package here for guests, you know.'

'You think so?'

'Heavens, yes! I think, marketed correctly, this place would be rammed.'

Marco looked mystified. 'Rammed?'

'Busy... popular. It's a London word...'

For the rest of the day, when she wasn't bed making or decorating, Millie took photographs of the tree, the decorations, of Elena at work in the kitchen and even their small private chapel, decorated with winter greenery for Christmas.

Millie's family arrived in the early afternoon the day before Christmas Eve. After they had settled in, she showed them around the villa.

'It's too dark to see it all tonight, but tomorrow, I'll give you the proper guided tour – the silk farm, the vineyards, everything.'

'And you're happy here?' asked her father.

'Dad, I've never been so happy.'

'Well, your grandfather would be pleased. The idea that a Caparelli has come back to live in Italy after all these years would delight him. Shame it's not Lucca, where your cousins live, but you can't have everything.'

Bella's English grandparents, Jonathon and Pamela, arrived later that afternoon and Millie made sure they were comfortably settled into their room. Pamela caught her arm as she was leaving them to unpack.

'Millie... I just wanted to say – I'm so delighted that Lorenzo and Bella have found someone to look after them. I know my daughter, Caroline, would have been pleased too.'

Millie kissed her on the cheek.

'That means more than I can say. I love Bella so much, I promise I'll never let her down.'

On Christmas Eve the family assembled in the drawing room to hand out presents. Elena had bought Millie a set of kitchen knives.

'For your new kitchen,' she said, 'when you finally get one.'

'Oh, Elena, thank you! I can't wait to start using them – and we have something for you.' Millie smiled conspiratorially at Lorenzo, and went over and stood beside the easel in the corner of the room.

'I wondered what that was doing there,' said Elena

She removed the wrapping carefully, revealing the painting.

'Who is it?' asked Pamela.

'She's very beautiful; she looks rather like Elena, doesn't she?' observed Millie's father.

'It's one of Elena and Lorenzo's ancestors,' said Millie proudly. 'Her name was Anastasia Balzarelli and this is a self-portrait. She was an artist – she lived here in the villa, and owned a silk mill in Venice. She was also a famous silk designer. And now her designs – well, one or two of them – are to be revived, and she will be on the lips of the rich and famous at next year's Milan Fashion Week.'

Later that evening in the dining room, as the candlelight played on the pale apricot walls, the family sipped amaretto and toasted Elena's spectacular supper. She bowed and nodded to them graciously. Lorenzo whispered to Millie, 'Thank you for coming into my life.'

'Thank you for giving me everything I've ever truly wanted – a home, a wonderful daughter, a new baby and fulfilling career.'

'*What* did you say?'

'You heard me… You'd better get building, that's all I can say. We'll be four by next summer.'

Chapter Thirty-Nine

Villa Limonaia
April 1732

My dear Vicenzo,

How are you, my darling son? I hope all is well with you and Giulia and the new baby. I will try to come and visit you next week at Villa di Bozzolo, if the weather is good. I have only just come back from visiting your sister in Lucca. Polonia is very happy, and sends her love to you. I think she has made a good match with the Agnoli boy – he is so like his father, Luigi. Your father adored him so much and it would have made him very happy to know that his daughter had married Luigi's son.

Thank you for dealing with the sale of the mill for me. It was hard to let to go, but it was the right thing to do. Without your father, I struggled to keep it going. I was never comfortable staying in Venice, it held too many memories. I am happier now, without the burden of it all.

Life at Villa Limonaia goes on. As I write to you from your grandfather's old study, the sunlight is playing on the lake and there is a flock of geese flying low over the water. Francesco, who looks after the gardens for me, took me out in Marco's old boat yesterday. We sailed over to a little village nearby and I sat and painted for a while. It reminded me so much of the early days with your father. I miss him so much – more every day. I cannot believe it is nearly a year since he died. But I am not unhappy, *caro*, I still have my painting, and I design a little. My old friend James Leman, in London, wrote to me and said he liked a new design I sent him. It is good to know that my work will be there after I have gone.

I found your grandfather's copy of 'The New Book of Flowers' by Maria Sibylla the other day. It took me back to my time with her in Amsterdam. What a remarkable woman she was! She was just a little older than I am now when we first met. I hope she realised how grateful I was to her. She wrote to me several times after I left, giving me her news. I was so sad when she died, but her work lives on.

I hope the mulberry orchards do well this spring. Are the silk farms getting ready? The feast of San Marco will be here any day and the whole cycle of life will begin again.

Remember, Vicenzo, we are simply the caretakers of a precious inheritance. There were silk farms before we came, and they will be there when we are gone.

Your loving Mamma,
Anastasia

Acknowledgements

I am grateful to the following people, collections, authors and companies who have helped me with the writing of this book:

My family for their unwavering love and support

My publisher and editors Claire Bord and Natasha Harding for their help and encouragement

My friend Alannah Barton who first suggested Maria Merian as a subject for one of my novels

Chrysalis – Maria Sibylla Merian and the Secrets of Metamorphosis by Kim Todd
 Pub: I.B. Tauris, 2007

Marriage Wars in Late Renaissance Venice by Joanne M. Ferraro
 Pub: Oxford University Press, 2001

Italy in the Seventeenth Century by Domenico Sella
 Pub: Longman, 1997

Women on the Margins – Three Seventeenth-Century Lives by Natalie Zemon Davis
 Pub: Belknap Harvard, 1997

The Queens Gallery, which held a wonderful exhibition of the works of Maria Merian in 2016.

For more information visit: www.royalcollection.org.uk

Villa Sagramoso near Verona. This fabulous villa was the inspiration for Villa di Bozzolo. I visited it several years ago in one of the hottest summers they had ever experienced, and knew that it would form the central part of a novel one day.

www.villasagramososacchetti.it/en

D'Orica This wonderful jewellery company based near Verona was the inspiration for the silk spinner in the modern section of the novel. In real life D'Orica is owned by Giampietro Zonta and Daniela Raccanello, who are leading the way in the regeneration of the indigenous Italian silk industry.

www.dorica.com

Luigi Bevilacqua This stunning eighteenth-century mill in Venice, which produces some of the most spectacular silk and cut velvet in the world, was the inspiration for the Bordignon mill. I am indebted to them for letting me spend so much time in their beautiful mill, learning about the weaving process and studying their incredible historic collection of fabrics.

www.luigi-bevilacqua.com

Serica 1870, a silk and wool mill in Follina I visited to observe the modern silk milling process. I spent a fascinating afternoon watching top designer fabrics destined for the catwalks of Chanel and Max Mara, among others, rolling off the mills.

www.serica1870.com

The Silk Worm Museum, Vittorio Veneto. This museum was a fabulous resource, enabling me to understand the complex process of silk production. It is beautifully laid out, with visually creative displays, and I spent a wonderful day there. I was so grateful to the curator Elisa Bellato for her patient explanations and delicious impromptu hospitality complete with local prosecco!

www.museobaco.it

CAST OF CHARACTERS:

In all my books I make it clear who is a real-life character and who is fictional. Real-life characters are in italics:

1704–1706:

Villa di Bozzolo – somewhere in the countryside near Verona.

- Ludovico Balzarelli – silk farmer and vineyard owner
- Polonia – his wife
- Anastasia and Marietta Balzarelli – their daughters
- Angela – the cook
- Magdalena – the maid
- Giuseppe – the footman

Villa Limonaia – on the shores of Lake Garda.

- Vicenzo Morozoni
- Marco – his son
- Giancarlo and Alessandro – Vicenzo's brothers
- Tobias – Marco's cousin on Lake Como
- Caterina – Tobias's wife.
- Luigi Agnoli – Marco's friend from Lucca

Venice:

- Anzolo di Zorzi – the mill owner
- Veronica – the maid
- Juliana di Luna – the midwife
- Signor Bertucci – his lawyer

The Legal Team:
- *Zan Jacomo Gradenigo – the lawyer*
- *Giovanni Venier – the Procurator*
- *Gianalberto Badoaro – the Patriarch of Venice*
- *The Vicar of the Cathedral of San Pietro*
- Maria Teresa Pinottini – the cleaner of the church of San Zan Degolà

Amsterdam:
- *Maria Merian – artist*
- *Dorothea Merian – her daughter*
- Sébastien Benoît – musician and Huguenot silk merchant
- Jean-Antoine and Angelique Benoît – Sébastien's parents

Spitalfields:
- *Peter Leman – Huguenot silk weaver based in Steward Street*
- *James Leman – Peter's son and famous silk designer*
- *Christopher Baudouin – famous silk designer*
- *Joseph Dandridge – famous silk designer*

2016–2017
Spitalfields:
- Camilla Caparelli – journalist
- Max – her editor and lover
- Katje – Max's wife
- Tabby and Lottie – Max and Katje's twin daughters
- Freddie Caparelli – Millie's brother
- David and Marion Caparelli – Millie's parents
- Kitty – Millie's best friend

Villa di Bozzolo:

- Lorenzo Manzoni – owner of Villa di Bozzolo
- Elena Manzoni – Lorenzo's sister and co-owner of the villa
- Lino and Angelo – her sons
- Bella – Lorenzo's daughter
- Antonio Moretti – the silk entrepreneur

Venice:

- Signor Giovanni Bordignon – mill owner

Note from the author

I hope you have enjoyed reading *The Silk Weaver's Wife*. As anyone who has read my two earlier novels, *The Girl with Emerald Eyes* and *Daughters of the Silk Road*, will know, I enjoy integrating fact with fiction. I am inspired by the stories of real people who have achieved extraordinary things, but who may have been overlooked by history.

This story was inspired by my 'discovery' of the artist Maria Sibylla Merian (1647–1717). She was born in Frankfurt; her father was a successful printer and artist who died when Maria was just three years of age. Her mother then married the talented flower painter Jacob Marrel, who taught his stepdaughter to paint in watercolour. Maria married her stepfather's apprentice, Johann Andreas Graff, and the couple moved to Nuremberg, where they had two daughters – Johanna and Dorothea, both of whom became artists in their own right. In 1681 Maria's stepfather died and she returned to Frankfurt to care for her mother. Together with her daughters, they moved to a religious community, the Labadists, living a life of austerity and piety. But her fascination with the Labadist movement faded, and Maria divorced her husband and moved to Amsterdam with her daughter Dorothea.

Maria worked as a watercolour artist, developing a technique to paint directly on to silk, and learned how to engrave copper plates. She brought this skill to her first book – a collection of watercolours in three volumes entitled *The New Book of Flowers*, which remains a remarkable record of her artistic ability. But what marked Maria out from her contemporaries – male or female – was her knowledge of entomology. Maria had shown an interest in silkworms since childhood, but it soon developed into a fascination with the metamorphosis of butterflies and moths, and the wider life cycles of insects. Unusually for that time, she preferred to examine and paint insects in their real-life habitats, which culminated in her extraordinary visit to Suriname in South America, aged fifty-two, accompanied only by her daughter Dorothea, in 1699. She remained in the Dutch colony for two years, exploring, studying and painting.

She returned to Amsterdam in 1701, suffering from a tropical illness, and spent the next four years preparing her ultimate work, *The Metamorphosis of Insects of Suriname*. She was described by the Royal Society in 1710 as 'that great Naturalist and Artist' and her collections were widely collected by such luminaries as Peter the Great, Sir Hans Sloane and the Duke of Newcastle. Today Her Majesty the Queen owns a stunning collection of her works, which I saw myself in the Queen's Gallery at Buckingham Palace in 2016. Maria Sibylla Merian is still considered by no less an authority than David Attenborough to be among the most significant contributors to the field of entomology.

The second real character who inspired the novel was Anna Maria Garthwaite (1688–1763). I originally intended her to have a larger part in the story of my fictional silk designer Anastasia Balzarelli. But Anna Maria moved to Spitalfields from her home in Yorkshire in 1728 – twenty-two years after my heroine left London. I am not comfortable cheating with dates, and so was forced to leave her out. But her existence – and her importance in the field of silk design – was proof, if any were needed, that women in the seventeenth and eighteenth centuries were capable of extraordinary artistic achievements.

lds in the early eighteenth century was brimming over nted silk designers. Men like James Leman, a young man of eighteen when his father Peter, a French Huguenot escaping religious persecution in France, put him in charge of the family firm. James was obviously a man of enormous talent and maturity, and produced the earliest known collection of silk designs in the world. As my character Anastasia was just nineteen at the time I set the novel, it seemed a natural fit for them to have met and become friends. James's silk designs are displayed in the V&A next to those of Anna Maria Garthwaite.

Throughout history, women have shown they are capable of huge artistic achievements. What is remarkable about the real women mentioned here is that they broke with convention and tradition to follow their artistic desires. They all achieved fame in their lifetimes – an extraordinary accomplishment in itself.

If you have enjoyed my novel, please leave a review on Amazon for others. And if you'd like to keep up to date with all my latest releases, sign up here: www.bookouture.com/debbierix

🐦 : @debbierix

📘 : DebbieRixAuthor

🖥 : www.debbierix.com